Nozomi's Battle

A Cutters Notch Novel – Hope Spencer Book II

Michael DeCamp

Michael DeCamp
7/11/2021

In honor of my dad, Ralph DeCamp. This story is begun on his birthday. He would have been 105 years old today

Copyright © 2020 by Michael DeCamp

Published by Jurnee Books, an imprint of Winged Publications

Editor: Cynthia Hickey
Book Design by Winged Publications

All rights reserved. No part of this publication may be reproduced, stored in a retrieval system, or transmitted in any form or by any means—electronic, mechanical, photocopying, recording, or otherwise—without the prior written permission of the publisher. The only exception is brief quotations in printed reviews. Piracy is illegal. Thank you for respecting the hard work of this author.

This book is a work of fiction. Names, characters, Places, incidents, and dialogues are either products of the author's imagination or used fictitiously. Any resemblance to actual persons, living or dead, or events is coincidental. Scripture quotations from The Authorized (King James) Version.

Fiction and Literature: Inspirational
Thriller Suspense Mystery
Paranormal
Young Adult

ISBN: 978-1-952661-29-7

Acknowledgements

Writing a novel is a big deal. The process is complicated and involves multiple levels of support along the way. If it is a success, the author gets all the accolades, but he or she would never see success without the assistance of many other people. This page is dedicated to those folks, the incredible humans who helped make Nozomi's Battle a reality.

First, I want to thank my wife, Nancy DeCamp for her never-ending confidence in my story-crafting imagination. Without her patience and encouragement, this series may have ended with book one. Or, perhaps, never even started.

Second, I thank my agent, Sarah Joy Freese from Wordserve Literary for hanging with me through the publishing process.

Third, I thank my publisher, Cynthia Hickey from Winged Publications for believing in the story and bringing it to the world.

Fourth, I thank my beta-readers, Jeremy Garrison, Anni Carter, and Kristina Seifert, who provided the first feedback, refining the story in critical ways.

Fifth, I appreciate my editor, Sherri Stewart of Stewart Writing for fixing so, so many things. She made the story readable. Thank you, Sherri.

Finally, I thank you, the reader for indulging my imagination. I hope you enjoy the wild and crazy world of Cutters Notch and the Arboreal Realm.

Prologue
Late June

Russell Bray was proud of his new Chevy Suburban with its digital dash, its leather upholstery, and its large sunroof. His wife liked to say that it rode like a truck, but he didn't mind because in his estimation, it *was* a truck. Maybe it didn't have the large open bed for hauling sheetrock or cow manure, but it had the horsepower and the towing capacity that he craved. He was more than proud of it—he loved it. He adored it. It made him feel like the testosterone was surging in his arteries again.

"What are you thinking about?" Annette asked.

"What?" His wife always seemed to ask that question when his mind was somewhere it shouldn't be. When he was younger, that usually involved some pretty girl who'd caught his eye. Now, it was his obsession with the SUV.

"Oh, nothing," he lied. "I was enjoying the scenery, and my mind's just jumping around and landing on nothing in particular."

"Well, I was wondering if maybe you'd given some thought to where in the world we are," she said. "The kids are getting tired. I know I am."

Russell glanced at his children in the rearview mirror. They didn't look tired. They looked oblivious. Patrick and Patricia were twins, sixteen years old and off in their own universes. Trick, as he preferred to be called, had earbuds in his ears and his eyes were closed, but his head was bobbing up and down to some song Russell likely hated. Patti had her nose in a book, as usual, along with her own set of earbuds—she liked pop rock. She read constantly—usually some fantasy-ridden, young adult, pseudo-romance. More than likely, the story included a dragon. How she could read and listen to music at the same time was beyond his comprehension.

"Hey." Russell snapped his fingers several times to get their attention.

Both teens looked up with their bright green eyes and pulled one earbud loose in nearly an identical move. They were born different genders, but they shared all the other qualities of identical twins. Even the waves in their red hair flowed across the crown of their heads in the same way.

"What?" they asked in unison.

Russell realized that he was also getting tired and hungry. They'd left Lake Geneva, Wisconsin, on the last day of their summer vacation earlier that morning and had lingered in downtown Chicago a little too long after lunch. Then, he had unilaterally decided to make an adventure of the drive back to Lexington by detouring through the hills of southern Indiana. Now, the sun had dipped below the ragged horizon behind them. The residual light slowly disappeared in his rearview while they wound their way through the crazy curves, dips, hills, and forest somewhere in the Hoosier state.

The truth that he couldn't admit to Annette was that he really wasn't sure where they were at the moment. There wasn't much around anywhere but trees, as far as he could tell, but stubbornness was a family trait, so he kept his course and figured he'd find something eventually. "Your mom says she's getting tired of driving and wants to stop."

"Yes," they replied in unison. "I want a Starbucks," Patti said.

"Ugh," said Trick, "let's get Qdoba."

"You two obviously have not been looking around much," Russell said. "Do you see anything remotely like a fast food restaurant?" He checked the clock on his dash. It read 9:55. Daylight Savings Time at the western end of the Eastern Time Zone in late June meant the sun would go down really late. "Besides, it's getting late enough that anything around will be closing. We'll have to get some food out of the cooler."

"Ahh, man," was their unified response.

"I'm going to start looking for a motel," Annette added. "I saw a sign for a little town coming up. Maybe there'll be some place to stop there."

"Maybe," Russell replied. He ran his left hand through his own crop of red hair. He had no doubt about the fidelity of his marriage, but if he did, the red hair he shared with his twin children relieved any stray suspicion. His wife's whole family sported dark brown tresses. "I did see a beaten-up billboard for a motel a couple of miles back. Something called 'The Notch Inn.' Maybe we can get a room for the night."

"I am not sleeping in the same bed with Trick," Patti interjected. "I'm not doing it. I'll sleep in the Suburban first."

"You won't have to bunk with your brother," Annette reassured her. "We'll get two rooms—one for the boys and one for the girls." That seemed to satisfy the girl. She settled back and reopened her book.

The family rolled past a sign that read: *Welcome to Cutters Notch*. The forest fell back and a small, dilapidated town filled the landscape. First, a few small cottages sprang up. Built with limestone blocks, most were dark, but a few had lights in the windows. Then they cruised into what must have been a downtown sometime in the previous one hundred years. A street with larger buildings. On their left sat a boarded-up school building with broken windows in the upper stories. On their right stood an old salvage yard with a chain-link fence hugging a jangled mess of wrecked vehicles. One large gate hung crooked on its hinges and swung free in the wind.

Russell slammed on the brakes, and everyone lurched forward.

"What the—" Annette shouted. "Dad!" the twins added together.

"Sorry. A raccoon ran in front of me. I didn't feel like killing anything tonight."

"Geesh," Trick said, smiling as he felt around his chest. "You might have broken one of my ribs." Patti giggled. Annette glared at her husband.

They sped up again until they approached an intersection. Another boarded-up building stood on their left—it looked like an old bank with large limestone pillars. Diagonally across the intersection on their right sat a brightly lit gas station. A large lighted sign read, General Store. The green and white sign on the corner said the crossroad was Robbins Creek Road.

"Russell, maybe we can buy some food in there," Annette suggested. Even as she said the words, the sign went dark and the lights went off inside the store.

"Nope. Don't think so," he replied. "Closing time." He looked at the clock on the dash. Ten o'clock on the dot.

The family continued to cruise the rest of the way through Cutters Notch in silence, perusing the town. There wasn't much else to see other than the large, old stately homes that sat back in the shadows on their left. As with the smaller homes on the edge of town, some were dark and a few had some lighted windows. *Those grand homes must have been something to see back in their day.*

They were approaching the eastern edge of town when a neon sign flickered into view. It read *The Notch Inn* in bright, cursive blue letters. Below that in red letters, *Vacancy* flashed on and off. Unlit and below the neon was another sign. It read: *Robbins Stone.* An arrow pointed past the motel.

"Here it is," Russell announced with muted enthusiasm. "The next leg of the experience that we call, *The Bray Family Adventure.*"

A muffled "Yay" was the less than enthusiastic response from the back seat.

***

Russell Bray's adored Suburban wheeled into the drive toward The Notch Inn. Overnight, the vehicle sat in front of a lonely motel room door collecting dew on the windows, but early the next morning, a large tractor hooked it to a chain and pulled it deep into the forest.

The next *Bray Family Adventure* really had just begun.

One
Saturday
Mid-October

It was 4 a.m., and Josh Gillis was restless. He couldn't sleep well following the ordeal from two weeks earlier. His best friend, Hope Spencer, had been abducted by their mutual neighbors, an elderly couple, Faye and Earl Hicks. He and his best friend, Danny Flannery had nearly died in their efforts to find and rescue her. Tack on the other weird and wild things that happened, and the result for Josh was night terrors.

First, he had met a group of friendly elves from a parallel dimension, Gavin Allwind of the Trees and his two brothers, Gronek and Smakal. They could enter and exit his dimension through portals called "shimmers" that presented themselves in mirrors. But more importantly, Josh realized that he really, really liked Hope. He and Danny along with their State Trooper neighbor, Rick Anders, had rescued Hope with the help of the elves. She was safe and they survived. But a third thing occurred during the ordeal that now left him terribly tormented and robbed him of his sleep. An encounter with the evil entity the elves called a *specter*—and the specter became aware of him, too.

Josh glanced with sleepy eyes at his closet door. It stood open with its light shining into his darkened room. The light reflected off the mirror and brightened up his various collections—superhero posters and sports paraphernalia. His bedroom door also stood open, hall light shining through. The house was quiet. The only sound was the soft tick, tick, tick from the clock in the family room. The sound was comforting.

His mind slipped into a fitful sleep and flitted like a bird from situation to scenario to situation. At one point, he and Danny were building a fort in the woods. At another, he was holding hands with Hope. At yet another, he was sitting on the grass in his backyard, brushing the excess fur out of Sheba's coat. He'd brushed so much out that he had a pile bigger than her doghouse and he didn't know what to do with it all.

Suddenly, his dreaming mind became aware that he was in his own bed. His closed eyelids glowed with the light from the closet. The clock ticked. His covers had all been kicked off, but he absolutely could not move. No matter how hard he tried, he could not budge his arms or his legs. Josh tried to call out, but he couldn't get his voice to utter even a squeak. He was paralyzed.

His eyes opened and there it was. Again. The specter. It floated mere inches above his face. The black, dark, swirling cloud of a thing with the red, pinpoint eyes. It stared at him, and even though he couldn't see a mouth, he knew it was smiling. He could feel its smirk.

Josh tried again to scream but couldn't. He tried again to get up, but he couldn't budge. He tried to squirm, but he was locked down like his body was wrapped to his bed with plastic wrap.

Somehow, he knew it was only a dream. It had to be. Still, despite that knowledge and despite how hard he tried, he couldn't will himself awake. The thing just hovered above him—smiling, tormenting him.

"Hello, Joshua," it said into his mind. "*Are you afraid? I sense that you are afraid. It tastes like you are afraid.*" Then, it cackled as it slurped his anxiety like melting ice cream.

"You can't hurt me," Josh's mind shouted back at the specter. "You can't touch me."

"*True,*" the specter acknowledged, "*but, I know who can. He's coming for you, Josh. He's coming very soon. He's also coming for Danny, for your parents, and of course, he is coming for the girl, too.*"

Josh's mind rebelled against the words of the specter. With enormous effort, the boy pushed his mind forward and burst from his sleep with a scream. He was sitting up in bed, sweating and breathing hard when his parents rushed in.

His mother wrapped him in her arms. "It's okay, honey," she said. "It was just another dream. Just a nightmare. You're okay."

"Mom, it said it was going to get me, again. Why won't it leave me alone? It's going to get me; I just know it. It's not going to go away. Ever."

***

Cindy Gillis held her son to her chest, rocking him back and forth. She brushed her blond hair away from her face and looked up at Roger, her husband, with a look of desperation. Roger peered back, equally concerned. For the fourth time that week, Cindy and Roger helped their son to get up, walk the twenty paces to the master bedroom, and then positioned him on their bed between them. As he drifted off to sleep, they stared at one another from their pillows.

"We need to get him some help," Cindy whispered.

"Yeah, we do," Roger whispered back.

***

In the darkest corner of their bedroom, up near the ceiling, the specter looked down, satisfied. *Yes, this is coming along nicely.*

***

Gavin stepped clear of the trees and into the huge clearing that surrounded the mouth of the great cave. As he stood there glancing around at the place that had been his home for the first 150 years of his life, a strange interaction of weariness and excitement battled for dominance in his mind. He had not been home for many years, but it had been a long journey, and he was bone tired and quite dirty. Still, he knew he had to present himself upon arrival. It was both customary and a matter of respect to the queen. All visitors to the elf queen's compound were required to make their presence known before doing anything else. *But first, I am going to sit down on this rock and rest my feet.*

He had followed protocol and reported the entire episode surrounding Hope Spencer's kidnapping and subsequent rescue to the royal office by attaching a scroll to the leg of a fairy, sending the fairy southward. In the human realm, fairies had passed into extinction, but as with many other species, his elfin kin had managed to rescue a representative number into the Arboreal Realm. In the subsequent centuries, their descendants had multiplied until their population was stable, even slowly growing. Many of them served the queen as messengers.

After two days, the fairy had returned with the summons:

Gavin Allwind of the Trees

Proceed to the Queen's Presence Forthwith

Of course, he had left his forest as soon as he received the summons, taking only enough time to change clothes, gather some food, and say goodbye to his brothers, Gronek and Smakal.

Now, here he was, sitting with his dirty elbows propped upon his dirty knees and his dirty chin cupped inside his dirty hands. Gavin wanted a bath. Pools sat nearby, but he was required to present himself before any activity—dirty or not. He could not tarry long in his rest, lest that be considered a violation of protocol, as well.

***

The journey had taken more than a week, and he had needed to cross many lands left barren by human destruction. After leaving the forest where he and his brothers served, he found that the trees were sparse and the earth lay bare into trenches, divots, and sometimes large canyons that were the result of the manmade roads, buildings, and other infrastructure in the Human Realm. Those man-made things, both large and small, did not appear in the Arboreal Realm after they had been tooled out of their natural state. Only natural fauna and material were visible. Though, the impact of the human manipulation was evident in the destruction of their natural state.

After two days' journey, he had reached the great river that divided the land to the south of his forest at a point of heavy devastation that the humans called Louisville. The sun was setting as he arrived, and thousands upon thousands of shimmers appeared on both sides of the river's flowing waters. The sea of dimensional portals stretched up into the glowing night sky to the extent that it mimicked the twinkling aura of his forest. He had forgotten about the odd artificial beauty created by the human cities. It was an illusion, he knew because in the morning, the land would appear— a wasteland, devoid of all but minimal botanical life. There would be deep craters and ridges of rock, pits of water and rivers that seemed to flow through the air.

That night, Gavin bedded down along the riverbank near where the water ran shallow across an ancient fossil bed. He drifted off to sleep wondering about the multitude of lives that were represented by the shimmering lights that filled the horizon.

The next morning, the sun began to melt the frost that had formed on Gavin's blanket, and a cold drop soaked through the fabric and landed on his warm cheek, waking him up. As he stretched, his feet and arms splayed out in four directions and he yawned widely, his face still tucked underneath the tattered cotton cover.

"Are you going to want a ride across?" asked a deep, booming voice that seemed to be right over the top of him.

Gavin reached up and gripped the blanket with the two thumbs of his right hand, pulling it free of his face. Sure enough, a ferry ogre was glaring down at him. His red, oversized eyeballs were as big as baseballs, only a couple of inches from the end of the elf's nose. His orange head was round and as big as a large pumpkin. He wore homemade trousers that resembled bib overalls with ropes that draped over his muscular shoulders. Two burlap bags, loosely stitched together with twine, covered his chest. His huge, hairy, calloused feet remained unshod.

"Yes," Gavin answered and then sat up when the ogre backed off a couple of paces. "I would be most grateful if you would carry me to the far shore."

"Well, then, get up. The sun is high, and you have slept far into the morning. I mean to shove off in two minutes." Ogres were grumpy but basically harmless. They preferred hard work and often took the chores that were too difficult for others in the queen's service.

The elf stood and gazed over to the far side of the river. When he did, his heart sank. The destruction was immense with huge piles of open soil surrounding massive barren canyons and deep fissures. Here and there was the occasional small tree, or even a little copse of trees that the humans would call a park, but these were so sparse as to be of little account. It was to one of the parks on the far shore that the ogre would transport him.

In these zones of human devastation, it was critical to stay near the trees because out in the open wasteland, the earth could open up at any moment, driven by one of the monstrous machines that the Realm of Men contained. One moment, you would be walking along with nothing of note happening, and the next, a huge fissure would appear and the soil would fly through the air, falling into a new pile nearby—maybe on the hapless elf that happened to be standing there at the wrong moment.

The ogre's raft, which consisted of cobbled-together buoys and barrels tied to wooden pallets, all pulled through various shimmers over time, delivered Gavin safely to a tiny park on the southern shore. After providing payment, a small bag of Slumber Dust, he began to thread his way through the oaks and magnolias, then carefully into the wasteland.

The human cities provided odd sights in the Arboreal Realm. Ivy hung with angular shapes in midair. Likewise, moss seemed to cling to nothing but formed various squares and rectangles of green. Pools of water floated above his head and flowed through invisible channels. Occasionally, an unexpected concentration of forced air struck him, driven, he knew, in the Human Realm by great fans in their heating and cooling systems. As the sun rose higher, weird shadows formed as human buildings blocked the sun, not visible to Gavin's elfin eyes.

As he moved from tree to tree, trying to limit his exposure to the dangers of the turbulent city, he happened upon three of his own kind—fallen ones—elves who had allowed their natures to be corrupted. Two were asleep, holding large glass bottles with a small amount of golden liquid resting in the bottom. One sat with her back against a tree. She wore a human woman's nightgown and a pair of leather sandals. Her greenish skin was paler than normal with hints of yellow and was peeling around her neck and shoulders.

Glancing up at Gavin, she asked, "Do you have any bourbon?"

"No, young one," he replied. His heart ached for her. Influenced by evil desires, she had damaged her aura and was slowly snuffing out the light of life.

"Are you sure?" she tried again. "I could pay you for it." Then the female elf sat a little more upright and gave Gavin a twisted wink. When she did, the gown's strap fell off her left shoulder.

Gavin turned and hurried away, deeply saddened. His concern deepened as he encountered other small groups of fallen elves before he left the wasteland. It was normal to see an occasional fallen one, but he had passed by dozens, perhaps more than a hundred. He would have to discuss this with the queen.

***

Gavin rested on the rock as long as he could justify, then he stood, stretched, and began to head toward the cave. A certain amount of trepidation occurred naturally when one entered the presence of the queen. Still, Gavin was eager for the reunion—too many years had passed since he had last seen her sharp yet warm eyes.

As he entered the mouth of the cavern, the twinkling aura of millions upon millions of microscopic plants living in the crevices of the walls provided a warm glow. It was nearly as bright inside the cave as it was in the sun outside. The initial chamber wound to the right and emptied into the main royal hall. Two sasquatch stood guard with spears crossed, barring entry.

"I am Gavin Allwind of the Trees. I have been summoned into the presence of the queen."

The guards uncrossed their weapons and stepped apart. A short hallway angled downward to the left. Gavin stepped along, taking his time, allowing his left hand to trail along the wall. He could feel the dampness of his home through his fingertips. Raising them to his long nose, the smell awoke memories of his youth.

The queen's secretary met him as the path spilled into the huge royal chamber. "Gavin. My friend," he exclaimed, "it has been so long. My spirit has ached for our reuniting."

This elf was shorter than Gavin, and rounder—the result of administrative duties—yet his color was a deep green. His friend was in good health. The secretary wore a formal tunic of maple leaves. Dipped in wax and strung together with golden thread, they formed a one-piece tunic that draped over his shoulders across both the front and back, overlapping at the sides. A sash of interwoven grape vines secured it at the waist.

"Maxle. My heart leaps with joy to see you again, old friend." Gavin threw his arms around the shorter elf and embraced him warmly. "We must converse and reprise our times while I am home."

"Yes, yes," Maxle agreed. "Indeed, we must."

"The queen has summoned me," Gavin informed his friend. "Before all else, I must present myself to her."

"Indeed," Maxle replied, then he turned to the great hall to announce Gavin's arrival to the room. In a voice that boomed more loudly than his short stature would imply, he shouted, "Gavin Allwind of the Trees to see Queen Agahpey Hesed of the Southern

Queendom."

The queen, wearing a full-length golden tunic of painted magnolia leaves, turned to face Gavin, and a huge smile spread across the smooth skin of her angular face. A crown of chestnuts interspersed with pinecones rested upon her head. Her piercing green eyes sparkled and latched onto Gavin's own eyes. "Gavin, my son, it has been too many seasons. Come and embrace your mother."

Following his reunion with his mother the queen, Gavin was excused and given time to clean himself, eat, and rest.

***

Sunday

The next morning, he stood before the high council and answered questions. At the moment when a debate replaced the interrogation, Gavin looked around at the assembled dignitaries. There was Maxon, his uncle from his father's side, and Maxle, his friend—they were both seated to his mother's left. Also present were Dargo and Dorcas, seated to her right. He considered each of their functions: Dargo was Director of Security Forces, and Dorcas was Minister of Community Support.

All four of the council members were dressed similarly to the queen in tunics of waxed magnolia leaves, the primary difference being that theirs lacked the golden tint and retained their natural dark green color. Dargo also donned a black bowler hat and had a dagger strapped to his waist. Dorcas accentuated her tunic with an emerald strung onto a simple gold necklace.

Dorcas winked at Gavin. In response, blood flushed into his face.

"The young prince has placed all our kind in great danger," stated Maxon, the Director of Imported Goods, which was a fancy title for the person who oversaw the material acquired and imported through shimmers across the queen's realm. "We cannot let this go without consequences." As he spoke, bracelets jiggled on his arms and clip-on earrings dangled from his ears and his short scruffy beard. He obviously had an affinity for human costume jewelry.

"That is ridiculous," Dargo replied, "he only revealed himself to children. Furthermore, he has been very valiant in taking such personal risks to stop the heinous acts of those fallen humans. He even suffered an injury. Look at his wounded ear. We could use more of our kind who have such valor." Dargo was another of Gavin's long-time friends.

The prince smiled and nodded his appreciation for the supportive words, even as his hand unconsciously went to his missing ear tip. A bullet had taken it off as he worked to rescue the human children.

"Valiant or not," Maxon continued, "the children revealed us to the man, Anders."

"He never saw us," Gavin said.

"Nevertheless, it is a slippery hill. You have acted foolishly, valor or no valor."

"What do you know of valor, Director Maxon?" Dargo asked. "I would say that your most valiant act has been to slip into the human realm long enough to snag another discarded bauble."

Maxon reacted with clenched teeth. "Do you challenge me in the Queen's presence, Director Dargo? I am not the one putting our whole community at risk. We are peaceful beings, and you have few actual security worries." The angry elf paused and glared at his fellow council member. "That could all change due to the careless decisions of Prince Gavin."

Dargo began to stand, but Dorcas placed a hand on his arm and pulled him back into his seat. "Maxon," she began, "there is no reason to attack one another. We are only here to listen and evaluate the details of the situation. The queen will determine any steps that need to be taken, and I trust her judgement. Personally, I agree with Dargo that Gavin's actions were brave." She turned toward Gavin and smiled again. His eyes met her gaze, and a warmth once more drifted up into his face. "He saw evil deeds of the most heinous kind and took action. True valor."

"It may have been brave—" Maxon began.

The queen raised her hand, and the room fell silent. "That is enough bickering," Hesed said. "I have heard enough. My sons have all been taught from their earliest moments to seek good, to always do what is right, and to protect those who are innocent. From the explanation Gavin has provided, he had no choice but to act despite the potential dangers. I will not punish him for following the core teachings that have been drilled into him from his infancy."

The four council members bowed and tugged on their right ears to indicate their agreement. Even Maxon seemed settled on the matter.

"Further," the queen added, "we may have need for more of our folk to show valor in the days to come."

Her last statement startled Gavin. That one phrase raised warning bells in his mind. They lived in a peaceful dimension. Other than the sadness of the fallen ones, rarely a conflict occurred among their kind except for the occasional dispute over some scavenged article or perhaps a misunderstanding over some food. The fact that Dargo directed a security team was merely a traditional holdover that dated back to long before Gavin was born. He had often wondered if it was a waste of resources. "Is there some danger, mother?" Gavin asked. "Is there some new peril to our people?"

"Indeed, there is," a voice boomed from behind him.

Gavin turned to see a robust elf dressed in a garment of waxed roses, daisies, and carnations, all interspersed and painted in alternating shades of silver and blue. Behind him and towering above him was a blond sasquatch sporting two sword scabbards, one over each shoulder. Gavin had heard of the yeti, but he had never seen one prior to this encounter.

"Gavin, my son and dear council members," the queen said, "let me introduce you to Ambassador Karma from the Ancient Kingdom. He brings us disturbing news."

Gavin moved up and stood next to Dargo in order to give the ambassador an audience. "A need for valor, and disturbing news?" he asked. "What has happened?"

Karma looked each council member in the eyes before continuing with a somber inflection. "Bayal has begun to reassert himself into our realm and by proxy into the realm of men."

All those listening gasped, save the queen herself. The council members murmured among themselves.

"As I reported to the queen earlier, he has dispatched hundreds of specters among our folk," Karma continued. "His goal is to influence our fallen ones to deeper levels of depravity. Furthermore, he is preparing to send them into the human realm to commit atrocities."

Remembering those he saw in the Louisville wasteland, Gavin

turned to his mother and said, "I saw many fallen ones in the northern wastes. There were so many that I lost count. Some were very bold with me, but I avoided them and continued my journey."

"How many years has it been since Bayal retreated into the Pit?" Dargo asked.

"Many generations," Hesed replied. "Over two thousand years. He fled as the Mighty One unveiled his solution in the Human Realm."

"What do we do?" Dorcas asked. "How do we respond?"

It was Karma who answered. "We are yet unsure. Still, we must raise our vigilance and enhance our security. If Bayal is successful in raising an army of our fallen ones and sends them through the shimmers, our life as we know it will be destroyed. The realm of men will fall into complete devastation, leaving our Arboreal Realm wasted beyond all imagination."

***

It was Sunday, a couple of weeks after Hope's rescue had made the news, when Kenny Burton finally decided to visit Cutters Notch. Of course, when he first saw Megan's and Hope's faces on his TV screen, he wanted to throw everything away and rush right down, but that voice in his mind urged caution. *"Think it through and plan it carefully,"* it spoke directly into his brain, *"then, go down there and kill them slowly, painfully."*

He had listened, studied the maps, read the news stories, and considered his options. Now, he was on a reconnaissance run. No action yet. Planning was his only intention.

The big V-8 rumbled under the hood of his old Ford Gran Torino as he cruised westward past the town line. The sun shone bright in the sky and the colors of the fall leaves were on full display.

A glance to the right showed the huge bluff from which the town derived its name. Large trees rose like feathers from its top. At its base, Kenny passed a seventies'- era school with light yellow bricks and metal framed windows. A large gymnasium rose on the western end. After the school, the forest swelled back toward the road only to recede once again at the entrance to a motel. *Interesting possibilities.*

Scoping out the area, he was looking for places where he could hide out or maybe take Hope or Megan, or both. *Megan might go by Maggie now*, he thought—a shortened version of Margaret, her middle name—*but she will always be Megan to me.* He was looking for a place to do the deeds.

He needed anonymity, seclusion, easy access, and escape. The motel had some of those qualities. Obviously, he could get on and off the road easily enough, but it lacked seclusion. Someone might see him taking them in or out of the room. He kept rolling.

On his left were small, random houses, some with broken windows and patchwork roofs. Others were in better condition with vinyl siding and painted trim work. The forest encroached right behind them and sometimes in between. Various businesses and town features interspersed the small homes. An auto repair shop. A self-carwash. A local government building. Even a small park. On the right, below the bluff, were larger, more stately homes. They sat back off the road behind hedges and under large old oaks and sycamores. These houses sported wraparound porches with large pillars and covered balconies.

Kenny spotted one in the middle of the bunch that appeared recently burned. Black smoke stains ringed the upper windows and the bottom ones were mostly boarded up. The siding was charred. He swung into the driveway for a closer look. *Hmm. Maybe. Secluded, but with homes on either side. It could work, though. Maybe the trees and brush will be enough cover.*

He backed out again and continued through town. Kenny paused at the main intersection, knowing that his ex-wife and her brat lived down the road to his left. Someone honked at him from behind, so he rolled on, passing the abandoned bank building and then the dilapidated old school. *More possibilities, but a little close to the intersection.*

The voice in his head wasn't helping. Sometimes, it was like he could feel it creeping around inside his brain, poking and prodding. It gave him a sense of power, but it was also frightening. Normal people didn't hear voices that they knew were distinctly not their own. Those who did had mental issues. So, on one level, he felt sort of insane, but still he heard the voice. It had to be real. Further, it would not let him ignore it. Right now, though, it seemed to be somewhere else as he explored Cutters Notch.

At the far end of town, he made a U-turn and returned to the intersection with Robbins Creek Road. This time he turned right.

He needed to see where they lived and understand the lay of the land around them. Again, the forest was everywhere, deep and dark. The tires roared as he sped over an old steel frame bridge. He knew from Google that their neighborhood was just ahead on the left, so he slowed down.

A street marker read Basketball Court. Two small roads connected the neighborhood to the county road, and a narrow row of low bushes created a perpendicular line between them. As he passed the first of the roads, he glanced to his left. There was Hope. She was standing with her back to him on the basketball court that filled the area between the roads. He could tell immediately it was her from the way she leaned to one side and held the ball on the opposite hip. It had been over two years, but that was the brat.

"*There she is,*" the voice roared inside his head. It was completely unexpected and so loud that Kenny swerved and nearly ran off the road. "*And there is the man-child, also. You must kill him along with the girl.*"

Kenny regained control and kept rolling by. He didn't want her to turn and recognize his car.

"*Do you understand?*"

"Yes," Kenny responded in a whisper.

"*Do you understand?*" The voice shouted the question into his head again.

"Yes," he replied, this time with more apparent enthusiasm.

As he drove a little further south, Kenny came upon an old farmhouse on the right that was overgrown with weeds. A gravel drive wound through the brushy yard, so he pulled in to check it out and turn around. *Another interesting option.* Like so many other places, the bottom windows were boarded over, and the paint was peeling from all exterior surfaces. Upstairs, the screens were torn, and a few windows were broken. Behind the house and off to the right, an old lonely, gray, grain silo loomed out of the weeds with its domed metal roof. Between the house and the silo, the rear end of an old jalopy jutted out, likely abandoned. *This has potential. Everything I need. And not far away either.*

Kenny had seen what he needed to see. He'd scoped out the lay of the land and identified some potential locales for his project. It was time to head home, so he backed out of the driveway and sped past Basketball Court toward town. He'd make one little pit stop for some smokes and a Coke, or maybe some beer, then he would head back to Muncie.

The bell dinged as he strolled into The General. He walked past the auburn-haired fat woman behind the counter—her name tag said "Rose"—and headed to the cooler for his drinks. Carrying the refreshments, he returned to the counter, plopped some money near the register, and asked for his favorite brand of cigarettes.

A round cooler was loaded with clumps of red carnations— carnations just like he used to give to Megan. *Hmm. Maybe just a little fun before I leave town.* He glanced out the window. The sun was headed west. *It'll be dark in a little while, so maybe I'll stick around for a bit.* Retrieving his wallet, he pulled out another ten and yanked some carnations from the cooler. *Maybe I'll even get an early start.*

***

October in Indiana can be blustery, and this day resembled that description, despite the sun still sitting high in the western sky. A chilly wind blew down out of the north, bringing with it the possibility of some early snow flurries. Hundreds of colorful leaves swirled around the little neighborhood as the three friends played basketball in their hoodies and jackets. Overhead, a flock of Canada geese soared toward the south in a V formation. Josh threw a bounce pass to Hope, which she scooped up and performed a perfect layup despite her bulky clothes.

Grabbing her own rebound, Hope stopped with her back to Robbins Creek Road and faced her two best friends. She leaned slightly to her left and propped the ball on her right hip. The boys were facing her with their backs to the cul-de-sac. She could see the Hicks' vacant house over Josh's right shoulder. She wanted to tell her friends her whole story—but she couldn't. Not yet.

"So, how did it happen? How did they start—you know what I mean?" she asked. "I mean, do you wake up one morning and say to yourself, 'Self, I think I want to eat someone today'? I just can't see how you ease into something like that."

"Beats me," Josh replied. "It's so gross. I get queasy just thinking about it."

"We may never know," said Danny. "Some people are just sick."

Hope glanced down at her left hand. There were still some tape burns on her skin from when the duct tape had been pulled off. "Guys, I don't know if I can get over this. I'm afraid of people and I'm jumpy."

***

The truth was that all three of them were scared. Both boys were having nightmares and Josh had taken to sleeping with a light on. In fact, Josh's parents had just told him that morning that they were looking at the possibility of him seeing a therapist. The only thing that really distinguished the three friends was that Hope was the first to admit the fear openly to the other two. Josh had told Hope about his nightmares but had otherwise worked to keep up a strong façade.

***

Just as she had admitted her fear, a car rumbled past the intersection behind her. The sound stirred a memory. Tires squealed and an engine gunned. Suddenly, it hit her. Her dad's car. She spun around. It was too late. All Hope saw was some dust floating above Robbins Creek Road. The vehicle had moved beyond the trees that edged up to the road on the south side of their neighborhood. "Did you guys see that car? Wha'd it look like? What color was it?" She spun back to her friends.

"I didn't see it," Danny said.

"Me either," Josh replied.

"We were looking at you," Danny explained.

Hope turned back toward the road. "See? I'm freakin' paranoid."

"Let's go inside," Danny suggested. "I'm cold, and there's an alien movie on Starz."

"Works for me," Josh added. "I'm getting cold, too."

The three friends collected their things and strolled off the ball court toward Danny's house.

***

Behind them, an old Gran Torino quietly cruised by, headed back toward town. Above them, a dark, undulating shadow weaved through the upper tree limbs.

Two
Sunday Night

The three friends were over midway through their second alien flick as Maggie knocked on the Flannery's door. When the door opened, Annie's friendly, freckled smile greeted her.

"Come in, Maggie," she said. "Come right on in." As Maggie stepped through the door, Annie babbled on. "I'm so glad to see you. Do you want a cookie? I've got some fresh oatmeal raisins in the kitchen."

Maggie glanced around the room, taking in the large collection of ceramic knickknacks. They covered the tables, the shelves, and filled various glass cabinets. Antique cups, old decorative perfume bottles, cheap souvenirs from various sightseeing spots. Below one overloaded shelf to her left, Hope sat on a sofa between her two best friends, zoned into a movie that was booming from a flat screen TV across the room. Hope's and Josh's fingers were interlaced. Maggie wasn't sure how she felt about that.

"Okay, I'll have a cookie—just one anyway." She followed Annie to the kitchen, pausing long enough to get Hope's attention. "How much time is left in the movie?"

"It's almost over, Mom. Maybe fifteen minutes."

"Good. We need to get home. You have school tomorrow, remember?" Her daughter smiled at her and nodded before her eyes drew back to the flashing screen.

In the kitchen, Annie was leaning her torso over the center island. A plate overloaded with large cookies took up the prime spot in front of her. Two yellow coffee cups lined up on one side. "I love oatmeal raisin cookies," she exclaimed with a smile stretching from ear to freckled ear. Her red hair was pulled back into a ponytail, but one tuft fell over her forehead. "Do you want coffee? Or, maybe some milk? I've got some two-percent in the fridge."

"A little milk would be nice," Maggie replied. "I can't stay long tonight. Hope has school tomorrow—her first day back." Since that crazy day and night two weeks earlier, Maggie had spent many hours with Annie and Cindy, Josh's mom. She had spent all her time at one of their homes, driving Hope to a doctor or counselor, or having a meal with Rick. *I hope Rick comes over tonight.*

"Right, Hope's first day is tomorrow. Do you think she's ready to go?"

"Yeah, I guess so. It's probably me that's not ready, but I have to let go sometime."

Hope had seemed to be incredibly resilient. She claimed to be ready to go back to school that first Monday, but Maggie insisted on keeping her baby close. It could be that the counselors she'd arranged for her little girl were more of her excuse than a real need. Still, she thought they were a good thing, even if they were an excuse. Hope may be tough, but she was still a young girl. "As much as I want to, I can't keep her locked up inside forever."

Annie poured the milk for Maggie and then some coffee for herself. She handed the cup to her neighbor and asked, "Have you seen Rick today?"

Maggie took the cup and raised it to her lips, a slight tremor making the milk slosh around a bit. "I saw him walking out to his new car this morning."

"He looks good in his new sheriff's uniform," Annie said. "Right?" She smiled at Maggie, swirled her coffee, and lifted it to her lips.

Maggie did like the way Rick looked in his new clothes, but she would like how he looked if he were wearing baggy sweatpants and a greasy t-shirt, too. "Yeah, he does," she replied. A smile brightened her face.

"Do you think he'll make it permanent in the special election next spring? Has he said anything to you about it?" Annie poured a little of the milk in her coffee.

Maggie picked up a cookie and nibbled off the edge. "He might. I mean, he hasn't really said much since they appointed him to fill Dunlap's spot, but he likes working closer to home."

Just the week before, the county council had asked Rick Anders, her neighbor, state trooper, and the man who helped save her daughter to be the interim sheriff. The previous sheriff, J.B. Dunlap, had died during Hope's ordeal.

The cookie was delicious. Maggie stuffed the rest of it in her mouth and grabbed a second one.

"He really likes you, Maggie," Annie stated. "I mean, the way he looks at you." The woman added a touch more sugar to her cup and mixed it with a spoon.

Maggie began to blush. She could feel the heat in her cheeks. "Do you really think so, Annie?" She felt a little like a schoolgirl with a crush. She'd been attracted to Rick before he saved Hope, but after…well…now she was truly smitten.

"Oh, yeah," she said. "He is all about you, girl. I mean, I'm a student of body language, but I don't need it to figure this one out. He can't stop smiling anytime he's around you." The woman nibbled her own cookie and took a sip of coffee before adding, "You really like him, too. Don't you?"

Annie's question shoved more heat into Maggie's face, but she reveled in it. "Yes, I do. I really hope there's more between us down the road." As she said that, the pain of her last relationship snuck up and bit her heart. Her eyes moistened and her lips quivered. "After Kenny, though, I'm afraid—" She couldn't continue. Instead, she turned around and buried her face in her hands, one cookie crumbling into her curly black hair.

Annie rushed around the island and pulled her into a bear hug. "Now, now. It's okay. You don't need to worry yourself about that Kenny. Rick ain't no Kenny, honey."

Maggie returned the embrace and lowered her head to Annie's shoulder. It was so comforting to have a friend nearby, and she sensed Annie really cared. The woman cared about her pain and was making herself available for support, both moral and tangible. She'd been on her own with the burdens of life for a long time now, and Annie's friendship was a welcome relief.

Annie pulled away and retrieved a tissue for her neighbor. As Maggie dabbed her eyes, Hope walked in. "What's wrong, Mom? Are you okay?"

"I'm okay, sweetie," she replied. "Annie and I were just

talking, and I got to thinking about all the stuff with your daddy."

Hope gave her mother a hug that mimicked Annie's from a few moments earlier. Annie took the opportunity to get a paper plate out of the pantry and began to load it with cookies.

"The movie's over," Hope said. "Let's go home so I can get my clothes ready for tomorrow." Maggie couldn't find words, so Hope pulled her toward the door. "Thank you, Mrs. Flannery," she added.

"Here, take these with you." Annie handed Hope the plate of cookies. "If you heat 'em up in the microwave for ten seconds, they're great for breakfast." The robust woman smiled warmly. "And they're great with a glass of milk."

Hope said her goodbyes to the boys and gave Josh a little kiss on his cheek, while Maggie hugged Annie and thanked her for her hospitality. As Maggie stepped outside onto the Flannery's stoop, she spotted taillights leaving their cul-de-sac, and a big engine revved from a car that sped away. Unconsciously, she put her arm around Hope's shoulders and pulled her close. There had been a steady stream of gawkers since the events two weeks prior, but the rev of the muscle car engine still unnerved her.

A chilly breeze rustled through the forest and blew fallen leaves here and there through the neighborhood. They swirled and danced in the middle of the cul-de-sac. The evening was very dark, and low-hanging clouds blocked the moon. Two streetlamps near the basketball court provided the only light not connected to a house. Maggie shivered. Hope, holding the plate of cookies in her right hand, used her left to pull her mother closer. Annie switched on her porch light, and they began to make their way down the sidewalk.

"Oh, hey there," a voice called to them from their right. Startled, Maggie and Hope stepped back in response. Turning toward the Hicks' vacant house, Maggie saw the shape of a man standing behind a large, older car parked in the old couple's driveway. He wore glasses, and the light from the porch reflected off the lenses as if they were mirrors. A mother-bear instinct caused Maggie to shove Hope behind her.

"Did I scare you?" the man called out. "I'm so sorry."

The man began to walk in their direction, so Maggie and Hope backed up toward Annie's stoop.

"Who is it, Mom?" Hope asked.

"Shh. I don't know."

"Oh, don't be afraid," the man said with a friendly tone. "I'm harmless, I promise. I just wanted to introduce myself."

"Are you a realtor?" Maggie asked, her voice shaky.

"Oh no. Nothing like that," he answered. "Actually, I also want to apologize to you and your girl. On behalf of our family. My name is Al Havener. I'm Faye's nephew. The family has asked me to take an inventory of the house and prepare it for sale on their behalf."

At the mention of the man's connection to Faye Hicks, Hope bolted back to Annie Flannery's front door, ready to knock. Maggie held her ground, but the hair stood up on the back of her neck.

"Ms. Spencer, my whole family is just sick about what happened. I know you can never forgive my aunt and uncle for what they did, but our hope is that you can resist the temptation to blame our extended family. We didn't know what they were, and we're so sorry that they did what they did." What little hair the man had was flying around in the breeze. He kept reaching up to push it back down, a lost cause. He approached to within twenty feet and then hesitated. Stuffing his hands in his front pockets, he smiled. "Is there anything we can do to ease your anxiety?"

"Mr. Havener—"

"Please, call me Al."

"Mr. Havener, we just need time. Time, and space. Please give us that and don't contact us. I bear no grudge against you, but you'll understand if I'm hesitant to trust strangers these days."

"Of course," he replied. "I understand. I'll leave you alone." He paused; then he abruptly turned, walked up to the Hicks' front door, and went inside.

"It's okay, honey," Maggie said to Hope. "He's gone now. Let's go home."

Her daughter rejoined her at the street, and they cut across the cul-de-sac to their little ranch-style home. It looked much like all the others on the street except that it was well lit. Maggie had been sure to turn on all the interior lights, plus the front and back porch lights before she left. They shuffled though the leaves toward their stoop.

Suddenly, Maggie stopped short, grabbing Hope's arm.

"What is it, Mom? What's wrong?"

Maggie pointed. There on the porch, just to the right of the storm door, was a small bouquet of red carnations. All the blooms were bent over, the stems kinked. Grabbing Hope, she quickly unlocked the door and shoved her inside.

"He's found us," she exclaimed. "Your dad found us."

***

"Hey there, Sheriff," Rose said to Rick who'd entered the General. Rose's cheeks flushed, and her lips curled up in a smile. "Lookin' good there in your new uniform." She gave him a flirty wink.

Rick smiled at the redhead who worked as the manager of the Cutters Notch General Store, lovingly called 'The General' by the locals. She was mid-thirties, bright, and quick to banter with anyone who walked through the door. Some might claim that she carried a little too much weight, but Rick felt her size suited her well. If he didn't already have eyes for Maggie, Rose might have captured his attention.

"That's 'interim sheriff,' Rose," Rick said in reply. "You know that but thank you." He smiled at her warmly. Despite his deflection of the title, he appreciated the compliment. His tan and brown county uniform was still new enough that he could feel the starch in the collar. His radio crackled, and he reached for the mic fastened to his shoulder, but it stayed silent—false alarm.

"Just 'til the spring," the woman answered. "Then you can make it permanent."

"We'll see," Rick responded and headed back toward the cooler. "We'll see."

"You've got my vote." Rose winked again.

He wasn't sure if he wanted to run for office or not, but he knew he had to decide soon. This new job was sprung on him only a few days after Sheriff Dunlap died. *Was that really only two weeks ago?* He had taken a couple of days to think it over before accepting. Now, here he was just a week into the responsibility and folks were already asking him if he was going to make it a career move. Rick hadn't even sorted out his new office yet.

Officially, he was only on a temporary, extended leave from the Indiana State Police. Work for the state or work for the county?

Hold elected office and worry about being reelected every few years or go back to the security of a state police job for maybe twenty more years? These were huge questions. One thing about this new role did appeal to him, though—he liked working close to home. He liked being near Maggie and Hope. *Maybe I can even see my son more often.*

"Are you just coming on shift?" Rose called out from the front of the store. She busied herself rearranging the products under the lip of the counter.

"Nope. I'm close to my quitting time. Well, as close as I can get in this job."

As he reached into the cooler for a bottle of water, his cell phone rang. His hand came back out with a drink, but he dropped it in among the chips so he could answer the call. Maggie's number played on the screen, and a warm feeling flushed his face. "Hello?"

"Rick!" Her voice was frantic. "He's found us. He was here."

"Maggie, please. Take a breath. Who's been there? Who're you talking about?"

"Kenny. He left a bunch of broken flowers on my porch. Where are you? Can you come?"

"I'll be there in two minutes."

He left the cold bottle of water sitting between the barbeque and sour cream chips and waved at Rose as he rushed out the door. "Gotta go, Rose."

***

He's a good one, Rose thought. *Hope we can keep him.*

***

"How do you know it was him?" Rick asked, holding Maggie in a loose hug on the front porch. "I mean, anyone could have left those there. There's been a lot of people reaching out to you since we got Hope back."

"Look at 'em," she replied. "They're all broken. All of 'em."

Rick hesitantly released the frightened woman. She smelled good and he enjoyed the embrace despite the desperate nature of the situation. He felt needed and…well, connected. Whether it was acting as a protector or a friend, and maybe one day as a lover, he enjoyed the connection he was building with this woman whom he found to be remarkable, beautiful, and vulnerable.

Reaching down, he picked up the damaged bouquet. As she

had said, each flower stem had been snapped and kinked over. *That is weird and definitely not a good sign.*

"He used to give me red carnations before we were married. After we were married, he'd still bring them once in a while—to make up after a bad fight. When we stepped out of Annie's house tonight, I saw taillights leaving the court, and I heard the rumble of his car's engine. It sounded familiar, but then I was distracted by that guy at the Hicks' house."

"What guy?" Rick glanced over to see lights on in the former home of his cannibalistic neighbors.

"Oh, some family member who's supposed to clear out the house. You know, sell their stuff and put the house on the market. I told him to give us space and not bother us."

He examined the flowers and asked, "Why are all the stems broken?"

"I don't know," she choked out. "I think he's messin' with me. Trying to scare me." Maggie pressed forward and wrapped her arms around Rick's waist again. She rested her cheek against his new uniform.

Rick let her stay that way. She needed a sense of security, and Rick was becoming that source of safety in a world that had been completely insecure to her for a long time. He cupped her face. Tilting her chin up, he stared into her eyes. "I'll call it in and have my deputies keep an eye out for his car." Maggie smiled at him, and his heart surged a touch. "Tomorrow, I'll make some calls and get the lowdown on what he's been up to. I promise you," he added, "Kenny Burton is not going to hurt you. Not you. Not Hope. Not ever. I won't let him."

Maggie pulled back a little, keeping her hands on his waist. "I'm really scared. Hope is too," she added. "Can you stay in the house with us? I know you're probably—"

"Yes," he answered before she finished. "I'll not leave either of you alone tonight."

***

Gronek and Smakal, two of the three elfin brothers that had assisted in Hope's recent rescue, emerged from the trees in their dimension's version of Basketball Court. The aura of life was falling like rain all around them as the leaves made their annual journey to the forest floor. The bare limbs left behind were glowing varying shades of a dull, pulsating blue. Soon, the entire forest would take on that simple blue aura until the spring season pushed the winter aside.

The two brothers, standing there with coats of sycamore leaves worn over discarded long johns and with satchels hung across their shoulders, scanned the clearing that was the home of their friends in the human dimension. In their own realm, it was an odd-looking place full of geometric holes in the ground, rounded off shrubbery, and plants that seemed to float in the air. At night, as it was now, the clearing glowed with various shimmers of multiple sizes and shapes. It had become their practice for the last two weeks to visit nearly every night so that they could look in on their friends as they slept, sort of keeping watch.

This night seemed to carry a sense of tension in the air. Sheba, Josh's dog across the way, barked nonstop. The dog was barking toward the boy's house rather than toward the forest as she normally would. Then, the barking abruptly stopped, and Sheba appeared to be wolfing down some food.

"It is an odd time for a snack," Smakal remarked, "but maybe the humans are awake exceptionally late tonight for some reason."

Gronek shrugged.

"You go look in on Hope," Smakal continued as he absently straightened his new—to him—Indianapolis Colts hat. "I will go across to check on Josh and meet you at Danny's shimmer."

Smakal had seen Josh thrashing in his sleep during some of his previous visits, and it worried the elf. Even though neither he nor Gronek had seen the specter hanging around, he had real concerns that it was terrorizing the young ones. When Josh had screamed at it during Hope's ordeal, the specter had heard him. Smakal knew then that the evil entity would seek the boy out.

"Agreed," Gronek replied as he pulled a knit hat down on his head, making his ears stick out on each side. He ambled off toward the rectangular hole where Hope's dwelling stood in the other dimension.

Smakal strolled through the space that split the manmade canyons that represented Rick's home and the home of the evil couple. The elf shivered as his mind considered the deeds they had committed.

***

Gronek approached the shining portal that provided passage to Hope's bedroom, careful not to step on the fall flowers that her mother had planted in the soil below. Rising on his tiptoes, he pressed his nose to the wavering light and peeked inside. The room was empty.

Perhaps, she is still in the main living space. Gronek edged his way around to peer into that shimmer. He could see no movement, but a large man, the human they called "Rick" was asleep on the sofa. No sign of Hope, though. *Perhaps, she is with her mother.*

Gronek retreated around the invisible home to the portal that represented Maggie's bedroom and peered into that space. *There you are.* Hope was snuggled up next to her mother. Maggie's arm was wrapped around her daughter in a protective hug; a sheet covered them to the waist. They were wearing cute, matching pajamas. Gronek would watch for them to be discarded. Assured of Hope's safety, he turned toward Danny's home. That was when he heard Smakal call out.

***

Smakal headed toward Josh's shimmer after passing between the large policeman's canyon and the hole that represented the darkness that had almost cost his friends everything. A touch of pride welled up in his heart at the way that he and his brothers had worked with the boys—and the man—to rescue the girls, both Hope and the other unexpected one, Faith. But by the way that his brother, Gavin, had been called before the queen, they would have to answer for the human contact. He did not regret it, though. *No, I do not regret it one bit.*

As the elf crossed the space between where the human homes stood in the other dimension, three shimmers appeared in an unusual spot. Small ones. Two stood at Smakal's eye level, a few feet apart. Oval in shape. A third one split the distance between the other two and stood a foot higher. This oval was longer and narrower. Smakal recognized the orientation as representing a human transport vehicle—a car.

Stopping, the elf considered the position of the human transport machine. By his estimation, in the human realm, this vehicle would be parked on the oval road in front of the dwellings but positioned just between Danny's and Josh's homes. He had never seen a set of shimmers in that position before. He lifted the Colts cap off his head and scratched the tiny tuft of green hair on his crown. The elf peered into the closest of the miniature shimmers. The metallic form of a fender was visible. *Hmm.* He had no explanation, so he continued on toward Josh's shimmer.

As he rounded into Josh's backyard, he expected Sheba to greet him. She always did. He even looked forward to her slimy affection. It was one of the Mighty One's gifts that allowed the humans' pet canines to coexist between dimensions. This time, though, she did not come ambling over with her tongue hanging out. Instead, he found her lying unconscious on the grass near the rear of the yard. Her breathing was deep, but she was unresponsive when he reached down and stroked her fur. Fear rose up in his heart.

Bolting upright, Smakal considered the unusually placed shimmers and the unconscious dog. *Something is wrong.* Hurrying to Josh's shimmer, he peered inside. His friend was not in his bed. The bedclothes were scattered about. The elf caught movement to the right side of the room where the boy's window was positioned. He saw a man. The man was carrying Josh. As Smakal watched in horror, the man shoved the boy through the window and then followed him through to the outside.

"Gronek! Come quickly. Hurry. Something is very wrong."

"I am coming," Gronek called back.

As Smakal waited for his brother to meet him, drag marks appeared in the grass. They were headed toward the unusual shimmers, where the unexpected car was parked. Gronek ran right through them as he approached.

"What is wrong?"

Smakal quickly explained what he had found—the dog, the man, the tracks. Gronek spun around toward Josh's shimmer.

"Must you always see for yourself?" Smakal exclaimed as his brother checked the boy's room. "We must check on Danny before it is too late."

"I am sorry. I do not understand what is happening."

Having had more time to process the facts, Smakal knew exactly what was going on. "They are being abducted," he explained. "We must find a way to help them. Come on, let us check on Danny."

The brothers reached Danny's shimmer together and peered

inside. They were dismayed to see that the boy was being dragged out of his bed toward his bedroom window.

"What do we do?" Smakal asked. "Do we dare intervene again?"

"It is too dangerous to our kind," Gronek answered. "Give me a moment to think."

"Danny only has moments," Smakal pointed out.

Gronek rubbed his chin with both thumbs of his right hand, a habit he had when he was working on an idea. "Do you still have that tennis ball in your bag?"

"Yes."

"Give it to me." As he spoke, he dug into his own satchel. After a moment of rifling through it, he came out with a stubby pencil and a piece of lined notebook paper. Quickly, Gronek scribbled on the paper.

Smakal squeezed the ball, his anxiety making him fidget; worry for his human friends compressed his heart just as he compressed the small, fuzzy orb in his hand.

When he finished scribbling, Gronek looked up. "Do you have a rubber band?"

"I am unsure. I will look."

They both fished inside their respective bags. Seconds later, Gronek produced one. Then he used it to fasten the note he had made to the tennis ball. "Follow me," he said, then sprinted away toward Hope's shimmer.

Smakal kept his eye out for the unusual shimmers as he followed Gronek. Still there. There was still time.

Gronek reached the shimmer that opened into Hope's living room just ahead of his brother.

"What do you plan to do?" Smakal asked, stopping beside him.

"Rick, the policeman, is asleep on their long, soft chair. I will lean inside and throw the ball at him. With any blessing from the Mighty One, he will awaken, find the message, and come to our friends' rescue. Boost me up a little. I can see in, but it is too high for me to enter."

Gronek stepped onto Smakal's knee while his brother steadied him. Peering inside, he could see Rick still slumbering on the sofa. The elf leaned his body through the portal to the waist. As he dangled there midair, he flung the ball at the man. His aim was good, and the ball bounced off Rick's forehead, ricocheting over to a side table before striking the television and falling to the floor.

"What the—" Rick bolted upright, pulling his weapon.

Gronek made eye contact with the man before ducking back through. "I think he saw me. His eyes met mine."

Smakal shook his head. "This is not good. Humans are not supposed to see us—especially adult humans. Did you say anything?"

"No," Gronek replied with slightly less than the full truth. "I saw his eyes and then ducked out."

The two elves stood on their toes and peeked inside again. Hope and the adults gathered around the ball. "Perhaps this will work," Gronek said.

Turning around, Smakal watched the unusual shimmers begin to move. The lights circled the open area in front of them before moving away through the flanking trees. "It is too late," he said, fear for his friends gripping his gut. "We should have intervened, despite the peril."

***

Rick Anders patted his boy on the head. "Come on. Let's go," he said. "Let's have some fun while the sun is shining." Ricky was sitting on the floor, tying his shoes. The boy couldn't seem to get it right, so Rick knelt down and laced them up for him. Then, they were at the door. The sun, just above the treetops, cast long shadows across the court.

Stepping outside onto his stoop, he used his right hand to pull his son against his leg. A ball glove was on his left. Ricky had a similar but smaller glove on his left as well.

"Hi, Rick," a young voice called out. It came from one of the older kids playing hoops on the basketball court. He waved with the gloved hand.

Taking a deep breath, Rick could feel the smile creeping across his face. All was right with the world. "The only thing that would make this day better," he said, "would be if Maggie were out here with us."

Suddenly, there she was, standing at the end of his walk, a ball glove on her hand, as well.

The three of them walked together onto the cul-de-sac and spread out so they could toss the ball back and forth. Rick positioned Ricky so the sun was behind the boy. He didn't want him to lose the ball in the light and get hurt. Looking over, he saw Maggie. His face flushed. He couldn't help but smile when she was around. Rick loved how her long, dark hair curled around her pretty face. He tossed the ball to her. "Be careful when you throw it to Ricky," he said. "He's pretty new to baseball."

Maggie caught the ball and then zinged it over to the boy. He caught it with no problem. *Wow, he's already pretty good.* Ricky turned toward him. Suddenly, the boy was much bigger, a teenager. He flung the ball at Rick, and the man lost it in the sun blazing over his boy's shoulder. *It missed his glove and slammed into his forehead.*

"What the—" he blurted.

Rick was shocked awake. Something had hit him in the face, so he grabbed his weapon and lurched upward. A ball was rolling around on the floor. Glancing to his left, he caught movement. There, hanging half out of the wall mirror was an odd little face and two arms. The small strange being had a slight greenish tint to its skin, and it wore a pink stocking hat pulled down. Ears pointed out on each side. Their eyes locked. The little green face gave him a grim smile. A small green finger pointed at the ball rolling on the floor. Then, it was gone. The elf—*it was an elf*—dropped back through the glass of the mirror like a turtle might drop its head under the surface of a pond.

Jumping to his feet, Rick knocked over the coffee table. A glass of water, a pile of books, and a tray of flowers crashed onto the floor. Ignoring the mess, he rushed to the mirror. Nothing but his own startled face with a round, slightly red spot on his forehead stared back.

"What's going on?" Maggie rushed in from the hallway with Hope at her heels. "Are you okay?"

"I'm fine," Rick replied. He waved them back. "But I think I just saw one of Hope's elf friends." He reached up and rubbed his forehead with his left hand. A gun still dangled from his right. Glancing at the weapon, he returned it to his holster.

"What?" Hope blurted. "Where?"

"He was hanging out of the mirror. Kinda green. Had a pink stocking hat on his head. Apparently, he hit me in the head with that ball." He pointed to the tennis ball that had come to rest near

the sofa. "Hey, what's this?" he asked. Rick picked up the ball and found a folded piece of paper attached to it with a rubber band. Maggie and Hope gathered around him, Maggie on his left and Hope on his right. Carefully, he pulled the paper from the ball and unfolded the message:
The boys are being taken
Help them
Hurry

"Does he mean Josh and Danny?" Hope asked, fear riding on her words.

Rick rushed to the front window facing the cul-de-sac. Nothing moved, but the trees to his right, where Basketball Court emptied onto Robbins Creek Road were illuminated in red. Taillights. The crimson lights moved away. He couldn't tell which direction. Pulling out his phone, he dialed Roger Gillis, Josh's dad, and waited while it rang. It seemed like the hours were ticking away with each ring.

"Hullo?" A groggy voice answered. "Rick, is that you?"

"Roger! Quick. Check on Josh. Make sure he's okay."

Rick bobbed from foot to foot while he waited for Roger to return. Thoughts laced with fear rushed through his mind, but he kept shoving them back. *It's probably nothing. It's just some prank. Or maybe I'm still stuck in some weird dream.*

There was a rustling sound, then Josh's dad picked up his phone. "Cindy, get up quick. Call Annie and see if Josh is over there," he said before speaking to Rick. "Rick, he's gone. His window is open, and his bedcovers are dragged over beside it. You've got to find him!"

***

Ten minutes later, they all gathered in the Flannery kitchen. Kevin Flannery, Danny's dad, was making coffee. Annie dumped a sheet of fresh cookies on a plate resting on the countertop, picking up strays that fell off the sides. Roger sat at the table next to Cindy, her head in her hands.

Rick stood facing them with Maggie holding Hope behind him. "Annie," he said. "Please sit down."

The woman stopped. Her face was flushed. The plate of cookies fell from her hand and landed hard on the tabletop. Covering her face, she burst into tears and fell into her husband's grasp.

"They've probably snuck out again," Roger said. "I'd have to nail Josh's feet down to keep him inside." Cindy peered up to Rick, hoping against hope.

"I don't think so, Roger," the sheriff replied. "I have reason to believe they were taken by someone, both of them." Annie let out a sob. Tears welled up in Kevin's eyes.

It was Cindy who responded. "But, Rick, how do you know that? And who could it be? Earl and Faye are locked up. They're just kids."

Rick hesitated. He had no way to explain how he knew what he knew. *What am I supposed to say*? If he told them that an elf with a pink hat popped through Maggie's mirror and hit him with a tennis ball that had a note attached... Well, that would be the end of his credibility.

"It's Kenny," Maggie blurted. "It has to be. He's trying to hurt us...I mean, he's trying to hurt Hope by hurting her friends. Kenny left those flowers last night, and now he's kidnapped the boys."

Rick turned toward Maggie. Her eyes held so much pain as she stood there holding her daughter, the anguish causing her to shiver. He shifted his gaze to the girl. She was as tall as her mother. Hope's eyes were full of pain, too, and something else...then, he recognized it, sadness.

"Flowers? What flowers?" Annie piped up.

"Someone left a bouquet of broken carnations on Maggie's porch last night," Rick explained. "It's just the sort of thing her ex would do. I was planning to have one of my buddies on the Muncie PD go by and have a chat with him later today."

"Rick," Maggie asked, "how do you know he's in Muncie?"

"I had him checked out. First, I confirmed that he was out of prison. He got out in August. Then, I looked into where he lived and what he's been doing. He lives in a rundown house in Muncie and works at a grocery store, stocking shelves."

"Well," Roger said, "if it is him, then he's not at home right now. Can you call Muncie now and have someone go over there?"

"I already did," Rick replied. "I'm waiting for their response." As if on cue, his cell phone rang. He stepped into the other room to take the call.

***

Cindy stared at Maggie, her pale complexion streaked with flushed splotches. "Why would he do this?" she asked. "Why would your ex-husband want to hurt our boys? He doesn't even know them." A tear spilled from her left eye.

"He's an evil man," Maggie looked away from Cindy, unwilling to make eye contact. "He didn't used to be. When I first met him, he was a big teddy bear. Something changed, though. Now, he's just evil."

Hope buried her face into her mother's chest. All the memories of her Monster Night, the night her father had tried to kill her, flooded back into her mind. *He took my friends in Muncie away. He took my dog away. Now, he's taking it all again.* She hurt deep inside. She wanted to hate her dad. Still, somehow, she couldn't. She couldn't find the hate within herself. All she could find was pain and loss. It was all happening again.

"He's not at home," Rick announced. "They went by. The place is all dark. They banged on the door multiple times with no response. His car isn't there." Rick Anders paused and observed the distraught parents. "I want you to know," he added, emotion leaking from his voice, "that I've got my entire team out looking right now. I've called in all the off-duty deputies and I'm heading out now, too. We will find them."

***

Danny stirred. He opened his eyes, and the world rose like a tunnel above him. He could see the moon. It was a crescent way up above, shining like a dull memory. Around it, his vision swirled. He lifted his right hand to see if he could touch the moon. *That's crazy, but I've gotta try.* As he watched, his fingers stretched out in a long line toward the sky. *Maybe I can.* He giggled. The sound seemed silly, so he giggled again.

Next to him, he heard someone moan. He flopped his left hand in that direction. The back of his hand landed on a face.

"Ow," a sleepy voice said. "What are you doing? Why'd you hit me?"

"Oops," Danny said. "Sorry." He looked over. It was too dark to see the owner of the voice, but it sort of sounded like— "Josh, is that you? What are you doing in my room? How can I see the moon? Did you cut a hole in our roof?" He felt weird.

"I don't think we're at your house," his friend replied. "It's really dark in here."

"I had a weird dream that I was dragged out of my bedroom window."

"Me too," Josh said, "but I don't think it was a dream."

Danny was starting to regain his senses. The world was returning to reality and his ability to think was riding with it. Danny's fingers, which he continued to stare at, began to retract to their normal length. He stared at their silhouette against the light of the moon. "I'm cold," Danny said.

***

"Me too," Josh answered. "Any idea where we are?"

"Not a clue. We're on something hard and dirty. Concrete, maybe."

Josh began to feel the area around him. He spread his fingers and reached out to his left. His palm met a hard, smooth-surfaced wall that seemed to have a bit of an arc. Bringing his hand down to the floor, it brushed against something soft. That soft thing squealed and scurried away. The boy sat bolt upright. "Danny, I think there's a rat in here with us."

Danny quickly sat up, also. Josh grabbed his friend's arm and pulled himself next to his buddy. Sliding back against the curved wall, the boys sat huddled together while the moon slowly crossed out of view above them and the little light they had faded away.

Three

Gronek and Smakal continued to watch the humans through the various shimmers. They observed as Rick Anders used his radio and his phone to call for assistance. When Rick, Maggie, and Hope exited the house, the elves skittered from shimmer to shimmer until they found them again in Danny's kitchen. The boys' mothers were crying, the fear obvious on their flushed faces. The fathers seemed anxious and paced about as if they were restless for some sort of action. It became obvious to the brother elves that the human boys whom they considered friends were in grave danger.

"What shall we do now?" Gronek asked, his eyes moist.

"I wish Gavin were here," Smakal replied. "He would know what action to take."

The brothers sat down on the damp grass beside one another, neither speaking for several minutes. Gronek pulled his legs up and wrapped his arms around them. Resting his chin on his knees, he let out a sigh. Smakal splayed his legs outward in a V shape and crossed his arms across his chest. He took a deep breath and slowly exhaled, the vapor visible in the chilly night air under the moonlight that had begun to slip through the clouds.

Finally, Gronek reached into his pouch and pulled out a little tube. "We need Gavin," he said before blowing into the tiny cylinder. His fingers fluttered up and down twice. After two minutes, he repeated the action. Thirty seconds later, a fairy fluttered down and landed on his left arm. "Smakal, write a note to our brother. We must send for him at once."

Smakal jotted down some words on a tiny strip of paper and then rolled it up like a miniature scroll. Taking a piece of string, he tied it to the fairy's luminescent leg.

Gronek lifted the little winged creature up before his eyes. Its wings sparkled with hundreds of golden lights. Streaks of blue and green pulsated randomly down through its torso. "Please carry this message to our brother, Gavin. He is with Queen Hesed at her home. Proceed with all haste and without detour. It is most urgent. Do you understand, little friend?"

The fairy cocked its head once to the right and once to the left to indicate understanding. Then, it bowed deeply and sprang into the air. After swirling around their heads twice, it darted into the southern sky.

Gronek turned to face Smakal. "Now, we must do what we can."

"Yes," his brother replied. "We must search the shimmers before the sun breaks the horizon."

***

Patrick Bray opened his eyes and stared at the rough planks that formed the roof of the shack. The dirty little place had been his home for over three months, ever since he and his family were snatched from their rooms at the little motel. Trick exhaled and watched the moisture turn to mist in the cold air. On the cot next to his, his father coughed in his sleep.

"Dad? Hey, Dad. Wake up," Trick said, leaning over toward his father. "It's six o'clock. They just rang the bell. Time to get up." He was sitting on the side of his hard bunk in the dark. Light filtered in through the cracks in the outer walls. The boy stretched his legs out. The chain shackled to his right ankle rattled at the movement. His dad didn't reply. He coughed instead.

Pulling the coarse blanket over his shoulders, Trick stood up in the space between their beds and leaned over his father. Russell Bray had his back to his son. Trick checked to see if he was okay and tapped him on the shoulder. His father's bright red hair was long now, longer than he'd ever seen it. Its oily waves spilled out on the thin piece of foam their captors considered a pillow. The man barely moved.

"Come on, Dad. It's time to get up. They'll be here any second to unlock us. Are you okay?"

The boy shivered. When they'd first been taken, it was hot back in this shed against the rock wall. Mosquitoes ate them alive. Now, the seasons were changing, and the nights were getting cold, very cold. Winter would be upon them soon, and Trick was starting to worry that they wouldn't be able to survive it. Reaching down, he touched his father's cheek. It was hot; his Dad was burning up with a fever.

"Dad," he exclaimed. "Wake up." He shook him harder.

Russell mumbled, coughed loudly, and then rolled over on his back, but he didn't wake up. Then he started to cough heavily. He coughed and coughed before rolling over again.

The door opened, slamming back on its hinges, and a flashlight shone in. "Get up," the figure ordered. "I've got your grub, and then you need to get working. Lots of stone to haul outta that mine today, fellas."

"My dad's sick," Trick answered. "I can't wake him up. Please help him. He's burning up with a fever and keeps having coughing fits. Can you get him a doctor? Please?"

"Nope. No doctors," the man replied. Shoving the boy aside, the man stooped over Russell. He shook him. Touched his forehead. "Well, obviously he can't work. He'll just have to stay in bed. I'll have Mabel come down and check on him. Best I can do."

After stepping back outside for a moment, he returned with a keyring and a bowl. "Here's your oatmeal," he said, handing Trick the bowl.

Trick sat down and stretched out his right leg, as he had been conditioned to do. The man unlocked his shackle. "You've got five minutes, then we're headed to the mine."

Trick looked over at his sleeping father. He used to long for the days when they were a family, fussing over music or food. Trick missed arguing with his sister. He gave up that fruitless emotion. Now, he just wanted to survive—he wanted his dad to survive. Hopelessness circled his heart like a buzzard.

***

Rick felt that weird sense of déjà vu. Not in the locale he found himself in, but in the overall situation. It had only been two weeks since those intense hours searching for and then rescuing Hope. Now, here he was, smack in the middle of another search for missing kids. This time, there was no mobile command post since they were sure the boys were taken away from the area in a vehicle, but all the other factors were in play. The Indiana State Police were notified. The FBI was contacted. Flyers were going up at convenience stores and truck stops. His deputies had been out all night looking for unusual vehicles, driving behind buildings, passing through various parking lots. Still, nothing turned up.

The Muncie PD confirmed several times that Kenny Burton had not returned home, so at six a.m., Rick decided he was going to head to Muncie himself. This was his investigation and Kenny being his prime suspect, Rick wanted to be there whenever the man did show up. At nine a.m., he sat on a rickety lawn chair on a wooden-plank front porch on West 17th Street waiting for the big man to come home. He took a deep breath and then watched the mist billow out and dissipate as he exhaled the chilly morning air.

Rick tried to get a feel for the man from his front yard, the sun peeking over the tops of the trees behind the homes across the street. The house was a small, white cottage with wood trim. The paint was flaking off everywhere. There was a front door with a broken screen, flanked by two windows with purple trim. The wooden porch slats and the concrete sidewalk that stretched to the street also had the residue of purple paint. *What's with the purple? School color?* A small lilac bush sat off to his left and some rose bushes gone wild lined the edge of the porch. Beside him sat a small metal table with a full ashtray surrounded by crumpled beer cans. A small rubber mat in front of the door read, "Go Away!" *Lovely place.*

He heard the growl of a big engine. Glancing up, an old muscle car rumbled toward the house, slowly.

***

Kenny Burton had had a late night and now what felt to him like an early morning, so he was tired and feeling a little ragged around the edges. He rolled into Muncie along Hoyt Avenue with its mishmash of small houses, industrial businesses, and biker clubs. He was eager to get home, have a beer, and then catch a couple more hours of sleep before he had to be back at work stacking cans of green beans. The voice in his head was silent. He was grateful. It was the only time he could really rest.

As he crossed Cowan Road, he glanced in his rearview mirror at a police cruiser that had just pulled out of a gas station and began to follow him, the sun reflecting off its light bar on top. Out of instinct, he let up on the gas and checked his speedometer. He wasn't speeding. *Relax. I'm mostly sober and I'm not speeding.*

Nothing to worry about.

He turned onto 17th Street. The cruiser followed. A bead of sweat formed on his left temple. A cigarette was burning in his left hand, so he took a drag.

As he rounded a small bend, he saw a car in his driveway, a man sitting on his porch, and another police cruiser parked perpendicularly across the road. He was boxed in, trapped. *Well, looks liked I'm screwed.*

The voice in his head still had nothing to say.

Kenny pulled up in front of his house and parked parallel to the street. For a few moments, he just sat there. The city cruiser that was following him stopped alongside his car. Yet a third car pulled up behind him, now completely blocking him in. If he decided to bolt, he'd have to smash through the barricade or take off on foot.

Car doors opened and closed. Men circled his Torino, their hands on their weapons. The cop on his porch stood. Kenny recognized him from the news—the state trooper who'd helped to rescue Hope. *Your little girl*—it was a random thought out of nowhere. He rejected it.

The trooper was wearing a sheriff's uniform now. Kenny placed his hands on the Torino's steering wheel. The cigarette was smoldering between the fingers of his left hand. He wanted a drag, but the nicotine fix would have to wait.

"Get out of the car, Burton," the man on the porch ordered. "Keep your hands visible as you exit."

He unlatched the door. *Maybe those flowers weren't such a good idea.*

***

Rick stepped off Kenny Burton's porch as the big man exited his vehicle. Kenny flicked a cigarette into the grass and then rose to his full height. *Wow, he is big.* Rick was no small person, but this guy was huge. *I'm glad I've got some backup with me.*

"Where are the boys, Kenny?" Rick demanded. "In your trunk?"

"Where's who? What boys? I don't know what you're talking about."

"Open your trunk," Rick ordered.

"You got a warrant?" Kenny countered. "You still gotta have a warrant to go searching my stuff."

Rick sighed. "C'mon, Burton. I'm going to look in that trunk. Just pop it so I won't damage the lock," Anders said. "Open it up, big man."

Kenny stared at Rick for a long moment. "Okay, okay," he finally replied. "Look, I don't know what you're lookin' for. I ain't done nothin' wrong, but if you wanna look in the trunk, then have at it." He jiggled the keys in his right hand and turned toward the back of the car. With his left hand, he pushed his black-rimmed glasses up on his nose.

Rick watched Kenny walk around his car, the outline of muscles rippled through the shirt covering his upper arms. His shoulders were massive. Despite all the crushed beer cans lying around, the guy had no gut. He was looking at a dangerous man.

The trunk latch popped; the lid rose on its own. Kenny stepped back and motioned for Rick and the others to take a look. "Nothing in there but junk," he said.

Motioning for the officer behind Kenny to watch the man, Rick stepped over and peered inside. A spare tire, a few more crushed beer cans, a few wrenches, a Doritos wrapper, and a bag from a hardware store. "What's this?" he asked as he picked up the plastic bag. Kenny didn't reply, so he looked inside. "Duct tape and zip ties." Turning to face his suspect, he said, "Interesting supplies. What are they for?"

"I'm working on a project," Kenny answered. "Look, there's no law against possession of tape and zip ties."

"There is a law against kidnapping teenage boys," Rick countered. "Where are they?" Despite the cool weather, sweat beads formed on Kenny Burton's forehead. "Did you stash them somewhere? You'd better not have killed them. I'm telling you right now, if you killed them, I'll deal with you personally."

"Look, dude," Kenny answered. "I don't know what boys you're talking about. I've been gone on a little trip and I didn't get much sleep last night, so I'm tired. Look at whatever you want, but I need to catch a nap before I go to work."

"Trip? Where'd you go?" one of the cops asked.

Kenny glared at the man. "I tracked my old lady down to some broken-down place in the southern part of the state. Cutters Notch, I think it's called." Looking at Rick, he added, "That's where you live, ain't it?" He paused a second, and then continued. "I drove down there to check it out. It's a free country, right? I wanted to see where my ex was living. Anyway, I hung around for a while, checked out the area, and got a really late start back. Ended up stopping at a fleabag motel down in Indy because I couldn't keep my eyes open anymore. I don't know anything about any missing boys. Whatever happened to them had nothing to do with me."

Rick was surprised at his candid answer. He expected him to deny being anywhere near Cutters Notch. "So, it's just a coincidence that your daughter's two best friends went missing on the same night you happened to be in my little town?"

"Guess so," he said. "I bought Megan some flowers and tossed them on her porch to say hello. If something happened to those boys, you got the wrong guy."

"Can you hold him?" Rick asked one of the Muncie officers.

"Sure. For twenty-four hours, anyway."

"Oh, man, come on," Kenny exclaimed. "You're gonna get me fired, and it was the only crappy job I could find."

As Kenny was being cuffed, Rick circled to the driver's side and yanked a motel receipt from the front seat of the man's Gran Torino. "I'll check this place out on my way back. We'll see if your story holds." Then he folded up the paper and stuffed it in his shirt pocket before stepping into Burton's personal space. "No more trips to Cutters Notch for you," Rick said through clenched teeth. "No more flowers for your ex-wife. You stay away. You got it?"

"Yeah, I got it." Kenny glared back at Rick.

"That better be the case," Rick warned. "Don't even come into my county." At that, he waved to the Muncie PD before jumping in his own vehicle to head back home. With there still being no sign of the boys, worry was gaining a grasp on his heart.

"You've got the hots for her, don't ya?" Kenny called out to Rick as he was being stuffed into the back of a cruiser. "I can see it in your eyes."

Rick didn't respond. He just looked at the giant. He wasn't sure what he saw, but the look in the man's eyes sent a chill down Rick's spine.

***

While stirring the scrambling eggs, Maggie glanced at Hope, whose face was buried within her crossed arms on the kitchen table. Bacon sizzled inside the microwave. She'd always considered the microwave to be the cheater's way to cook bacon, but on this particular morning, she didn't have the patience or the desire to make the mess that would undoubtedly happen by frying it up. Scrambling the eggs was almost too much. She was tired. They both were. Neither had slept at all since the boys had been taken. They spent the balance of the night taking turns holding one another.

When the sun cracked the horizon, Hope announced there was no way she was going back to school without her friends. Her mother had neither the energy nor the will to argue.

"Mom, they rescued me. There's gotta be a way I can help find them."

***

Overnight, when Hope wasn't being held by her mother or returning the favor, she had scurried from mirror to mirror, searching deeply into each, ignoring her own image and hoping to see one of her special friends. "Where's Gavin, Gronek, or Smakal?" she asked her mom, lifting her head from her arms long enough to speak. "I wish they'd let me help 'cause I know they're doing what they can."

***

Maggie didn't know how to respond to that question. She wasn't sure she even believed those creatures were real. Hope was adamant about it, and both the boys had confirmed it was true. Apparently, Rick had seen one of them himself just last night. Still, it was all a little too fantastic to believe. *Maybe I should mention these creatures to Hope's therapist. It could be some sort of PTSD thing. Maybe a group hallucination?*

"Hope, sweetie, I'm sure they're just wrapped up in trying to find Josh and Danny. Plus, they probably don't want to involve you. You know...to keep you safe."

"Ugh," the girl said and put her head back down. "That's just stupid."

Maggie turned away from the cooking eggs and stared at her daughter. The girl was taking up half the table with her strawberry blonde hair spilling over her arms. She couldn't help but harbor a sense of relief that it wasn't her little girl this time. Yes, she was relieved, but she also felt a little guilty because of that relief. The boys were obviously in real danger. She didn't know what Kenny was up to, but she knew what he was capable of doing. Consciously this time, she rubbed her tongue against the scar on the inside of her lip and rubbed her lower back as she remembered that terrifying night when he'd nearly killed both her and Hope.

The microwave dinged, jerking her back from the memory. The eggs were getting a little crispy, so she scooped them onto two plates. "Come on, Hope," she said. "Let's eat. Then, we can figure out how to help the boys." She hoped they still could be helped.

***

Danny and Josh spent the night huddled together against the odd curved wall. They were too tired to stay awake but too cold and too scared to sleep. The result was a fitful night of drowsy fear. Neither of them, having been pulled directly out of bed, was dressed for the exposure to an October night. Danny wore a simple white t-shirt and blue flannel pajama pants. Josh had on a mixed-up set of pjs—Superman shirt and Ironman pants. The chilled air left Josh's exposed toes numb, but Danny was marginally better since he'd worn a pair of white socks to bed. The cold, moist floor numbed his butt. The combination of the cold and the fear had driven out any macho ideas, and they wrapped their arms around each other for warmth and at least the sense of mutual security.

Eventually, as the sun rose, the strange triangular gap in the area above their heads began to fill with light. The palpable darkness dissipated. Birds chirped outside the hard wall at their backs. Slowly, objects around them emerged like monsters out of the fog. The triangular gap became a hole in a round, domed ceiling. Light penetrated down the inside of the walls, revealing them as a composition of layers of interlocking blocks, each about a foot or maybe eighteen inches high.

The curved wall at the boys' backs wrapped around in a complete circle and rose way up high to the domed ceiling. It was so high that it felt like they were looking into a funnel. A cable draped from the center of the ceiling all the way to the floor where it was connected to some sort of mechanical contraption. Steel supports, a motor, and a drive chain appeared from the darkness, and some sort of blower unit with a curved outlet stared at them like a rectangular eye.

"We're in a silo," Danny announced.

"A what?"

"A grain silo. You know, those tall round things on farms where they keep the corn."

"How do you know this is a silo?" Josh asked. "Have you been stuck in one before?"

"Well, no," Danny answered, "but my uncle has a big farm over by Seymour. He has a couple of 'em on his property. We go over there sometimes, and he took me inside one. That machine with the cable is the unloader. It empties the corn through windows that open up in the sides."

As the minutes passed, the room continued to brighten. There was moss on the concrete floor. Across the circular room, an opossum poked his head out of a crevice in the wall and glared at them. Josh found a crumbled Coke can near his leg. He picked it up and tossed it at the critter with angry-looking teeth. The thing hissed and retreated into the hole.

Now that they could see the whole room, it was obvious that it hadn't been used for grain in a very long time. Rather, it appeared to have been used for everything from storage to a dump to a clandestine clubhouse. A couple of broken lamps reclined by the wall near the critter crevice. Dozens of crumbled cans—some soda, some beer—littered the floor. Cigarette butts lined up like a weird chain-smoker's collection about ten feet around to their left. Above their heads, ropes dangled from the ceiling, connected to one another and anchored to the block walls as if in a trapeze artist's dream. The lowest one draped a couple of feet above their heads. A mouse skittered across one of the cross ropes and disappeared into another crevice about twenty feet up.

"I bet it's a hundred feet to the top," Danny said. "That's stinking high. You wouldn't catch me swinging around on those ropes."

"So, if all this stuff is in here, where's the door?"

"Well, there really isn't just a door," Danny answered as he slowly turned in a circle, "but those windows come all the way down... There it is." Danny pointed to the area just beside them to their right. "See?" He rushed over to it. "It should just push out." He tried pushing it, but it wouldn't budge. "Help me, Josh."

Josh joined his friend, and together they shoved on the bottom window covering. Even their combined strength couldn't move it.

They tried the one above it. Same result.

"Hold me up, Danny," Josh said. "I'll try the ones above."

Same result. Nothing moved.

"I guess we're locked in," Danny announced.

"Ya think?" Josh answered as he hopped back to the floor. He looked at his friend. Then, he looked at the covered window in front of him. Out of frustration, he threw his shoulder into it. That hurt, but still nothing moved. Finally, he plopped back down with his back against the wall and pulled his knees into his chest.

Danny sat down beside him. "I'm hungry," he said.

Josh looked over at his friend. "Humph," he grumbled. Then he smiled, "yeah, me too. Which do you want? The mouse or a cigarette butt?"

Danny laughed. Josh always made him laugh.

Four

It was just after 10 a.m., and Hope was still desperate to get involved; Maggie was going a little stir crazy herself. They hadn't heard from Rick, and Maggie didn't want to bother him by calling too often. *Maybe Cindy and Annie will have some new information.* She grabbed her keys and her purse off the dining room table. "Come on," she said. "Let's go see Annie and Cindy." Hope was at her side immediately.

They stepped outside, the sun fully over the treetops. A light breeze from the north was putting a little chill in the midmorning air. Leaves blew off the large trees, circled the neighborhood, and swirled over the cul-de-sac. Maggie's phone rang. They stopped on the walk to take the call. The screen read Rick's name.

"Have you found them?" she asked.

"No, I'm afraid not," Rick replied with a tired voice. "But Kenny is in custody. He finally drove into his driveway about an hour ago."

"Did he tell you where they are?"

She glanced up. A big, dark blue Lincoln Continental, perhaps twenty years old, pulled across Basketball Court and stopped in the Hicks' driveway. Al Havener's balding head bobbed behind the wheel. Her eyes met his in his driver's side mirror. Maggie quickly looked away.

"He claims not to know anything about the boys."

"That's crap. He was here last night."

"He actually admitted to that," Rick said. "He said he was messing with you but didn't know anything about the boys going missing."

"Where was he all night then?"

"He said he got tired on his drive back to Muncie and stopped at a motel near Indy," Rick answered, "I'm about to check that story out. I'll let you know what I learn. Just wanted to give you an update. Gotta go. I need to call Cindy and Annie."

"Hope and I are heading over there now. I can fill them in."

"Okay, thanks. I'll call back after I stop in at that fleabag motel."

"Rick, that man is back at the Hicks' house this morning."

"What man?" he replied.

Hope was gripping Maggie's non-phone arm and standing behind her. As they watched, Al Havener stepped out of his car and peered over at them. He smiled and waved. Both Maggie and Hope, almost in unison, averted their eyes. The man shrugged and headed toward the front door of the empty house, the thin, gray hair on his head blowing in the wind.

"That Havener guy," Maggie answered. "I told you about him last night. He stopped Hope and me as we were headed home from Annie's house. He's Faye's nephew and he's supposed to inventory their house. Remember?"

"Oh, yeah," Rick replied. "With all the excitement, I forgot about him. I'll check out his story today, too."

"Rick, I—" Maggie started. She couldn't complete the sentence. *I love you.* She was definitely feeling it, but she couldn't bring herself to say it.

"What?" he asked.

"I dunno what I was gonna say," she lied. "Call me back when you can. Okay?"

"Sure thing," he answered.

They clicked off the call. Maggie pulled Hope in for a hug. "It's okay, honey," she said. "I've got you." With that, they crossed the cul-de-sac, skirting away from the Hicks' former home and knocked on the Flannery's door.

***

It was nearly noon when Gavin sat down with his mother, the queen, for a private meal. They sat around a flat rock on a ridge in the middle of what the humans referred to as Kentucky, gazing over a vast forest. He was thankful that the forest was still so vibrant, despite the regular appearance of new points of devastation originating in the Human Realm. The sun was high in the sky, but a thick mantle of spruce boughs protected them.

His mother had arranged for an array of white china plates with a decorative golden trim swirling on the edges. The feast spread before him. Fancy crystal goblets filled with a reddish-blue liquid stood within reach. Her serving staff gleaned the plates and glasses through the shimmers from wealthy humans who often discarded items for no apparent reason. Roasted rose petals and stalks of rhubarb, all drizzled with honey covered Gavin's plate. He took a sip of his purple drink, grape juice. He scanned his brunch, then looked over and smiled at his mother. It was his favorite meal, and she had remembered.

"Do you still enjoy this meal as much as you did as a young one?" she asked.

"Oh, yes," he answered. "Very much so. Thank you."

Queen Hesed smiled, and Gavin looked closely at her face. She looked much the same as their last visit, which had been years ago. There was, perhaps, another little line in the skin around her eyes, but otherwise, she had not much aged. He was pleased to see that the pallor of her skin was still a healthy shade of green and her aura of life was strong.

Gavin paused to think about how long it had been since their last meal together. *At least twenty years.* The concept of the time is different for elves with their extremely long lives, so the passing of decades felt to Gavin as the passing of years would feel to a human. Still, he had missed his mother greatly.

Glancing back to his plate, he picked up a stalk of rhubarb between the thumbs of his right hand, shoved it through the drizzled honey, and then crunched on it greedily. A huge smile formed at the treat his mother had prepared. It was not their habit to converse during a meal, so he followed that first bite with several rose petals. As he chewed, he watched his mother enjoy her meal. *I truly have missed you so much.*

After a quarter of an hour, their plates were empty. Gavin took a sip of the purple juice from the goblet and looked over at Queen Hesed. "Mother," he began, "please tell me about this Bayal."

The queen frowned and dropped her gaze. "But, my son, I would like to hear more about this Hope Spencer you wrote about." She glanced up again and forced a smile back onto her face.

"Yes, I am eager to share," the prince replied. "Yet, I am

anxious regarding the news that I heard yesterday. May we clear that from my mind?"

"Very well," Queen Hesed replied, "we shall cover that ground first." She also took a sip from a goblet on her side of the stone table. After dabbing at her lips with a decorative napkin, she closed her eyes as if she were sifting deep memories. "Bayal is of our kind, but is very, very old—even by our standards. As you know, I was born just over two thousand years ago. Your grandmother was born three thousand years ago. Your great grandmother was born approximately five thousand years ago. Oh, Gavin, I wish you could have met her. She brought so much joy. Ah, I digress. My apologies.

"It was during your great grandmother's youth that Bayal began his forays into the human spectrum. He learned that we could venture into their realm through the mirrored waters, and he found the journeys exciting. It was also around this time that the shimmers began to appear as the humans learned to polish metals and stone to form their mirrors. That only expanded Bayal's access, and he took full advantage.

"Humans were very primitive during that time, simple-minded and warrior-like. They were easily fooled. Bayal took advantage of his ability to appear and disappear in order to create the persona of a god. It wasn't long before the humans began to worship him. At first, he found it flattering, but as it progressed, he proceeded to encourage their praise and the sacrifices that came with it. Bayal carried the spoils of those sacrifices into our realm for his own enjoyment. Others of our kind saw the materials he was acquiring and envied his growing collection."

The story mesmerized Gavin. Servants passed through, collecting their breakfast dishes and refilling their crystal goblets, but he did not even notice. He sat with his elbows on the table and his six-fingered hands holding up his chin. The day was bright with the sun filtering through the blue glow of the spruces overhead.

"Bayal used their envy," she continued, "to grow his influence among our kind. It was not long before he had thousands of worshippers in the human world and hundreds of followers in ours. His influence among our communities led to power, and power can be addicting. He was addicted."

"Did he become violent?" Gavin asked before taking another

gulp of the juice. "Did he seize power?"

"Not at first," Hesed replied. "It took many decades for his influence among the humans and among our own to grow enough for him to see that he had the potential to rule both realms. It came to a climax around the time of my birth."

"What happened?"

"It was during the season when the Mighty One inserted himself into the realm of the humans, providing the sacrifice required to bring them back into alignment with his purpose and love. Even though much of the human race had moved on to other idols, Bayal still held sway with many, and he used other personas to duplicate his ploys among them. He was a false god. In our world, his followers grew in number and mimicked his strategies. Under his direction, they challenged the regional governments of our various kingdoms. Your grandfather led a coalition of defenses to stand against him, while in the human realm, the Mighty One drove aside all evil influences. Bayal was expelled from both dimensions. He fled into the Pit."

"Where is this Pit?" Gavin asked.

"Deep in the forests of the southern hemisphere, there is a portal into a dark dimension. Bayal had no other choice. He could no longer abide among the humans, and we would not accept him among our kind, so he fled into the dark. It is our understanding that he has bided his time there…until now. It seems that he has arisen, and the humans are again listening to his false message. This news is fresh to my ears, so I do not yet know much more of the current situation beyond the fact that my fellow queens and kings are quite concerned.

"Enough of Bayal," the queen said. "I want to hear about your friend, Hope."

A huge smile formed on Gavin's face as his mind shifted to his human friends. He absently scratched under his left arm. Gavin was wearing a tunic of painted magnolia leaves, and his skin was no longer accustomed to the royal garments. "Mother, she is remarkable. Her aura of life is unlike any I have ever witnessed among her kind. In our world, it was as if she were a walking and talking lantern. I am convinced that she is special, but just do not know in what way. I wish you had seen her."

"Perhaps, I shall."

Gavin perked up even further. "Oh, Mother, that would be wonderful. I cannot bring her here. Are you thinking of visiting our forest?"

"Perhaps." Hesed smiled warmly at her son.

At that moment, a sasquatch stepped into the shade of the trees. Looming over the top of the two elves with his twin swords sticking out from over his shoulders, he held out his right hand. Sitting in his palm was a fairy. It looked exhausted with its four wings drooping and its head hung over. A small piece of paper was strapped to one leg. Still, when the guard extended his hand, the fairy fluttered over and landed on the rock in front of Gavin. It sat facing him and extended the leg with the message attached.

While the queen looked on, Gavin carefully removed the message and read the note from his brothers. A look of distress came over his countenance. His hands began to tremble.

"What is it, my son? What is wrong?"

"Hope's friends…my friends—" Gavin choked out. "The two human boys…Josh and Danny—" Emotion was making it hard for him to speak.

"What?" she asked.

"They have been kidnapped and are missing," he finally blurted out. "Gronek and Smakal searched the shimmers for hours with no success in finding them."

The queen whirled and motioned for the guard to approach. When he was at her side, she stood. "Sacqueal, have my carriage prepared," she instructed. "Gather my council. My son and I will be departing within the hour for the forests north of the river."

***

Mabel Robbins, the matriarch of her wing of the Robbins family, proprietor of the Notch Inn, and owner/director of the Robbins Stone Limestone Mine, sat on the edge of the cot where Russell Bray lay shivering. The lighting wasn't good inside the makeshift cabin, but she could see that her involuntary employee was sick and very weak. After dipping a dingy washcloth in a pail of water, she carefully folded it and then placed it on the man's forehead. He barely moved.

"Maybe we should move him up to one of the motel rooms," her son Robert said, leaning over her shoulder. "He looks cold."

"Ain't doin' it," Mabel replied, "and of course he's cold. It's really chilly down here...but he either makes it or we'll have to acquire a replacement. Is the boy sick?"

"Don't think so. He seemed okay when I put him to work this morning."

The old woman reached up and scratched behind her right ear, then she scratched beneath the gray hair pulled up into a bun on the back of her head. She lifted one of the man's eyelids and checked his pupil. Pulling his chin down, she motioned for her son to hand her a flashlight, snapping her fingers a few times for emphasis. Looking at his throat, she could see swelling, white splotches, and lots of redness. Her concern rose.

She wasn't particularly concerned for Russell Bray. He was just a tool to her. A tool used to extract limestone from the hillside. If a tool broke, she'd get a new one. Her concern was for the acquisition of a new tool. It had been a few months since they'd gassed this family in the night and forced them into their personal labor pool, but not long enough for her to feel comfortable doing it again.

If Bray were to die, two things became a problem. First, she would lose a bit of her leverage in controlling the women, Russell's wife and daughter, whom she used to clean the motel rooms. By keeping them apart, she could threaten one against the other. Fear for their family kept the workers in line. Second, the reduced labor force would require her to look for a new tool. In order to maintain production levels, she would need to gas another room. She would need to grab another unsuspecting laborer in the night—always a tricky prospect. *Maybe we should take another one anyway, just in case.*

Grabbing a new laborer needed to be done carefully. They needed to pick their target from the select few who were not easily traced to Cutters Notch. Plus, they needed to space the snatchings out so that it seemed random. If Bray died, it would require her to grab another worker a good deal sooner than she normally preferred.

As the old woman sat considering her options, Russell erupted in another fit of coughing. He curled up and coughed and hacked and wheezed before finally expelling a disgusting wad of phlegm.

"Bring down some chicken noodle soup and try to get this man to eat," she instructed. "Bring him some Gatorade, too. If he don't eat and drink, he's definitely gonna die, and that would be very inconvenient." She reached into the leather satchel draped over her left side and pulled out a bottle of water and a plastic medicine container. "Mr. Bray," Mabel spoke to the man. "I've got some medicine here for you. You need to wake up enough to take it." She pulled three pills out of the small bottle.

"What are you giving him, Momma?"

"Ibuprofen and an antibiotic," she replied. "I hope he's not allergic. If he is, we'll probably lose him for sure. Bring his boy in from the mine early. Let him look after his father. Don't bother shackling him tonight, either." Mabel raised Bray's head, pushed the pills into his mouth, and held the water to his lips. Almost involuntarily, the sick man swallowed.

"That'll reduce production," Robert pointed out.

"If he dies," she replied, "production will be cut even further. Do as I say. Start with the soup." She took another hard look at the sick man on the cot and then glanced around at the makeshift shelter with the water dripping down the stone wall on the back side. *We should definitely secure another worker.*

"Okay, Momma," her son replied. Then he stood there looking over her shoulder at the sick man's pale skin.

"One more thing," she added as an afterthought. "Get something to cover the cracks in the walls. We need to block some of the cold air from getting in here."

"Okay." Robert continued to stand there looking at Russell.

"Now." She stood up and shoved her son out the door. "Get moving. I've gotta get back to the office and see what his wife and daughter are doing."

***

Rick cruised into the east side of Cutters Notch early in the afternoon. He had checked out Kenny Burton's story by stopping at the Sleepy Eyes Motel off Pendleton Pike in Indianapolis. The dumpy place was flanked by a small barbeque stand on one side and a cocktail lounge on the other. The dull, flaking gray motel consisted of two wings of simple rooms with red doors, each in a strip, connected in the middle by a breezeway that held both ice and soda machines.

The attendant had not been on duty when Burton checked in but was there when he checked out. The man said he saw Kenny get into his car and that he had no luggage. He also confirmed that Kenny was alone. He simply turned in his key, jumped in his muscle car, and left. The attendant remembered him clearly because of the car.

Rick had the attendant walk him over to look at the room. The door opened to a cockroach scurrying under a TV stand, but nothing else moved. The single bed was still unmade, so it was clear that he'd been there alone. Nothing else was disturbed. So far, the man's story checked out. *Where could the boys be? What did he do with them?*

Those questions haunted Rick all the way back to Cutters Notch. He'd tried to envision which route Kenny might have taken and the points along the way where he might have left the boys. He didn't want to consider the implications of what condition they'd have to be in to be left behind, using all his training and force of will to block out his emotions.

As he passed the Notch Inn, it occurred to him that maybe Kenny had spent the night in Cutters Notch the night before last, the night before the boys had disappeared. He considered that maybe he should check with his local motel staff to find out what they might have seen. After doing a U-turn in the middle of highway 257, he pulled past the combination motel/limestone mine signage and drove up to the motel office.

Once parked under the overhang near the office entrance, Rick watched a woman with long, dark hair roll a service cart down the sidewalk toward the room furthest from where he sat. A scarf held the hair back from her face, and she wore what looked like nursing scrubs. Small, dirty tennis shoes adorned her feet. She kept her head down and never looked over at him.

The interim sheriff stepped out of his car and looked around the nearly empty lot. A small convertible BMW was parked about halfway down the row of rooms. Apparently, no other patrons remained. The place was probably packed on weekends, since October was the high point of color in the fall foliage, but it seemed people had to return to work on Monday mornings. Since it was now afternoon, any weekend leftovers had already departed—save the driver of the lone convertible.

Rick stepped back from the building to take it in. Turning a full circle, he gathered the ambiance, what little there was of it. It wasn't a particularly nice place, but he supposed it fulfilled a need. Stepping back a few feet, he tried to look further down the lane toward the limestone mine, but he couldn't see anything that resembled an industrial operation. He knew it was operational because trucks came and went, but otherwise, one would never know it was there without the sign out by the road. The forest completely hid it. The motel parking lot was paved, but it changed over to gravel as it met the tree line. Then, the gravel disappeared about fifty feet further when the lane curved to the left.

"Humph," he mumbled. Grabbing his utility belt, he adjusted its position and then strolled to the office. It was a simple entryway positioned under a canopy. A newspaper box sat to the right. It was empty and looked like it hadn't been touched in two decades. An empty soda can sat like a sentinel on the top. To the left of the door was an oversized flowerpot filled with sand. Cigarette butts grew like little orange or white sprouts from the top.

Inside, a display of tourist flyers lined a paneled wall to the left and a countertop lined the wall immediately to the right. A padded orange sofa sat opposite the door. Rick stepped up and rang a little bell.

There was an inner office behind the counter; the door stood ajar and light leaked out. Someone was moving around, but no one emerged. He rang the bell again. Thirty seconds later, he rang it a third time.

"I know you're in there," he said. "Could you please come on out here?"

"Mabel will be back in a few minutes," a female voice replied. "I'm not supposed to interact with customers."

"That's okay," Rick replied. "I'm not actually a customer. I'm the sheriff. Can I ask you a question or two?"

"I can't talk right now. I'm cleaning up this room."

"I won't hold you long," Rick promised. "I just wanted to ask you if you'd seen anyone unusual over the weekend. We had a couple of boys go missing, and we need to find them."

A head poked out the door. Long red hair and green eyes. The hair had a similar scarf holding it back as the woman's outside with the cart. Just as quickly, the head ducked back into the office. "Please come out here for a minute." Rick hesitated for a moment, then repeated, "please."

Slowly, the person emerged. The teenage girl also wore similar scrubs to the cleaning woman. *Trisha* was the name etched into the brass name tag. She kept her gaze down.

"As I said," Rick continued, "two local boys were abducted last night. My deputies and I are doing an intensive search. Did you see anything unusual? Any person or persons with two boys? Anything at all?"

"No, sir," the hesitant girl answered. "There was only a couple of guests last night. Nuthin' really weird."

Tricia finally made eye contact. She held Rick's gaze and seemed to want to say something else.

"What?" he asked. "Did you see something else? Something odd?" He noticed her hands were shaking.

The girl glanced out the windows as if to see if someone else might be approaching. Rick followed her gaze. An older woman walked toward them from the gravel drive that led down to the mine.

"There was another car—kinda weird—I've gotta get back to work now—but, I can give you the license plate number." She blurted her words out in a flurry and then started scribbling on a pad of paper. She ripped the paper free and handed it to Rick. "I've gotta go," she said before ducking back into the office.

Rick took the note and then turned to watch the old woman approach the door. Since the door was full-length glass, he could see her clearly. Just over five feet tall with gray hair pulled up into a bun, she wore a one-piece dress with some sort of paisley pattern. It ended just above her ankles. Scuffed-up brown shoes poked out from underneath. She carried a satchel over one shoulder, and she was smoking. Stopping just outside, she took one more long drag before planting the butt in the sand-filled flowerpot alongside the others. Then she jerked the door open and stepped inside.

The woman stopped short and looked at Rick as he casually stuffed Tricia's piece of paper into his right breast pocket. "Are you the new sheriff or are you some deputy I haven't met yet?"

Rick smiled. "I'm the interim sheriff. The name's Rick Anders."

"Mabel Robbins," the old woman said. "I own the place. How can I help you today, Interim Sheriff Anders?" The woman was no nonsense and a tad gruff but not in a belligerent way. Her mouth almost formed a smile but not quite. She walked past Anders and took up residence behind the counter.

"Ms. Robbins—"

"Call me Mabel," she interrupted.

"Mabel, we had a couple of boys go missing last night."

"Again?" Mabel exclaimed. "What's going on in our quaint little town?"

"That's what I hope to clear up. We have a person of interest, but there's still no sign of the boys. I thought I'd stop in to see if you noticed any unusual activity come through your motel this weekend. Especially on Saturday night."

"Nothing strange around here," she said. "It was a normal tourist weekend—folks coming in to see the color in the trees and the like. No one seemed out of place to me. We've only got a couple of guests left over today. The place will be pretty dead until Friday now."

"Did you see a big green Ford Gran Torino maybe on Saturday night? It would have had white stripes across the sides. Or maybe have a guest named Kenny Burton?"

Mabel scratched her chin and frowned. Then she started typing on a keyboard and stared at a screen. "I don't remember any such car," she said. "I'll check the name in the register." She looked at the screen for a minute more. "Nope," she finally said. "No Kenny Burton or any name similar. Guess I'm not gonna be much help on this one."

Rick stood there for a moment more. Then, he looked over Mabel's shoulder toward the inner office. He could still hear Tricia rummaging around. For some reason he couldn't place, he felt a tickle in his gut.

"Anything else I can do for you, Sheriff?" Mabel asked. "If not, I have a few things I need to attend to."

Rick was pulled back from his thoughts. "Uh, no," he replied. "I guess that's it. Thank you." He turned to leave, then stopped. Pulling out a small card, he turned back. "Oh, Mabel, here's my phone number. If you do think of something, please call me."

"Will do," she said. "Nice to meet you."

"Nice to meet you too," Rick said and stepped outside.

***

Mabel Robbins stood at the motel office door and watched

Rick Anders until he got into his cruiser and backed out. Worry lines formed on her forehead and around her eyes. It was always a risk leaving Trisha and her mother alone at the motel, and she didn't like doing it, but with Russell Bray being sick, she'd had to take the risk. Finding the new interim sheriff alone in the office with Russell's daughter was disconcerting, to say the least.

Turning away from the counter, she stepped over to the office. Looking in, she saw Patti Bray, whom she had renamed *Trisha*, on her hands and knees. A bucket of water sat beside her. She was hand scrubbing the tile floor just as she'd been instructed. The girl didn't look up or acknowledge her presence.

"Tricia," Mabel said. The girl didn't react but kept scrubbing away as if she hadn't heard her captor. "Tricia, stand up and face me." She didn't care if she hurt her. As long as she got the work she needed out of this young woman, Mabel was pleased. People don't care if the tools they own like them or not, and that's all this girl was—a tool.

***

With her back still turned to the old woman, Tricia dropped her scrubbing rag into the bucket of water and slowly climbed to her feet. Turning around, she dropped her gaze as she faced Mabel. Tricia was taller by about four inches, but she was careful not to make eye contact. Instead, she focused on the woman's scuffed-up shoes. She'd been kicked more than once by those brown leather-covered toes.

"Did you speak with the sheriff just now? What did you tell him?"

"I didn't talk to him," the girl lied. "I stayed quiet and pretended I didn't hear him."

Mabel grabbed the girl's shoulders and shook her.

"Tricia, look at me. Look me in the eyes."

When the girl refused to look up, she shook her again—hard. "Look at me."

This time, Tricia raised her head and looked at the woman's hazel eyes. She couldn't conceal the hatred oozing from her own green eyes as they stared hard into the old woman's.

Mabel lifted her hands from Tricia's shoulders and placed them on each side of her face. "Are you telling me the truth?"

Tricia nodded, working hard to keep her emotions at bay. "Are you sure?"

The girl nodded again.

"You'd better be telling me the truth," Mabel said. Then, she grabbed Tricia's hair in her left hand and jerked her over toward the desk against the far wall. "Do you see that red button right there? Don't forget what happens if I push that button."

Tricia knew exactly what would happen if Mabel pushed that button. The old woman had made it patently clear on their first day under her control—the day she'd gone from being a fairly well-off and spoiled teenager named Patti and became a helpless teenage slave under the control of a twisted mind, somewhere in southern Indiana.

"Let me remind you," Mabel continued. "If I push that button, a light will flash in the mine and my son, Robert, will hurt either your dad or your brother. He'll hurt one of them bad. Do you remember that?"

Tricia nodded. "Yes," she affirmed.

Mabel continued. "If I push it twice, one of them will die. Do you remember that?"

Tears welled in the corners of Tricia's emerald eyes. "Yes, ma'am."

"And, one of them would die long before that sheriff or any of his deputies ever even found the entrance to the mine. You got that?"

"Yes," the girl replied as tears began to flow down both freckled cheeks. The corners of her mouth were quivering.

"So, let me ask you again. What did you tell the sheriff?"

"Nothing. I just ignored him and kept working. Just like you told me to do if anyone ever came in while you were away. I did what you instructed. That's all."

"You sure?"

Tricia nodded again.

Reaching over to her desk, Mabel grabbed a tissue. Then, she grabbed two more. "Here," she said and held them up to the girl. "Wipe your eyes, blow your nose, and get back to work."

***

Once the girl went back to her chores, Mabel returned to the counter in the outer office. She had a choice to make. Activating the computer by swirling the mouse around, she clicked on the icon that opened up the current occupancy list. There were two rooms still occupied for this coming night—two potential new tools from which to choose—one was a sixty-eight-year old retired woman from Fort Wayne and the other was a forty-seven-year old single man from Missouri. The retiree from Fort Wayne hobbled around with a cane, so her choice was easy. The man from Missouri would be joining the others in the mine tomorrow. As far as anyone would know, he'd disappear somewhere along the road home to St. Louis.

***

Rick Anders brought his new cruiser to a stop in his driveway. Bone tired, he backed up toward his garage door. He'd been up since that crazy event with the elf in the mirror, and the weariness was catching up with him. Rick decided to go home, call Maggie to check in, eat a bowl of soup, and hopefully, catch a short power nap. He sat in his car for a few moments while he checked his phone for messages. There wasn't anything new from his deputies. Everything seemed to be a dead end.

From his position, Rick had a good view of the cul-de-sac. He took a deep breath and studied each house. It seemed so peaceful, but the reality of the matter was anything of the sort. Catching movement to his left, he glanced at a man emerging from the Hicks' former home and approaching an older model Lincoln Continental in the driveway. Rick jumped out of his car. "You must be Havener," he called out to the man. "Have you got a minute?"

"Sure," the man replied. Al Havener strolled to the rear of his car to wait as Rick walked over. He smiled at the sheriff and leaned casually against a fender.

Rick looked him over and quickly noted the vehicle, too. Dark blue. A dent in the rear fender. Missouri plates. A man in his mid-forties.

"My neighbor tells me you're Faye Hicks' nephew. You're here to liquidate their property on behalf of the family?"

"That's right," Havener replied. A breeze fluttered his sparse hair around. The man smiled big and stuck out his hand. "I'm Al Havener and it's just as you said."

"That's fast," Rick said and hesitantly shook the man's hand.

"The county just released the scene this week."

"Yes, we realize that. Our family just figured we'd better jump on it. Might as well put it behind us—all of us." He gestured at the neighborhood.

"What's your authority to sell off someone else's property?"

The man chuckled and stuffed his hands into his front pockets. "That's a great question, Sheriff," he said, "and luckily for me, I've got a legitimate answer. You see, my aunt and her husband are divorcing even as they prepare for their respective trials. They both know they'll never again see the world from outside a jail cell, and they need money for lawyers and such."

The wind gusted, blowing the trees to and fro. A large crow circled overhead. Rick heard the bird call out and glanced up. The sun was starting to trek toward the western sky. The day was nearly lost, and the boys were still missing. "Do you have any documentation to prove your authority?" Rick probed some more. "And, where're you from? What do you do?"

Al Havener laughed again. It was an easy sort of laugh. He had a personable demeanor. It was almost so personable as to be artificial—plastic. "Sure do. It's in the car, on the front seat." He moved to open his driver's side door, and Rick reacted instinctively by placing his hand on his service weapon. "Whoa, Sheriff," Havener said. "I'm harmless. Just getting you the paperwork, I promise."

"Just a precaution. In my line of work, I can't take chances."

"I understand. I'll just move sort of slow. Okay?" He opened the door and leaned inside. When he turned back, he had a manila folder in his hands. "Here you go." He handed the papers to Rick.

Rick flipped open the folder and scrolled through the paperwork. "Seems in order. Now, tell me about yourself. I see the Missouri plates. Give me your details, please."

Al chuckled. "You're really a no-nonsense fella, aren't you? I'm from Chesterfield," he answered. "It's just west of St. Louis. I'm a pharmaceutical rep. Single. Divorced, actually. I've taken two weeks off from work to take care of the house. That's about it."

Rick studied his face. A day's growth covered his chin and slightly plump cheeks. His hands were soft with no calluses. The guy wore a Polo golf shirt and cargo pants. His forearms were tanned, probably from a season full of golf outings. *Pharmaceutical rep, huh? A sales guy. That explains his artificial friendliness.*

"When did you get here and when are you leaving?"

"I drove over on Saturday. Man, this place was busy then. So many people driving around staring at the leaves. Didn't come over here to the house 'til yesterday. I don't know how long I'll be around. Guess it depends on how long it takes me to finish my business. Maybe a week or two."

Rick forced a smile onto his face. "Good enough, Mr. Havener."

"Please call me Al."

"I'll stick with Mr. Havener for now," Rick replied. "And, do me a favor. Keep your distance from anyone in this neighborhood. They're a bit on edge right now. Besides what your aunt and uncle did, we just had two more boys go missing last night."

"What? Really? What happened?"

"They were taken right out of their bedrooms. We're searching, but so far there's no trace. So, keep your distance. Okay?"

"Sure will," Havener answered, "and I'll keep my eyes open for the boys. Do you have a card? So, I can call if I see something?"

Rick removed another card from his pocket and handed it to the man. "Thank you, Mr. Havener," he said and turned to head back to his own place. He was so tired that he felt sort of wired. There was a buzzing in his head. He needed that power nap, and he needed it now. Maggie and his soup would have to wait.

"You're welcome," Al Havener said as the sheriff turned away. He studied the card and smiled. "I'll be happy to keep an eye out for the boys."

***

Stuck in the silo, Josh could tell that the sun was beginning to drop into the west. The light was no longer falling directly through that open triangle above their heads. He'd watched the sun spot on the wall travel up, up, and out. It was nearing the end of a hopeless day.

His eyes tracked down the various ropes dangling above his head. Josh let his imagination consider how they got there and for what purpose. It had probably been some teen boys who created the rope maze as a sort of dangerous climbing playground. Those boys were most likely men now because the ropes looked pretty old. Each was anchored to the wall with a steel ring. Some hung loose and others crisscrossed over each other and were anchored on both ends. Had he found himself in the silo under different circumstances, he'd be excited to play around up there, swinging back and forth. It was high, though. The ropes went nearly to the top, stopping just a few feet short of the hole in the roof.

Dropping his gaze, he looked over at Danny. His friend looked so sad. He'd cried a little. They both had. They'd long given up the pride that kept their emotions in check. Instead, they decided to share the fear that replaced their usual playful arrogance.

Both of them were hungry and thirsty, too. A full day had passed with no food or drink.

After the initial realization that they were locked in a corn silo with nothing to eat and no water, they'd filled their time in various ways. A few times the boys just sat in silence. Eventually, Josh set a bunch of soda cans along one of the edges of the unloader frame. They took turns throwing pieces of broken concrete, trying to knock them down. That was fun for about an hour.

A game of strategy followed the knock-over-the-cans game. Each of the boys set up makeshift forts a few feet apart. They used spent cigarette butts as infantrymen, placing them behind various objects in their respective forts. When each fort was ready, they used their thumbs and forefingers to fling small pieces of concrete at one another's forts. The boy with the last infantryman standing won. Danny won that game. That whole process took a couple of more hours.

After that mega battle, they sat with their backs to the wall in silence again until they both drifted off into a nap. An hour later, they reset their forts and repeated the battle. Danny won again. A second game of knock-over-the-cans followed, and Josh won that.

During one of their unnecessary rest breaks as they sat against the wall, Danny put Josh on the spot. "Do you love Hope?"

Josh stared at him. He didn't answer at first. Normally, he wouldn't answer that kind of question at all, and Danny wouldn't have asked it. But being trapped all day in a corn silo loosened up the conversation.

While Josh considered his answer, Danny followed up. "I

mean, I know you like her and all. She's your girlfriend now. I know that. But, do you think you love her? Like, for real?"

Josh continued to stare at Danny for a bit. Then seriousness overtook his face. "You know, I think I do."

They were quiet again after that and just sat there. There wasn't much else to do. Even the opossum stayed away. Every once in a while, Danny would announce that he was really getting hungry. Sometimes, he alternated it with how really thirsty he was.

Now, Josh returned his view to the sky through that seemingly unreachable opening in the roof. As he watched, a large crow landed on the edge and peered down at them. "Hello, Mr. Crow. How are ya?" Josh said. "We're kinda hungry down here. Do you think you could go get us something to eat?"

"Cawww," the crow responded. It glanced at them one more time and then leapt into the air and flew away. One small black feather fluttered down through the ropes.

Five minutes later, the crow was back and cawed. The boys glanced up in unison to see it zip across the open roof. "Caw, caw," it repeated. As it passed over the opening again, something white fell from one of its clawed feet. The object dropped though the hole, bounced off a horizontally strung rope, ricocheted off the center cable, and landed at Danny's feet. The boys stared at it. It looked like a Payday bar—king size.

Danny looked at Josh. Josh looked at Danny. It was Danny who moved first. He bent over and snagged it out of the mess on the floor. Sure enough, it was a brand new, still-in-the-wrapper Payday bar. "I can't believe this," Danny exclaimed. Then, he looked up at the bird and said, "Thank you."

"Caw."

Josh was on his feet, too. They stood together as Danny ripped the cover off the candy bar. "This is awesome," Danny said. "I'm starved." He started to take a bite but hesitated. "I'm sorry," he said to his friend and tore the treat into two equal pieces, handing one over. "This is awesome," he repeated.

"Thanks," Josh said. He held the sweet food in front of him and considered it for a moment. Peering up, he saw the crow perched on the rim of the roof again. It was watching them. "And thank you, Mr. Crow," he added. "Any chance you could scrounge up a bottle of water, too?" Then he laughed and took a big bite.

"Caw, caw," the crow answered before fluttering away into the sky again.

"Josh, a crow just gave us a candy bar," Danny remarked. "This place is sometimes pretty freaking weird, but right now, it feels pretty freaking awesome."

As they sat back down in their spot by the wall, gravel crunched under tires from outside. A moment later, a car door slammed shut.

"Help," Josh yelled. "Help us! We're locked in the silo. Help."

Danny joined his friend and they continued to call out. Outside, footsteps approached. They stopped just beyond the locked access window.

"Can you hear us?" Josh called out. "We're stuck in here."

"I hear you," a man's voice responded. "I'm glad you both woke up. I was a little worried I'd overdone the dosage. I just sell the stuff; I don't usually administer it."

The boys stepped back from the access portal—suddenly afraid. This was the person who'd put them in this place. He'd drugged them and locked them in the silo.

"Dude," Josh spoke up. "Let us outta here! We're cold and thirsty, and it's getting dark again. Please let us out."

The man laughed. "Oh, I don't think so," he said between chuckles. "You're going to be in there a very long time. I'll be long dead before anyone finds you. But don't worry. I'll come and pay respects to your remains periodically while I'm still breathing."

"Please, mister," Danny cried out. "Please let us out." He looked at Josh, terror in his eyes. His arms were shaking.

"Why?" Josh screamed. "Why are you doing this to us?"

"I'll answer that," the man replied. "You need to understand why you're going to dry up like raisins in that pitch-dark chamber."

Pitch dark? Maybe he doesn't know about the hole in the roof. A desperate idea formed in Josh's mind.

"You see," the man continued, "you put my aunt in a cell for the rest of her life, so our family has decided that you should suffer the same fate—you two boys plus your friend, the girl."

"Hope?" Josh blurted. "You leave her alone."

The man laughed. "Oh, she should be in there with you right

now, but she wasn't in her own bedroom last night. I'll get to her soon, though. She'll join you in there. Who knows, maybe you'll still be alive to see her. Well...I guess it'll be too dark to see her, but maybe you can talk a little before you fade away."

"Someone will find us," Danny yelled. "We'll get out of here."

"Oh, that is highly unlikely. You see, you are tucked away in an old silo on private property. You're on a vacant farm and no one comes here. Ever. It's been in our family for decades. My dad and his twin sisters, Faye and Maye, grew up here. Me and my cousins used to have the run of the place. We even built a sort of fort right in there where you're standing...or sitting...or, whatever you're doing. Anyway, our family still owns the place. It's in a trust. I'm the caretaker. Nobody else ever comes here. So, face it. This is where your lives will end."

It was quiet for a few moments. The boys stared at one another through the fading light. Tears streamed down Danny's face. Fear played in Josh's eyes, but there was something else there, too. Something Danny had seen before. Determination.

"I've gotta go now, boys," the voice said. "Maybe I'll come back tomorrow and see how you're holding up."

Laughter accompanied the man's footsteps. Josh wrapped his arms around his sobbing buddy. A car door slammed, and an engine started up. Soon, wheels crunched gravel and the sound faded away.

Josh stepped back from Danny but held him with both hands on his friend's shoulders. Looking him in the eyes, Josh said: "Danny, he doesn't know about the hole in the roof up there. Maybe it's new. Maybe a tornado took off a little section and he hasn't noticed."

"So?" Danny asked. "It's like a hundred feet up in the air."

"So," Josh replied, "we're climbing those ropes and getting outta here. I've been studying 'em and I think we can get all the way to the top. I've gotta get to Hope before he does."

"Caw, caw, caw," came a familiar sound from above.

The boys glanced up to see a bottle of Dasani water drop through the hole in the roof. It fell cleanly through the ropes, and Josh caught it in his right hand. "Thank you," Josh called to the bird as it fluttered away again. Then he twisted off the lid and downed half the bottle before handing it over to Danny.

"Here. Drink this," Josh said, "and let's get climbing."

Five

Hope sat on Josh's bed and stared through the window at the forest in the fading light of the late afternoon. Being October, the days were starting to shorten. Sheba was reclining next to her. The dog had been found in the yard asleep—drugged. Now, she was lethargic and, perhaps, as worried about her master as was Hope herself. Hope ran her hand across the canine's brown fur. The dog was soft, and that provided a tiny touch of comfort. She still missed her own dog—a painful memory piled upon a painful reality.

Hope glanced over to the large mirror attached to Josh's dresser. Reaching to the bedside lamp, she clicked on the light. She knew that light activated the shimmer that would allow the elves to connect with her world. They needed to connect. Hope was desperate to see them, helpless. The boys had risked everything to save her just a couple of weeks prior, and now, she had no clue what to do to help them. *Where are you? Oh, please be okay.*

The adults were in the other room. Hope wanted to be alone. They wanted answers. She wanted action. Rick was responding, doing what he could. All she could do was sit, listen, and wait for a little green nose to poke through Josh's mirror.

Rick was explaining that her father, while a key person of interest and in custody in Muncie, had nothing incriminating in his possession. There was no evidence that he had taken the boys. There was nothing, with the exception of his presence in the area, to tie him to their disappearance. Still, Hope was conditioned to believe that he was the bogeyman at the window, the creature under the bed, the shadow in the darkness. Her mother was sure that he was behind it all. As a result, Hope feared him.

Hope feared her father and not without reason, but she also

harbored a yearning for him. She could still remember being a toddler when he pushed her in the swing in their backyard. She could still smell the scent of his hair when he hoisted her onto his shoulders for a walk down the block. She'd grab his ears, and he'd act like she was hurting him. Sometimes, she sat on his lap, and he tickled her or blew raspberries into her belly. She'd giggle and laugh.

Those memories brought her so much joy but also pain. Those days were lost to her. Hope missed them so much. She missed her dad. The truth that she couldn't say to her mother was that she still loved him. Despite all the pain and the danger, despite all that he'd done, she harbored hope that he would someday reemerge from the dark place into which he'd fallen. *I love you, Dad, but did you take my friends? What did you do with them?*

As she sat there, her eyes darting from the window to the mirror and back, the sun dipped below the tree line. Darkness quickly fell like a blanket across the forest. The voices continued down the hall, but she sat in silence. Sheba whimpered a little. *Please, Gavin, let me help. Gronek? Smakal? Are you out there?*

Her eyes drifted from the mirror back to the window. Then, they made the return trip. Back and forth, back and forth. She looked down at the dog's face drooped across her legs. Sad, tired eyes looked back up at her. She was stroking Sheba's shoulder when the dog's ears suddenly perked. It stared over toward the mirror, whining.

Hope felt a subtle change in the room. She followed Sheba's eyes. The surface of the mirror rippled and began to bulge. Hope's heart raced and she bolted up in anticipation. She nearly shouted when she saw Gavin's face as his whole head popped through the mirror.

***

"Hello, my friend," he said. "Come. We have much to do. I have someone for you to meet and we must find the boys."

As the little green fellow stepped through and stood on Josh's dresser, Hope rushed over and gave him a hug. Then, she planted a kiss on his cheek. He flushed a deeper shade of green but hugged her in return. "I'm so happy to see you," Hope exclaimed. "You have no idea."

"I am sorry to be so long in coming, dear one," Gavin replied.

"I have been away and have only just arrived back. My brothers have informed me of the situation. They have been searching for the boys to no avail. Still, we have more eyes now. We must rush to check every shimmer we can reach while the night lasts. Let us go quickly."

"I need to leave a note for my mom," Hope answered. "She'll freak if I disappear again."

Gavin was perplexed—should he leave or stay? Maxon had lectured him and accused him before the queen's court. His uncle deemed him guilty of causing danger to his kind by revealing himself, and that fear was not without merit. If the elves were revealed, the human scientists and governments would stop at nothing to penetrate their world. Everything his kind found precious would be compromised.

Now, he had a predicament. Should he bring Hope into his dimension to join the search, which would require the note? Or, should he do his best to reassure her but leave her here?

"Does she know of us?" Gavin asked.

"Only a little. She isn't quite convinced that you're real. She thinks you may be just a side effect of PTSD."

"Pee tee ess dee?" the elf inquired, drawing out each letter. "I am not familiar with that phrase."

"It's an abbreviation," Hope explained. "It means Post Traumatic Stress Disorder. You know…from when I was taken."

"Oh, yes. I see. Still, you must not reveal us any further. It will greatly endanger my people. Choose what you will do. You may come with me, but you cannot leave a note. Or, you may stay here, and I will report back to let you know of any developments."

Hope paused for a moment. She peered over at the door from behind which the adult voices rose and fell. She looked down at the dog. Sheba smiled back at her. The poor thing was still so lethargic that she hadn't risen to greet her elfin friend. As she considered her choice, Hope's eyes drifted to the window where darkness now hid the world beyond. Josh and Danny were out there somewhere. They needed to be found. This may be the only way. She had to go.

"Okay," she finally said. "I can't stay here. Mom will just have to be okay without me for a little while." After one last glance at Josh's bedroom door, which sported a giant Avengers poster, Hope climbed up on the dresser and took Gavin's hand in her own. "Let's go."

***

Kenny Burton, Hope's dangerous dad, sat on the side of a bunk in the Delaware County Jail. He'd tried to lie down, but his feet dangled off the end at his calves. His elbows rested on his knees and his hands cupped his face. He was bored and discouraged. First, he almost certainly wouldn't have a job when he got out. Second, he couldn't figure out what was up with those boys—boys who he was supposed to deal with himself. Kenny felt a little deprived.

He looked around. It was now late afternoon on a Monday. This cell probably had been packed over the weekend, but by noon this particular Monday, everyone else had cleared out. Eight bunks hung from frames imbedded in the cement walls—four down low and four up high. They had no structural supports, a feature designed to prevent suicides. LED lights lit the room behind thick plastic lenses well up and out of anyone's reach. There was one door across the room and slightly to his left with a thick window up top and a slide-out tray down below. The dull gray floor held questionable stains scattered here and there. A single toilet with a built-in sink hung off the wall to his right.

It had all stopped being interesting about two hours earlier. Even the voice had not visited him. He was alone. Kenny hated being alone. As much as the voice was annoying when he tried to sleep, it kept him company at other times. To him, it seemed like the voice of truth in his chaotic world.

"Where are you?" he shouted. "Why have you left me hanging?"

Nothing.

His hands began to shake. "I need a drink," he said to the air. His head was pounding behind his eyes. He closed them and tried to rub the ache away. Instead, an image of his daughter formed behind his closed eyelids. Anger welled up inside. A need to squash something or someone surged to the forefront of all else. He grabbed ahold of the flat, worthless mattress he sat on and squeezed. Kenny imagined it was Hope's neck. Then, another feeling formulated and tried to reach the surface but failed to do so. He couldn't quite understand it.

"*You'll be out soon,*" the voice suddenly made its presence known. "*They have no reason to hold you here for very long.*"

"Where have you been all day?" Kenny asked his sometimes unwelcome, internal friend. "Can you get me out of here? I need a drink bad."

"*Like I said, you will be out soon. You'll have your drink. I will make sure of it.*"

"What's up with the boys?" Kenny continued. "I thought I was supposed to kill them. That state cop who's now the sheriff down there said they were missing. He thought I'd done it."

"*I found another way. It presented itself, and I am enjoying the experience.*"

Kenny's face glowed red with anger. Again, he grabbed ahold of the flimsy mattress. The veins stood out on his neck. "But it was my job," he complained. "I was supposed to kill them. I spent time planning it out and thinking it through. You're cheating me."

"*You still have your little girl to kill. I will savor that one. You will make me very pleased; I am quite sure.*"

Again, that unfamiliar emotion tried to break into his mind. And again, it was shoved back down. It was like an imaginary trapdoor that kept slamming shut in his brain. "Yes," he said. "I know. But I wanted the boys, too. I thought you wanted me to kill the one named Josh especially."

"*Oh, the man-child. Yes. I do expect to enjoy his demise.*" The voice had the tone of great expectation. "*I will savor him over the next few days. It will be glorious.*"

Kenny placed the balls of his hands against his temples. He pushed. Suddenly, he felt like squeezing his own head until it collapsed in on itself. Kenny yearned for the voice, but he hated it, too. He missed it when it was gone, but when it came, he just wanted it to vanish again. On top of all that, Kenny now began to realize that this voice in his head was playing with him. It was messing with him. "You are cheating me," he screamed.

"*Ha! Of course, I'm cheating you. Did you expect anything less? Do you think you are the only weak-minded, ignorant human I can use?*"

"Maybe I won't—" Kenny enjoyed a brief thought of rebellion as another part of him surged to the surface.

"*Sleep,*" the voice interrupted. "*Sleep now.*"

The big man's eyes rolled back in his head and his eyes closed. His body teetered back and forth for a few seconds and then slumped to the side. Kenny landed with his right shoulder on the bed, but then he simply rolled forward onto the floor. He began to snore.

***

"Paaatrick," Russell Bray moaned. "I need a drink of water." Beads of sweat gathered on his forehead, and his neck was moist. At the same time, he was cold. Russell shivered almost uncontrollably.

In his rough cabin, Patrick had been sitting on his bunk watching the light slowly fade through the slats in the hardwood that formed the walls. When Robert had retrieved him from the mine and brought him back to care for his dad, he noticed sheets of clear plastic had been tacked up on the inside of the walls. It didn't help much, but he appreciated the change, nonetheless. They also left two large pills in a little sandwich bag. "One tonight and one in the morning," Robert said.

At least his dad was speaking now. That was something. Robert hadn't shackled him either. That was something new.

"Paaatrick, please. I'm thirsty."

"Sure, Dad. I'm sorry. I was just trying to figure out what to do." The boy got up and poured some water in the small plastic cup left beside the water bottle. Sitting on the edge of his father's bunk, he helped his Russell lean forward, and tilted the cup so he could sip. The man's red hair fell in clumps around his head. Patrick had never seen his dad with this much hair. His beard was full now, too.

When Russell had enough to drink, Patrick returned the cup to the little wooden table between their bunks. He remained on his father's bedside. Patrick surveyed the ramshackle hut around him, the wooden slats, the stone back wall, and the web-filled rafters above his head. Outside, their little enclosure was itself enclosed within a steel chain-link cage with only one gate for entry and exit. It was locked at all times with no way to escape.

As he sat there, he kept thinking that he had to do something. His dad was in no condition to help him, either. In fact, if he didn't take some sort of action, his father wouldn't survive the coming winter. He would freeze to death—they both might.

Patrick looked down at the denim coveralls that they'd given him to wear. Threadbare. The work boots he wore to work in the mine were heavily worn, as well. He had a long-sleeve thermal undershirt over his upper torso. That was it. His hair reached down to his shoulders, and his scraggly beard had grown down over his neck. Patrick was cold all the time now.

"Have you seen your mom?" Russell forced out and then began to cough. "Your sister?"

"No," he replied. "Not since that day a couple of weeks ago when they let each of them come see us." The boy rested his left hand on his dad's shoulder. "We can't go on like this. I'm going to have to escape and get some help."

"Trick," Russell replied using his son's preferred name, his voice so weak that the boy had to lean down to hear him. "That could get us all killed. Robert wears that pendant with the buttons. If he pushes that red button, Mabel will kill them."

"I know Dad, but if I don't do something and soon, you—"

"Don't worry 'bout me. If you go, don't look back. Go straight to your mom and sister. Make sure they're safe."

Patrick could see that his dad was using all his strength just to speak to him. Coughing fits interrupted the few words he said. He squeezed his dad's shoulder. "You rest now, Dad," he said. "For right now, I'm only going to take care of you. Okay?"

Russell said nothing more. He shifted and rolled over toward the outer wall.

Patrick gripped his dad's arm, gave it another squeeze and a little rub. He hadn't realized how much he loved his family until now. Patrick had never even given them much thought. They were just always there. Patti annoyed him. His father ragged on him. His mother smothered him. Now, Patrick missed all that and needed everything to go back to what it was before that night when they were snatched out of their beds.

After moving over to his own bunk, he began to think through what he might do. Robert did wear that pendant around his neck. Whatever he did, he couldn't let him touch it. If he pushed that button, his family would die before he could ever reach them. Mabel had made that clear. His captor also carried a Beretta nine-millimeter on his right hip. A large hunting knife sat on his left hip. Usually, he had another man with him—part of their twisted, extended family.

Escaping was not going to be easy, but Patrick didn't see any other options. Things had reached the point of desperation. It seemed hope was a thin, frayed thing, and he was only holding on to a thread. Before, he was holding back, waiting for his dad to come up with something. Now, it was up to him. If Patrick was going to do something, it was going to have to be soon.

He sat on the bed, the sun dropping behind the trees. The lights kicked on outside, bathing their enclosure in LED light. Someone was watching him. He'd seen the cameras mounted on the trees nearby. Nothing to do about it now. Pulling off his shoes, he huddled under the flimsy covers and closed his eyes. Think. That was all he could do right now. Think and sleep. Maybe an answer would present itself. Maybe tomorrow he would make his move. Maybe.

***

Danny looked up at the hole at the top of the silo. Through the tangle of ropes, the sky had turned reddish orange in the fading light. Soon, it would be too dark to see his hands in front of his face. The prospect of climbing all the way up there in dim light was too much. "Are you crazy?" he asked. "It's too high. We'd fall and break our necks."

Josh stared up, too. "It's high, but we can do it. We have to get to Hope before that man takes her. It's our only way out," he reasoned. "We have to get out. Come on. Let's do it."

"It's getting dark and pretty soon we won't be able to see anything. I can't climb all that way. I just can't." The ropes looked secure, but they'd been there a long time. Plus, he had once fallen from the hayloft at his uncle's farm. Fear tucked itself into its familiar place in his mind, effectively nailing his feet down. "It's too high and I can't do it."

"Well, I'm gonna do it," Josh said, giving voice to his determination. "I can't sit in here any longer, especially with Hope in danger. You can stay here if you want. No problem. I'll go get help and get you out, too."

"What if you fall?" Danny asked. "What then?"

"Fall?" Josh replied. "I'm not gonna fall. I climb like a monkey." He laughed and jumped around, making sounds like a chimpanzee.

Danny's gaze fell. He was embarrassed because of his fear. Of the two, he was always the one who worried. The top of the silo was, in fact, very high. He looked toward the ceiling again. "Please be careful."

"Aren't I always?"

This time Danny laughed. "Ha, not really." One of the reasons he liked Josh so much was his willingness to try so many things that he, himself, was too afraid to attempt. His friend was fearless.

"Here I go," Josh said, as he jumped up, grabbed the center cable, and pulled himself upward without using his feet. Two or three seconds later, he balanced on the first horizontal rope line. His feet wavered back and forth as he found his center. "Hey, is there any way down on the outside once I get up there?" He asked, shinnying up to the next level.

"There should be a ladder somewhere out there. Usually, there's one fastened to the outside. The farmer would've used it to climb up when he needed to start unloading the silo. But who knows if it's still there? It could've rusted off by now."

***

Josh pulled himself up two more layers. He was nearly halfway. "I hope it's there. It'll be bad if I get all the way up and there's no way down." This time, Josh jumped off the rope and grabbed the next horizontal rope. The distance was too far for his feet to be any help, so he swung freely. He started moving sideways back toward the center cable. One hand slid over, then then the other would meet it. He could feel the strain in his forearms. Reaching over with his feet, he hooked them around the cable and climbed up another level. Two thirds there. "Man, there are a lot of cobwebs up here." Looking down, he saw Danny staring up at him. Gaining yet another level, he smiled and waved. He was holding on with one hand, and his feet were again dangling loose. Danny waved back.

It was at that moment something crawled across his hand, the one gripping the cable. Startled, he let go to fling it off. Immediately, he tried to grip the cable with his other hand, but it was too late. He was already falling. His back caught briefly on the next horizontal rope, but he couldn't get a hold. It flung his head and torso forward and his feet backward so that he was falling face first. Reaching with his right hand, he was able to snag a rope crossing perpendicular to the others, but his momentum prevented him from holding on. All it did was slow his descent and flip him back around.

He landed hard just a few feet from Danny. His right leg got caught in the unloader machine and twisted as his head glanced off the side of the old electric motor. His leg snapped. Josh screamed in pain. Blood soaked into his pajama pants and ran across his face.

Danny rushed to him; Josh's left collarbone was bulging through the skin. "What do I do?" Danny sat in the dirt and cried; this time, his greatest fear of the moment realized.

Six

While Rick was filling them in on the developments of the investigation, Cindy Gillis was heating up a pot of chili. She'd make it weeks before, then saved it in large freezer bags. Cindy listened to her neighbor's words while she stirred the frozen clump floating in the middle. *A few more minutes.* She gave it another quick stir and sat back down at the table.

"So, there is nothing to directly tie Kenny to the boys other than he happened to be in town?" Maggie asked. "Footprints? Fingerprints? There's gotta be something."

Cindy looked over at Maggie, her face framed with new worry lines, but she held Annie's hand and rubbed her arm.

"We checked the footprints," Rick replied. There were a couple in the landscaping—"

"Kenny wears size thirteen," Maggie informed him.

"The prints weren't that big," Rick replied. "Only about size eleven. Typical of any number of guys."

"Yeah," Josh's dad spoke up. "I wear that size."

Rick continued, "The only fingerprints we found weren't useable. They either belonged to one of you or weren't in any database. They could have been from the boys, for all we could tell. Kenny Burton is in the system, so they don't belong to him."

Cindy stepped back up to the stove. Steam rose out of the big, stainless steel pot. The red, meat-filled stew was bubbling nicely. "Looks like the soup's ready," she said. "Maggie, would you go get Hope? She's probably hungry, don't you think?"

Maggie stood and headed down the hall.

"So, unless something else comes up, the Muncie PD will have to let Kenny go in the morning. There's nothing to hold him on,"

Rick said.

Maggie rushed back into the room, her eyes wide with terror. "Hope is gone!"

***

Hope, holding Gavin's hand, emerged from the shimmer into the world of the elves, promptly losing her grip and falling to the ground. She hadn't remembered that the portal was a good five feet above the yard. Quickly, two familiar green faces were at her side helping her to her feet.

"Gronek. Smakal. It's so good to see you. You have no idea."

From where she stood, the beautiful, colorful aura of the natural world overwhelmed her. The forest sparkled in hues of blue, green, red, orange, purple, and yellow. Plus, a myriad of variations within those colors. All around, twinkling lights left the trees and swirled to the ground, fading as they fell, leaving the pulsating blue bones of the trees behind. Hope knew the brilliance of the arboreal world was around her all the time, but she simply couldn't see it on her side. The spectacle tugged at her, as if begging her to stay on this side. Yet, she couldn't. She might visit, but she couldn't stay. It wasn't her place.

Gavin, after releasing Hope's hand, moved away as his brothers moved in to help the girl up. She looked around and spotted him a few feet to her right. He wasn't alone. Beside him stood a female elf dressed in golden, leafy splendor. She shared the bright green aura of skin that her friends sported, and her eyes shone like emeralds in the shimmering light. She wore a white rope sash around her waist and golden shoes to match her dress. Hope couldn't tell from what material they were made, but they were lovely. Her head carried a crown of a variety of nuts and cones. *She's beautiful. Stunning.*

"My dear friend, Hope," Gavin said, "please come meet our mother, the queen."

"Your mother?" Hope answered. "She's a queen?"

"Yes, yes," the elf replied. "We have only arrived by her carriage a few moments ago, and she is eager to make your acquaintance."

Glancing beyond the royal elves, Hope could see a carriage. Reindeer grazed beside it. She stepped up before the queen, and the majestic elfin woman smiled at her. Gavin's mother looked her over, head to toe.

"Ah, my son is correct. Your aura is remarkable. Rarely do humans bear such a powerful life force. Come nearer, dear girl."

Glancing back at Gronek and Smakal, she hesitated for a moment. They nodded for her to proceed, so she stepped over to meet the queen. Hope lowered herself until she was eye to eye with the royal elf.

"I am Queen Agahpey Hesed of the kind that you know as elves. Welcome into my realm." As she spoke, the queen raised her two six-fingered hands and placed them gently to each side of Hope's face. "My son has told me of your ordeal and of your bravery. Truly remarkable. I am honored to meet you this evening."

Almost overwhelmed, Hope forced her mind to focus. "Your Majesty. Uh, Queen Hesed," she said. "Please, can you help me find my friends? They've been kidnapped, and we can't find them anywhere."

"Of course, we will work diligently to find your friends. I must meet them, as well. I have brought help, and more help arrives as we speak." The queen motioned to her right toward the forest.

When Hope looked toward the trees, she spotted a large, hairy creature with two swords draped across his back. The hilts were visible over each shoulder. Before she could look away, another individual moved to stand with the creature. *A man*? He wore leather trousers and a leather shirt. Beads adorned his neck.

The queen followed Hope's gaze. "Please meet Sacqueal. He is my personal guard. He hails from the Sasquatch Nation. Next to him is Tomo, the Guardian. He lives near here. His people have made this forest their abode for thousands of years. They will assist us as we look for your friends."

Hope looked back at the queen mother. Tears formed in her eyes, one trickling down her left cheek. "Our neighbor, the sheriff has all his men out looking, but they've had no luck. Josh and Danny have disappeared."

The queen began to respond, but Smakal broke in. "Dear Hope, your mother is in Josh's room for sleeping. She looks very upset."

Hope rushed to the shimmer and peered inside. Sure enough, her mother was distraught. Her hands covered her mouth, she was trembling. Before Hope could say anything, she sensed the queen at her side, her green fingers gripping Hope's shoulders. "I have to go back," Hope said. "I can't do this to her."

"Yes, dear," the queen replied. "You must. Be assured that we will search everywhere and check back with you periodically through the night. Watch for us." The queen turned Hope to face her. She again placed her hands upon Hope's cheeks. "Your name is Hope, but this day, I rename you Nozomi. That will be my special name for you."

"What does it mean?" Hope asked.

"It means 'beautiful hope' in the language of the people from the island that you call Japan. I visited there many, many years ago. The name captures the beauty of your aura and the spirit of your name. To me, you are now my Nozomi. We will find your friends. Now, you must go back to your mother."

Hope looked back through the dimensional window. As she did, her mother rushed out of the room.

"Go," Hesed urged. "Go, quickly, before she returns. We will search every shimmer for miles around. I will send one of my sons to report to you every hour."

"Thank you," Hope replied. Then Gronek and Smakal hoisted her up, and she stepped back into the human realm.

***

"What do you mean?" Rick asked from where he stood in the middle of the kitchen.

"I mean she's gone. I went to get her, and she isn't in there. It's all happening again." Maggie covered her face with her hands and fell against Rick's chest.

Rick wrapped his arms around her, something he longed to do without there being some sort of crisis. In the last two weeks, he could only think of two things—his new job and Maggie. Rick pushed his thoughts back down. Now was not the time—still. *Will it ever be the time?*

"Are you sure she wasn't just asleep or maybe in the bathroom?" Cindy asked.

"Josh has a walk-in closet, right?" Annie asked. "Maybe she was in there."

"That's probably it," Roger said. "Half the time, Josh can't hear us when he's sitting in there playing with this, that, or the other thing. She was probably in there exploring his toys and games."

"Besides," Kevin Flannery said, "we would have heard it if someone broke in. Roger and I secured all our windows and doors this afternoon."

"I'm telling you she wasn't in there. I looked everywhere," Maggie said. Tears flooded her cheeks.

The women gathered around Maggie. Roger and Kevin stood, leaving the cups of coffee they were nursing on the table. Rick cupped the back of Maggie's head. She leaned back against his touch, and he could read the despair in her eyes.

"Let's go look again," Rick said.

Just then, a thump came from down the hall. All six adults rushed to Josh's bedroom, Rick leading the way. When they burst through the door, Hope stood in front of Josh's dresser with a sheepish look on her face. She was holding a picture frame with a broken lens.

"I'm sorry, Mrs. Gillis," she said. "I accidentally knocked this off the dresser."

Rick's eyes shifted to the mirror. He could almost make out other images in the reflective glass. Without speaking, he knew. She *had* been gone. She'd gone through the mirror and come back again.

"Where were you?" Maggie asked in a rush. "I couldn't find you." She wrapped her arms around her daughter.

Hope gave her mother a quirky smile. "A girl has to go to the bathroom once in a while."

***

Queen Hesed watched through the shimmer until Hope and the others had left Josh's room, and then she turned slowly around to speak to her entourage. "My son, you were right in wanting to introduce me to Nozomi. Although she is young, her life force is remarkable. It is quite rare to see such force present in humans. In fact, it is something that I have never seen in my two thousand years of life."

"Mother," Gronek said, "do you have any idea what she may be capable of doing?"

Hesed pulled her son in for a motherly hug. "No. I do not. Her gifts will only be discovered as time unfolds and as the Mighty One decides to reveal them. We know that certain reindeer can fly in our realm due to their aura. We know that the sasquatch can pass into and out of the human realm by vocalizing certain rhythmic sounds. We know that Tomo's people have learned to do the same in this forest."

Tomo joined the queen and her sons near the shimmer. Sacqueal followed closely on his heels. "My queen, I am here at your request. What may I do to assist you?"

"Tomo, my friend," Hesed replied. "It is nearly as pleasant to see you again as it is to see my own sons. Have the years been pleasant for you? Is your family well?"

"Yes, they are all well. The Mighty One has blessed us these many years in this forest."

"We must visit more. I want to hear stories of your children," the queen said. "But for now, we must do that for which I have come. We must locate Nozomi's two missing friends. Spread out to all the shimmers in the region. Check every portal for any sign of the young humans. With the passing of each hour, you will all report to Smakal of your progress. Smakal, you must remain here so that you can update Nozomi."

Gavin, Gronek, Smakal, and Tomo nodded their understanding. Sacqueal nodded and growled deep in his throat.

"Start with the town," she continued. "There will be many shimmers there. Then spread out in all directions. Go now."

Without another word, they all turned and rushed away.

***

In the quickly fading light, Danny assessed Josh's injuries. His friend was bleeding in several places, but the worst seemed to be from his forehead. Without a thought to himself, Danny pulled his t-shirt off and wrapped Josh's head. There were other scrapes and cuts. Josh's collarbone was broken. With all of that, what worried Danny most was his friend's twisted right leg. It was wedged into the unloader machinery as he hit the ground. The momentum of the fall had caused his body to turn, but the leg was trapped and held tightly in place. The resulting snap had been loud. Josh screamed until he passed out.

Gingerly, Danny tried to pull the leg free from the machine, but it only caused Josh to writhe in pain. He was afraid to touch it again. The way it was positioned, it looked like an extra joint protruded just below the knee.

By the time he finished caring for Josh as best he could, darkness again encompassed the two of them. The sky had grown cloudy, so there wasn't any light even from the moon. Danny could no longer see his hand in front of his face. All he could do was sit with Josh's head in his lap and think. And he could pray.

"Dear God," he called into the blackness that surrounded him. "Please help us. Please send someone to get us out of here." He prayed that same prayer over and over, and over again, but there was no reply.

Josh would occasionally mumble or moan. A few times he woke up and called out in pain. Danny held him as still as he could so the injured young man wouldn't yank his leg and cause more damage.

"Caw. Caw, caw," the crow said from somewhere up above. It seemed as if the bird was checking to see if they were still there.

"Mr. Crow," Danny answered. "Josh fell. He tried to climb up there where you are, but he fell. Now, he's hurt bad, and I don't know what to do."

"Caw," the crow answered before flying off again.

For a while, Danny thought from within his hungry, dehydrated, weary state that maybe it would go find help, but then he realized that it was only a bird. There was no way for a crow to find any way to help them get out. His heart raced with despair. They were locked in an old silo on an abandoned farm in the middle of nowhere. No one would ever find them. There was nothing he could do about it. Josh would probably die from his injuries tonight or tomorrow. Maybe the next day. Then, Danny would follow him by dying of thirst a few days later.

"There's nothing I can do, Josh," Danny said. "I'm sorry."

As he said those words, he realized they weren't true. They were lies he was telling himself to avoid facing the obvious. There was, in fact, something he could do. He looked up toward the sky, and as he did, the clouds briefly cleared, and he could make out the shapes of the various ropes strung from place to place. There was something he could do. If Josh was still alive when morning came, Danny decided he would do it. He would do what Josh had tried to do. He would climb out of this trap and get help to save his friend.

Seven

Patrick Bray, known to his family as Trick, was sleeping fitfully on his hard cot in the cold shack at the base of the bluff. He was worried about his dad, and he had to do something about it. His mind was working on the problem as he slept, but there were so many issues. They were locked in a cabin which was positioned inside a steel cage. His mother and sister were being held under threat somewhere else and used as hostages against anything he might try. When they moved him during the day to the underground mine, his captors were always in pairs. The main captor, Robert, was armed and wore that pendant around his neck. All the man had to do was push the button on the pendant, and his mother would punish Trick's family. *If I could only get him alone...*

His dreaming mind conjured the images of his confinement. *He was sitting on the side of the cot. Sun was filtering past the colorful trees and slipping in through the cracks in the cabin walls. His father shivered on his own cot.*

The door flung open. Robert stood there and motioned for him to get up. It was time for work. He wanted to stay with his dad, but Robert wouldn't allow it. There were limestone blocks to cut from the cavernous walls in the mine. Patrick's dream-self stepped outside into the morning light. The sky appeared a swirl of red and yellow. His captor stood at the open gate, motioning him to pass through, waving his gun.

Patrick glanced to his right. There was a row of other cabins in other cages. They lined up along the rock wall, hidden by the forest canopy. A trail led past them to the mouth of the mine. He stepped out of the cage and turned toward the worksite. Robert walked alongside him on his left, near the forest. Today, there was no guard. It was just the two of them. The pendant around Robert's neck was on a lanyard. The button was in a square, plastic transmitter. Rather than dangling free around his neck, Patrick could see that Robert had it tucked into a breast pocket.

Two other captives entered their cabins, men who had been there much longer than him. They were just returning from their nighttime shift. The mine was underground, so day or night, there was work to be done. They were skinnier than Trick. They looked weaker as well. Did they have families? Were they missed?

His sleeping mind gazed down at his own hands. They looked older, stronger. His forearms were muscular now. The work had developed them. Gone was the baby fat that had doggedly clung to his frame into his teen years. Will I look as scraggly as those guys eventually?

They passed the last caged cabin and came to a bend in the trail. The path turned to the right toward the rock wall. A pin oak stood there with a low-hanging branch. Robert ducked to pass under. His head dropped down and toward Trick. All Trick would need to do is reach out with his left arm and wrap it around Robert's neck. One hard twist, and everything would change.

I just need the chance, Patrick's dreaming mind said. I just need him to come get me by himself and give me a chance.

"You'll get that chance," a voice replied. "I'll see to it."

Trick's mind was confused. He heard the voice, but he didn't recognize it. It came from outside and slipped inside his head as if he were listening through some sort of internal headset.

"Be ready in the morning," it said. "Your opportunity is at hand."

***

Kenny Burton's mind was forced to sleep by the specter. That specter would not let him awaken, but instead returned multiple times through the night to feed the same imagery into Kenny's alcohol-fogged brain. His dream was like watching a video in loop mode, so Kenny experienced the same dream again and again.

It's morning. Kenny is sitting on the side of his bunk staring at the cell door. Rather than a deputy, the actual sheriff comes to see him. "Okay, big boy, time to go home," the sheriff says. "Let's get you outta here."

In the next vision, Kenny finds himself outside. He looks up and the sky is a weird swirl of red and yellow. He walks the two miles back to his rented house in the Shedtown neighborhood of Muncie. A train stops him on Hoyt Avenue. He continues on his way and stops at the grocery store where he's been working. "You don't have to fire me," he says. "I quit."

When he arrives home, instead of going inside, he jumps into his Gran Torino and heads out of town. He's going back to Cutters Notch despite the warning given by that new sheriff—the one with the hots for his ex. He's going to deal with the girl. He's going to do it now.

The next image has him in Cutters Notch. He's driving up to the burned-out house. Hope is in the trunk. There's no explanation as to how she got there, but he has her. He finds himself around the back of the large old house. The back door is boarded up. He rips the two-by-fours off and kicks the door in.

He finds himself at his trunk. As he opens it, Hope is staring up at him. There is duct tape over her mouth. Her hands are bound with zip ties, her feet as well. He looks into her eyes. He sees within them just how much she hates him. The hatred radiates out in waves. Her eyes are boring a hole into his brain. Jerking her out of the trunk, he throws her over his shoulder and turns to go inside.

Stop. Reset. Play the images again.

***

Tom Bennett, the Delaware County sheriff, woke up in the middle of the night. He jerked upright in his bed in the master bedroom of his West University Avenue home in Muncie. There was one primary thought that had been driven like a spear into his brain: *Release Kenny Burton.*

He felt watched. He felt invaded, soiled. It was like the inside of his mind was covered in some sort of slime. He looked over at his wife of twenty-five years who was sleeping peacefully with her back to him and placed his hand on her side. She had kicked their blanket off revealing her silky pink nightgown. Her breathing came deep and smooth. She was okay. He took a deep breath and then let it out slowly, trying to calm himself.

A cold draft shot across the back of his neck. Goosebumps raised on his arms. In the darkened room, nothing seemed out of the ordinary. He listened, but all he heard was the ticking of the grandfather clock in the dining room.

"I must have had a dream," he whispered to himself. "It feels so weird."

He reclined back on his pillow and closed his eyes. Still, the one thought that wouldn't leave him was to release Kenny Burton. It was as if a broken record kept skipping back to the same point in his brain. *Release Kenny Burton. Release Kenny Burton. Release Kenny Burton.*

Pulling the blanket up around his neck, he stared at the dark ceiling. He was wide awake. He was very cold.

Eventually, the adrenaline drained away and he began to drift off again. His mind fell into a fitful series of incongruent images. He tossed. He turned. Then, *"Release Kenny Burton!"*

He jerked up in his bed. It felt like someone speaking through a direct line into his brain.

Stop. Reset. Play the images and the message again.

***

Al Havener had driven forty miles to Washington, Indiana, to eat dinner at an Amish buffet. Cutters Notch had a gas station with a few hot items and a diner that was open for breakfast and lunch, but there was no real full-service restaurant in the whole town. Unless you had a kitchen or you liked pre-made deli sandwiches, you pretty much had to drive somewhere else for an evening meal. It was after ten in the evening when he returned to his room at the Notch Inn. He drove past the neon sign that announced there were vacancies and parked directly in front of his unit. Ten minutes later, his teeth were brushed, he poured himself a small amount of bourbon into one of those clear plastic cups, and he crawled under the covers.

Al was too tired to watch television, so he sipped his drink and thought about those boys in the silo. A smile crept across his face. By now, they were parched and starving. Cold and dirty. Most of all, and the thing that really gave him the jollies, they were terrified. They had to be. *I would be if I were them.*

He was going to be in Cutters Notch for at least three more days, maybe a week. He had lots to do in his aunt's house. To a degree, he resented being sent to the little nowhere town to deal with those kids and liquidate the property. He had no love for his Aunt Faye or her husband. Their crimes disgusted him. Even as a criminal himself, some lines should not be crossed. Cannibalism was one of those lines.

Al's mind began to slowly leak toward sleep. *Maybe I'll skip checking in on the boys tomorrow.* He'd wait a whole extra day. It would build the anticipation within himself, and it would be even more devastating for those brats. *Besides, I need to figure out how to get that girl.*

There was a tiny amount of the amber liquid left in the bottom of his cup, so he slurped the last of it. He liked the sting it brought. It was some good stuff. Smooth going down. Placing the cup on the nightstand, he picked up a paperback book. Maybe he could read two or three pages before sleep caught up to him. It was a novel by Michael Connelly. He loved crime novels. To him, they were like everyday life. They fed his imagination and gave him new ideas.

He laid the book back down. Al was just too tired. Stacking up two pillows, he reclined and peered around the tiny motel room. Two lamps flanked the headboard of his queen-sized bed. Across from him, a small, flat screen TV sat on a low dresser; its rectangular black face stared back at him from above his feet. To his right was the door to the tiny bath. There was barely enough room to turn around, but it did what it was supposed to do. All the fixtures worked as they should. All in all, it wasn't a bad little place.

His eyes scanned the drop ceiling and spotted a smoke detector. The whole inn was non-smoking. He could tell that the owner smoked in the office, but the rooms were clearly free of the effects of tar and nicotine. He also spotted some sprinkler heads. *Wow, this place is more up-to-date than I thought.* There were four sprinkler heads in the ceiling—one in the far right corner, one in the far left corner, and two spaced apart in key places in the room. *Seems a little excessive, though, for such a small room.*

Al gave the sprinkler heads no more thought before reaching over and switching off the light. Closing his eyes, he quickly drifted off to sleep.

"You've done a good job," a voice softly whispered into his mind.

Under the blanket, he shivered. It would be many hours before he awoke again.

***

At midnight, Mabel Robbins and her son, Robert, were in the lobby of the Notch Inn. Robert was seated on the orange, vinyl sofa. Mabel stood over him barking orders. Outside, the parking lot was dark. They had turned off the exterior lights and the lighted neon sign near the road. Underneath the sign, they closed the long, swinging gate across the entrance to the parking lot and padlocked it to its mating post. By morning, they would need to reopen it because being closed-up in the light of day would draw its own attention. For now, though, they wanted no unexpected guests while they performed their overnight tasks.

Mabel was dressed in a pair of coveralls with a paisley blouse blooming out of the shoulder straps. Robert was dressed all in black. He even sported a black stocking hat.

"I want you to have Boyd stay over in the morning to handle the shift change with Parker," Mabel instructed. "You're going to have your hands full getting our new worker settled into his new accommodations tonight and orienting him to his new responsibilities tomorrow. Not to mention the sick one that you'll need to see to."

"And the boy?"

"Let Patrick sleep in just a little. He can check on his father when he gets up. Be sure to give Russell another antibiotic tablet. Then, take the boy on down to the mine later in the morning."

"If Parker is already down at the mine, I'll need to transfer Patrick on my own."

"He's a boy and you're a man," she answered. "You can handle him. Now, have you brought the tractor up so we can tow Havener's car down to the pit?"

"Yep. It's just around the bend in the woods."

"Excellent. We're ready, then." Mabel walked into her office, opened a small metal box affixed to the wall, and pushed a small black button. No noise emitted. No lights flashed. Nothing seemed to happen at all. But, down the row of units, where Al Havener lay sleeping, a little hiss emanated from the two sprinkler heads in each corner as an invisible gas permeated the room.

***

Havener was normally a deep sleeper, but his sleep, which was often a flurry of unrelated dream images, drifted deeper and deeper until there was nothing but a numbing darkness. He was so far gone that he didn't hear his door open. He didn't feel the covers pulled back from his bed. He didn't even feel Robert pull him, feet first, off the bed and onto a wheeled cart. Even as his head bounced up and down when the cart rumbled down the path, he didn't rouse from his gas-induced slumber. He would be quite surprised when he awoke to see his new cabin inside the steel cage along the base of the stone cliff wall.

***

As Robert positioned Al onto his new cot, Mabel removed any remnants of the man's stay. His book, some paperwork, along with his keys and wallet were placed in a plastic tub. His bottle of bourbon was tucked into a pocket of her coveralls. His suitcase, which was standing open next to the TV stand, was zipped up and tossed out the door. His toiletries were rounded up from the bathroom, dropped in a ziplock bag and placed into the plastic tub alongside the wallet and keys. As she backed out of the room, Mabel took one last look around and was satisfied. It looked like any other room vacated by a guest. She'd have Annie Bray clean it thoroughly in the morning.

***

Within the hour, Robert had finished supplying Al's cabin with his new work clothes as the man snored on his cot. He jumped on the tractor and drove it up to the parking lot. Lining it up with the back of Al's car, he linked the two with a chain. Using the pilfered keys, he put the car into neutral and pulled it away, down the road through the forest to the mine. Inside the gaping mouth of the mine, he turned to the right, found the vehicle storage chamber, and positioned the four-door sedan next to the Brays' family Suburban.

After unhooking the large car, he stepped back and looked at the row of vehicles in the huge limestone garage. A row of incandescent bulbs had been strung along the ceiling for about a hundred yards. The glowing orbs illuminated the scene. The vehicles were now three rows deep. Jeeps, Chevys, Fords, Toyotas, Hondas, and even a few Kias. This collection was in addition to the long row that lined the rim of their old surface mine. Soon, he would begin to line up row number four. It was such a waste to leave all these in the depths of the mine simply to rust away, but there was nothing to be done about it. They couldn't risk them being used on the streets. The vehicles had to disappear.

A thought occurred to him. *Maybe we could part them out. Hmm.* He decided to bring it up with his mother. *Why not make a little money off them? Most of the parts aren't traceable.* Robert was still considering that possibility as he headed off to see Boyd about staying over a couple of hours in the morning. He yawned. It had been a long day, and he had an even longer night ahead.

***

It was after ten when Rick finally gave into his weariness and went home to catch some sleep. Upon entering his front door, he was again reminded of the loneliness that had saturated his life since his wife took his son and moved away. For a while, hopelessness had gripped him, and he had contemplated taking his own life. He'd often left his service weapon on the counter or on the table where he could see it as he considered that ultimate option. These days, though, he locked it and his backup weapon in a gun safe. Maggie had rekindled his heart, and the rescue of Hope had revitalized his spirit.

After locking the door behind him, he walked into the dark kitchen and opened his refrigerator. There wasn't much to see: a bottle of ketchup, a bottle of mustard, some American cheese, a half-gone package of bologna. He found a pint of milk, opened the top, and chugged it down. He almost wiped his mouth on his shirt sleeve but then remembered he planned to wear it again in the morning. Instead, he yanked a paper towel from the dispenser. Closing the refrigerator door, he made his way down the darkened hallway, making a pitstop in the bathroom.

Finally, he stumbled into the bedroom he used to share with his wife. *My ex-wife,* he reminded his brain. He flicked on a bedside lamp and looked around. The room was devoid of anything remotely feminine. Rick had no pictures on the wall and there was no bedspread, only a thin blanket over some formerly white sheets.

Rick opened the folding, louvered door to his closet and fumbled with his shirt buttons. Pulling the shirt from his torso, he hung it carefully on a wire hanger. Then, he removed his utility belt and weapons. After placing the guns in the safe, he hung the belt from a hook beside the closet. Finally, he stepped out of his trousers and hung them on a different hook. As he headed toward the bed, he yanked his socks from his feet and tossed them toward a clothes basket in the back corner. He missed. They rimmed out. He didn't care.

Rick sat on the side of his bed and thought through his day and the short night he'd had before the sun had risen. He was so tired that he felt tingly. After checking his alarm, he reclined on his pillow, pulled the covers over himself, and immediately fell into a deep sleep.

His dreams seemed to be a battle of wits between two parts of his psyche. The part of himself that loved life and loved people, the kind, generous, and happy Rick Anders battled with the part of himself that seemed to want to prove he was a broken-down, worthless loser.

Images of mistakes flooded his mind. The times when he said hurtful things to his ex-wife. The times when he was harsh with his son. The time when he couldn't save a four-year-old girl who'd been attacked by some feral dogs. She'd bled out in his arms. He lost her.

Those images would be replaced by happy memories. He saw himself with his own father on the bank of the White River, fishing. He saw his boy licking an ice cream cone with sweet dribbles on his chin. He saw another little girl—the one who had drowned in Lake Monroe, but he'd revived.

Back and forth, the images flew. They pulled his emotions first one way and then the other. He tossed and he turned, and he woke once with tears on his cheeks. Rick woke again later laughing out loud.

In the end, his mind turned to Maggie, and as it did, the negative energy that had been battling for control disappeared. He saw her smile. He saw her beautiful, curly hair. He saw her sparking eyes. In his dream, she reached out and took his hand in her own. His heart leapt.

Then, the dreams came to an end and he just slept.

***

Hope had kept a vigil in Josh's bedroom. She stroked Sheba's fur and watched the mirror, hoping against hope. To pass the time between Smakal's reports, she immersed herself in Josh's collection of *The Walking Dead* graphic novels. They were sort of gross, but they kept her mind distracted.

Smakal checked in three times, but there was no news. Just before the fourth check-in, her mother stepped in and announced they needed to go home for the night.

Hope glanced at the digital clock on Josh's nightstand. "Can I have ten more minutes?" she asked. She held up one of the books as if that were the reason. Her mother agreed to ten more minutes, but then they had to go.

Five minutes later, Smakal popped his head back through the mirror.

"Dearest Hope," he said, "there is still nothing to report. I am so sorry." The elf truly did look sorry. His eyes were moist and even his pointy green ears drooped. There was no hint of his normally cheerful smile.

"The next time you report, please come to my shimmer, the one at my bedroom. Okay? My mother says we need to go home. I'll be watching for you there."

Smakal agreed and ducked back out.

Fifteen minutes later, Hope was holding a similar vigil in her own bedroom. She'd positioned herself in a chair in front of her vanity and rested her chin on her arms. Her curly blond hair hung loosely around her shoulders. Staring into the mirror, she willed herself to stay awake.

She failed.

***

Maggie stepped into Hope's room to check on her and found her sound asleep at the mirror. As carefully as she could, she hoisted her teenage daughter, which was no easy task, and carried her into her own bedroom. Placing her on one side of her queen-sized bed, she crawled in next to her and wrapped her arms around her treasure, her sweet, sweet Hope.

***

Hope slept peacefully. When Smakal went looking for her, he saw her curled up next to her mother. There would be no more need to check in that night, so he joined the search.

***

It was a long and difficult night in the silo. Danny sat in the dark with his back against the machinery and Josh's head on his lap. He was shirtless and bitter cold. Josh slid in and out of consciousness. Sometimes, he'd sleep for thirty or forty minutes, but then he'd awaken and call out in pain. All Danny could do was hold him. When Josh called out and thrashed about, Danny held him down. When Josh drifted off to sleep, Danny would cushion his friend's head and try to sleep a little himself. He had nothing to rest his own head against, so it kept bobbing. Other times, he'd awaken to find himself leaning to one side.

He could hear the scurrying of little feet in the rubble on the floor. Mice. He'd seen the opossum. His imagination also conjured up other creatures lurking in the darkness—rats, bats, tarantulas, giant snakes. At one point, something rushed across his socked feet and he kicked at it. That caused Josh to stir and cry out, and Danny regretted his reaction.

Above their heads, the sky eventually cleared, and the moon poked through the angular hole in the roof. The light backlit the tangle of ropes. As much as he feared heights and dreaded climbing anything, he found that as the time passed in the dark, he began to yearn for morning and his journey up through that network of hemp, nylon, and cable. Nothing, absolutely nothing, could be more torturous than what he was doing as he stared upward into the dark.

Sometime in the middle of the night, a fit of shivers overtook him. He shook uncontrollably. Gooseflesh covered his arms and torso. The only warm spot on his body was the small area under Josh's head. Again, his shivers woke Josh, who then cried out in pain.

"Ahh," Josh cried. "It hurts, Danny. It hurts so bad. And that thing won't leave me alone. It's laughing at me. It's going to get me. I know it is." Josh then slipped into sobs and deep groans before his mind shut down again, forcing him back into unconsciousness.

"I've got you," Danny said. It was all he could think of to say. "I'm right here, and I've got you."

After finally drifting off into some extended semblance of sleep, Danny opened his eyes, again. His head was lying back, and he could see the first hint of light in the morning sky. As dawn flooded into the morning air, hope flooded into his adolescent heart. He could feel Josh's breathing. His friend had made it through the night. Danny had done everything he could to comfort him in the darkness, but now it was time to act. Now, it was time to rescue his friend and himself. It was time to climb those ropes.

The crow landed on the edge of the triangular hole in the ceiling. "Caw," it said. "Caw, caw."

"I hear ya," Danny answered. "And I'm coming." With that, as carefully as he could, he slipped out from under Josh's head and stood up. His joints were stiff, and his arms, torso, and hands were icy cold. He jumped around to get the blood pumping and rubbed his hands together in the growing light.

"Josh," he said, "I'm going to get help. You hang in there."

His friend didn't reply.

Finally, Danny took a deep breath and steeled his will. It was time to climb.

Eight

Danny stood in the dim light that barely illuminated the inside of the silo. He was stiff and cold—and scared. His fingers ached. His toes ached. His neck ached. He took a deep breath and exhaled. His breath came out, a visible vapor cloud in the chilly air.

As he worked his fingers and rubbed his hands together to generate a bit more warmth before starting his climb, he looked down at his friend. Blood had seeped into the t-shirt that he'd wrapped around Josh's head, but the good news was that he didn't seem to be actively bleeding anymore. Danny was encouraged and happy that Josh was breathing. It was shallow and made only small, visible clouds of vapor, but it was there. His friend was still unconscious, and that was probably a good thing.

Danny looked up. More light was flooding inside. Condensation gathered in the spider webs that interlaced the tangle of ropes. One path was cleared of any webs—the path that Josh had followed when he first climbed but had subsequently fallen back through. The spiders had not rebuilt in the night. Apparently, it was too cold for them.

Returning his gaze to the silo floor, he began to move around, careful to avoid stepping on anything sharp with his socked feet. *I've got to get some blood flowing.* He swung his arms around and jumped up and down, occasionally slapping his hands together. All the while, he was opening and closing his fists, moving his fingers. Danny willed the blood to flow into his extremities.

After a couple of minutes, the time had come. As a boy in the process of becoming a man, there was a part of him that was still fighting for the false safety that came from being frozen in fear. But, as a man trying to explode out of a boy's body, he knew he had to act. There was no room for the paralyzing fear he knew so well. Josh's life, and his own, depended on his willingness to make the dangerous journey up through those ropes.

"I'm not gonna get any warmer," he said aloud to himself. "I need to get this over with."

Danny knelt beside his friend. Gripping Josh's face between his hands, he felt the warmth of his skin. "I'm going for help, Josh. I'll be back. You hang in there." Josh's only reply was a low moan.

"Caw! Caw, caw," the crow called out from above.

Danny peered up. "I know," he said. "I'm coming." The sky was a weird, swirling combination of yellow and red.

Standing up, Danny looked down at his feet. His socks and his pajama bottoms were covered in the dirt and dust from the silo floor. He pulled his socks up snuggly against his feet and then carefully climbed onto the unloader frame. The steel cable was rough and cold when he gripped it. Danny took a deep breath and blew out a plume of vapor. Then he leaped and grabbed the cable as high as he could, wrapping his feet around the end dangling under him.

He pulled himself upward. Danny needed to climb about ten feet before he'd reach the first crossing rope. As he pulled with his arms, he tried to use his feet to support his weight. One of his uncles had taught him a technique for climbing that included a way to wrap a rope around your feet and sort of stand on it as he climbed. Unfortunately, the steel cable wasn't very flexible, and it limited the usefulness of that skill. Still, it helped some. Every little bit was important.

Danny pulled with his arms and shoved with his feet, making headway upward. The muscles in his arms and shoulders began to burn. They weren't used to this level of exertion. After reaching the first crossing rope, he stood on it and rested. He looked up and was struck by how far he still had to go. Danny looked down and saw his crumpled friend. He had to go on.

He jumped again and grabbed the cable, a repeat of the move he'd made below. It didn't gain him much, the leap of a turtle but, every inch counted. Danny pulled and he pushed, pulled and pushed. His muscles were screaming. He made it to the second horizontal rope line.

Leaning on the center cable, he looked up and down again.

Josh was smaller and the roof was closer, but he had a long, long way to go. Danny was breathing hard. His hands throbbed. As he stood there, a mouse bustled across the rope supporting him. It stopped a few feet away, looking at him with its tiny eyes.

"Oh, no you don't," Danny told it. "You just go on back where you came from."

As if it understood English, the mouse reversed course and skittered away. It stopped at the silo wall and glared back at the boy for a few seconds and then slipped into a crevice. "If only I could get out so easy," Danny said to no one.

He leaped. Again, he pulled with his arms and he pushed with his feet. Again, his muscles screamed. His hands were getting numb, but at least he no longer felt cold. He reached the third crossing rope—about halfway to the top. Feeling something on his arm as he rested again, he lifted his numb right hand off the cable and found blood running from a blister in the meaty portion of his hand under his thumb. Danny wiped the bulk of the red liquid onto his pajama pants.

Leaping yet again, he repeated the same process to the next horizontal rope and then the next one after that. He found himself just one level below the top. The sun was now bright in the sky, but he could barely make out Josh's form on the silo floor below him. He was almost out, but he was so exhausted. Danny wasn't sure he could reach that one last level near the top. In comparison to how far he had climbed, it wasn't that far, but in his state of physical exhaustion, it seemed like miles and miles. It may as well have been.

"Danny?" Josh moaned below. "Where are you? I'm scared. That thing is still here. It won't leave me alone."

Danny looked down at his friend sprawled out in the shadows so far below. Josh was squirming, moaning, and crying out in pain.

"I'm up here," Danny yelled down. "I'm going for help. You hang in there. Just a little while longer."

With his resolve steeled, Danny leaped one more time. But, as he tried to grip the cable with his feet, his toes cramped up. The big toe on his right foot was violently pulled downward by the spent muscles. He cried out in pain and dropped back to the rope he was on. His left foot missed, and he landed with the cross rope supporting his butt. Quickly pulling his right foot up, he massaged it with his left hand until the cramp released. He leaned his forehead against the center cable and cried. Tears mixed with sweat ran in streaks down his dirty face.

Carefully, Danny drew himself upright again. He teetered on the rope as he clung to the center cable with a shaft of light shining down through the roof, illuminating his face. Just as the muscles in his foot were cramping, so was the fear in his heart. It knew him so well. It told him that he couldn't do it. It told him that he'd fall. It told him that he'd let his friend die.

Something cold passed across his neck. Placing his head across his right forearm, he stared down through the tangle of ropes at Josh sprawled on the floor below. *Josh is gonna die, and I can't help him. I can't do this.*

"Caw! Caw, caw!"

Danny glanced up, and the bird was there again. It was only about ten feet away, perched on the lip of the open roof. He could see its black eyes as it turned its head, first one way, then the other, looking at him. It hopped to the right, then to the left, flapping its wings. "Caw, caw."

Somehow, Danny felt a sense of urgency in the bird's calls. As he focused on it, the fear that had frozen him at the cusp of his escape slipped away. Something about that crow drew him upward. Its avian voice sliced across his self-doubt and told him to get up and get going.

"Caw, caw," it said again. Danny heard it as, "come on."

Determination reestablished itself in Danny's heart. He took a deep breath and leapt again. Without using his feet this time, he grabbed the cable and pulled. He pulled and pulled and pulled, one hand over the other, until suddenly his feet found a footing on the very top rope and he was able to see horizontally straight through the hole in that domed roof. He'd reached the top.

The sun was bright outside. The hills undulated, lifting the forest and lowering it. The colors of autumn were shining brightly far into the distance. The cut of a road wound through the trees. Somewhere in the distance, a train whistled. It was spectacular, but he had to get to the side lip of the silo, and he still needed to find a way down.

With a great flutter, the large crow jumped into the air and soared into the sky. Danny wished the crow had a line tethered to him so it could pull him to freedom. Still, if he were going to get out of this, it was going to be because he did what was demanded of him. He had to complete the mission.

Looking down, Danny examined the rope. It was tied off just to the left of the angled hole in the roof. Looking up, he saw a frame of steel that supported the cable apparatus. One of the supports ran on a straight line from the center of the dome down to just above the tethered rope.

Slowly and carefully, he held onto the steel support and edged his way across the rope toward the lip of the silo. He needed to reach the spot where the bird had been perched. The rope swayed back and forth, so he was constantly readjusting his balance. Soon, his head cleared the roofline where it curved downward, and his view widened. But it became harder to move across as the distance between the support and the rope narrowed. It was forcing his exhausted body into a tighter and tighter crouch, even as he fought against his unstable footing.

Eventually, he couldn't move any further without losing his toeholds on the rope. It was now or never. He had to go for it. Danny let go of the support, used his feet to propel himself, and surged to the top of the silo wall. His head and torso cleared the edge, and he caught the rim of the concrete cylinder with his lower abdomen. On the inside, his feet were dangling free. On the outside, his head and chest were in the cold morning air. He was holding himself in place with his elbows.

A breeze carried the icy morning air. It stung his nose and blew his dirty, oily red hair around on his head. He could see the roof of an old farmhouse. The front porch had collapsed and there were holes in the green shingles. Looking to his left, Danny could see glimpses of a road, but it was a good hundred yards away behind a barrier of trees.

"Help," Danny screamed. "Help us."

No one responded. No one was around. Down below, a bunny rabbit nibbled the leftovers of the previous summer's growth. Off to the right, two deer ambled across an open meadow. A barn sat across the yard. There were no people nearby at all. He was alone. If he was going to get Josh any help, he was going to have to find a way down.

Danny pulled himself further up by his elbows and upper arms.

His muscles continued to scream at him. Then he swung his right leg up and caught the rim with his big toe. There was a ridge of steel protruding from the top of the silo, and it was digging into his gut. He used his foot to pull his torso further up onto the rim. A rusty screw grabbed his leg through his pajama pants and gouged into his skin. Ignoring the new pain, he pulled himself upward until he sat straddling the silo wall—one leg out and one leg in. The effort left him out of breath.

"Josh, I'm at the top," he called down to his friend. He could see him sprawled out on the floor below like a large insect.

Josh flailed his right arm around and moved his head from side to side.

"You hang in there. I'll find a way down and get you some help."

Danny leaned over and scanned the side of the silo for a ladder or steel rungs. Support hoops hugged the outside every few feet, but they were mounted too tightly to be much help. Turning back to look the other way, he spotted a ladder mounted on the side. His eyes followed it to within ten feet of the top—that was where it stopped. The top ten feet had rusted loose and hung back from the silo at about a thirty-degree angle. Nothing remained attached to the silo, only rust stains from the mounting screws.

Danny's heart sank and he began to cry. He looked at the blisters on his hands. He looked at the stripes on his belly where the cable had cut into his flesh. Blood was pooling into the cloth on his upper right thigh from where the screw had gouged him. His muscles in his upper back and arms were like jelly. The toes of his foot were threatening to cramp up again. Without the exertion to keep his blood pumping, the sweat from the climb began to chill him in the cold air. All of that and he was stuck, perched on top of the silo wall with no way down. Tears flowed onto his soiled cheeks as he sobbed under a bright, sunny sky.

"Help," he screamed again. "Oh, God, please help us. Someone, please help us."

"Caw. Caw, caw."

Looking up and to his left, he spied the crow again. It was perched at the top of the silo dome. It turned its head back and forth, peering at Danny with its dark eyes. It jumped and ruffled its wings but settled back to the perch.

"Have you got a way for me to get down?" Danny asked the dark black bird.

"Caw," it replied as if to say, "of course."

"Well, what do you suggest?" Danny asked. *I must be going crazy. I'm talking to a bird.*

The bird jumped from the perch and flew off from the opposite side of the silo but then turned completely around and came straight back. As Danny watched, it did it three more times.

"You want me to come around on that side?" Danny asked.

"Caw. Caw, caw."

The dark hole in the roof angled like a triangle into the very top of the dome. Danny couldn't see the other side from where he was sitting. He stretched upward and tried to see more, but all that fell within his vision were the sky and some of the encroaching forest.

It was when he moved that he realized his muscles had begun to cool off. Not only was he getting physically cold again, but his hands were stiffening up, and his muscles were very sore. If he didn't get moving soon, he wouldn't be able to move. Again, he opened and closed his fingers several times and swung his arms around.

Danny scooted his way over to where the open hole met what was left of the domed roof. Ridges ran from the concrete rim to the pinnacle, and the angled sheets were fastened to them with screws. Dark rust spots bubbled through what used to be a pleasant coat of blue paint. He studied the structure, trying to figure out the best, safest way to work his way around. There was no going over the top. If he tried that and lost his footing, he would slide back down, and his momentum would fling him over the side. He had to go around.

The section he came through was obviously missing, perhaps blown off in a storm, but the next section seemed secure. Carefully, he pulled himself out of the opening, and using his cold right foot, he pushed his body up until he was prostrate, belly to steel on the roof. The metal had been heated in the morning sun and felt warm against his skin. Danny was grateful for that small comfort. Then, he edged his way around, feeling with his toes for each of the next foot placements.

He crossed three sections with no issue. When he reached the fourth, it flexed under his weight. Some of the mounting screws had rusted and disintegrated.

"Caw, caw, caw," the crow encouraged him.

Danny examined the section. He looked at every screw and pushed on the metal with his right hand. It was loose, but not in imminent danger of falling free. *What choice do I have?* He had to keep going, so he eased his way across. He checked with his toes, moved his feet, slid along the side, and used his spread hands for balance. Soon, he passed over the loose section, then across two more.

Finally, he reached the far side of the silo. The problem was that he was belly down. Danny couldn't see anything below without somehow turning over. Moving to the right side of that roof section, he then slid his left leg over until it was straight, in line with his body. Carefully, he pressed his body down against the steel and lifted his right leg and right arm. Trying to keep himself tight against the surface, he rolled.

After successfully flipping himself over, he took a deep breath and gazed up into the sky. He was now lying on his back, staring at nothing but a blue ocean of air. As he watched, the crow circled underneath a single, drifting pillow of a cloud.

"Okay," Danny said to the crow. "Why did you want me to come over here?" As he spoke, he slowly lifted his torso so that he could look down. "Really? That's your idea of how to get down?" Below was a very large blue spruce. The tree had probably once been planted about ten feet from the side of the silo, but now, decades later, it had grown to almost two-thirds the height of the silo and had wrapped itself partially around the curved concrete wall.

The crow again landed at the top of the dome. "Caw, caw," it said. Danny took that to mean "Go, go."

This is a completely insane idea, but, how else am I going to get down?

He studied the tree. The top point was ten feet out and about fifteen feet down. *Maybe I can jump down and grab around the main trunk. Then, I can just climb on down.* To his adolescent mind, it seemed like a reasonable idea, but Danny hated climbing trees. Mostly because he hated heights. Now, that fear was a moot point. He had to get down, and that looked like the only viable way. No more thinking about it. That Nike phrase jumped into his head. *Just do it*! He wasn't sure where it came from—maybe his dad used to say it. Regardless, he pushed further off the roof until he was balanced on the steel ring around the top of the concrete wall. The hard, cold, thin steel ridge felt like a knife on the soles of his socked feet. With one last deep breath, he leaped out and downward, aiming for the section of the trunk about five feet down from the top of the tree.

It wasn't like he'd ever done the maneuver before, so he misjudged the distance. He didn't have enough push-off to get his body across the gap to the trunk. Instead, he fell like a large rock into the branches. They gave under his weight, compressing like a spring and then propelling him backward toward the silo. He slammed hard against the concrete wall, banging his head and smacking his ribs. Something cracked. Crying out in pain, he continued to fall through the limbs, bouncing again and again off the curved, hard wall. Branches slapped him in the face and whipped at his legs. His left arm got tangled up between two limbs, causing his elbow to wrench out of socket. Finally, he dropped through the bottom of the tree and landed with a muffled thud on the bed of needles that had built up underneath.

Danny cried. Prone on his back, it hurt to breathe. Tears streaked his face. Blood seeped from his hands, his leg, his head, and his belly. His whole torso was scraped and scratched.

He tried to move, but pain shot through his side. Yet, he had to get up. He just had to. He had to get Josh help. For that matter, he needed help himself. He couldn't simply lie there. So, carefully, inch by inch, small move by small move, he pulled himself out from under the massive old spruce. It was perhaps the hardest thing he had ever done, but he forced himself to stand. He felt woozy. His vision was spinning.

With his sore feet on the ground, he got his bearings and stumbled across the weed-infested, overgrown lawn of the broken-down farmhouse, making his way to the road. Danny recognized it immediately. Robbins Creek Road. His road. The entrance to Basketball Court was only about a mile away. It might as well have been twenty miles, considering how he felt, but regardless, he hobbled toward home.

Danny spotted an approaching car. He waved his right arm for attention, but the action made his head spin. Closing his eyes, he felt the world swirling around him, but he didn't feel the pavement against his right cheek as his face smacked the road.

Nine

Sheriff Tom Bennett from Muncie, Indiana got an early start. His sleep had been wracked by disturbing dreams with one clear and razor-sharp point: *Get Kenny Burton out of your jail.* The interesting thing was that Tom Bennett had never before heard of Kenny Burton. Despite that fact, the man's name and the imperative demand to get him out of his jail wouldn't leave his mind. As a result, it was 5:30 a.m., and he was walking into the back entrance of the Delaware County Jail.

The sheriff spotted the deputy stationed at the desk. "Do we have a prisoner named Kenny Burton in this facility?"

The deputy looked up, surprise all over his face. He likely wasn't expecting his boss for another hour at least. "Uh, sounds familiar, Sheriff," he replied and carefully placed his coffee mug on a small heating plate next to a notepad. "Let me look." After a moment of clicking some keys on the desktop keyboard, he added, "Well, yes. He's on a twenty-four hour hold at the request of the sheriff down in Bowen County."

"Bowen County?" Tom questioned his subordinate. "Where on God's green earth is Bowen County?"

"I'm not sure, sir. I think it's somewhere down south. The county seat is some little town called Cutters Notch."

"Never heard of it. What cell is he in? As far as I'm concerned, his twenty-four hour hold just ended. Start processing him out. I'll retrieve him."

"He's in 22B, sir," the deputy replied. "I'll get started right away, sir."

The sheriff lumbered away. His rubber-soled uniform boots made soft echoes in the concrete and stone hallway. He didn't even stop in his office but instead proceeded directly to the first security barrier. This man, whoever he was, had caused him enough trouble.

***

Kenny opened his eyes. There was no window in his cell, but it felt like morning. He wasn't sure why. Perhaps, it was because the voice in his head seemed to have released its grip on his consciousness. Regardless, he sat up on the side of his bunk and looked around. There wasn't much to see, but seeing real things instead of the swirling dream images he'd experienced all night was a welcome relief.

He stood, used the commode, and then rinsed his hands and face in the tiny, stainless steel sink. After pacing the short length of his cell a couple of times, he stretched his large frame and sat back down. Placing his hands on his knees, he stretched his back, and glanced at the door.

The locking mechanism disengaged. The heavy door swung open, and in walked the sheriff. Kenny had never met the man, but recognized him from his election campaign billboards. They'd been placed strategically all over the county for months the fall prior to his previous arrest and subsequent imprisonment.

"Kenny Burton?"

"Yessir, Sheriff. That's me."

Kenny looked him over. The sheriff was wearing the typical tan and brown county uniform. His utility belt was laden with a holster, handcuffs, pepper spray, taser, and a few other things that Kenny couldn't identify. On the man's head sat a wide-brimmed sheriff's hat. He wasn't a small man, but Kenny knew himself to be bigger. He thought he could take him in a fight.

"Well, big boy, it's time to get you outta here," the sheriff announced. "Follow me."

A little over an hour later, Kenny walked out of the jail onto High Street. The sun was still early in the sky, shining in from low in the east. It was casting a weird reddish-yellow tone onto the fluffy clouds floating through the blue sky. So far, the day was going exactly the way his dreams had played out. A series of practice runs, really. As a result, he knew exactly what to do next. He began the walk home where he'd get into his car and drive to Cutters Notch. Today was the day. Today, he'd get that little wretch. Today, he'd watch the light go out in her eyes.

Kenny tried to smile. He tried to relish in the anticipation. He tried to lust over the impending violence, but without the voice in his head, he couldn't find that sweet spot. Another tiny voice kept saying, *"but..."* He didn't want to listen to that nagging voice. Maybe he couldn't control the louder, demanding voice that had dominated his psyche of late, but he could control this little, irritating one, so he shoved it back down and held it there until it shut up. Yet, the joy still wouldn't come, so he settled for determination.

As he walked along without the hateful voice controlling him, Kenny remembered that he had not always felt the way he currently felt. Once, he and Megan and Hope had been a nice, young family.

When the doubts first started intruding, he ignored them. When the hateful thoughts began to appear, he drove them away. Around the same time, he began to drink more, and it seemed that the more he drank, the more those thoughts intruded. And one day, he chose to listen. Kenny opened that door and welcomed the evil voice inside.

As he trudged along Hoyt Avenue, he muttered, "I'm gonna get Hope. I'm gonna take her to that place I picked out, and I'm gonna take my time squeezing the life outta her. Then I'm gonna go back and get her momma." There was no joy in the words he spoke to himself—only hatred. Kenny hated Megan because he'd bought into the evil thought that she'd cheated. He hated both Megan and Hope because he was convinced that together, they were the root of his deconstructed life.

Staring at the sidewalk, he repeated those words, drilling them into his brain, steeling his will, silencing any remnant of conscience that remained inside his heart. "I'm gonna get Hope," he repeated. "I'm gonna get Megan." Slowly, all other factors in his life melted away and the only thing left was revenge.

"but..."

"Shut up," he shouted at his own conscience.

***

Hope Spencer's dreamless sleep ended before dawn. She opened her eyes and immediately realized that she was in bed next to her mother instead of sitting in front of her mirror. Anxiety gripped her. She needed to know if they'd found her friends. Anger slipped in, too. She should have been able to stay awake. Carefully, she slid out from under the covers and made her way around the bed. The digital clock on her mother's nightstand read 5:55 a.m. It would be dark for a while yet.

Her mother's bedroom door was cracked open, so she silently inched it further, slipping into the hallway, then into her own bedroom. Moving quickly now, she darted to the mirror. As she approached it, a small green hand with four fingers and two thumbs emerged followed by Gavin's face.

"Dear Hope, please come with me," the elf said as he reached out his hand.

Hope reached out in response, but then hesitated. She quickly scanned the floor and found her slippers among the myriad of discarded clothes. Keeping her room organized was not her forte. She needed something on her feet. Slipping into the felt-lined house shoes, she climbed onto the vanity, took Gavin's hand, and ducked into the Arboreal Realm.

On that side of the dimensional portal, as usual, the world was aglow with a myriad of colors. The elves had their green auras. Sacqueal stood back near a tree and emitted a light orange glow. Tomo stood next to the queen with an aura of white mixed with blue. Her own aura lit up the ground around her feet.

The queen stepped forward and greeted her. Taking Hope's face into her hands, she pulled her down and placed her forehead against the girl's. "Nozomi, I so wish that I had good news for you. We have searched every shimmer for miles in every direction. There is no sign of your friends. I am so sorry." The others encircled them with their heads bowed.

Hope dropped to her knees and began to weep, covering her face with her hands. After a moment, she pulled her head back and screamed. "Dad! What have you done?"

Hesed knelt with the girl, pulling her to her into a hug. "There, there, dear girl. Do not give up. They may yet be found. We could not see everything, only what can be seen from one of your lighted rooms. Perhaps they were in the dark all night long."

The sobs subsided, and Hope regained some composure. Her skin was red and blotchy, and her face was wet. "Why would my father do this? Why does he hate me so much?"

The queen again took Hope's face into her hands. "Are you

sure that your father is responsible?"

"He tried to kill me before and he tried to kill my mother. He was in jail, but I guess he got out. He was in our town the night they disappeared. It has to be him."

"Perhaps you are right," Hesed replied. "In my many years of experience, when men do evil things, it is because their minds have been corrupted. Often the goodness that was their essence has been suppressed by darkness and cannot find its way back. Was your father always dangerous and full of hate?"

Hope paused for a moment and considered that question. "No," she replied, "not always. When I was little, he was just like any other dad. We weren't perfect, but we were happy."

"What happened to change everything? Was there some trauma? Did something happen to him?"

Again, Hope paused. "I can't think of anything. It happened sort of fast. First, he started drinking a little, but even then, we were mostly happy. Then, all the sudden, it was like he was a different person. He was scary. You could see it in his eyes."

***

Hope's mention of the eyes raised the small hairs on the back of Hesed's neck. "What do you mean when you say that you could see it in his eyes?"

"They were different," Hope explained. "They seemed darker, less color. He didn't blink as much, either. It was like they started oozing hate."

"Oh my," the Queen said with a hint of sadness mixed with fear, she dropped her gaze. "I believe that your father is suffering a fate worse than merely having a corrupted mind. There is only one answer for the ills that he is experiencing." The queen paused and examined the sad face of her new, young friend. She had rarely seen a human aura of such magnitude, but the girl's anguish was evident through the bright glare. Hesed's words had sparked something inside the girl, though. She could see it in her eyes. What it was, she could not say.

"There's an answer?" Hope asked. "There's a way to help him?" She stopped crying. Instead, she raised up and stared eagerly at the elf queen. Her aura had brightened even more, to the point that the others were shading their eyes.

Ah, there it is. She still loves him. "Yes, my dear, the only answer for your father is to—"

"Your mother stirs," Gronek interjected. "She has awoken."

The queen stood, pulling Hope to her feet. "I will explain tonight," she quickly said. "Come back through the shimmer when darkness falls again. Then I will help you to see your best course. Okay?"

***

Hope embraced the queen, then turned back to the shimmer. Smakal helped her up and she slipped back into her bedroom. Her emotions were ablaze. She worried desperately for her friends. She needed them. They had given her a new life, a life after the pain of what had happened. Josh had become more than a friend. Hope had to have them back. She was angry at her father, but at the same time, she yearned for the dad he had once been. She missed him terribly.

Yet, through the fear and the anger, another emotion found footing in her heart—an emotion she thought was long gone. Despite all the evidence and her experiences, she still had a love for her father. If there was an answer for whatever had made him turn so dark, she wanted it. She needed it. *No, he needs it.*

Her mother was in the kitchen making coffee. In the here and now, Hope needed her mother. She needed to hold her and to be held. She needed to smell the lotion on her neck and the fragrance of her shampoo. Again, she began to cry.

She found her mother at the sink when she entered the kitchen. "Mom," she sobbed. "Can you hold me?"

***

Queen Hesed watched as the girl she had dubbed Nozomi passed through the shimmer, returning to her own world. After the girl passed out of sight, the queen's entourage moved around to watch Hope enter the human kitchen and embrace her mother.

"Mother, as when you dubbed my brothers and I 'Allwind of the Trees'," Smakal stated, "I know that you will often give individuals new names that are special to you. Still, the name 'Nozomi' is odd to my ears."

"My son," she replied, "I explained the name earlier. Did you not hear me? Nozomi is a human term with several meanings, but the meaning that I find precious is 'my beautiful hope.' Would you not agree with that meaning? After all, the aura of her life dazzles the eyes."

"Oh, yes," the younger elf responded. His brothers tugged their ears.

"What of her father?" Gavin asked. "I saw the reaction in your face. What do you suspect?"

"Many human men are abusive," Hesed stated. "It has been an affliction of theirs for as long as they have walked the earth. Many of them will abuse their families. In nearly all those cases, they are choosing to act upon their own selfishness. They have corrupted themselves and have no inhibitions toward hurting others, even their own offspring."

"We just saw this with the evil couple who took Nozomi," Gronek blurted.

"Yes, son, Correct. That couple corrupted their own minds and allowed themselves to be influenced to do violent things. Despite the influences, they chose to do those things. They could have chosen to do good, but they chose to do evil. But, in rare occurrences, a human mind can be fully co-opted by the evil influence. When that happens, the human's only choice was in allowing the influence to take over by opening the door. What happens after that is no longer a thing that they have the power within themselves to change. You can see the presence in their eyes."

The three brothers looked at one another. Gavin shivered.

"What do we do?" Smakal asked.

"Tomo, please come to me," Hesed said, leaving her son's question hanging. "I have a request of you."

The tall Native American human promptly approached, the colorful, decorative stones he wore at his neck and wrists tinkling as he moved. "How may I assist the queen?" he asked.

"My friend," she said, "You are anxious to return to your family and to your duties as guardian of the Gate to Abandon, but it will soon be dawn and we will be unable to see through the shimmers again until nightfall. You are the only one among us who can pass across the dimensional barrier and then return during the hours of the sun. Look to the east. The sky is beginning to glow as I speak. I would ask that you pass through to the human realm and observe the events on that side. Please do this and report back as each hour passes. Will you do this for me?"

Tomo looked concerned. He was much taller than the Elfin queen, so he had taken a knee. Hesed gazed into his eyes. His brow pinched, and two furrows formed above his nose and between his eyes. "Queen Hesed, I am at your service," he said. "I will do as you ask. But please understand that I must return to my post no later than the setting of this day's sun. My own son is guarding the gate, and there have been rumors of the return of your Bayal. I fear he may have interest in what is contained beneath the stone cap."

The queen extended her small, six-fingered hands with their greenish aura and cupped the large man's face. His long dark hair fell to each side even as his aura glowed a bluish white in contrast. "My friend," she said, "your concern is justified. It seems that Bayal has returned. The gate is nearby. I will ask my sons to join yours so that they may all keep watch from this realm. They will ensure that no fallen elf approaches the gate while you are assisting me."

Tomo raised his large right hand and returned the affectionate caress by placing it against the queen's left cheek. "As I said, I am at your service. I will do what I do best. I will keep watch on your Nozomi and the activities in search of her friends." Upon making that commitment, he stood up again. He looked down upon her face even as she gazed upward toward his own. "I will report each hour." Then he turned and raced off into the forest, quickly disappearing.

"Mother, how does our friend pass into the human realm during the daylight hours?" Gavin asked.

"That is a closely guarded secret. He has not even shared that information with me."

"What is hidden beneath the great stone that would interest Bayal?" Gronek asked. "Would he really come here?"

"The story of the stone will need to be told at another time," Hesed answered her son with a kind tone. "Right now, we need to respect his concerns. I would like you and your brothers to proceed immediately to the ancient Gate to Abandon and be on guard for any approach by the fallen of our kind or any other creature that should not be there."

"Of course," the three elves stated in unison. Gavin added, "Will you advise us of any news from Tomo?"

"Yes. I will send Sacqueal if important news arrives." The

sasquatch grunted at the mention of his name. He was standing beneath a walnut tree, peeling the coarse green husk off the shell inside.

Gavin, Gronek, and Smakal each nodded to their mother before turning together toward the forest. Soon, they, like Tomo, quickly disappeared into the underbrush.

Queen Agahpey Hesed watched as they left her in the clearing between the forest and the rectangular hole in the ground that represented Nozomi's home. She loved her sons. Her heart yearned for them in the long periods of time when their respective duties kept them apart. Even though this situation was heart-wrenching, she was grateful they were all together once again. "I have good sons," she said aloud.

Sacqueal grunted again even as he bit down on the hard shell of another fresh walnut, trying to reach the rich meat inside.

Glancing over to the shimmer portal leading to Nozomi's kitchen, Hesed watched it fade away as the sun broke brightly across the top of the forest canopy.

***

Patrick opened his eyes to see daylight filtering through the cracks in the shack's eastern wall. He was surprised because lately they had been retrieving him before the dawn. He sat up on the side of his cot and rubbed his face with his hands. It had been a long night. Between the dreams and his dad's periodic coughing fits, he still felt very tired.

Glancing around, he again took stock of his cell. His shed inside a chain-link cage had no commode for bodily needs or stainless-steel sink for washing up. His only facilities consisted of a PVC tube that extended through the wall, and a bucket. A roll of toilet paper rested on a small, wooden shelf, tacked in between the wooden uprights in the frame. The white paper went well with the opaque plastic sheets someone had tacked up on the walls the day before. A box of tissues rested on the dirt floor beside his father's cot. Used ones were scattered around the sick man.

Russell was currently resting quietly. Trick was grateful. He had been up several times overnight as his father choked and wheezed and coughed up a lung.

"I've got to get him some help," Trick whispered to himself.

"He'll never survive a winter living in this shack." *He may not survive to see winter.*

As he considered his father's desperate condition, he recalled the dream that had played on a loop in his head overnight. He had been through it over and over again, even as limited as his sleep had been. Only one guard retrieved him. The sky was a weird color. Trick walked along the path beside his captor. He made his move at the low tree limb. It was almost like practicing a plan.

The chains rattled at the gate. Then, the lock on the shed door was released. The door opened and only one man entered. Trick looked past him to the sky. It was a weird color. Like his dream but real this time.

"How's the old man this morning?" Robert asked.

"He had a rough night," Patrick replied. "He can't stay out here like this. He needs a doctor."

"Can't help you there," Robert said, "but, see if you can get him to take another one of these pills." He held out a small baggy with one capsule inside. "I let you sleep in a little today, and I'm going to give you a few minutes to make sure he's set up before we go."

Trick stood up slowly. Reaching, he took the medicine from Robert's hand. *Was last night's dream some sort of premonition?*

"Here's some water, too," Robert added and pulled a small, plastic bottle from one of the pockets of his cargo pants. "One of us will bring him some soup in a couple of hours."

Patrick took the water from the man's outstretched hand and looked him over. Bags hung under his eyes. His posture seemed a bit slouched. Robert was speaking slowly, and his tone was not as belligerent. *He's really tired this morning.* The pendant with the red button hung loosely on the outside of his shirt. It was usually tucked inside. Over, and over again, Trick had been warned about the pendant. If he or his father made any trouble, Robert would push that button and his mother and sister would pay the price.

"Why are you staring at me?" Robert demanded. "Take care of your dad, and let's get going." Then, he turned and stepped back outside.

Trick noticed Robert's weapon was stuffed into his left hip pocket instead of in a holster on his waist. *He doesn't have his knife.* After Robert exited the shack, Patrick sat down beside his father. Retrieving the pill, he tilted his dad's head up and slipped the pill inside his mouth. Russell took a couple of gulps and then breathed heavily. "Ah," he groaned. "Son, I love you," he said and then fell back and closed his eyes.

Trick turned, sat with his back to his dad, and stared out the door. Robert was leaning heavily against one of the gate posts. His head was tilted downward. Then, the boy peered down at his own arms. The muscles in his forearms had grown even as his weight had dropped. They bulged out, forming deep ridges in his tight skin. *I have to do it. I have to take the chance. Today.* He made his decision.

Moments later, he stepped outside into the morning sun. Looking up through the treetops, he could see the sky was a weird yellowish red with the clouds swirling around.

Robert stood just outside the gate—alone. "Come on," he said and motioned toward the trail that led to the mine. Patrick joined him, staying to his right, keeping Robert positioned so the forest would be on the man's left.

The night crew was returning to their shacks. They didn't acknowledge him. Rather, they each slumped into their cages and crawled inside their respective shack. One shack had been empty, but now a man's voice came from inside. He sounded groggy. "Hey, where am I?" he said. "Help me. Let me out."

The low-hanging tree branch was just ahead. Robert slowed to drop behind his captive, but Trick slowed equally, keeping the man beside him. A moment later, they reached the large limb. It was smooth across the surface where men's hands had rubbed it over the years. From the corner of his left eye, Trick saw Robert ducking under.

Lightning quick, Trick pulled his left arm back and brought it up behind Robert's head. Reaching, using the man's own momentum, he wrapped his fingers around the back of Robert's head, driving his face downward. Simultaneously, Trick brought his left knee upward, and connected hard into Robert's face.

Blood gushed from the man's mouth and nose. He staggered. Trick drove his left elbow down with as much force as he could gather into the back of the Robert's neck. The injured captor fell like a lump into the dirt of the trail. The pendant, still wrapped around Robert's neck, rested in the dirt, blood pooling around it.

Trick jerked the pendant free and threw it deep into the forest underbrush. Looking down at the bleeding man, he kicked him one more time in the face. Then, ignoring the voices of the men calling out from the cages, he pulled Robert's gun from the man's back pocket and raced up the trail. He was pretty sure it led to the motel.

***

Rick Anders awoke to his alarm at 5 a.m. He sat up and rubbed his eyes. The night felt short, but after initially struggling with conflicting dreams, he'd slept well. Despite it all, his heart felt hopeful. It wasn't so much a hopefulness at finding the missing kids so much as it was hopefulness that his life was taking a new direction. Eventually though, the weight of Danny's and Josh's disappearance overwhelmed any residual sense of hope left over from his night visions. This day could go either way—it could lead to tremendous sorrow or tremendous joy.

He made some coffee and cooked himself some eggs, which he enjoyed while checking his email, watching the TV news, and looking at yesterday's *Indianapolis Star*. Finally, he showered and shaved. Then he dressed quickly, pulling the trousers off their hook and yesterday's uniform shirt off its hanger, re-hanging them on his own body. After collecting the balance of his gear, he stepped outside to climb into his dew-covered cruiser.

Rick stopped on the sidewalk. It was still mostly dark with just a hint of light in the east, casting the horizon in a yellowish red. The cul-de-sac was quiet, but the birds were singing in the surrounding forest. The only light came from the Maggie's kitchen window. "Boys," he said softly, "where are you?" He wished he could simply brew another pot of coffee and sit for a while on his deck, enjoying the stillness of the morning against the forest backdrop. That was not to be. He had to find the boys today. The longer they were missing, the more likely they'd never be found.

Thirty minutes later, after doing a slow drive around town, he walked into his new office. The desk deputy handed him some messages, then Rick sat down in what used to be J.B. Dunlap's chair. It was soft but worn. It leaned slightly to the left and creaked when it moved. It was well after 8 a.m. He enjoyed a donut from the General, courtesy of the desk sergeant, and another cup of coffee from the breakroom. The peanut and caramel pastry rested on a napkin. The coffee sat in his left hand as he flicked through the messages with his right. There was nothing particularly helpful or critical.

Morning light filtered through his office window, so he leaned back to glance outside. There was one message left in his hand. Rose from the General had called. He chuckled at the note. Apparently, a large black bird had been stealing things right out of the hands of customers as they exited the store.

Reclining in the chair that was now his, at least for a while, his eyes trailed over the room. Rick had only had use of the office for about a week, most of that time was spent in the field. After scanning the empty bookshelves, his gaze paused on the bulletin board that hung between the two office windows.

Much of it was covered in official information. One whole side was full of missing-persons reports. Another section was bare. That area had been where J.B. had tacked up personal stuff—pictures, phone numbers, and mementos. They'd been cleared off before Rick stepped into the sheriff's role.

J.B. Dunlap represented another example of sadness in Rick's life. In the few hours leading up to the final showdown at the quarry, he felt a kinship to J.B. He'd begun to really like the man. Then, in a flash, it was all over.

Rick's eyes fell again on the missing-persons reports. There were lots of young people—teenagers mostly. Some were younger and some were older, but most were runaways in their teen years. *Will Josh and Danny have their own official posters tacked on various sheriffs' office boards across the state?* He figured the results of this coming day would likely answer that question.

Finally, his eyes came to rest on a poster that represented an entire missing family—a mother, father, and two teens. He read the details. The family came from Kentucky. They had been on vacation the previous summer, having taken a road trip to Wisconsin. Then they vanished on their drive home. His attention was drawn to the teenage girl. She looked familiar, but he couldn't place her. *I'm going to need to dig into this one a little.*

Deciding to jot himself a reminder, he pulled his notepad from the center drawer. When he reached to his shirt pocket to retrieve his pen, he felt a piece of paper stuffed inside. He pulled it out. When he unfolded the note and looked at the writing, he suddenly knew why the girl in the poster looked familiar. She looked very much like that young girl who worked in the office of the Notch Inn. The hair stood up on the back of his neck as he read the license plate number that she'd given him: **3M 9J3H**

Rick stood, left his office, and darted into the men's room. He stood in front of the mirror, holding up the girl's handwritten note. Seen in the reflection of the mirror, it didn't take much imagination for the combination of letters and numbers to be clearly construed as two words: HELP ME.

Is this her asking for my help or is this a coincidence? Why would she be so afraid that she couldn't just ask me outright?

He wasn't sure if the letters and numbers were really a covert message or not. Still, the similarity between the girl's appearance and the picture on his bulletin board combined with the possibility of what could be a not-so-subtle cry for help demanded more investigation. If the girl was really that afraid, he was going to have to move cautiously.

Rick was considering the various angles of the situation when he walked back to his office. Then everything was driven from the forefront of his mind. His radio crackled and pulled his mind away from the Bray family.

"*Sheriff? Come back,*" the voice blurted. "*This is Gator.*"

"Deputy Randal," Rick replied. "This is Sheriff Anders. What's your situation?" Rick made a mental note to have a discussion with Deputy Randal about radio etiquette. He'd been told that the man didn't like his given name and had taken to being called Gator. Rick didn't care about that, but he expected his deputies to be more formal when using official channels.

"*Sheriff, I've got one of your boys. I'm out on Robbins Creek Road, south of Basketball Court. I found him walking down the road. You might want to get out here.*"

Ten

Rick was on the scene in minutes. Sirens sounded in the distance. The paramedic crew from the Cutters Notch Volunteer Fire Department and some of his other deputies were on their way. The morning sun was filtering through the overhanging trees, and a cool breeze blew fallen leaves across the road. He stood beside Deputy Randal's SUV. Danny sat in the passenger seat with blood and dirt covering his body. Randal had him holding a cold pack from his first aid kit against his face.

"Sheriff," Gator said, "I was cruising south past his neighborhood when I saw him in the distance. He waved at me and then fell over on the road. I got him up in my unit, gave him some water, and placed that cold pack on him. He's been mostly incoherent."

"Has he given you any idea of where he's been? Where he came from?"

"Just some mumbling about a silo. Oh, and about a big black crow that he says helped him get out. I don't know what to make of that. Probably hallucinations, I'd guess."

As the paramedic crew pulled their truck around Randal's Ford, Rick knelt beside the boy. "Gator, get me a moist cloth," he ordered before turning his attention to his young neighbor. "Danny, where've you been? Do you know where Josh is?"

Danny stared into the distance, his eyes unfocused. Tears streaked his dirty, bloodied, and bruised cheeks.

"Danny, please think. Do you know where we can find Josh?"

Upon the second mention of Josh's name, Danny came around. They locked eyes. It was as if he had suddenly awakened from a bad dream.

"Rick," he yelled. "You've gotta help him. He's hurt bad."

Danny tried to stand, but the pain drove him back down in the seat. "Aah!" he cried as he grabbed the ribs on his left side.

"Where is he, Danny?" Anders urgently asked. "Tell me where he is, and we'll go help him."

"He's still locked in the silo. He fell and he's bad hurt. His leg's trapped and he slammed his head, too."

"What silo?" asked Gator from over Anders' shoulder. "Where?"

The wounded boy pointed back toward the way from which he had stumbled. "Just over there. Past those trees and through the weeds. You can't hardly see it through all the bushes and stuff."

"The old Havener place?" Gator asked. "Right there?"

"Yeah." He winced again.

"Wait," Rick said. "Gator, what'd you call the place?"

"That's the old Havener farm. It's been vacant for probably fifteen, maybe twenty years."

Rick stood straight up, grabbing his radio mic. Gator backed off quickly to get out of the big man's way. "Unit three, what's your twenty?" the sheriff barked into the microphone.

"What is it, Sheriff?" Deputy Randal asked. "What's going on?"

"Gator, get Danny transferred to the ambulance, and then show me where that silo is."

Unit three answered Rick's call. *Sheriff, I'm on 257 near the General and about to turn onto Robbins Creek Road.*

"Three," Rick responded, "turn around and head to the Notch Inn. Find a guest by the name of Al Havener. Place him in cuffs and detain him."

Realization appeared in Deputy Randal's eyes. Moving quickly, he assisted the paramedics moving Danny to their rig. The medics placed a neck collar on the boy as they checked his pulse and bandaged his wounds. After one of the crew brought a gurney over, Gator helped them lift the boy onto the rolling stretcher before returning to the sheriff's side.

Rick felt pulled in three directions. He needed to make sure that Al Havener was found and detained. He needed to advise Danny's parents that their boy had been found. But priority one had to be to locate and rescue Josh. "Lead the way, Randal," he ordered and jumped into his car. "Show me that silo."

Gator hopped in his county vehicle and pulled away. Rick dropped the transmission into drive. As he checked his driver's side mirror, the reflection revealed a figure on foot, running at full speed toward the collection of emergency vehicles. Hope. She'd heard the sirens and could not be contained. When he turned his gaze back toward the front, he saw his deputy pull into a driveway about a quarter mile up the road. *She'll catch up.* He hit the gas and surged forward toward the abandoned farm.

***

Hope and Maggie were sitting at their kitchen table. The sun shone through the sheer curtains over the sink and formed bright spots on the light pine surface. Breakfast was over and Maggie had placed a doctored-up cup of coffee in front of her thirteen-year-old daughter. Hope didn't get coffee often, but Maggie thought she might need it today. Maggie took her own coffee black, but Hope needed a significant amount of sugar and cream in her cup.

"Mom," Hope started, "I just don't know what—" She couldn't continue. Tears formed in the corners of her eyes. One leaked down her left cheek, moistening the collection of light freckles.

"It's okay, honey. Let it out."

Hope swiped the tear with her left hand and took a sip from her cup before she could say anything more. Then, "I miss my daddy."

Maggie took in a big breath. She moved to kneel beside her daughter, placing her arm around her shoulders. Hope responded by turning and falling into her arms.

"I know he's bad. He's hurt us and he's probably hurt my friends, but I still love him. I can't help it. I just can't. What's wrong with me?"

"Oh, honey." Maggie squeezed her. "There's nothing wrong with you, nothing at all." Maggie wished she could come up with more words, but she couldn't find them. The truth was that any residual affection she may have felt for Kenny Burton had evaporated like distilled water sizzling on the surface of a hot iron. The man had used her, abused her, and injured her. He'd killed Hope's dog and nearly killed Hope herself. How her daughter could still feel anything for the man was beyond her comprehension. Still, she had to find a way to help her girl through this time. "He's your daddy," she said and stroked Hope's strawberry-blond hair. "It's natural for you to care about him."

The sound of a siren slipped in through the kitchen window. It was a rare sound in Cutters Notch, especially near their little neighborhood. Both mother and daughter perked up. Maggie hurried to the front of the house with Hope on her heels. Looking out the window, she didn't see any emergency vehicles, and the siren had ended. Turning back to her daughter, Maggie shrugged.

"Do you think they've found something?" Hope asked. "Could they have found Josh and Danny?" Excitement pierced her eyes. She was nearly jumping up and down as she darted from window to window to see through the trees.

"If they have, Rick'll call us. He'll let us know as soon as he knows."

Then, another siren blared in the distance. Maggie opened the front door and stood behind the storm door, listening. Hope crowded in next to her. The siren grew louder. Stepping out on their stoop, they could just make out a glimpse of Robbins Creek Road as it passed Basketball Court. The EMT rig blew by. Then, abruptly, the siren stopped.

"Sounds like they're right around the corner," Maggie said.

***

Hope dashed back to her room and threw on the first clothes she could find. Then she pulled on her basketball shoes, laced them as quickly as he could, and sped back to the front door.

Maggie was sitting on the sofa trying to get her own shoes on. "Hang on. I'll go with you."

Hope didn't slow down. Instead, she knocked the storm door open so hard that it banged against the tension of the restraining chain and lodged there. Leaping off the porch, she sprinted across the grass and out of the cul-de-sac. She passed across the basketball court and out the entrance to its namesake street and turned onto Robbins Creek Road in full stride.

In the distance, the Fire Department ambulance and two sheriffs' vehicles blocked the road about three quarters of a mile away—one was a Ford Explorer and the other was Rick's cruiser. Another shot of adrenaline drove her to run even faster. The back of the rescue rig was open. Danny was inside. She could see him in the shadows.

The sunlight formed bright spots across the pavement and red, orange, yellow, and brown leaves were scattered in her path. As she neared the scene, first the Explorer and then Rick's cruiser pulled away. When she reached the EMT vehicle, the Ford pulled into a driveway just up the road. Hope stopped at the open door of the ambulance and stared at Danny's pain-filled yet happy face.

"Hi, Hope," the boy mumbled. "I'm really glad to see you." He smiled weakly.

Hope smiled back, but she was shocked at what she saw. Her friend was sock-footed and wearing only a very dirty pair of pajama bottoms and a neck collar. His socks were soaked in blood. Danny was covered in dirt from head to toe and bleeding in several places. Bruises had formed on his sides, stretching all the way around to his belly. There was a large knot on his forehead.

"Where's Josh?" she asked in between pained breaths. "Is he okay?"

"I had to leave him to get help," Danny said with a wince. He squirmed on the gurney and moaned. "He's hurt pretty bad. He fell trying to get out."

"Where is he?"

Danny carefully lifted his left arm and motioned behind him with his thumb. "Back there," he said, grimacing. "He's locked in a silo at that abandoned farm."

Hope stood there a few seconds longer, staring at her injured friend. Her heart swelled both with love for Danny and concern for Josh. "I love you, Danny," she blurted, but before Danny could respond, she dashed around the rig and headed further up the road. She had seen the Explorer pull into a driveway. It hadn't come back, so that must be the place where Danny was pointing.

She recalled that old white farmhouse with its boarded-up windows sitting back in the trees behind overgrown grass and weeds. That must be where she'd find Josh, and Danny said he was badly hurt. Hope's speed surged. She had never run so fast in her life, but she had to get to him—now.

***

Josh had not truly slept all night. Rather, he'd gone in and out of consciousness. Sometimes he sank into what seemed like a deep lake of black, sticky muck that wouldn't let go of him despite his efforts to pull himself out. Other times, he stopped struggling out of exhaustion and let the muck have him. Near the surface of the blackness, he hurt. Josh hurt with a terrible intensity that he'd never previously experienced. When he let go and drifted deeper, the pain subsided, and his mind envisioned the people he loved.

He saw his mother pulling a tray of cookies from the oven, her bright blond hair dangling as she bent to withdraw the cookie sheet. He saw his dad in the garage tinkering with a birdhouse that he'd built from scrap wood. He saw Danny sitting cross-legged on his bed with a Superman comic lying open on his lap. Finally, he saw Hope. His heart sped up when she appeared to him. Just the thought of her made him feel warm. It was at those moments when he knew he couldn't stay in the muck. He had to fight back toward the surface—where the pain waited.

Nearing the surface, another face appeared to him. Not a true face, not exactly. It was more of the shape of a face, and *it* scared Josh. The face was a dark, undulating shape floating within the midst of the dark muck. Evil and hatred oozed from the glare of its red, penetrating eyes. It made him want to retreat, to drop back away from the surface. Josh sensed that if he completely let go, the evil face would leave him. The deeper he went, the safer he'd be.

As he dropped back, he heard voices. His mom was crying. His dad was calling to him from somewhere in the woods. Rick Anders' voice said he needed to come home. Once he heard Danny's voice, which seemed more real than the others, but somehow, fainter also.

"Hang in there," he said. "I'm gonna get help."

Each time he sank beyond the reach of the others, one specific voice called him back. Hope's voice.

"Hey Dork," she said. "You need to get back up here so I can kick your butt on the basketball court again." Each time she came to him, he resisted the sinking of his soul. He flailed in the muck and pulled himself back to the surface. He steeled his will against the dark face that awaited him, and he kicked and swam and pulled to free himself.

It was during one of those efforts to fight his way out that he screamed at the evil face in the dark muck. "Get away from me," he yelled. "You can't touch me. Get out of my way!"

Josh was shocked when the face answered him, *"Perhaps, I cannot touch you,"* it said, *"but still, I have put you here."* It laughed. The red eyes swelled. Josh sensed the weirdness, its evil joy. *"Your pain tastes wonderful, delicious, but soon you will sink too low and it will end."* It cackled. *"Not to worry, though. I still have the flavors of your friend, Danny, and the girl. Oh, yes, she will be the sweetest. The flavor of her pain will be delectable."*

When the wavering dark face spoke of Hope, Josh's anger flared. "You will not touch her. I won't let you. Get out of my way."

Strengthened by the power of his anger, Josh shoved past the pulsating form and swam with more intensity toward the surface. The muck began to thin. The darkness began to dissipate. He could almost see the surface. It was just past the end of his fingertips. With one last surge, he kicked his feet with all his might and broke the surface. He gasped for air and opened his eyes.

Then he saw her. Her blue eyes were staring into his own. Tears rolled down her cheeks. One dripped onto his lips. It tasted salty. Before he could say anything, she lowered her lips to his and kissed him. As the taste of her kiss lingered, something grabbed his leg, pulling him back down.

The pain surged. It smashed into his brain like a baseball bat to the head. He struggled to hold on to Hope, but he lost his grip. He kicked. He flailed. He tried through the sheer force of his will to keep his head above the surface of the sticky dark lake, but, yet again, he dropped downward into the muck.

***

The voice in his head came and went. It was during one of its periods of absence that Kenny Burton retrieved his car. It took him an hour to walk home from the jail. Along the way, he stopped into the grocery store where he worked just long enough to buy a bottle of water, tell them to kiss off, and punch his manager in the nose. Then, he rushed out before they called the cops. He didn't figure to be back anyway.

By the time he reached his Gran Torino, the sun was higher in the sky and the hazy bright blue of a Hoosier fall day was in full array, replacing the earlier swirling reddish yellow.

I should have punched that guy weeks ago. Kenny turned the key in the ignition. The voice didn't comment, but it would be pleased. It seemed to like it when people got hurt.

He turned on the radio. WERK was playing some stupid song from thirty years ago. Kenny preferred the local country station, but his old car only had an AM radio. He'd meant to buy a new system, but Megan put him in prison. There went his job. There went his money. There went his life. She'd pay for it now.

She goes by Maggie now, he reminded himself. Kenny didn't care. She was Megan to him and always would be. "It's that stupid kid's fault," he said aloud. Despite the resemblance around the eyes and how tall she had grown—tall like him—Kenny was still convinced that she wasn't his child. It was like those facts were erased from his memory bank. His mind was twisted into believing that Hope was the spawn of some illicit affair Maggie had while he was off at work, even though the pregnancy happened right out of high school. All the times he spent rocking her as a baby, changing her diapers, pushing her in the swing at Heekin Park, and bouncing her on his knee were almost wiped from his mind. The voice had told him about the affair. It convinced him because he chose to listen.

It started with whispers as he drank. After a few drinks, he'd get a buzz, and then little thoughts would pop into his head. *She's got a guy on the side. She runs around on you while you're at work. The kid isn't yours.* At first, he ignored the whispers, but the more he drank the louder they became. Eventually, the whispers became a full-blown conversation as he chose to engage the voice in his head, and he began to believe the lies. The brat had come between them, and Megan took the girl's side. They ran off to live without him while he sat in a cell.

Today is the day they pay. "Hey, that rhymes," he said, "I like that." He started repeating it—over and over. "Today is the day they pay. Today is the day they pay. TODAY IS THE DAY THEY PAY."

That phrase occupied the empty space in his mind left behind by the voice over the three hours that it took him to drive to Cutters Notch. Kenny was determined to make them pay. He was going to make them pay today. Periodically, another tiny, weaker voice whispered, *"But..."* Still, Kenny refused to give that other voice any space. Instead, he imagined a giant hand shoving it back down into a jar and then screwing down the lid. *Shut the hell up!*

He had made a choice. He had made it a long time ago. Kenny wasn't going to listen to his heart—not even when the voice in his head was absent, and he was all alone with himself.

***

In Cutters Notch, Unit Three was driven by Bowen County Deputy Calvin Churchill, the oldest deputy on the small force. At the sheriff's instruction, he looped his brown and tan Crown Vic through the General's lot and headed back toward the other end of the little town.

A man wearing a camo hat and an orange shirt waved from the gas pump. Calvin noticed the rifle on a window rack and a set of antlers protruding above the tailgate—an early hunting success. He found himself yearning for a few hours of solitude in his own tree stand. Calvin pushed those thoughts aside as he swung back out onto the main thoroughfare through town, Highway 257, and headed northeast. He grabbed his Yeti thermos and took a sip of coffee. He'd had two cups before he left home at six a.m., but his system ran on caffeine, so he kept the supply going most of the day.

He was disappointed at being redirected to the motel. Like so many others, he'd spent the entire day before searching for the boys. On top of that, he'd lost some sleep overnight as his mind raced from place to place, trying to think of where they might be. He couldn't shut it off. When he heard the radio chatter that one of the boys had been found, excitement and relief swept over him. He couldn't wait to get on scene, but that wasn't to be.

"Well, razzlesnatz. Who's this Al Havener, anyway?" he wondered aloud. "What's he got to do with anything?"

He did that sometimes. He rode alone in his county car for hours, so he took to talking to himself. It was how he thought through things and worked out questions and issues in his head. It was helpful to let his ears hear it. "I suppose it has somethin' to do with the boys. Comin' right on the heels of one of 'em being found."

Hitting the gas, he sped past the row of old, stately homes on the main drag. Calvin didn't pay attention to them on his way by, but he often wondered what it would be like to live in one. He loved how they were set back from the road and surrounded by the huge, old elm, oak, and sycamore trees. Several of them had front columns that stretched all the way to the roof lines almost three stories up. Calvin had studied architecture in high school, and those stately homes were the most interestingly designed buildings within fifty miles. His peripheral vision caught the burned-out house back in the trees. "Such a shame," he said to himself. "Probably be torn down eventually."

A few seconds later, the dual signage for the Notch Inn and Robbins Limestone came into view. He slowed down to let some traffic pass. There seemed to be a lot of cars coming through the area. "Probably the leaves." The unusually heavy traffic held up his turn. A few collected behind him as he waited. "Razzlesnatz," he muttered. He considered using his lights to get through.

Finally, the traffic cleared, and the aging deputy turned off the highway, passed the signs and a few trees, and entered the motel parking lot.

He hit his brakes as he took in the view of the parking lot. "Holy razzlesnatz," he exclaimed. "What in the wild world?" Grabbing his radio, he triggered the mic. "Unit Three to Unit One. Sheriff, come back."

A very long three seconds passed as he waited for an answer. *"This is One. Calvin, do you have Havener in custody?"*

"Negative, Sheriff. I'm going to need assistance and fast."

Calvin Churchill was looking through his windshield at a skinny young man with long hair and a scraggily beard, wearing tattered clothing. He was holding a pistol on old Mabel, who, in turn, was holding a long knife at the throat of a young girl in a housekeeping uniform. Another woman was nearby, hysterically waving her arms around and screaming at the standoff.

Eleven

Deputy Gator Randal rolled up along a gravel driveway to within twenty feet of the old silo. Rick pulled up right behind him. Both exited their vehicles and stared at the structure. It was built with concrete blocks and had steel support hoops set at intervals around the outside. The silo was dull gray with dying vines growing up the sides. The weeds were high all around except for a small path that led to the access panel near the bottom.

"The perfect place to put people you never want to be found," Rick mumbled.

"Do you think he's in there?" Gator asked.

"He must be. Are there any other silos within range that Danny could've meant?"

"Not that I'm aware of, but how'd the boy get out?"

"Good question."

Gator wandered around the concrete cylinder to the right while Rick approached the access door. The weeds were high, and cockleburs grabbed onto his trousers. "Hey, Sheriff, come see this."

"What is it?"

"The weeds are all tramped down on a line toward the road," Gator said as he pointed out the trail. The morning dew was still wet all around, and the boy's path was clearly marked through the trampled, moist ground cover. "Plus, look at that spruce."

Rick leaned further around the radius of the silo, took a few steps, and stopped to take it in. He was looking at a huge blue spruce that had grown to nearly two thirds the height of the silo and had wrapped its lower limbs around the structure. It was in good health, but on the silo side, many of the limbs were broken, recently snapped. Some were pulled free from the trunk and others were fractured in the middle, sticking out like broken bones. The walking path through the wet weeds toward the road started at the base of that spruce.

"Do you think that boy jumped from the top of the silo?"

"It seems so," Rick replied. "Wow."

"That took some real guts." The deputy shook his head.

Rick's heart filled with pride. He'd grown fond of Danny over the last several weeks—ever since their journey through the forest on the night they rescued Hope. The boy often seemed timid, but when the situation demanded it, he did what he had to do. "Let's get inside this thing."

As the two men reversed course to the access door, Hope ran up to join them. "Is Josh in there?" she demanded.

"I dunno," Rick replied, "but we're going to find out. Gator, do you have bolt cutters in your trunk? It's padlocked."

"I think so," the deputy answered. "I'll go grab 'em."

Hope rushed to the access door and grabbed the lock, jerking it out of frustration. "Josh," she called into the side of the panel. "Are you in there? Can you hear me? We're coming. We're gonna get you out."

Gator stepped between them, Rick to his right and Hope to his left. He positioned the cutter's snips onto the lock's loop and grasped the ends of the red handles. Bracing his feet, he squeezed. The steel ring snapped, and the lock fell free.

Rick pulled the access door open. Hope shoved herself in front of him and stood on her tiptoes to see inside. What met their eyes was horrifying. The sun was shining through the open roof, and a ray of light was blasting onto one of the inner walls. It provided enough illumination that they could see Josh's crumpled body on the floor. He wasn't moving, there was blood on his face, and his leg was twisted and lodged in some mechanical framework. Danny's blood-soaked t-shirt had slipped off and fallen into the dirt.

Rick was about to scramble inside when his radio crackled. "*Unit three to Unit one. Sheriff, come back.*" The voice sounded urgent.

Rick paused and grabbed the mic. "This is one. Calvin, do you have Havener in custody?"

"*Negative, Sheriff. I'm going to need assistance and fast,*" Calvin replied.

"Situation?"

"*I've got a scraggly-looking young man holding a pistol on Mabel Robbins, who, in turn, is holding a knife to the throat of a young girl in a maid's uniform.*"

Rick was immediately torn between the two desperate situations. In front of him was his young neighbor, who was obviously seriously injured, but down the road, a hostage situation was going down at the same time. His mind raced back to that picture on his office cork board and the note that was still stuffed inside his shirt pocket.

"*Sheriff?*" Calvin's crackled voice said through the radio. "*Can you get me some help? Please?*"

Anders looked around for Deputy Randal and found him already sitting behind the wheel of his Explorer. "Gator, go help Calvin," Rick ordered. "I'll call the station and get some more help moving."

"Roger that," Gator replied. He gunned the engine and spun around in the gravel as he left the abandoned farm, lights flashing and sirens blaring.

"Unit Three, help is on the way."

Rick glanced around. He didn't see Hope anywhere, but he couldn't stop even for a moment to track her down. With active scenes in two places, he needed back-up. "Unit one to dispatch. Judy, you there?"

Judy Steinkamp was his assistant and the dispatch operator. She'd come in the door just as Rick ran out, racing to this scene. A stern, older woman with deep crevices in her face, she ran a tight office and didn't hesitate to set one of his deputies straight. She'd even corrected Rick himself a few times over the last week. "I don't care if you rescued the President of the United States from a troupe of terrorist morons," she said. "Don't put an empty coffee urn back on the hot burner."

"*Dispatch,*" Judy replied.

"Judy, call the other deputies back in."

"*Already done,*" she answered. "*I've been monitoring. Unit Four will head your way and Unit Five will assist Units Two and Three.*"

"10-4," the sheriff replied. "Thank you," he added, but Judy didn't respond. "Judy, get me another rescue unit out to the old abandoned Havener farm on Robbins Creek Road. We've located the other boy and we need medical assistance ASAP."

"*Roger that,*" the woman said. "*I'll get 'em rolling.*"

With those duties covered, Rick turned his mind back to the immediate situation in the silo. He still didn't know where Hope had gone, but he had a strong suspicion, which was confirmed when he leaned through the silo access door. Hope was sitting on the silo floor, cradling Josh's head in her hands, crying.

He climbed into the silo and approached the injured boy, assessing the scene as he drew near. The boy's leg was lodged between parts of the mechanical framework and was twisted like a pretzel. There was one too many bends in his leg. A large knot stood out on Josh's head, dried blood caked his face, and bloody scrapes covered other places. Josh could have any number of internal injuries in addition to the obvious external damage. Not only did he need a rescue unit, he needed a chopper, too. The boy would need to be taken to the nearest emergency trauma hospital.

"Hey, Dork," Hope choked out, "you come back to me. I need you. Come back so I can stomp you in basketball again."

Josh's eyes fluttered before locking onto Hope. She bent close and kissed him in response, but when she lifted her head again, the boy cried out in pain. Then, his eyes rolled back, and he was again unconscious. Rick clicked his mic. "Dispatch."

"*Go ahead, One.*"

"Judy, get a rescue chopper in the air, pronto."

"*10-4.*"

"Also, make sure the rescue squad brings their Jaws of Life."

"*Roger that.*"

"Judy?" Rick added.

"*Yes, Sheriff?*" she responded.

"Tell 'em to hurry big time."

Rick had finished his radio requests when footsteps rushed up outside. Whirling around, he saw Roger and Cindy Gillis reach the access door. Cindy screamed and covered her mouth with both hands. Roger's stricken face was drained of all color.

Rick went to them. "Josh is alive. He's still with us." He raised his hands to both console them and to slow them down. If they weren't careful, they could hurt Josh more. "He's breathing. He called out in pain a few moments ago and moved his head. He can move his body, but he may have suffered internal injuries and his leg is caught in a machine."

Cindy Gillis climbed inside and tried to push past Rick. He restrained her, wrapping his arms around her to hold her back.

"Let me by. That's my boy," she demanded.

"Be careful, Cindy," he said. "Don't try to move him. Help's on the way." Rick released Josh's mother and turned to see Hope, who was looking at Cindy with tears flowing down her face. The woman joined the girl, and they held one another even as they held on to the boy that brought them together.

Roger finally climbed inside and examined the unloader system into which Josh's leg was lodged. "This is tricky," he said. "It's gonna be a bugger getting his leg out." It was obvious the man was trying desperately to approach the situation from a logical perspective. His hands were shaking as he walked around the unloader, considering how to get his boy free.

Rick understood just how difficult that was to do. "Yep," Rick replied. "I've got the Fire Department on the way." Sirens sounded in the distance as if on cue. "They've got some special tools that can make light work of this mess."

"How did you find him?" Roger asked.

"I didn't." Rick glanced up through the tangle of ropes and cables. A large crow perched on the opening at the top of the silo. "Apparently, Danny climbed up to the top and jumped out."

Roger Gillis' mouth dropped open.

"Caw," the crow said as it leapt into the air.

***

Mabel Robbins had a short night too, but unlike her son, she got some sleep. After getting the women working, as the sky shifted from the weird yellowish-red to a clear blue, she was sitting in the plush leather chair behind her desk in her small office just off the Notch Inn lobby. Trisha Bray was mopping the linoleum floor in the other room. Mabel glanced at her calendar. Only two, maybe three, more weeks remained of the fall season. When the last of the tree tourists dried up, she'd shut down the motel for the winter. At that time, Trisha and her mother would be moved down to the mine. They'd then learn what real work felt like. The old woman smiled. When she had taken the two females, they seemed a little prim. Their vehicle was new and nice. Their wallets were flush with cash and credit cards. They were soft. That was then. Things were different now.

Swiveling around, she pulled a ledger out of her credenza. Mabel had avoided electronic documentation. Her son wanted to upgrade to some sort of digital bookkeeping, but she knew enough about it to know that there were a thousand ways that electronic accounting could come back to bite her. No, she would stick to the tried-and-true method of pencil and paper. In a pinch, she could just toss the ledger in a fireplace and all the evidence would vanish into smoke. She swiveled back to the desk, placed the book on the desk-pad calendar—a gift from the janitorial-supply company—and opened it, so she could add to the last entry.

Mabel wrote with her right hand while she rested her left on the oak surface of the desk. Her free hand brushed against something. She glanced over. It was the large hunting knife she always kept nearby. The blade measured eight inches long, and the knife had a stained, hardwood handle. She kept it in a light brown leather sheath.

Pick it up. The thought came from thin air.

Putting her pencil down, she lifted the big blade. After unsnapping the clasp, she pulled it from the cover and examined the edge. It was sharp. She kept it that way. A dull knife was useless. Mabel turned it over and then back again, gazing up and down its shiny, steel surface. Turning the edge toward her face, she carefully passed her thumb across the thin, deadly surface.

She was about to return it to the sheath when another thought came to her like a mental text message. *Look outside.*

Standing with the knife in her hand, she leaned past the credenza and peered out toward the parking lot. First, she gazed toward Highway 257. Nothing moved. Then, she glanced back toward the gravel drive that led to the mine. "Well, burnt biscuits," she blurted. Patrick Bray was running out of the trees carrying a gun.

Mabel lurched away from the window and moved as quickly as her old legs would carry her around the desk and into the lobby. Moving the knife to her right hand as she maneuvered around the check-in counter, she wrapped her left arm around Trisha's neck and jerked her toward the door, dragging her feet behind her. The girl's face caught the corner of the door's window frame, ripping a gash into her forehead.

Mabel dragged the now-bleeding girl into the parking area and screamed at the boy, "You stop right where you're at, boy! I'll gut her like a pig. You'd better believe I will."

A woman screamed behind her. Mabel glanced back. It was the twins' mother, Annette. She was standing outside of what had been Al Havener's room. Annette was tasked with removing any trace of the man. She wore rubber gloves and a bandana that held back her dark brown hair.

"Mabel, no," she bellowed.

Mabel swung the girl right and left, trying to keep the boy and his mother within sight. Blood from Patti's face was running across the old woman's arm and dripping freely to the pavement. "I'll do it. I'll drop her intestines right here on the driveway."

***

After knocking Robert out cold and swiping his gun, Trick hoped to take the old woman by surprise. He ran up the gravel drive before diverting the last few hundred feet to pass through the woods between the mine and the motel. If she saw him coming too soon, she'd hurt his family. He had to be quick and he had to be careful.

The boy paused at the tree line. There was a significant gap from the edge of the trees to the motel office. It was the one risky place she might see him coming. Trick could see Mabel's office window, but with the light of the morning, he couldn't make out any details. With any luck, she wouldn't be looking out when he rushed out of the trees.

Trick made his move. He darted out, crouching low to make himself smaller as he trotted across the open space. He hadn't quite made it three quarters across when the lobby door crashed open and he knew luck was against him.

Stopping, he saw the sun glint off a large blade that Mabel held to his sister's throat. He heard the old woman's words. He heard his mother scream. Time seemed to freeze. He felt the sun on his face. He felt a slight chilly breeze as it ruffled his long, shaggy red hair. Drops of sweat dribbled down his forehead at the same rate his sister's blood dripped on the ground. A few red drops hit

Mabel's boots. The old woman threatened his sister. Trick saw the truth of her threats in her eyes. He raised the gun and took aim.

"Hold it right there," a voice ordered.

Four sets of eyes turned in unison to see the sheriff's deputy standing behind his open driver's side door. The man had his service weapon pulled and pointed. "Everyone—freeze right where you're at," Calvin Churchill ordered. "And I mean everyone."

Mabel wasted no time in creating a scenario. "Thank heavens you're here, Cal," she exclaimed. "These three here are trying to rob me. I managed to capture this girl and hold 'em off, but if you hadn't arrived…well…who knows?"

"She's lying," Trick shouted. "She kidnapped us. She's been holding us, making us work in her mine for months."

The old woman laughed, and she swung the girl back to face the teenage boy, the knife still held to the Patti's throat. "Now, that's just silly. I gave you all a place to stay, and now, you're trying to rob me?" Mabel turned her attention back to the deputy. "They were homeless and came here looking for a place to sleep and maybe some work. I gave 'em beds and some food and something to do. Now, they're tryin' to steal my cash."

Patrick kept his weapon trained on Mabel. "We aren't people to you. We're just tools!"

***

"Now, Mabel," Calvin said, "why don't you just lower that knife, and I'll make sure all this gets straightened out." A siren blared in the distance. *I sure hope that's my help.* "You too, son," he added. "Lower your weapon."

"He's not lying," Annette chimed in. "Our family was on vacation. We stopped here for the night. She must have drugged us somehow because when we woke up, we were prisoners. My husband is being held somewhere down by the mine."

"Mom, he's bad sick," Trick said. "He needs a doctor."

"They're all lying," Mabel shouted. "Calvin, you've known me for years. My family has worked this motel and this mine for decades. These people are trying to rob me."

I have known her for years. Calvin's mind was racing. Both conflicting stories seemed wild and extreme. *But how could she have been giving them a place to stay for so long and I've never noticed them around town? Could she have actually kidnapped them from their room and forced them into slave labor?* He wasn't going to figure this all out while they were at a stand-off. He had to get that gun and that knife safely into his possession. "Mabel, let the girl go, and drop the knife. Son, you do the same with that gun," he added. "Everyone, stand down and I'll sort this out."

"I'm not dropping this gun until she lets my sister go," Trick said. "She's an evil, old witch."

The siren was getting louder. Calvin heard tires enter the drive, then a vehicle pulled up next to him. "Young man, my gun is drawn, and I'll protect the girl. Stand down, now. Lower your weapon."

Trick looked over at the deputy. He saw the second deputy exit his vehicle. After a moment of consideration, he lowered the Beretta and dropped it on the ground. The boy followed it down, collapsing into a lump, and began to sob. Annette rushed to him and held him while keeping her eyes on her daughter and the old woman.

"Mabel, now drop that knife," Gator chimed in from Calvin's side. "You put that weapon down. Right now." He angled to the left so that she couldn't block them both with the girl's body.

More sirens sang in the distance. The usually sleepy little hamlet of Cutters Notch was suddenly alive with action. Every resource they had at their disposal was being activated to cover the two simultaneous crime scenes.

"This is crazy," Calvin whispered to Gator.

"Yeah," he replied. "Sure hope nothing else happens."

***

Tomo stepped out of the forest and approached Queen Hesed. She was seated at a small table in the clearing between the forest and the gaping hole that represented Josh's family home. Sheba was curled up at her feet, her head on her front paws. Sacqueal was nearby with another walnut in his hairy hands. Hesed's face was turned toward the sun, as if she were absorbing its energy. The warm green glow of her aura emanated from the skin of her oval face.

"My queen, I have news," Tomo announced.

Sacqueal dropped the husk of the walnut he was working on and put the nut in a small pouch, then he stepped forward to stand at attention behind his queen. Holding the straps that fastened his twin swords over his broad shoulders, he listened intently.

"What has happened, my friend," Hesed replied. "Do you have good news?"

"The news is worrisome yet good. Both boys have been found. One is injured badly and was flown away in one of their flying machines. The other one is hurt also, but his injuries appear to be less severe."

Hesed sat up straight, anxiety visible in the creases on her face. "Where were they found?"

"One was found on the road and the other was found in a strange building on a vacant farm. I believe it is called a silo. They were nearby here."

"Does Nozomi know?" Hesed asked.

"Yes. She has seen them both."

Queen Hesed was relieved at that news.

There was a loud crack. Tomo and the queen looked over to see Sacqueal pulling a walnut shell out from between his large teeth.

"He really likes walnuts," the queen stated with a smile. "Go on."

"After they carried her friends away, she and her mother returned to their home."

"Sacqueal?" Hesed called.

The sasquatch dropped the rest of his walnut into a pouch and approached. "Ergh," he grunted.

"Sacqueal, please retrieve more of my persimmon juice from my carriage and prepare a drink for Tomo."

"Ergh, og," he replied. Then he nodded before trotting off toward the royal transport.

"They have rescued both boys, yet one is badly injured. They flew the injured one away for medical treatment," Hesed summarized. "Hmm. This *is* good news, but we must beseech the Mighty One to bring the boy safely through this trauma. Is there anything more?"

"Not much," Tomo replied.

"Thank you," Hesed said with a smile.

"I am pleased to serve you, my queen," Tomo stated. As he spoke, Sacqueal handed him a wooden cup. It looked small in the large man's hand, but he smiled when he tasted the contents. "May

I return to my people and my post?"

"Tomo, I am sorry," she replied, "but, I have need of you yet a bit longer. You may check in with them, but I will need you to keep watch on Nozomi throughout the day. I want to know how things progress until we can see for ourselves when evening returns."

"As you wish," Tomo answered. "I will visit my son and return before the sun reaches its peak." Tomo then nodded, handed the cup back to the sasquatch, and trotted into the forest.

"Give my love to your sweet family," Hesed called after him.

"I will do so," he answered before he faded from sight.

***

Kenny steered his green Gran Torino with the white stripe off Highway 257 about ten miles outside of Cutters Notch. He pulled into a driveway for an electrical substation and backed up so that he was mostly hidden behind some shrubbery. It was late morning, the sun was nearing the top of its daily arc across the sky. It felt good as it shone through his windshield. He cranked the glass fully down, then rested his left arm on the open window.

Glancing to his right, he considered the six pack on his passenger seat. It had been over twenty-four hours since he'd had a beer. That was an unusually long dry spell for him. Except for his stint in the Pendleton Reformatory, he hadn't been more than a few hours away from a drink in several years, nearing a decade. Even in prison, he was able to snag a smuggled one occasionally. The brews were like magnets to his right hand. He could feel their pull. He'd been feeling it since he'd bought them a half an hour earlier in French Lick.

The beer was going to be his extra shot of courage. This was the day. This was the hour. It was now or never. He would get Hope and he would get Megan and he would make them pay. His right hand gave into the magnetic force and pulled a can from the plastic loop that bound them together. He guzzled it.

Deep in his core, Kenny Burton felt alone. He had lost his wife. He had once thought he had a daughter, but the voice in his head told him that was a lie. She was someone else's kid. He had no friends. They had all deserted him when he'd gone to prison. They didn't want to be associated with a felon. Finally, even his mother didn't want him around. They'd had a falling out after he demanded his car back when he was paroled. His only companion was the voice in his head, and even that had been silent all morning. Kenny was left to his own thoughts and they were in conflict. He needed more liquid courage, so he grabbed another can.

Closing his eyes, Kenny rested his head against the headrest and let the sun soak into his face. It was warm for October. *She'll always be Megan to me, not some jacked up middle name.* The girl he knew and once loved was Megan. That love was gone. Now, he wanted to hurt her bad. *I'll take the brat first. Make her squirm. Then, I'll come and get her, too.*

He didn't have a plan yet, at least not one that could be written out on paper. He was counting on the return of the voice. *It* would lead him through the steps he needed to take. *When I take her, I'll drag it out. I'll take my time. In fact, I'll take my time with the kid, too.*

A small voice from deep in his mind tried one more time to be heard. *What if she really is your child? Don't you remember holding her? Carrying her on your shoulders?*

"Shut up," he said out loud.

And, you don't really believe Megan was cheating, do you?

"Shut up, I said."

Kenny tossed the second can out the window where it joined the first one on the gravel near the fenced utility equipment. He grabbed a third brew, rested his head against the seat, and took in the warm sun. Then, a familiar chill swirled around his neck. It slunk down his arms and wormed down his spine. The warmth of the sun disappeared, and the presence of the voice returned.

"*It is time,*" it clearly spoke into his brain. "*I have set the stage for you. All the local authorities are distracted and fully engaged with other duties.*"

"What do I do first?"

"*Drive your car,*" the specter said. "*Go to your wife's house. I will tell you what to do with each step.*"

"But—" Kenny began.

"*GO,*" the presence ordered. "*GO NOW.*"

Kenny Burton pushed his own thoughts aside, started the car, and sped away. It didn't matter what he thought anymore. His own thoughts were irrelevant. The voice was back, loud and in charge.

Besides, *it* was his only friend.

***

Josh was deep within the enveloping darkness. There, pain did not exist, and he was able to rest. He could think. He could imagine. He could fear. He was alone.

Josh knew he couldn't stay there. He had to rise back to the surface. That was where the people he loved waited for him. His smart mom with her general-like orders flowing through a sweet smile. His goofy dad who tried to be cool but just came off as even goofier. His buddy, Danny, who was always there to go on any adventure he could concoct even if he was reluctant. Then he thought of Hope. Her pretty eyes. Her cocky attitude. He sweet smile. She was up there, too. His heart swelled with emotion—and determination. He didn't care if that thing waited for him just below the surface. He had to get to them—to her.

Josh began to fight his way back up. He imagined kicking furiously with his feet and clawing desperately with his hands. He pulled and he pushed. He squirmed and he struggled. He fought until he could see some hint of light begin to dispel the darkness around him.

"Ah, there you are," the specter spoke into his mind. "*I've been waiting for you to make another attempt. Your determination guaranteed me another taste of your fear.*"

"Get away from me," Josh screamed at the evil spirit. "Get out of my life."

"*It is yet to be seen if you will even have more life, young one. Regardless, you will never be rid of me. Now that we are acquainted, you and I must stay in touch.*"

Josh tried to push past the shadow of darkness billowing in front of him. As he neared the surface, the light began to filter down, giving the darkness a form. The shape of the specter stood out against the lighter backdrop. Out of anger, Josh kicked at it, but his foot simply slipped through as if it were only a mist.

"*Ah, relax, young Joshua. I will let you pass for now. I have other business to attend to. Look for me, though. I will be in touch again. Soon.*"

The mist dissipated. It drifted away and spread out until it was no longer there. Turning his attention back to the surface, Josh renewed his struggle toward consciousness. The specter's words remained, though. He pushed them away into the back of his mind, but they were still there. *"You will never be rid of me"* and *"I will be in touch again."* In that moment, a new tenant took up residence in Josh's heart. Terror.

Finally, Josh broke the surface. Someone held his hand. He opened his eyes. Hope. She was smiling at him, but tears streaked her cheeks, making her freckles moist. Warmth surged within his soul, banishing the fear he'd just felt. It was like a surge of electricity. The love in her eyes drove out the terror that had just moved in. He smiled.

Then, he screamed.

They were working to free him. They moved his leg. Pain shot up and hit his brain like a bat hits a fastball. His body jerked into an arc and he screamed again. A stick punctured his arm, followed by the sensation of something cool flowing into his shoulder. The pain ceased and the silo disappeared. His mind and soul took a trip.

***

Josh found himself sitting on the beach in Panama City. The surf was surging back and forth across his feet and up his legs. The sun was shining on his face and across his shirtless chest.

He glanced to the right. There sat Batman in the sand with the surf splashing on his boots. He was in the full Batman uniform with the mask, the utility belt, and the cape blowing behind him in the wind.

Josh looked to his left and saw Spiderman sitting there. Spidey was in full uniform too, but his feet were bare. A web umbrella shaded his face.

"Are you guys allowed to be in the same place together?" Josh asked.

"Well, not in the real world," Batman answered.

"Yeah," Spiderman said, "but, in your dream we can hang out. No problem."

Josh smiled. "Cool."

Twelve

Rick stood along the inside of the silo wall, watching the EMTs and firemen work to extricate Josh's leg from the dirty, old piece of machinery. Josh's father stood to his left. Roger was fidgeting, obviously nervous. Maggie was leaning against Rick, his arm wrapped around her waist, her hands over her face. The softness of Maggie's side felt comfortable in his grasp, and he was grateful for the opportunity to provide her some comfort.

A few feet in front of them, Cindy Gillis rested Josh's head in her lap. He had already been fitted with a neck brace. She held an icepack against the knot on his scalp. Hope was across from Cindy, stroking Josh's hand.

Josh remained mostly unconscious. He'd awoken briefly but then he screamed, his eyes flared, and he fainted. Both Hope and Cindy continued to speak to him, urging him to stay with them.

The Cutters Notch Fire Department was a volunteer service, but they had the use of modern rescue equipment. The team seemed competent. Rick had seen the Jaws of Life and other tools used many times during his responses to traffic accidents on the state's highways. As he watched, they were preparing the tools to force the framework of the machinery to spread open so they could pull the boy's leg free without causing more damage.

"Come on, Josh," Hope pleaded, "stay here with me. You're gonna be fine."

"We're going to get you outta here," Cindy added. "Danny got you help, and the fire department is going to free your leg. It's going to be okay." She struggled not to sob.

Cindy and Hope continued to speak to Josh, to encourage him, to urge him to hang on. An EMT just behind Hope's right shoulder prepared some medicine. Rick looked at the boy's soiled face. Smudges of dirt mixed with blood were smeared around his eyes and on his cheeks. Hope's tears had dripped onto Josh's face and formed streaks through the stains.

Josh opened his eyes. He glanced up at Hope. Recognition reflected in his gaze. There was a spark of happiness.

Suddenly, the rescue team began to operate the Jaws, and the metal framework stretched open. Josh's leg shifted. The boy writhed in pain and screamed out again. In response, one EMT held him down, and the other immediately injected something into his shoulder. Moments later, Josh relaxed into unconsciousness.

"Lift his leg out very carefully," one rescuer said to another. "We'll need to place him on a board to move him through that opening."

Rick leaned over to Maggie. "See if you can get Hope to step back long enough for them to move Josh outside."

While she spoke to Hope, Rick urged Josh's parents to climb out, as well. Neither Hope nor Cindy wanted to let go of Josh but reluctantly climbed outside to wait for him.

Surrounding the silo, a small crowd had gathered. A Cutters Notch Fire Department engine, an EMT rescue truck that doubled as the county's second ambulance, and another Sheriff's Department cruiser had joined his car on the scene. A handful of people from town had followed the lights and sirens down Robbins Creek Road to see what the excitement was all about. Old Willie Robbins stood among them. He was wearing a gray Indianapolis Colts hoodie, so his long white hair and scraggily beard almost blended in with the fabric. The old man waved, his shaggy brows furrowed. Rick nodded at him and gave a small wave in reply. He hadn't seen much of his old neighbor since Hope was rescued, and he still wasn't sure how he felt about him.

"Is it the boys?" Willie called out. "Are they okay?"

Rick walked over to his neighbor. As he approached, the older man stuck out his right hand, and Rick gave it a shake. "Hi, Willie," he said. "Yeah, actually Danny got out and is already on his way to the hospital. Josh is still in there, but he's hurt pretty bad. The EMTs should be carrying him out any second."

Willie shook his head and rubbed his white beard. It was stained a dark brown around his mouth and below his nose. After his experience in the old man's basement a couple of weeks back, Rick understood why.

"I just don't understand all this craziness," the man said, shaking his head. First, those nasty buggers from our own neighborhood and now this. Did somebody lock them in there?"

"Seems so. Do you know a guy named Havener?"

"Well, this here is the old Havener farm. It belonged to Faye Hicks' folks and their folks before them. I saw that young man coming in and outta their house this week. Is he a relative? Do you think he had something to do with this?"

"Maybe," Rick replied. "He's Faye's nephew. I don't know for sure, but we're going to look into it anyway."

"Unit one? Sheriff?" Gator's voice crackled through Rick's radio speaker.

"This is one," he answered. "Go ahead."

"Sheriff, we have a real weird situation down here at the motel. We're going to need you on scene as soon as you can. I'm not sure of the facts but looks like we've got an active hostage situation."

"Copy that," Rick said. "Control and contain. I'll be there as soon as I can get this situation handled."

"Ten four."

Rick was feeling torn, but he was going to have to trust his team. Despite the sleepy nature of the little town and surrounding rural county, sometimes more than one thing would happen at once, so he had to allow his deputies to carry their share. He couldn't be everywhere at the same time. Leaving the old neighbor, he rejoined Maggie just as they began to maneuver Josh through the silo access door.

One EMT climbed out and waited. Two firemen positioned themselves, one on each side of the door. Soon, the top of Josh's head became visible as the team inside handed the backboard off to the team outside. With the EMT guiding them, the firemen on each side grasped the board and carefully pulled the boy out into the late morning air.

They carried him until they were well clear of the silo, placing him on the ground so the sun could help warm him. Then, they placed a blanket over his body. As soon as she could, Hope returned to her boyfriend's side and again took his hand into her own. Cindy Gillis joined her.

One EMT called out, "We need to get some saline going. He's dehydrated." The other EMT pulled a bag of clear liquid free of their supply case while a fireman positioned a steel pole. Soon, they inserted an IV and hung the bag from a hook at the top of the IV support rod. Josh wasn't moving. The pain medicine was apparently doing its job well.

An arm slipped around Rick's waist and a hand gripped his side, low down near his utility belt. Maggie had moved up close and embraced him. He raised his left arm and pulled her in. She was crying. "It's okay," he said. "He's going to be okay."

"Did Kenny put them in there?" she asked.

"Actually, I don't think so. It seems his presence here *was* a pure coincidence. I think he was telling the truth."

"Who was it then?"

"I'm not one hundred-percent sure, but I'm leaning toward that Al Havener character. This abandoned farm is his family's old place."

Maggie squeezed up tight against Rick. He felt the warmth of her body against his own, and a surge of energy shot up his spine. He pushed it back down. *Not right now.* He hoped there would be a time, though. *Soon, maybe. If all this weirdness ever ends.*

"I knew there was something off about that guy."

A few minutes later, an approaching helicopter whirred above. The noise grew intense as it cleared the tops of the surrounding forest and maneuvered toward the ground. It touched down in a clear spot where an old pasture used to feed dairy cows. The wind pushed the dying grasses vertical and swung them back and forth as the air whipped from the whirling blades.

It didn't take long to load the boy. Hope tried to climb on board, but Cindy climbed on instead. Maggie corralled her daughter, and they stood aside. Cindy called down to her husband for him to meet them at the hospital. Her voice was lost in the overwhelming noise of the helicopter engine, but her soulmate seemed to get the gist anyway.

In moments, the bird lifted off and swung away across the treetops. The chopping sound faded into the distance.

"Where're they taking him, Mom?" Hope asked. Her face was streaked, her eyes red.

Maggie peered at Rick. "Do you know?"

"I'll check," he answered, "but probably the trauma hospital in Bloomington. It's the closest option."

"I've gotta go," Hope blurted. "I've gotta go be with him. Please, Mom?" she pleaded. "

"I'll drive you both up," Rick said. "Right now, go back home and catch your breath. I need to check on a situation in town, and then I'll come get you. Okay?"

"Are you sure?" Maggie said. "You don't mind?"

"Of course, I don't mind. I'd be going to check on him anyway. We might as well go together."

The fire engine pulled away. Rick peered over Maggie's shoulder and watched them go. More sirens sounded in the distance. He had to find out what the story was at the Notch Inn. "Go on home," he repeated. "I'll be back in a little while, and we'll head up there." He looked over to Hope. "Josh is going to be okay, now. He's safe and in the best hands possible."

Glancing around, Rick saw that the last of the fire department crew had left. The crowd had dispersed. Willie was gone. It was only Maggie, Hope, his deputy, and himself. "Go on now," he said.

After Maggie and Hope turned to walk home, Rick shifted his attention to the work still to be done. The scene needed to be secured. He had to make sure that any evidence was protected, and that no one could come in and screw things up. The rescue had already trampled over everything, but he needed to limit further contamination.

The deputy pulled some crime scene tape out of his cruiser, and the two of them strung it around the periphery of the silo. That only took a few minutes. When they were done, Rick stood back. The sun was high overhead. The silo stood like a cold, dark stone finger out of the grass-covered earth. Medical wrappers were strewn over the drive that led to the stolid structure. The weeds were smashed down from all the boots, truck tires, and helicopter wind.

"Jerry," Rick said to his youngest deputy, "take pictures of everything. Then pick up the trash and guard the scene. No one comes in or out of the area without you clearing it with me first."

"Yessir," he replied.

Jerry Steinkamp, at twenty-five, was the youngest deputy on

his team and the son of his dispatcher. He still had his youthful, athletic frame. While Rick now needed to work out regularly to keep in shape, this young man had the metabolism to maintain his form without too much effort. He had a light complexion and a big smile with lots of straight, white teeth. Judy had obviously sprung for braces.

"When you have the area documented and cleaned up," Rick added, "turn your car around so that no one can come onto the property without you noticing. You don't want to be surprised."

"Got it, Sheriff," he responded.

Rick moved toward his cruiser, then stopped. He was being pulled in so many directions that he was in danger of making a mistake. He needed to get to the motel. Gator had said it was a weird situation. Yet, he also needed to be sure that this scene was well protected. The evidence that might be sitting right here could possibly be critical to any future prosecution. On top of all that, Maggie and Hope would be anxiously waiting for him. He was under pressure, so he needed to take a moment to think, to make sure he was covering all the bases. Rick turned back toward his deputy. "Jerry—" he started.

"Sheriff," Jerry interrupted. "I've got this. I know what to do." The young man probably read the conflict in his new boss' face. "I promise, I do. You get on over to the motel."

"Thanks." Rick jumped in his Crown Vic and sped out onto Robbins Creek Road, fishtailing as he hit the pavement.

He flicked on his lights. *No need for the siren. What a weird couple of days. How much weirder can it get today?* He was so wrapped up in the multiple emergencies, concern for Josh, care for Maggie and Hope, and his need to reach the motel that he didn't even notice the green Gran Torino with the white stripe down the side that passed him on the bridge over Robbins Creek.

***

Trick had dropped Robert's gun on the Notch Inn parking lot. Even so, Mabel had continued her standoff with the deputies. Gator and Calvin were pleading with her to relent and let the girl go. She was hesitating, and time was ticking by.

"Now, Mabel," Gator said, "the boy has lowered his weapon. You need to let the girl go and lower yours."

Mabel Robbins was a fixture in the Cutters Notch community.

Gator had known her all his life, although he'd rarely interacted with her. Like everyone else, she stopped into the General and chatted with people. The woman always seemed pleasant to him, friendly even. Still, as he watched her now, there was something in the way she held that knife on the girl with the blade turned up and pressed into the skin that gave him pause. She was claiming self-defense, but he wasn't quite buying it. "You need to drop it now," he ordered.

"Gator," she said, "this here girl was in on it, too. All three of 'em. They're trying to rob me."

"I hear you, Mabel," Gator replied, "but the boy is now unarmed. You need to stand down." Sweat ran down the young girl's cheeks. The bleeding from the cut on her head had stopped, but blood still covered one side of her face. "Come on now. Let her go and drop the knife."

Annette found her voice. "Deputy, this woman has held us captive for months. This is my son and that's my daughter. She's been forcing us to work by keeping us separated and under threat. She's got my husband down that road in a cage somewhere. Please help us."

The two deputies had formed a forty-five-degree triangulation. Gator looked over at Annette as she bent to hold the boy. They didn't look much alike, but then again, he didn't look much like his own mother. *Maybe they were running a scam on Mabel.* That seemed more plausible than the idea that Mabel was holding them as captives.

"Look," Calvin shouted toward the woman and the boy, "kick that weapon toward my partner here, and then you sit down on the ground next to the boy. Do it now!"

Annette complied. She kicked the pistol, and it spun across the pavement, stopping about five feet in front of Gator. Then she sat beside Trick and wrapped her arms around him.

"Mabel, the boy and the woman are no longer a threat," Gator reasoned. "Please lower that knife. Let us sort this out."

***

Mabel refused to comply. Instead, she glared at Patrick and Annette. Then, she glanced beyond them toward the forest and the gravel road that led down to the mine. Finally, she looked back at the deputies. All the while, she kept the knife pressed into the soft flesh of Patricia's neck. A little dab of blood oozed out under the weapon's edge.

She was about to let the girl go and place her hopes in her own ability to talk her way out of this train wreck of a predicament when her walkie talkie crackled, fastened to her waist. The volume was turned up high so she could hear it whether the girl was running the sweeper or not.

"*Mom,*" Robert's voice boomed out of the tiny speaker. "*The boy escaped,*" he shouted. "*He got out. And he's got my gun!*"

The jig was up, and Mabel knew it. Her only hope now was to escape somehow. She had a hostage, and she wasn't going to let the girl go. Mabel redoubled her grip around Patricia and pushed the blade in even deeper. More blood oozed out of the girl's neck.

Sirens blared in the distance.

***

Gator reached for his mic attached near his collar. "Unit One? Sheriff?"

"*This is one,*" the sheriff replied. "*Go ahead.*"

"Sheriff," Gator said, "we have a real weird situation down here at the motel. We're going to need you on scene as soon as you can. I'm not sure of the facts but it looks like we have a hostage situation."

"*Copy that. Control and contain. I'll be there as soon as I can get this situation handled.*"

"Ten four," the deputy confirmed. More sirens sounded in the distance. He hoped they were headed his way. This thing was getting to be more than he could handle.

***

Quickly, Mabel twisted together a plan. Keeping the knife tightly against the girl's throat, she used her other hand to retrieve the walkie talkie. She kept her eyes on the two deputies with their guns pointed in her direction, and she could hear the additional sirens in the distance. "Robert," she replied. "We're screwed. I want you to get Parker and Boyd. Lock up the workers and then get the AR15s out of the locker. Get four of 'em—one for each of you and one for me. I'll meet you at the mine."

Mabel glanced back toward the forest. She needed to reach the cover of the woods. She was too vulnerable in the open parking lot.

"*The ARs?*" Robert asked.

"Yeah. The ARs, Robert, and don't screw around. The sheriff's department is here, and we're screwed. We're gonna have to go deep." Gator and Calvin could hear her orders, but it didn't matter. They wouldn't understand anything except the AR15 part, and that would give them pause.

A third county cruiser pulled into the lot. It angled itself across the last remaining open exit to the road. Mabel didn't care. Her plan didn't involve Highway 257.

"Get the ATVs ready, too," she ordered her son. "Like I said, we're going to need to go deep." *A little misinformation never hurt.*

"*Got it, Mom,*" Robert replied. "*We'll meet you at the gateway.*"

"Yep," she said. "No more talking. Get moving."

Returning her attention to Gator, Calvin, and the new female deputy she didn't recognize, Mabel slowly backed up toward the forest. "You deputies stay back," she ordered, "or else I'll slice this little girl right through the carotid artery. I'll do it. Don't you doubt me."

"Judy," Gator said into his own walkie talkie mic, "we're gonna need a lot more help."

"*Roger that,*" a voice replied. "*I'm on it.*"

Mabel took two more steps backward, dragging Patricia with her.

"Mabel. Stop now," Calvin ordered.

"I ain't gonna," she replied. She took three more steps back. The forest was only a few more feet away. "Y'all are going to have to catch me the hard way. Put on your big boy pants, 'cause you're gonna need 'em."

***

Queen Hesed was pacing. She had worn a path about fifty yards long on the grassy ridge that edged up against the forest. Sheba rested alongside a tree in shorter grass where her yard existed in the human realm. The dog watched the queen as she trotted to one end and then back again. The royal elf was worried. Tomo had not returned from checking in with his family and she didn't know what was happening with Nozomi and her friends. The daylight hours were like a wall she could not see through.

Sacqueal stood under a small grove of walnut trees gathering a collection of fallen nuts, still in their husks, into a canvas bag. He had removed his swords so that he could move more freely. They were propped up against a large stone.

"We have those trees near our home, too, you know," she pointed out as she pivoted for another return trip. He grunted in reply.

The queen traversed another cycle of her worrisome path. "You can bring those home but only one bag," she advised. "Do you understand?" Again, Sacqueal grunted and picked up another husk with a large black spot on one side. He must not have liked its looks because he tossed it into the forest.

"Where is Tomo?" she asked, pacing in front of the large sasquatch. "He should have returned by now."

"I am here." The Arboreal Realm's Native American emerged from the forest behind the sasquatch.

Hesed spun at the sound of his voice. "Is everything okay? You were gone a long time."

"There was some excitement," Tomo answered. He gestured for those behind him to step out of the forest, as well.

Gavin and Gronek emerged from the underbrush. They weren't alone. Each had another elf in tow, bound with leather straps, gagged, and hobbled at the ankles so they couldn't run. The captive elves wore threadbare garments from the human realm, obviously taken during excursions through the shimmers. These elves, though, had weakened auras and large bags under their eyes. Unkempt and dirty, they refused to look at the queen. She knew at once. These were fallen ones.

"What is this?" the queen asked in a strong yet compassionate voice. "Where were they found?"

It was Gavin who responded. "Mother, they were in the forest near the ancient Gate to Abandon. They refuse to tell us their purpose in being there."

Turning to the new arrivals, she addressed them directly. "Where are you from and what is your purpose here?"

The two bound elves offered quick glances in her direction but remained silent, their heads turned down toward their dirty bare feet.

Sacqueal had dropped his walnut-laden canvas bag when they appeared and replaced his swords across his back. He stepped forward and glared down at the two fallen elves. "Grr."

"Children," the queen said. "You cannot refuse me. You know that. Answer my questions. Answer them now, so that I will not need to resort to the Leaf of Necessity."

Gronek's captive didn't react, but the one Gavin held had obviously experienced the aftereffects of the Leaf's power before. It was from a tree that grew exclusively in what the humans called Africa. Its first effect was to remove all defense from telling the truth. But the aftereffect necessitated finding a spot to relieve the bowels—thus, the Leaf of Necessity. Severe stomach pain always accompanied the bowel distress. The effects were temporary and non-lethal but intense.

The elf under Gavin's control raised his face, and his eyes were as large as those green walnut husks. He dropped to his knees. "No, please," he pleaded.

"Answer my questions now," she ordered.

"Yes," the elf replied. "We are fallen. We are from the great human wasteland to the north."

"The one they call Indianapolis?" she queried.

"Yes. That is the one."

"Why are you here?"

"We received word that Bayal has returned to our realm." At this, the weakened elf again lowered his gaze to his feet. It seemed he still retained his ability to feel shame. "The message instructed us to join him at the Gate to Abandon. We were the first to arrive."

"For what purpose were you to travel there to meet Bayal?" she asked. "What does he want with the Ancient Gate?"

"We were not told. We were only told to meet him there and he would restore us to strength. It gave us a sense of hope, so we came..." His voice dropped and trailed off. "That is all we know."

Gavin spoke to Tomo. "Do you have any sense of what Bayal would want with the Gate?" Turning to his mother, he added, "What is hidden beneath the stone?"

Hesed stared at Tomo. Tomo stared at Hesed. Their gaze communicated much, despite no words being exchanged. "There is a great darkness contained there," she said.

"It must never escape again," Tomo added.

"Again?" the queen asked. "It has escaped before?"

"Yes, a few seasons ago. It briefly escaped, and if not for the intervention of one of the Mighty One's emissaries, a Bright One, we would have all perished."

"That is news that did not reach me," the queen stated. She pivoted away and paced a few steps. "I must think for a moment. Sacqueal, secure the prisoners until I decide our next actions."

***

As the queen returned to her pacing pathway, considering the next moves, Gavin and Gronek whispered to one another. They had no idea that they were living so close to something so dangerous. Sacqueal tied the two fallen elves to the trunk of a large walnut tree. When he stepped away, one green-husked nut dropped and popped one of them square on the head. The big, hairy bodyguard stooped down and picked it up. He looked it over, grunted, and placed it inside his canvas bag.

Hesed returned to the little group. "We will need to call a large force of our own to this region. I will send word. In the meantime, we still have the situation with Nozomi and her friends. Sacqueal will guard the captives. Gavin and Gronek, you will return to your brother and continue to guard the Gate. Tomo, I need another report from the human realm. Check on Nozomi, learn what you can, and then return to me."

Gavin and Gronek headed back into the forest. Tomo did not appear pleased, but he complied. After bowing once, he also disappeared into the woods.

***

Queen Hesed whistled a sharp little tune and sat down in her royal chair, an old folding lawn chair—the plastic straps having been replaced with strips of bamboo leaves. As she picked up her wooden cup to take a sip, a fairy fluttered down and rested on her left arm. "Ah, there you are," she said. "Give me a moment."

A few minutes later, she fastened a note to the little creature's leg and sent it off. "Take this to Dargo, the Director of Security Forces. Quickly, my little one."

Finally, alone with her thoughts, the queen took a sip of her tea. After she swallowed, she took a deep breath and let her head fall back so the sun would strike her green, oval face again. Worry lines had formed between her eyes and across her brow. *I had hoped we would never see those evil times again. Oh, Mighty One, please guide my actions,* she added in prayer.

***

I like this place, Josh thought. He continued to sit in the sand with the surf soaking his feet again and again. Batman and Spiderman were out in the water, waist deep, tossing a frisbee back and forth. Behind him, Wonder Woman and Aquaman were playing a game of two-on-two sand volleyball with the Black Panther and Black Widow. *Could life be any better? I wish Danny and Hope could see this.*

The Hulk lumbered up with a couple of hotdogs in each hand—ketchup and mustard smothered each one. He sat squat-legged in the sand.

"Are any of those for me?" Josh asked. "I'm starving."

"Nope, big boy," the Hulk replied. "Get up and take care of yourself."

Josh tried to stand and discovered he couldn't. His legs wouldn't move. For one second, that worried him and then the concern dissipated. *Oh, well, I guess I'll just lounge around and watch the guys goof off in the water.* Turning his attention back to the surf, he saw Batman send an errant frisbee soaring toward deep water. Spidey shot a web and pulled it back in.

"Watch what you're doing, Batboy," he yelled.

"Sorry, Arachnid-head," Batman replied.

Thirteen

Kenny slowly rolled into Cutters Notch. He passed the consolidated school. A couple of yellow buses were lined up by the main door, and the parking lot was three-quarters full. A few ratty-looking houses began to spring up on his left. Despite how small and rough they looked, he could tell most were occupied due to the debris in the yards—or lack thereof. In some cases, clunky plastic toys designed for toddlers littered the front walks and the tiny porches. At the other end of the spectrum, the leaves were all collected and bagged, and flowerpots lined the porch railings. They were either young parents just getting started in life or they were retirees enjoying the time they had left.

"*Look to your right,*" the voice instructed.

Kenny was passing the Notch Inn. Several police cars with flashing lights formed an arc between the road and the motel office.

"*That will keep them busy while you do your work.*"

Kenny slowed down even more. Just like any normal rubbernecker, he was curious about what was going on.

"*Keep going, you idiot,*" the voice ordered. "*I want you in place when the time is just right.*"

Kenny pushed on the gas and sped up. His window was still down, and his left arm dangled in the cool air. Sirens were getting louder. They sounded like they were behind him. A moment later, he passed the stately houses that sat behind the huge old trees and back from the road below the bluff. He looked down each driveway, examining each home as he passed. *Ah, there it is.* He passed the one that had been burned out.

"*Yes,*" the voice said, "*that is a good place to complete your task. What a delicious setting,*" it added. "*Turn at the store and head toward their home. We will not go straight there, but we will pass by and then wait for the optimum moment."*

Kenny slowed and made the left at Robbins Creek Road. As he turned, he glanced over into the general store on the corner. The redhead leaned behind the counter. He thought of the flowers he'd purchased for Megan. Somewhere deep inside, a yearning sense of loss rippled like tiny waves in a pond.

***

"Megan always wanted to control you, to keep you from enjoying your life," the voice said, and added, *"She was always manipulating you to do what she wanted, when she wanted."* Kenny was blind to the fact that it was the specter doing the manipulating.

That counter-thought that had been shoved into his brain successfully sublimated the softer feelings that were riding underneath.

"Now, you are in the driver's seat, and you will do what you want to do," the voice lied. The reality was he was doing what the voice wanted him to do, but the lies were so strong and so frequent that he'd come to buy into them. *"You will show that woman and her little brat what it's like to pay for the pain they've caused you."*

***

He passed by the store and accelerated down the country road. It wasn't far. Just ahead, across the bridge and on the left. A sheriff's car was headed toward him. Fear struck his heart like a hammer. "Oh, he's gonna see me!"

"Keep calm. He is not going to even notice you. His mind is in other places, and he thinks you are still in the Muncie jail. Keep your speed steady and drive straight. He will go right by you."

They passed on the bridge. Kenny forced himself to face forward, but he followed the driver with his eyes. It was that neighbor. Anders. The guy who had put him in jail the day before. As the voice has promised, the man didn't seem to notice him.

"I want him, too," Kenny exclaimed.

"We will see. For now, slowly pass by the entrance to their neighborhood. Look at it as you go by."

Kenny complied. He slowed to a roll and let momentum take him past. As he eased by, he glanced across the basketball court and into the cul-de-sac—all was quiet. No one in sight and few vehicles. "Where is everyone?" he asked.

"*That is the trick,*" the voice cackled. "*I have cleared the way for you. All are occupied elsewhere. The parents of the boys are either at a hospital or on their way. The Hicks are gone. Their nephew is not there. The sheriff is otherwise occupied on the other side of town. The only people home are your ex-wife and her brat. I have set this up beautifully,*" the voice added with an air of self-appreciation.

"Do you want me to go now?" Kenny asked. "What if someone comes home?"

"*No! Not yet. The time isn't quite right. We need to be sure that the sheriff is fully engrossed in the other situation. Keep going until you round the bend ahead. Then, you will find a little drive into the forest that leads to an old storage shed no one uses anymore. Pull in there and wait for my signal.*"

"Are you leaving again?" Kenny asked the voice.

"*Yes, but I will be back soon,*" it replied. "*Drink the rest of your beer and wait for me to tell you when to go.*"

Kenny passed the abandoned farm, rounded the bend in Robbins Creek Road, found the overgrown driveway, and backed into place. Suddenly, he found himself alone. His mind became an empty room. He found it interesting that he could almost feel the voice leave. It was like a wind blowing through an open window, except outward instead of inward. With the voice absent, other feelings began to resurface. Emptiness. Loneliness. Resentment. Anger. Rage. Yearning. Loss. Somewhere, down below all of those resided one tiny voice. Occasionally, it penetrated the cacophony of noise in his mind. It would force its way through and shout a counter-thought: *What if...*

What if Megan didn't really cheat?
What if Hope IS your daughter?
What if you are just a selfish, angry, violent idiot?

"Shut up," he shouted at himself. "She never respected me. She never loved me. The brat is not mine. No way." He retrieved another beer and guzzled it in only a few swallows. Then, he grabbed another, guzzled it, and then grabbed yet one more. It was the last one. Between the brews and his emotional outburst, he again silenced that little voice. Instead, he embraced his anger and began to imagine what it would feel like to have his hands around

Megan's throat, to choke her until her lips turned blue and her eyes bugged out. As his imagination took over, he sipped his beer and rested his head back. *Oh, this is gonna be fun. I'm gonna enjoy every minute of it.*

***

Yet, somewhere down deep in the big man's gut, that other voice waited. *No, you won't,* it whispered. *You won't enjoy it one little bit.* It was biding its time, though, looking for another opportunity to counter the lies to which Kenny was otherwise listening.

***

Rick pulled his vehicle into the parking lot of the Notch Inn just ahead of Sheriff Clem Downey from the next county to the east. Four other official vehicles were already there. Both men exited their cruisers simultaneously.

"Heard you found those missing boys, Rick," Downey said.

"Sure did. One's hurt pretty bad, but we've got 'em."

"That's good. What have we got going on here?"

"More craziness. This town seems to have it in droves. Apparently, our local motel keeper has been keeping some missing people as unwilling employees in her operation."

"Hey, Sheriff," a voice called out. "We need you over here." Both sheriffs turned to look at the same time. It was Gator. He motioned Rick to approach the motel office. Rick headed over with Sheriff Downey on his heels.

"Hey, Clem," Gator acknowledged the visiting sheriff.

"Hey, Gator."

"What's the situation, Deputy Randal?" Rick asked.

"It's sorta off-the-hook," Gator answered. "When we got here, there was a standoff between a young man, who it turns out was on our missing-person's list along with the rest of his family—one Patrick Bray—and Mabel Robbins. Mabel was holding a knife to a young girl's throat, who it turns out was—"

"Patricia Bray?" Rick asked.

"Yes, how did you know?"

"I met her yesterday. She slipped me a cryptic note, and I just started sorting it out this morning before all hell broke loose. Are they inside?"

"Just the boy," the deputy replied. "His mother is with him.

The boy is saying that his father is very sick and being kept in a shack down near the base of the bluff on the road to the mine."

"Where's Mabel?" Downey asked. "Do you have her in custody?"

"No sir," Gator replied. "She dragged the girl back into the woods with the knife still at her throat and disappeared into the underbrush. Right now, we're setting up a perimeter so she can't slip past us."

"Has anyone ventured down toward the mine yet?" Rick asked.

"No sir. Calvin is itching to go, but I thought we needed more backup to get the perimeter set before we approached."

Rick turned and stared at the woods and the gravel road that disappeared into the old growth forest. Calvin had moved his vehicle down to block the entrance to the mining road. He was considering the various factors of the situation. The old woman obviously had a hostage. Maybe more than one. There was a mining operation down there, so she probably had accomplices. She knew the terrain and he didn't. "Gator," Rick said, finally embracing the nickname, "do we have anyone on our team who has ever worked at this mine?"

"Probably not, Sheriff," he answered. "This has always been a family affair. They pretty much keep to themselves."

"Lot of that around here," Rick quipped.

"*Perimeter set,*" Calvin's voice announced from the radio clipped to Rick's shoulder. "*We're ready to roll.*"

"We're gonna need a chopper," Rick pointed out. "With these woods and the size of their compound, we don't have the manpower to cover it all. Clem, I'll take my team in. Can you provide backup and quarterback from here? Maybe see if you can get a bird in the air from someplace? Nearest is probably Bloomington."

"Roger that," Sheriff Downey replied. "You got it."

"Gator, you're with me," Rick said. "Get your semi-auto from your vehicle. Are you vested up?"

"Yessir," Gator replied.

"Good. We're going down that road."

Gator gave him a crooked and excited smile. "Amen," the man added before trotting off and popping open his trunk. Rick followed suit, retrieving his own semi-automatic weapon. After they were both geared up, they joined Calvin near the mine entrance. Rick sent Calvin to the right to flank down through the woods and Gator to the left to do the same. He himself headed straight down the gravel road, his eyes darting everywhere.

***

Unseen by anyone, the specter floated overhead, soaking in the emotional energy. It slunk between the upper limbs of the massive oaks and slipped between the branches of the old sycamores. It watched as the three law enforcement officers maneuvered below, smiling an invisible smile as Rick moved further and further down into the forest.

The time was just about right. It had set the table for its gourmet meal. It was now time to bring out the food. It was time to start nibbling on the appetizers. *"Ahaha,"* it laughed hysterically. *"Oh, I have set this up perfectly."*

***

Down below, Rick stopped. He looked up into the massive trees that towered overhead. He could have sworn he'd just heard someone laugh from high above. It was high-pitched, almost a cackle. *Probably just a bird.* Putting that distraction aside, he focused again on the job at hand. He pushed all thoughts of Maggie, Hope, Josh, and Danny aside. Rick needed to deal with the immediate danger. What was ahead of him he couldn't fathom. It could be an ambush.

***

Kenny was dozing off. He'd finished his last beer, tossing the empty cans into the dying weeds outside the car. A cigarette was burning down to the filter in his left hand as it hung out in the cool air. His head rolled back against the headrest.

At first, he was eager to go. When he'd moved to this spot from the last place the voice had made him wait, he'd thought this was it. Then, it told him to park here and wait again. The excited rush he was feeling when he passed that sheriff's car earlier had soon passed. All his energy had leaked out. Now, he was just sleepy.

He was pulling his hand back inside to take one last puff off the spent cigarette when the door to his mind crashed open. Whenever the voice returned, it was like a storm was blowing inside his brain. The force of its energy would shove everything else aside and suck any semblance of control away from him. When it came during the rare times that he was sober, he could almost withstand the maelstrom, but when he was under the influence of alcohol, the voice just shoved him back on his mental butt.

"*GO!*" the voice screamed. "*Go straight to the house. Park along the curb. Kick in the front door. I will give you the rest when you get there. Now go.*"

Immediately, Kenny sat up and started the big Ford V-8 engine. Moving the gear-shifter to first, he revved the engine and engaged the clutch. Loose gravel scattered as he swung the green and white car back onto Robbins Creek Road. Sixty seconds later, he was around the bend and approaching the little neighborhood. The big man only slowed enough to keep the car from flipping when he swung into the cul-de-sac, then he gunned it past the basketball court and looped around past the neighboring homes. The tires screeched when he slammed on the brakes in front of Hope's house.

Kenny left the engine running. Moving as quickly as he could, he sprang from the car, popped the trunk, grabbed the roll of duct tape, and approached the front door. *No reason to slow down now.* He stepped up and kicked in the door.

"That was easy enough," he said aloud. Stopping long enough to examine his handiwork, he saw that the deadbolt had broken clean through the wood frame. "Ha. I guess I do know my own strength."

His peripheral vision caught movement racing toward him. He stepped inside to deal with it. A stream of some noxious fluid caught him square in the face. The can that it came out of followed the stream and struck him in the mouth. A door slammed somewhere. He didn't know where. He didn't dare look. Whatever that fluid was, it was still all over his face. Stinging.

Now, he really was mad.

***

Maggie was relieved, anxious, and exhausted. Here it was, only two weeks after Hope had been through her ordeal, and now this crazy, frightening mess was happening with the boys. She had only just begun to sleep well again over the last week. Now that improvement was wiped out. She'd had fitful dreams in short bursts the last two nights. Her daughter was upset as well. Then again, maybe she was just projecting. Hope was a teenager, after all. They seemed to be able to sleep anytime, anywhere.

"Do you want some lunch?" she asked her daughter. The digital clock on the kitchen stove read almost noon. "Maybe some grilled cheese and tomato soup?"

Hope didn't respond. She was sitting at the table with her eyes a million miles away. She was holding something in her hands—a silver chain with a silver metal plate attached. The little dog-tag ID necklace Kenny had given her when she was little, before their lives had blown apart. Hope fiddled with it, rubbing it with her thumbs.

Maggie remembered their conversation over breakfast. Despite everything, Hope still yearned to have her daddy back. Her heart broke for her daughter because she knew that Kenny was totally lost to them. She didn't understand it, but somehow his heart and mind had gotten lost. Maybe it was the alcohol or maybe it was his own lost dreams. Regardless, the Kenny she knew was gone from their lives for good. "Honey?" she said. "Did you hear me?"

No response.

"Hope," she said again, a little louder this time.

That broke the invisible barrier. "Uh, yeah?" the girl said, startled back to reality.

"I was asking you about lunch. Do you want a grilled cheese maybe? And some tomato soup?"

"Sure," she replied absently and then went back to rubbing on the dog tag.

Maggie went about preparing the lunch, pulling the slices of cheese from the refrigerator, getting the bread out of the pantry, and grabbing a couple cans of soup. The pots and pans hung over a center island in the kitchen, so she retrieved a skillet and a small pan, placing them both on the stove.

The sun was glaring through the window above the sink, brightening up the whole room. Maggie heard a buzzing, she glanced through the white sheers that hung over the window frame. A wasp was flitting back and forth on the inside of the window, tapping on the glass, over and over. She knew from experience that a wasp sting was incredibly painful. Maybe she should have tried to capture it and put it outside, but fear drove her to defend herself.

Reaching into the cabinet under the sink, she pulled out an aerosol can of wasp and hornet killer. She aimed. She pushed. A stream of insecticide burst from the nozzle and smashed into the dangerous bug, and it immediately fell to the windowsill—a goner.

Where there's one, there's more. She placed the can on the counter—just in case. Then, she went back to her lunch prep.

Maggie let her own mind drift back to the early days, the days when she, Kenny, and Hope were a cute little family. She was happy then—in a simple way. They didn't have much in that little house on South Monroe. They were too young. Still, they liked being with one another. It was tough making the ends meet with her staying home, so Kenny worked a lot of hours at the foundry. Then, those hours he was away started stretching even more as he'd stop by the Stag for a brew with the boys. Soon, one brew became two, then three. Finally, he started staggering in at all hours, reeking of spilled beer and cigarette smoke. All the joy fled from their home like a dissipating mist.

Maggie had hung in there, though. She maintained the house and cared for Hope. She even started babysitting to augment their income, to put some extra food on the table. Eventually, that backfired. One evening, the father of a child she was caring for picked up his baby about the time Kenny was staggering in from his latest brewfest. That was when the accusations started.

The end of their relationship had come quickly, then. It was like a switch had flipped inside Kenny's mind. He no longer seemed himself. Even his eyes looked different.

A burning smell yanked her from her daydream. The grilled cheese was smoking, so she quickly turned off the burner and shifted the skillet. Pulling two plates and two bowls from the cabinet, she set up the table and sat down.

"Mom?" Hope said.

"Yes, honey?" she replied.

"Spoons?" Hope rose to retrieve them from their drawer.

"Oh," she said. "I'm sorry. My mind was somewhere else."

"That's okay, Mom. I gotcha."

As Hope sat back down, a big engine revved, tires squealed, and brakes screeched. Maggie jumped up to see what was going on outside. Everyone else in the neighborhood was gone to some hospital, except Rick, and Rick was busy with some other mess in town. She walked into the living room and glanced through her front picture window just in time to see Kenny closing his trunk, a roll of duct tape in his hand.

"HIDE!" she screamed and ran back to the kitchen.

***

Ever since she and her mom had returned home from the silo, Hope had been lost in her thoughts. She was desperately worried for Josh. He'd looked so bad, so messed up. It tore her heart out to see that helicopter rise and soar away, without her. Of course, his mother would get priority, but it still tore at her emotions. They had grown so close since she'd moved into this little neighborhood and especially so over the last few weeks. He had rescued her, but she had been helpless to rescue him.

Hope also hurt for her dad. Every time something scary happened, he got the blame and except for that one violent night, he was innocent. When the Hicks had kidnapped her, everyone, herself included, had assumed her dad was behind it. It wasn't so. Now, when Josh and Danny had disappeared, her dad was blamed again. She heard the talk. He was even put in jail up in Muncie. But Rick said he had nothing to do with them or that silo, either. It just wasn't fair.

On the other hand, she remembered the terrible things her dad had tried to do to them. He had killed her dog. Those memories of *Monster Night* were extremely painful. Hope really wanted to hate him. She wanted to despise him. But she just couldn't do it. Something in her heart wouldn't let the hate have a foothold.

Gazing down, she fingered the little silver necklace in her hands. She cherished it. It was the one thing her dad had given her that she still possessed—besides her eyes and the shape of her nose. It looked like a military dog tag, but it was made of actual silver. It carried her name—the one she was born with: Hope Megan Burton. Normally, she kept it in a small wooden box tucked up in the corner of her closet, but she was missing him, and this was her only connection.

Hope's mother had interrupted her thoughts a couple of times about lunch, but Hope had returned to her memories after each occurrence. She thought about how her dad had walked her down the road to the park and pushed her on the swings. Her feet would get tired, so he'd hoist her up to his shoulders. Sometimes, they'd sit in the grass under the huge old trees and pick dandelions together. She would put them over her daddy's ears, and he'd wear them proudly home, taking them off only after retrieving a small glass of water to display them on the table.

Then, she thought about going to the fair. They rode the Ferris wheel together and he held her on a wild-looking horse on the merry-go-round. Later, they walked down the aisle with all the carnival games holding hands. She munched on a huge swirl of cotton candy, and he sipped a lemon shakeup. Hope missed him so bad. It hurt so much she could feel it in her chest.

She missed sitting on his lap and the smell of his cologne. She missed his large, calloused fingers and his clunky glasses. She missed his kisses on her cheek and the raspberries he would blow on her belly. She thought about him. She missed him. She loved him—desperately—despite it all.

A big engine roared outside, brakes screeched. Looking up, she watched her mother investigate.

"HIDE!" her mother screamed.

"What?" Hope asked, rising from her chair. "What's going on?"

"HIDE," her mother screamed again as she rushed into the kitchen. "It's your dad. He's outside and coming up the walk. He's got duct tape in his hand." She appeared frantic as her eyes scanned the kitchen. "Hurry. Get out the back!" Then, she grabbed the can of hornet spray and darted back into the living room.

Hope was dumbfounded. *Dad? He's really here? I thought he was in jail.* For a moment, a sense of hopefulness sprang to the surface. She wanted to see him again. She didn't want to run. *Maybe he wants to see me too.*

Instead of running, Hope stepped around so she could peek over her mother's shoulder, waiting for him to knock. "Maybe he just wants to see us," she said. Then the front door came crashing inside. Splinters of wood flew across the room. The heavy door swung all the way around, driving a small table into the drywall and then hung crookedly from a broken hinge.

Her dad stepped into the space the door used to occupy. His left hand was in a fist and his right hand carried the tape. He was backlit by the sun outside and stood like a silhouette in their entranceway. He examined the busted doorframe, then grinned.

"Run," her mother spat out between clenched teeth. Then she sprang forward, aimed the can, and let a stream of hornet killer fly at Kenny's face. It struck him on the forehead, angling down across his glasses and his right cheek.

As Kenny sputtered and coughed, Hope ran toward the back of the house. There was a small breezeway between the kitchen and the garage, flanked on one side by a door to the backyard and the other by a small broom closet. She paused in that tiny space to think. She was terrified, but she couldn't just leave her mom. Hope looked outside. She looked at the garage door. She looked at the closet. Behind her, her dad was still coughing and muttering some unpleasant words. Her mother was screaming for him to get out. Hope made a quick decision.

She opened the door to the backyard and slammed it shut again. Hard. Loud. A diversion. Then, she tucked herself into the tiny closet, squeezing into a corner. She slipped the silver necklace over her neck. Hope didn't know what she could do, but she wasn't going to leave her mom to face her dad all alone.

A fight broke out. Things breaking. Her mother screaming, then whimpering. Hope started to cry. Sobs wracked her body, but she worked with all her might to contain them and stay quiet. Terror again drove any warmth for her dad out of her heart.

From the kitchen, Hope heard duct tape being pulled from the roll, first one strip, then a second and a third. Her dad was muttering the whole time, as if he were talking to himself.

After a moment, he grew quiet. Then, "Hope? Where are you?" His voice carried a playful tone.

Her mind raced. Frigid fear froze her in place. She didn't know what to do. It was dark inside the closet, so she tried to remember what was stored in the tiny room. She groped around, searching for something, anything, she could use for a weapon. Her hand landed on a broom handle. Too light. Reaching behind her, she found her old aluminum softball bat. It would make a good weapon if she had more room. The space was too tight to swing it. In front of her was the sweeper. Beyond that was a set of metal shelves with cleaning supplies.

I should have run outside. I could've gone for help.

Hope had left the closet door slightly open so she could see out through a crack. First a shadow appeared, then her father stepped into view. Just a few minutes ago, she'd sat in the kitchen yearning for him. Now, here he was only three feet away, and Hope was frightened out of her mind.

"Come on out, sweetheart," he said. "I know you're here, so come on out to daddy. I just want to see you. I miss you so much."

Sweet words, but she could see his face now. His eyes didn't match his words. She could hear her mother groaning in the kitchen, struggling against some sort of binding. Hope assumed it was the duct tape. She tried to shove herself further into the corner, willing herself to be invisible.

In the breezeway, her father stopped a long time, probably considering his options. His eyes darted from the garage to the back door. Suddenly, he looked up as if listening to someone speak. "Right," he said. Then he whirled around to face the closet.

Hope gripped the aluminum bat behind her. The last time she was this close to her dad, he'd killed her dog and tried to kill her. Her mother had used that same bat to save her life. She pulled it up and aligned it with her right leg.

Maybe if I can just get a good shot in, I can rush past him. She had used that tactic successfully on Faye Hicks and then again on the old woman's husband, Earl. It had worked on them, so it could work one more time.

Then her father pulled the door wide open. They stood face to face. He was so much bigger than she remembered.

"Hello, sweetie," he said with a huge grin. "We're going to have so much fun together. Our day is all planned out. I've got the perfect spot for our little father-daughter day back in town there."

"I have other plans," Hope replied as she swung the bat up in an arc toward Kenny's crotch.

"Thought you might try something like that," he replied and caught the bat in his left hand. "Now, come on. Let's go." He jerked on the weapon, pulling her out of the closet. His right hand grabbed a handful of her strawberry blonde hair and dragged her into the kitchen. "After all, we need to get our little date started."

"Mom," Hope screamed. She could see her now. Maggie was lying on the floor with her hands and legs taped together behind her back. A strip of duct tape was wrapped around her face, covering her mouth. She struggled to free herself, but it was hopeless. There was too much tape. Their eyes met. Hope could see the terror residing there.

"Dad, why are you doing this?" Hope screamed. "Please don't do this anymore." In her heart, the sympathy that she'd generated for her father during their separation evaporated in an instant. As her dad pushed her past her bound mother, Hope twisted and tried to break free. "I love you, Mom," Hope managed to say.

***

Kenny shoved Hope into the living room and forced her face-down on the carpet. The smell of spent insecticide permeated the air. There was no second-guessing, no doubts. The Voice was in full control. *"Tape her up,"* it ordered. *"Her hands, her feet, and her mouth. Just make sure she can breathe. We don't want to lose her before I've had my fun."* The big man complied. It was almost like he was just along for the ride or watching a movie. Or, better yet, it was like he was inside one of those virtual reality video games.

The tiny part that used to be Kenny Burton, what was left of his conscience, was huddled in a corner of the man's mind. That little remnant of a man was horrified, but ever since he had ceded control to the specter, he no longer had enough power to overcome the lies, hatred, and evil thoughts.

After Hope was on the floor, Kenny straddled her back and sat his weight against her butt. Pulling her arms back, he strung duct tape tightly around her wrists. Then, he reversed position and repeated the process with her feet. Finally, he pulled a long strip of the gray tape free and covered the brat's mouth. The house was suddenly silent except for a clock ticking somewhere and Megan's moaning.

"Now, put her in the trunk and get going."

"What about Megan?" Kenny asked.

"You'll come back for her. It will be hours before anyone discovers what you have done."

What I have done… What have I done? Quickly, those thoughts were obliterated.

Kenny rose to his feet and towered over the girl that he'd been duped to believe was his daughter. He glared down at her, allowing his resentment and pain to relish in the conquest that was at hand. A grin swept across his face. He reached down and picked the girl up like she was nothing more than a sack of potatoes or a rolled-up rug, tossing her across his shoulder before heading outside. At the door, he turned back to see Megan still fighting against the tape, squirming on the floor, now in the dining room.

"I'll be back in a while, honey," he said. "Then, we'll go out and have a good time, too."

Kenny Burton laughed all the way down the sidewalk to his car. He laughed as he opened the trunk. He was still laughing after he dumped Hope inside, closed the lid, and jumped behind the steering wheel. He could hear the laughter in his head and the laughter coming out of his mouth, but somewhere, deep down inside, there was a part of him that was only a spectator—that part of him that used to push his little girl on the swing at the park. That part of him wept.

***

Queen Hesed was enjoying her tea, but worrisome thoughts plagued her mind. The sun was high in the sky and the aura of the forest was dimmed in its glaring light. She could see clouds moving in from the western horizon. The impending conflict surrounding Bayal hung over her mind like those vapors in the sky, and she needed to consider her options as the leader of the Elfin people within her region. Worry lines had formed on her forehead. Between the greatly increased number of fallen elves, the danger that lurked beneath the stone nearby, and the re-emergence of the greatest of the fallen ones, her long reign over a realm of peace seemed about to come to an end.

Taking another sip of tea, she gazed out over the clearing carved from the forest and saw the specter glide smoothly into the middle of the little barren circle the humans called a 'cul-de-sac.' The appearance of a specter was a bad omen. They always followed the opportunity for impending violence, feasting on the intense negative energy.

This specter moved too smoothly, she noticed. Normally, they would flutter to and fro like a butterfly, expanding and contracting as they moved about. This one moved in a straight line as it cruised into the area, following the line of the barren soil that designated the human road. As it reached the circled area, it flowed around it and came to a stop in front of the spot that Hesed had come to know as the location of Nozomi's home. A great fear arose within her as the specter moved directly into the space that the home occupied.

"Sacqueal," she called out. "Sacqueal, come quickly."

The sasquatch dropped yet another walnut and moved quickly to his queen's side.

"Retrieve my sons," she ordered. "Find them and bring them here as quickly as you can."

Queen Hesed could not see what was happening in the human realm. The sun prevented the shimmers from being accessed. But the presence of the specter could only mean evil. As she sat there alone in the clearing watching the specter move about—a dark, shuddering shadow in an otherwise bright midday—her heart ached for what it must mean for Nozomi and her mother. Until the sun began to set, she had only one option. Prayer.

Queen Hesed began to pray to the Mighty One.

***

Tomo emerged from the forest behind Willie Robbins' pasture in the same spot where he had been standing that chilly morning when he saw Hope bolt from her house. He'd followed her and witnessed each of the boy's rescues. Now, the sun had driven the night chill away, and the day was a little warmer than normal for October. A few fall flowers skirted the edge of the forest where some bees were gathering last-minute nectar.

The large Adena leader was worried. His people had guarded the stone-covered gateway for many, many, generations. They stood against any effort to tamper with the capstone, and the words from the fallen ones regarding Bayal were evil tidings. They weighed heavy on his heart. It seemed that his people's long period of peace was about to come crashing to an end.

Looking down upon the modern human neighborhood, he saw a green and white power wagon, what his distant, modern human cousins referred to as a car, sitting in front of Nozomi's home. "Hmm," he muttered to himself. "I have not seen that one before." He found the power wagons to be interesting. They came in so many shapes and sizes. His people had no use for them, but still, his curiosity drove him to understand how they functioned and how his modern cousins used them.

Movement in the sky caught his eye. A large crow circled above Nozomi's home. "Caw, caw, caw." Tomo sensed an urgency in its calls, the hair on the back of his neck stood up. The bird soared, then suddenly diverted in his direction. It flew directly at him, but just as it reached him, it reversed direction and flew back over to circle the house again. "Caw, caw, caw," it screamed.

Tomo didn't understand the meaning of the bird's calls, but he knew that special creatures inhabited the area. There had been legends passed down for hundreds of years about how the Creator had designed special beings to live in the forest nearby. The legends held that these creatures were both intelligent and aware. His instinct told him that he was now seeing one of them.

The bird flew toward him again only to repeat its maneuver and return to the house. "Caw, caw, caw," it continued to scream.

His eyes moved away from the soaring black bird to the house below. A sense of urgent trepidation came over his mind. *Something is very wrong.* No sooner had that thought rammed into his brain than he saw movement near that green and white power wagon. A large man had emerged from Nozomi's house carrying something across his shoulders. It looked like a large bag, or perhaps, a rolled-up rug. Then, the object squirmed, and the man was having trouble keeping it on his shoulder.

Panic hit Tomo like a hammer to the face. Nozomi was being taken. Again.

For a moment, it was as if his feet had grown roots and were anchored to the forest floor. Terror washed over him when the girl was dropped into the storage compartment at the rear of the wagon. Breaking free of his initial shock, he moved to charge across the pasture. Unfortunately, the power wagon roared to life before he had crossed the first fence, and it sped away. The crow followed from above the treetops.

Tomo changed course and raced as fast as his feet could carry him through the trees, toward the human path known as Robbins Creek Road. *I will cut him off. I will stop him on the road.* He crashed into the brush, ignoring the tangling of the brambles and stickers, and pushed into the woods. He passed behind Willie Robbins' barn and emerged onto the road within seconds.

He was too late.

The car sped across the bridge and accelerated toward town. He stood in the middle of the road, his hands on his hips, his breath coming in surges, and watched as the modern machine grew smaller in the distance.

"Hey, what's going on?" a voice yelled from behind.

Tomo whipped around. An old man with long, white hair stood along the edge of the road next to a pile of cut brush. He held a pruning saw in his hand and sweat trickled down from his brow. It was the old man who lived in the old white house near the entrance to Nozomi's tiny village. He had lived there for as long as Tomo could remember.

"Someone has taken the girl," Tomo stated. "Go, check on her mother." Without another word, Tomo darted back into the forest, disappearing within the ancient trees. His only hope for finding Nozomi again resided in the queen. He needed her help, and he had to return to his own realm to get it.

Frantically, he searched for a passage. Tomo ran past oaks and maples, chestnuts and birches, hackberries and elms, and then, there it was—the ancient sycamore. Majestic with its towering limbs and gray and white speckled trunk, it towered over the other trees. Only a few oaks challenged it for the supremacy of the forest. All the neighboring trees kept their distance as if making room for their king. That left a small clearing beneath the lower limbs.

Tomo recited some ancient words that he himself did not understand, bowed once, and then ran at full speed directly toward the trunk of the massive tree. Just as he was about to smash into the side of the sycamore, the fibers of the tree's trunk opened, and a bright, sparkling hole formed. He darted inside the shimmering crevice.

The crevice closed behind him and the forest returned to normal. Tomo was gone.

***

"I hate these things." Willie Robbins clipped yet another Japanese honeysuckle out of the underside of his hedge of burning bushes. The hedge was alive with its signature red color, making the honeysuckles stand out like Santa Claus at the Easter parade. The removal of the pesky plant had become an annual ritual. Every year, he cut them out and every year they grew back. "Ugh," he groaned and clipped another stem as close to the earth as he could reach.

The old man stood up and looked south along his ten-foot-high row of shrubs. He was proud of what they had become. He trimmed them back and shaped them regularly, working them so that they grew together and blocked any view of his back and side yards. He'd already cleared the invasive weeds from about sixty or seventy feet of the brush, he only had about ten more feet to go. A pile of clipped stems stretched in a low line along the edge of the road.

The old man slipped over to the next bush. "Oh, I must have missed you last year," he said to a honeysuckle. "You're kinda thick." Placing the clippers down, he picked up his pruning saw. "I'll get you this year, though." He dropped down on his knees and ground away at the side of the overgrown weed.

An engine revved. It sounded like the one that rushed into the cul-de-sac a few minutes prior. Then tires squealed causing him to look up just in time to see a green Gran Torino skid as it rushed back out onto the main road. "What in the—" He stood to watch it speed past him. "Slow down," he yelled at the man with the dark-rimmed glasses who was driving the muscle car. Spinning, he looked north as the car sped toward the bridge over Robbins Creek. Just before the Gran Torino reached that old iron bridge, a man broke out of the forest and rushed to the middle of the road as if he'd been trying to cut off the driver.

Willie couldn't see the man's face, but he recognized him. He'd seen him at various times over the years, but only in glimpses. The man was one of the People of the Forest. He could tell by the deerskin trousers and the deerskin shirt. Plus, the man wore feathers in his long black hair. Willie was pretty sure that he had seen this particular man over the years, walking under the cover of the trees. He never got close, at least not close enough to speak. Once, as a young boy, Willie told his grandfather about seeing another similar man. His grandfather had only smiled and told him about his own experience in meeting one of those "Indians" back when he was a boy himself. Now, he found himself standing within twenty feet of the elusive man. Close enough to speak.

"Hey," he called out. "What's going on?"

The man spun to face Willie. Colorful stones, seeds, and shells adorned the front of the man's shirt. Elaborate stitching decorated his waistband and the front of his pants. His sleeves flared at the hands, and more colorful stones, seeds, and shells were strung together on bands looping each wrist. The native's eyes were open wide above his deeply tanned cheekbones. A large knife was strapped to his hip.

"Someone has taken the girl," he declared. "Go, check on her mother."

The man said nothing more. He briefly looked Willie square in the eyes, turned to look back toward the direction that the car had sped, and then rushed back into the forest.

Willie stood there motionless for several seconds, processing what the man had said to him. He glanced toward town and then turned and peered the other way. Finally, he faced toward his own house. *Did he mean Hope?* Hope's home stood on the other side, beyond his pasture. Panic rushed through him and surged into his feet. Dropping the saw, he smashed through his shrubbery, angled around the front of his house, and hurried as fast as his old feet would carry him toward that sweet little girl's house.

It took longer than Willie would have liked to reach Hope's front door. At his age, his body refused to run anymore. He had too many aches and pains, too many nagging injuries. The worst was his left knee. It felt like someone was poking an icepick into it whenever he moved too fast. When he finally reached the concrete walk that led up to their little porch, he could see that the front door had been smashed in. Splinters poked out from the frame.

He stumbled up to the open entryway. Out of breath, he leaned against the broken casing. A piece of wood poked into his shoulder. Then someone moaned from inside.

As he entered, the sun was shining through the side windows and clearly illuminated a large lump lying on the floor where the living room met the dining room. Maggie. Frantic eyes stared in his direction. She moaned as loudly as she could muster through a strip of duct tape. Wiggling back and forth, she struggled against her bindings.

Willie hobbled over. Bending to one knee, he eased the tape from her mouth.

"Call Rick," Maggie screamed. "He's taken Hope."

Willie tried to free her hands. "Where's your phone?" he asked Maggie.

"Forget about me," she insisted. "Our phones are in the kitchen. On the counter. Call Rick."

The tape was wrapped around her wrists and ankles and then more tape was used to connect those two sets of appendages together. It was a mess, but he tugged away at them. Suddenly, he remembered the pocketknife he carried.

"I said, 'forget about me.' Go, call for help," Maggie repeated.

Willie sliced quickly through the tape on the woman's hands, freeing her to move around. Then, he handed her the knife and headed to the kitchen for the phones.

"Do you have a land line?" he asked as he returned.

"Of course not," Maggie answered. "Nobody has one of those anymore. Give me the phone."

"That's unfortunate," the old man muttered as he handed over the phones.

"What? Why?" Then, Maggie looked at the crushed phones that Willie held down in front of her. "He's smashed them! Damn that wretched man to hell," she cursed. "Willie," she said, "give me your phone."

"I can't do that, Maggie," he said.

"Well, why the hell not?" she demanded.

"All I have is a landline."

Fourteen

Rick maneuvered down the gravel road toward the mine. The surface was uneven with heavy wheel ruts on both sides of the road. Large puddles of water from recent rains gathered into some of the deeper ruts. Off to his right, he caught glimpses of Calvin slipping between the trees. Rick peered left and caught sight of Gator moving through the brush. He was constantly amazed at the sheer size of the trees in the local forests.

Overhead, a large black bird swooped in and took up a spot on a limb. "Caw, caw, caw," it called out. Rick ignored it.

Ahead, the road curled to his left. The bluff rose like a moist wall just beyond it. Following the moss-covered stone upward, Rick lost sight of it behind the trees. The sun, bright as it was, barely penetrated the canopy. The air held a chill.

Rick reached the bend in the road and stood on the left side behind a tree. Calvin joined him. There was no more room for a right flank. The bluff blocked that path. Glancing around the side of the large oak, Rick considered the path ahead.

"There are shacks on the right up against the cliff," he told Calvin. "They have large steel, chain-linked cages around them."

"How many?"

"I see five. Maybe six. The road veers to the left through the trees again. There's a walking trail along the front of the cages."

Calvin leaned around Rick and took a quick look of his own. "I'll cover the trail. You stick with the road. Sound good?"

"It's a plan," Rick replied. Then, he fingered his radio mic. "Gator, we're about to turn down the road. Stay in the trees and be our left flank."

"*Roger that*," Gator answered.

"Calvin," Rick instructed, "you swing around and hug the cliff.

I'll cover you to the first cage. Then, I'll start moving up the road again."

"Got it." He slipped back across to the trees and made his way to the stone wall.

Rick watched him move. He had to admit that he had some good deputies. They knew their stuff. Even Gator with all his quirkiness was a professional. He really needed to get to know these men. *And women.* Rick also had a couple of female deputies. He needed to understand their backgrounds and their training—what made them tick and what lit their fuses.

"Caw, caw, caw," the large crow called out again. It now rested on one of the upper cross supports of the cage surrounding the first shack.

Weird.

Calvin moved into place. On the left, Gator had taken up a position across from Calvin. *Time to move.* Rick slipped around the corner and hugged the tree line on his left, moving slowly, carefully forward. The road sloped slightly upward to left, away from the shacks and the stone wall, allowing for a strip of forest between itself and the trail. Trees continued to provide a natural cover overhead.

When Rick had matched his deputies' advancement, the three began to move forward again. Gator slipped ahead on the left. Calvin moved around the front of the caged shacks, checking each gate as he went. Each were padlocked, but violent coughing came from one of small buildings.

After about another hundred yards, the walking trail rejoined the road as it crested a small hill. Two large limestone columns marked the spot with an iron sign connecting them at the top—Robbins Stone Works. The columns reminded Rick of the large stone blocks at the abandoned quarry a couple of weeks prior. Gator stood on the far side of the one on the left. Rick joined him. Calvin took cover behind the one on the right. A twenty-foot gap allowed the road to pass between them.

The crow cawed. Rick looked up. That same bird was now perched overhead on the iron sign. It was looking down at him and flapping its wings. "Caw, caw, caw," it repeated.

"Why is that bird following us?" Rick asked his deputies.

"Who knows?" Gator replied. "Weird stuff happens around

here all the time."

Rick peeked around the stone column and down toward the underground mine at the bottom of a small pit. A row of cars, trucks, and SUVs lined the far wall of the pit. The opening of the mine itself resembled the gaping mouth of a sad clown at the bottom of the bluff wall. A large piece of earth-moving equipment sat at the opening. Patricia Bray was tied to the machine.

A muzzle flashed and a bullet pinged off the stone above his head. The shot reached the stone before the bang reached his ears. The bird squawked and flew off.

"Sheriff," someone called from the mine. "Don't you come any closer." It was Mabel Robbins. "You'll never get across that gap alive."

"She's right," Calvin said from across the road. "There's no cover. They'd pick us off like targets at the range."

"Any ideas, fellas?" Rick asked.

"We could just wait 'em out," Gator suggested. "They can't stay in that hole forever."

"Mabel," Rick called down. "Can you hear me?"

"I can hear you."

"Why don't you throw your weapons down and come on out, so no one gets hurt? You can't stay in that hole forever," Rick added, echoing Gator's idea.

"I can stay in here longer than that there girl can stay attached to that machine," Mabel pointed out. "We got food. We got water. We got shelter. And, you can't get to her without us picking you off. Why don't you and your boys just back on outta here and leave us be? We'll let the girl go once you're gone. No harm, no foul? What do ya say?"

The sheriff glanced at each of his deputies. Both shrugged. "Mabel, I can't let this go. You know that. You just shot at me."

"Just a warning shot, Sheriff."

"Still, you've kidnapped a family and held them as slaves for months."

"Details, details," she answered. "Take all of 'em with you. Just leave us be."

"I can't do that. You come out now and I'll make sure you don't get hurt."

"Fine," the old woman yelled. "You just stay there, but just so you know what you'd face if you try to come down that hill—" She didn't finish the sentence with words. Instead, a barrage of rapid-fire gunshots exploded from the mine. Shots ricocheted from both columns from top to bottom. Chips of stone flew in every direction. The sound was deafening. Clearly, more than one gun was aimed in their direction.

The sheriff and his two deputies pressed their backs to the two stone pillars and flashed glances at one another.

"Razzlesnatz," Calvin shouted. "Looks like a big time standoff."

"Razzle what?" Rick asked.

"It's just something he says when he's a little stressed out," Gator explained. "He says that instead of cursing."

"*Unit one, come in. This is base.*" Judy's voice crackled out of all three of their radios simultaneously.

Rick snatched his mic. "Judy? We need more support. We have a standoff at the Robbins mine. Heavy weapons' fire. Check with the State Police and the other neighboring counties and see who they can send."

"*Rick, I've already done that. More support is on the way.*"

Rick noticed that Judy broke protocol when she used his first name. Trepidation grabbed his stomach. *Did something happen to Josh? Did he die?*

"Is something else wrong?"

"*Willie Robbins just called in. A man in a large green and white muscle car just kidnapped Hope Spencer from her home.*"

"Razzlesnatz," Calvin blurted.

***

Hope stared up in terror at the face of her father as he slammed the trunk lid over her. Darkness descended on both her face and her heart as he enclosed her inside his vehicle. Just a few moments earlier, she'd been waxing nostalgic for her daddy, but that had evaporated like mist in the morning sun. Now, as the engine fired up, she just wanted to wish him away. He was obviously not the daddy she remembered. Her mom was right. He was gone.

She lay on her back, but she rolled toward the rear of the car as he sped away from the curb. Then, she rolled back and forth as he swung the car out of her neighborhood. Hope had no control with her arms and legs taped together. It stunk in the trunk. She caught whiffs of oil, rubber, and stale beer.

Hope's mind cast her back a couple of weeks to when she found herself taped to that wooden chair in that dark room. She'd thought it was maybe her dad then, but it had turned out to be her neighbors instead. This time, it really was him. She remembered deciding to give them a real fight, a fight to the death. Now she would repeat that performance. *But they were old and weak, and he is so big and so strong.* Still, she had no choice. It was either fight or give in to whatever he had in mind.

The car rumbled over the old, steel-grated iron bridge on Robbins Creek Road. *He's headed toward town.*

Tears slipped out of her eyes and slid back toward her ears. Once again, her daddy was breaking her heart. For some reason, he'd begun to hate her, and she couldn't understand why. She thought back over the last three years, searching for something she had done, anything, that could explain his total change. *He used to love me. I know he did.* She remembered how his eyes used to sparkle when they were together. Now, they were full of darkness and hatred.

The car slowed to a stop. *We're in town near the General.* The car swung to the right. *Is he taking me back to Muncie?*

Hope tried to come up with some plan, some action she could take to fight back, but she couldn't see or move. She struggled against the bindings, but they were thick and tight. Something rolled against the side of her face. It was light and metallic. She could smell the residual odor of beer. Hope brought her knees up and tried to push against the trunk lid. It wouldn't move.

All at once, it was like the darkness inside the trunk suddenly got darker, thicker. Sucking in air seemed like sucking a milkshake through a straw. It was harder to breathe. A chill settled against her face like an icy kiss. Then, she knew. *It* was there. *It* was riding inside the trunk with her. That thing the elves had called a lesser demon, a specter. That thing that was haunting Josh's mind. She had been told about how Josh had challenged it. She could feel it against her skin. Goosepimples raised on her arms. A chill fluttered down her spine.

That thing's presence terrified her, but a light dawned in her mind. *It all makes sense now.* A spark of hope reignited in her heart.

Hope was surprised when the car slowed again so soon after making the turn onto Highway 257. They were still in town. The car turned and left the pavement. Gravel crunched under the tires. *Where are we going?*

The car swung right, and then swung back to the left. Then, it stopped, and the engine shut down. A car door opened and closed, followed by the sound of her father's footsteps on the gravel. He walked away and then came back. A key was inserted into the trunk lock, and the lid flew upward.

Hope had expected the sun to blind her, but instead she could see trees over her dad's shoulders. They were under a thick canopy of shade. A large bird perched on one of the limbs. Her dad was grinning from ear to ear; his unblinking eyes were intense.

"All right, you little brat," he sneered. "Time to start our fun." He reached in and pulled her from the confined space. She could see darkness in his eyes ... behind his eyes.

"Caw, caw, caw." The bird leapt into the air.

***

Kenny had no apparent internal conflict as he drove with Hope stashed in his trunk. The voice that had been directing his moves had taken full control, and those lingering doubts that often sprang up in its absence were shoved into complete submission. The specter had slipped smoothly into place on a slick surface covered in alcoholic lubrication. That six-pack Kenny had consumed on his way to do the deed had made taking control of him as easy as sticking one's hand inside an oversized glove. The feeble thing that passed for Kenny's conscience cowered in a corner of the man's mind.

"*Take the girl directly to the burned-out house,*" it instructed. "*Go quickly. All the authorities are otherwise engaged. You will find no one to interfere. Ahaha.*"

Kenny did as he was told. After carrying her out, draped over his shoulder, he dumped her into his trunk like a bag of river rock. He'd seen her look up at him with terror in her eyes. The thing in his head smiled a hideous grin. It was like he could almost see it with his own mind's eye. That grin translated to his face and stayed there all the way through the little town.

Now, as Kenny maneuvered the Ford through the trees that lined each side of the long, meandering driveway, he realized that the end game had begun. The part of his mind that he still controlled drifted to a memory from only a couple of months previous. He was standing outside the large iron gates at the Pendleton Reformatory after having just been released. The old guard told him not to come back, and he assured the man that he wouldn't. At the time, he had truly been determined to stay on the straight and narrow way. Instead of straight and narrow, though, he now found himself veering down a jagged one-way path. There was no turning back. Regardless of what he did next, his life was over. A line had been crossed that could not be uncrossed.

The driveway swung to the right and wrapped around the side of the house to the left, ending in front of a separate, two-car garage. It was impossible to see from the road and made for the perfect place for Act Two of his personal tragic play.

He killed the engine and stepped out into the midday air. It was cool under the shade of the huge trees. The place was rank, though. The acrid stink of the burned-out home hung in the air. Remnants of ruined furniture, melted housewares, and burned pieces of wood littered the backyard. A bird squawked overhead. As he looked up, it dive-bombed his face.

He ducked and swatted at it. "Stupid bird."

"Get her out and get her inside."

Kenny snapped back to the task at hand. He gained access to the house, then opened the trunk. He looked down at the person who used to be his little girl. There it was again—the terror in her eyes. The thing in his head grinned again, and again he felt his own lips curl into a matching expression.

"All right, you little brat, time to start our fun."

As Kenny reached in to yank the kid from the compartment, a tiny reflection caught his eye. A silver chain around her neck. Down deep inside, something registered. Something he had to force into submission. Something he couldn't let himself think about.

***

That little voice in the corner of his mind saw it, too. His mute conscience took note, but there was no traction for him to climb back to the surface. The specter still reigned over the alcohol-slickened hill that led to the control of Kenny's mind.

***

Kenny pulled her out and flopped her over his shoulder again. She was still struggling, but the tape kept her wiggling manageable. "Stop it." He slapped her across the side of her taped-up face. Inside, he dropped her onto an old metal kitchen chair with a vinyl seat and backrest. He grabbed more duct tape and wrapped it around her torso and the chair, securing her into place.

"*There you go,*" the specter said inside Kenny's head. *Now, we're going to have some real fun, some really delicious fun.*"

On the outside, Kenny heard his own voice say, "There you go. Now, we're going to have some real fun, some really delicious fun." He found it so weird to hear his own voice echo words he didn't initiate himself.

***

Unseen by anyone in the house, the bird left the limb of the tree and ascended into the sky above the canopy. It made a large circle around the house and then soared further to the east, along the edge of the cliff face toward the mine.

***

"Unit One to Unit Four," Rick yelled into his mic. "Jerry? Respond."

"*Unit Four,*" Deputy Steinkamp replied. "*Sheriff, how can I help?*"

"Hightail it over to Maggie Spencer's house on Basketball Court. Gather as much info as you can. Report back to me, ASAP."

"*Roger that,*" Jerry said. "*What about the silo scene?*"

Rick had considered that. The scene needed to be secured before a thorough search could be done, but he was out of manpower. The urgent had to trump the important. "Just leave it. We'll get back to it as soon as we can. Now, get moving."

"*I'm already on my way.*"

Inside, Rick was desperate. He was point-on-scene of a hostage standoff where heavy weapons were being fired on himself and his deputies. He couldn't just leave. Still, that's what his heart was telling him to do. He was terrified for Maggie and for Hope.

"Dispatch," he said into the radio. "Judy, call the Delaware County Jail up in Muncie and find out if they released Kenny Burton." *They must have. Who else has a green and white muscle car and would have taken Hope?*

"*I'm on it,*" Judy replied.

No sooner had Judy's words emanated from the tiny speaker than a barrage of gunfire erupted from the mine. Again, bullets bounced off the stone pillars sending shrapnel and stone chips in all directions. "Just a reminder," Mabel yelled from the dark, gaping hole down the hillside.

The shots pulled Rick's mind back to the here and now. He looked over at Gator, who stared back with eyes as big as quarters. Then, Rick glanced at Calvin. The older man was mumbling to himself and sweat dripped from his face despite the chilly October air. He needed more men up there. He needed that chopper. He needed to be in two places at once.

"Sheriff Downey, are you monitoring?" Rick radioed.

"*10-4*," Downey replied.

"Clem, we need more men up here, but have them flank the mine entrance and come in from further out along the cliff face. I want to make sure that there aren't any other ways in or out of the mine."

"*You've got it, Rick,*" Downey replied.

"Also, send a unit out to look for that green and white car. It's probably a Gran Torino."

"*Already done. I've also notified all the neighboring counties to be looking for it, too.*"

Rick was grateful for the assistance. *I'm going to owe him a dinner when this is all over.*

He had his back against the stone pillar. The hard surface gave him just a touch of security in an otherwise desperate combination of events. Rick looked up at the trees. Above them, the crow was circling in the sky, soaring on extended wings. Beyond the bird, the sky had darkened. A thick layer of clouds had moved in, enveloping the sunny sky. Between the tree canopy and the thick cloud cover, the day had darkened considerably. There was a bit more wind, too, making the air even chillier.

"Mabel," Rick called out. "Come on now. You know you can't maintain this forever. Be reasonable."

She didn't respond. Evidently, she had nothing more to say. Peeking around the corner of the pillar, he peered down toward the mine. Patricia Bray was still attached to the machine, and he could see the open mouth of the mine itself, but there was no sign of any other movement. Rick was desperate for a solution, but there was no solution to be found. He was stuck. Patricia was stuck. Maggie must be hysterical. And perhaps worst of all, Hope was lost.

***

Queen Hesed waited with intense trepidation for her sons to arrive. She had watched the specter move to and fro in the space that held Nozomi's home. Then, it moved out again and sped off on a line, making a ninety-degree turn and disappearing behind the forest. She was desperate for her new human friend. For once in her long life, she felt trapped in her own realm.

Within minutes, Tomo crashed from the trees into the barren clearing. He maneuvered deftly between the holes and rushed to her presence.

"Nozomi has been taken," he bellowed before he even reached her.

"Quickly, tell me what you saw."

"I had just taken up my position when I noticed a strange power wagon near her home." He paused to catch his breath. "Then, I noticed a large bird circling in the sky above. It went around and around and around. Suddenly, it flew directly at me, but before it passed, it swung back to circle Nozomi's home again. Then I knew something was wrong." He paused again, pulling in large gulps of air.

"A bird, you say?"

"Yes. A very large crow. It flew at me more than once. As odd as it sounds, I believe it was trying to alert me in some way. Then, a large man carried Nozomi from her home and enclosed her in his power wagon. Before I could stop him, he sped away."

"What did the bird do as the man drove off?"

Tomo stopped to think, to remember. "I rushed through the trees to cut off the human vehicle. When I reached, the road, I saw the wagon speeding away. The bird was above it in the sky. It was following the power wagon," he answered. "What does that mean?"

"It means that there are more than just humans and elves looking out for that young woman." Hesed was pacing again. She turned and started a new course along the edge of the forest. Her arms wrapped around her chest, her hands buried within the golden painted leaves of her royal garment. "It also means we may have a way to find her. Hurry back to the human realm. Find that bird. If you find the bird, you may find Nozomi."

Looking to the sky, she saw that heavy clouds had rolled in. The day was much darker, muting the light of the sun. Usually, she yearned for the sun and enjoyed resting within its warm rays, but today she couldn't have been more thankful for the darkness the clouds provided.

"This is a forest, my queen. How can I find one single bird within a forested area filled with birds?"

"My dear Tomo," she answered, "if what I believe is true, all you will need to do is look. It will find you. Go now."

Immediately, Tomo spun around and sprinted off into the trees, his long dark hair trailing behind him in the breeze. Hesed was still desperately afraid for Nozomi, but now a spark of encouragement found space to burn in the queen's heart. The Mighty One has many servants. *Perhaps, it is not too crazy to believe that a large crow could be one of them.*

Just then, Sacqueal came smashing out of the underbrush behind her. Gavin, Gronek, and Smakal were on his heels. "What is the problem, Mother?" Gavin asked, even as he worked to catch his breath.

"Nozomi has again been taken in the human realm. I saw a specter fluttering within the space that would be her home, and Tomo has confirmed my worst fears."

The three brothers stood aghast, looking from one to another and back again. Before they found words to speak, their mother continued. "Tomo says that they have gone toward the human village nearby. I have sent him back into their realm to search."

"What can we do?" Smakal asked, his voice raspy. "It will be hours before darkness falls and the shimmers reappear."

"Look at the skies, my sons. The heavy clouds have hidden the sun. Under the canopy of the trees, the shimmers may reappear while it is still day. We will hurry to the town and search through any shimmers we find. Perhaps the Mighty One will provide a solution."

***

Hope tried to lean forward as much as possible as her father changed her bindings, attaching her to the old, metallic kitchen chair. She tried to create as much looseness in the bindings as she could. Kenny shoved her back, and she found herself taped tightly to the metal frame. He had re-taped her hands in front of her, and her feet were now bound to the chair legs. She couldn't scream because a strip of the gray industrial tape covered her mouth.

The room was dark. Very little light penetrated the soiled window above the soot-laden sink on the back wall. Hope's nostrils filled with the acrid smell of burnt...everything. In the dim light, she could see the vinyl wallpaper drooping where it had melted on the walls, and smoke stains covered the areas that had not melted. She knew where she was. That huge, old burned-out house on the main road in town. Hope remembered the fire from the previous Christmas. A little boy had almost died.

Kenny left her alone for a few minutes. His footsteps echoed from other parts of the house. He had gone upstairs. She didn't know why. The only thing she knew for sure was her daddy that she loved was gone. He was gone, replaced by someone else, something else. This Kenny Burton, or whatever was inside him, hated her, and she was terrified of what he had planned for her.

Her mind drifted to Josh. Hope would never see him again—at least not in this world. She desperately hoped that he was okay. She yearned for his goofy smile and the feel of his hand in hers. *If only we had gone on up to the hospital.* Tears began to flow from her eyes.

Hope looked around again. Magnets connected pictures with curled edges to the refrigerator. A small plate still sat on the dirty kitchen table along the wall. Beside it was a crumbled soda can. Cabinet doors hung open. Smoke-soiled dishes still sat on the shelves. Last year's calendar hung by the back door, open to December. A key rack beside it held one key hanging on a hook.

A chill passed across the back of her neck. Goosebumps raised on her arm, and thoughts of hopelessness arose in her mind. "*You will never get out of this one,*" it seemed to say. "*You're going to die, and it will be your daddy who does it.*"

Hope defied the negative thought. Just as happened a few weeks back, a determination to survive rose up in defiance to the thoughts of hopelessness. She wasn't going to give up without a struggle. As long as she was breathing, she still had a chance.

His footsteps still echoed from upstairs. Using her toes to push the chair up and leaning her weight forward, she attempted to move toward the back door. Taking shuffling, tiny steps, she tried to make her escape, but her right toe caught on a burnt piece of debris. She lost her balance, toppling over. Her face landed flat and hard against the melted linoleum. Pain shot through her cheekbone. She started to sob. She struggled, but she couldn't get any leverage to get back upright.

Something skittered nearby. Her eyes shot from here to there in the dim light to see what it was. "Tick, tick, tick," it chattered. It skittered again and she spotted it. It was a squirrel with a large brown, bushy tail, tucked back under the overhang of the base cabinets. It paused in the corner space where the cabinets from two walls met at a lazy-Susan.

Hope looked at it. It looked back. It was as if she could see sadness in its tiny brown eyes. "Tick, tick, tick," it said to her. Then, it skittered around behind her. She couldn't see it, but she could feel it. It was sniffing at the tape holding her to the chair. *Am I going to be rescued by a squirrel?*

Then her father's heavy footsteps again echoed loudly through the charred, empty halls as they tromped down steps somewhere in the house. He was coming back.

***

Kenny carefully maneuvered the large, old, wooden-framed mirror down the tight steps from the rank attic. After he had secured Hope to the chair, the voice had told him to wait for its return, then left him.

While it was gone and he waited, he couldn't help his curiosity. Kenny decided to explore the huge place. He had been amazed when he pulled open what appeared to be a simple closet door on the second floor and found more steps behind a bunch of burnt and melted old coats. Jerking the coats off their hangers, he could just make out a little light slipping in from above. Once up there, he immediately spotted a large mirror against the back wall.

I'll drag that thing back down to the kitchen so she can see herself. It will like that. The idea sounded good. Whatever that thing in his head was, it seemed to enjoy toying with people.

Just what are you going to do? That thought arose from somewhere. It was a tiny voice, one he recognized as being his own, but with a huge question. "I don't know yet," he said aloud in response. "It hasn't told me."

Kenny took a break when he reached the ground floor. He was

standing in what must have been a pretty spectacular room at least twice—once when it was first built and again when it was aflame. Ornate archways and intricate trim-work remained, though charred and covered in soot. The remnants of a large Christmas tree slumped against the wall in one corner like a wooden skeleton. The hardwood floors were heavily burned and warped from the water used to extinguish the flames, but they had been real hardwood—oak, probably.

In another life, Kenny had loved architecture. He had even taken an introductory architecture class when he was in high school at Muncie Southside. The problem was that he sucked at geometry, and geometry was the math of architecture. Still, he loved the craft, especially the way it used to be done. Kenny found himself feeling a little sad at what had happened to this wonderful old house.

Architecture was just one of many of his dreams that had been lost. In school, he had been popular, an athlete. Girls hung on his arms. He could throw a ninety-five-mile-an-hour fastball. He was all-county in basketball. After high school, he was sure he was going to do big things with his life. Then, he'd screwed up with Megan and gotten himself tied down with her brat.

Your daughter, a voice whispered in an almost imperceptible, tiny voice. Again, a voice he recognized as his own.

His life had been one massive avalanche ever since. He'd been forced to forget college and get a job. The only decent one he could find with good money was at the foundry, and he hated that place. Working there led to the drudgery. Get up…work…sleep…get up…work. On and on and on. He could see no future, no light at the end. So, he'd begun to stop at the bar and have a little fun, a few drinks. Life, from then on, became a blur except when he got out of prison. Kenny had a clear memory of that day. But that touch of joy hadn't lasted very long.

He looked around the old living room again. Two windows flanked a solid wood front door. Both windows were broken with the glass missing. Plywood covered most of the openings, but not all. Strings of what looked like burned and melted Christmas lights hung from hooks on the walls. *Must have been quite a fire.*

"*Who cares?*" boomed the voice as it roared back into his brain. "*Get busy. I'm hungry.*"

In response, he picked up the mirror with both hands. It was heavy even for him. "Look what I got you." Carefully, he moved it down the short hallway to the kitchen.

"*Nice. Very nice.*"

Something skittered across the floor when he entered. *Probably a rat.*

"*Put that thing down and get her up off the floor,*" the thing in his head ordered. As he entered the room, he saw that Hope was lying on her side with the chair still taped to her body.

"How'd you do that?" he asked Hope as he placed the mirror against the wall between the back door and a window, blocking the calendar and the key rack. "Were you trying to escape?" He chuckled. "You were, weren't you? That's no good. No good at all. The rats 'll get you down there."

He picked her up and positioned her so she could see her own reflection within the large frame of the mirror. "Look what I brought you," he said, his voice excited. "I want you to be able to watch and enjoy what I'm gonna do."

Kenny looked down at the frightened girl. The voice told him to take the tape off her mouth. "*I want to be able to hear her screams,*" it said. He complied. "We are going to have so much fun," he heard himself say.

***

Hope screamed, but only two sets of ears heard it—one belonged to a squirrel and the other to her father. In front of her, her father adopted that grin that didn't really look like his. Behind her, the squirrel skittered underneath the edge of the base cabinets.

"It's too dark in here," her father said. "I need to find a way to get some light going...so we can see. I'll be back." Then, he paused, looking around as if he were considering options before exiting out the back door.

After she was sure he was fully outside, Hope urged the squirrel to help her. "I don't know if you can understand me or not, but if you can, how about you chew through the tape holding me to this chair, maybe come around and loosen my hands?"

The rodent ignored her. It jumped up on the charred countertop. Hope studied the mirror in front of her. It was a massive thing that rested in its own supported frame, legs and all, with detailed designs carved into the woodwork. The thing was probably six inches taller than Hope herself—almost as tall as her dad. It was a good three-feet wide. She hadn't seen one that large except for the ones that hung in her school restrooms.

"Mr. Squirrel, maybe my friends on the other side will see me in the shimmer." Even as she spoke, though, she realized that it was still afternoon. It would be hours before nighttime when light could activate the mirror, creating the shimmer portal.

Minutes later, her dad hadn't returned, but she'd been working the bindings around her arms and chest. They were a bit looser. The tape still clung to the chair back, but she'd wiggled until it came loose in the front with lint caking the adhesive.

The little brown squirrel dropped to the floor and stood on its hind legs in front of Hope. "Tick, tick, tick," it announced and then jumped up on her lap. It stared at her calmly, then sniffed at her taped hands.

Hope watched the little guy, willing him to chew the tape off her wrists. Its tail jumped and jerked. Little claws scratched through the fabric of her jeans. *Those teeth could cut through the tape like a warm knife through cold butter.*

She heard her father approaching the back door. "Quick," she told the squirrel. "Get down and start working on my feet." The squirrel jumped to the floor and scampered off into another part of the house, ignoring her feet.

Her dad stepped inside. "Believe it or not," he said, "I found a couple of lanterns with oil in 'em." He placed one on the 1960's-era kitchen table and one on the curled laminate countertop near the sink. He fished a small box of matches out of his left front pants pocket. She noted the large knife strapped to his belt. "Let's hope the wicks will light."

Hope couldn't suppress the question foremost in her mind and she didn't see that evil darkness reflected in his eyes at the moment. "Daddy, why do you hate me?"

Fifteen

Rick thought through his options. "Gator? Calvin? Do either of you have tear gas in your vehicles?"

"Negative."

"Negative. It's Cutters Notch, Sheriff," Gator added. "Who would ever dream we'd need tear gas?"

With his back against the stone pillar, Rick had a view of the trail that led past the makeshift cabins, ultimately reconnecting with the access road to the motel. Some men, raggedly dressed, watched him from the cages. *How many were they holding? Where are they from? How long have they been doing this?*

As Rick was considering the men in the cages, Sheriff Downey trotted up the road toward him in a crouch, carrying his own semi-automatic rifle. Rick motioned for him to squat lower. Downey complied immediately.

The neighboring sheriff ducked behind the pillar across the road from Rick, sharing it with Calvin. Rick saw him risk a quick glance down the hill and then duck back. Sweat gathered on his cheeks and beaded in his neatly trimmed, salt and pepper mustache.

"Anders, you're in a pickle," Downey pointed out.

"Excellent observation, Clem."

"You have two active situations," Downey continued. "This one is contained and the other one is not. Let me take charge here. You go find that girl."

Rick didn't immediately respond. Instead, he turned away and looked at the dark gray sky. That crow was still soaring on a line along the ridge of the cliff toward town, and then back again. He considered Clem's words. *Where am I needed more?* "Are you sure, Clem?" Rick asked.

"Absolutely," his fellow sheriff answered. "Look, I've got two more men working their way from each side of that bluff. We're well-positioned here. High ground. I've sent another deputy to retrieve some tear gas. We'll get that girl out safe and lock those turds up tight within the hour."

"Thanks. I owe you."

Clem Downey smiled. "Yes, you do. Now, get going."

Rick told his own deputies to follow Downey's orders and then slipped down below the mine's line of sight. He headed back up the trail toward the motel. As he passed the cages, he took in the faces behind the locked gates. Haggard and tired faces. A few called out for help. One face stood out from the others and stopped him cold in his tracks. Their eyes locked. Al Havener.

"Help me, Sheriff," he called out. "I've been kidnapped."

"Havener, you're right where you need to be. We'll be coming for you soon enough." *So, my kidnappers caught my kidnapper for me.* He made the turn toward the motel. *The weirdness just keeps coming.* As that thought passed through his mind, the crow dive-bombed him and then soared back into the sky, veering toward town.

"Caw! Caw, caw."

***

Tomo reemerged into the human realm at the edge of the forest behind a row of small homes. He had to be cautious. Rarely did he risk contact. His people couldn't afford for him to be lost to them. Only a handful of the Adena men and women had held the ability to cross the dimensional bridge in the centuries since they found refuge with the elves, and he was the only one who currently could do so.

Tomo aligned himself between two young maples and behind a young redbud. Pulling the barren limbs aside, he scanned the sky above the small, human community. To his left, a few small birds flitted from trees to wires and back again. He peered over the roofs of the tiny abodes. The trees below the cliff teemed with life, but none looked like the crow he had seen. He glanced to his right, and there it was.

The crow was soaring in line with the cliff, but then began to circle nearly straight across from his position. It made one, two, three loops. As it ended the third loop, the bird turned in his direction. Tomo was amazed when the creature diverted and soared directly at him, repeating the same maneuver it had performed earlier at Nozomi's home. It was calling him to follow. He was certain of it.

Tomo considered his course. He had to use stealth as he passed through the structures of his modern cousins. In front of him was the rear of a small, square house with a sloping roof. It was in poor condition with a large, gaping hole through the roofing material. The sky was dark but there were no lights in the windows. It was probably empty.

On the left of that home was a similar house but in better condition. Lights shone from the windows. On the right was a strange structure featuring large cubicles with tubes and hoses hanging from the ceilings. The sides and the tops were covered, but the cubicles were open on each end. He had no idea what that place was supposed to represent, but there were no people there. He could readily pass between the empty house and that odd building without being seen.

Moving swiftly, he reached the trail where the power wagons traveled. He paused to look in both directions. A small power wagon approached with flashing lights. After it passed, the course was clear, so he crossed into the relative safety of the trees on the other side.

As he emerged from the thin line of brush along the road, he saw that the undergrowth of the massive trees overhead had been cleared out. Far back from the road stood a large house among the trees. Oaks, maples, hickories, and sweet gums surrounded the house, but emerging over the roof of the huge home was a gigantic sycamore. Tomo smiled.

He darted from tree to tree, then crossed a trail that swung around the house to the right. The air smelled of burned wood and other odors of fire destruction. A massive blaze had almost destroyed the house. As he passed the front right corner, he spied the back of the green power wagon. Tomo smiled again. *Thank you, crow.*

As the Adena leader crept further along the side of the burned-out structure, he peeked through the various windows. Most were boarded-up, broken out, or so badly stained from sooty smoke that he couldn't see inside. He saw nothing until he reached the back corner. There he saw light glowing through a dirty windowpane.

Moving carefully, he ducked low and then came up slowly so that he could peek inside. First, he spotted Hope sitting in a chair. Then, he saw a large man, the man who had carried her out of her house. He was standing in front of her holding a very large knife. The light from a nearby lantern reflected off the blade. Behind the large man and weirdly out of place was a large mirror. *This is bad. Very bad, indeed. I must get help.*

Tomo ducked around to the rear of the house. He had a clear line to the huge old sycamore. Quickly, he said the words, bowed, and ran headlong into the tree—and disappeared.

***

The quickest way for Queen Hesed and her entourage to reach Cutters Notch was via her carriage. The queen, Gavin, Gronek, Smakal, and Sacqueal piled in, and the reindeer took to the sky. It was a short flight. In the twinkle of an eye, they found themselves parked in the groove in the earth that in the human realm was called Highway 257.

"Spread out," the queen instructed. "Check any shimmers that have appeared in the dimness of the day."

Gavin, Gronek, and Smakal took one side of the barren trail while she and Sacqueal took the other. Her sons ran this way and that, checking for shining portals. Hesed turned with her hairy guard following and ducked through the brush into the larger trees on the other side.

Immediately, they spotted a shimmer in the distance. It hung in a clearing of the trees well back from the main human trail. Large trees ringed the opening: oaks, maples, sweet gums. Sacqueal ran ahead and peeked through. He looked back and shook his massive hairy head. They weren't there. She glanced inside as she passed. An older human couple sat on a sofa together, holding hands and watching the floating images on a rectangular screen. *Human technology is amazing. May the Mighty One prevent it from ending us all.*

They kept moving and soon discovered another trail that led back to a shimmer in another clearing of the trees. This ring of trees included the same varieties as before but added one very large sycamore. Again, Sacqueal ran ahead and peered inside.

"Argh," he bellowed and urged Hesed to approach.

"Have you found them?" Hesed asked her large protector.

"Argh," he answered with a nod. He pointed for her to look through the shimmer.

What she saw through the dimensional window shot terror to her heart. Nozomi sat in a chair. She could barely see the girl because a large human stood between them with his back to the shimmer. He was waving a large blade.

"You are already here," a voice said from behind. Hesed recognized the voice of her friend, Tomo. "He has her inside. We must help her."

"Yes, my friend," Hesed said with a slight quiver in her voice, "but, the man is not alone. Look."

Tomo peered through the shimmer, and the same terror struck his own heart. Hope sat in a chair facing a large man with a knife, but a darkness was also there. The dark, billowing form of the specter floated around the ceiling inside the room. As they watched, it came down and enveloped the man. The undulating darkness began to move as the man moved. It went from fingertip to fingertip and from the man's toes to the top of his head. An orb of darkness surrounded his large head.

"Nozomi's father is only a puppet of the darkness, now," Hesed explained. "He is not simply being influenced. He is being controlled. We need my sons. Sacqueal, call them quickly!"

Sacqueal bellowed, "Arrrrrrrghhhh."

Inside, the specter paused its billowing. The man within the darkness froze in place for a moment before glancing back toward the mirror. Then, he turned his whole body to face his reflection. Hesed could see the man's eyes and his twisted grin, but she could also see the two red dots, the specter's eyes. They were floating in alignment with the man's pupils. The man said something. She could not hear the words, but she could read his lips.

"*Oh, we have an audience, now. I hope you enjoy the show.*"

***

Rick sat in his cruiser in the parking lot of the Notch Inn. The standoff was in competent hands with Sheriff Downey. Now, he needed to figure out what to do about Hope's abduction. He counted off the factors in his head. *One, the main roads were covered in the neighboring counties. Two, deputies were patrolling for that green car. Three, the perp could have gone off into the forest.* The last thought frustrated Rick. *They could be anywhere in this ever-loving forest.*

"I'll start with Maggie," he said aloud. "Maybe she'll give me some detail that'll point me in the right direction." Rick pulled out onto 257, headed toward the turn at Robbins Creek Road. He flicked on his flashing lights but didn't use the siren. *Where is everyone?* The previously busy roads were now oddly empty. *Probably the weather drove them inside.* The sun had vanished. *Typical Indiana weather. Wait ten minutes and it'll change.*

Rick started racing to Maggie's place but reconsidered. *I may as well look around as I go.* Instead, he cruised his way through the little community. He scanned the various structures, little houses on his left and the huge, old stately mansions on his right, focusing on the area between the houses, the area around, and the area behind the trees. Rick went past Floyd's Carwash, the old series of concrete walls with hoses where folks did their own spray downs. The place was useless now. Defunct. Still, it might make a good place to hide. Rick looked it over good as he went by. Nothing. The big old houses on the right were much harder to see.

About a hundred yards from the intersection, Rick was considering passing on through to check out the old, vacant school building when suddenly a shadow passed over his car. *That's not a shadow. That's that same crazy crow.* It soared directly up the road in front of him and then did a complete one-eighty and flew low over the top of his cruiser. Within seconds, it repeated the cycle.

Rick's mind shot back to Danny and then to what Gator told him: "*He was mumbling about a silo and about a big black crow that helped him get out. I don't know what to make of it. Probably hallucinations.*" He realized that he'd been seeing that crow all day. As he'd stood in the silo and looked up, there it was. It squawked at him in the forest and followed him down that road to the mine. It was above him when Mabel took her pot shots. He couldn't ignore it any longer.

Rick slammed on the brakes and came to a dead stop in the middle of the road. The crow repeated the same path twice more, directly in line with the road. *That crow's trying to get my attention. Is that why it's been dogging me?*

"I must be off my rocker," he mumbled as he turned his car

around. "But I'm gonna follow that bird." This time the crow didn't reverse course. Now that Rick was pointed where it apparently wanted him to go, it continued straight up the road. Rick followed.

They didn't go far before it made a low left turn into a driveway, which led back to the old burned-out house. He turned in and watched the bird soar along the drive's winding course ahead as it wound around to the right of the sad, charred place. Rick ducked his head so he could look up through the trees toward the top of the house. *Must have been something in its day.*

He slowed his cruiser to a crawl. It made sense. It was a secluded spot and was obviously empty. A good place to hide out.

Rick flicked off his lightbar and followed the driveway around a bend through the trees, then lowered his window to listen. Tires crunched on the gravel.

When he reached the point where the driveway angled back around the side of the house, the back of the green Gran Torino came into view. Braking, he grabbed his radio. "Unit One to base," he said. "Judy, respond."

"*This is base.*"

"Judy, I need every available unit to that burned-out house. I've got the car."

"*What's the address?*" she replied.

"I don't know the freaking number," he said with a bit too much bite. "It's that burned-out place on the main drag, on 257 in town."

"*Oh, the Brecker place. Got it. I'll get 'em moving your way.*"

"Roger that, and Judy, I'm sorry I bit your head off."

"*No worries, Sheriff. You've sorta got your hands full today.*"

Sorta. Rick hadn't taken his eyes off the house as he radioed in. He looked to the left, scanned the upstairs windows with their smoke-blackened frames, and then turned his attention to the ground level. As his eyes moved across, they landed on a man with long, dark hair ducking around the back of the house. "Hey—" he said. *I could have sworn that guy had on buckskin.*

Rick shut off the engine and exited the cruiser. Moving from tree to tree, he approached the house, skirted the side of the burned structure, and looked through the blackened windows that weren't boarded up. Some were broken, but he still couldn't see anything useful. He kept glancing behind him, mindful that whoever that long-haired man was, he could be looping around.

A light glowed through a rear, side window.

Carefully, slowly, he approached. He heard a man's voice. When he reached the still-intact glass of the lighted window and peered inside, his heart went cold. Hope, sitting in a chair, duct tape hung in ribbons off her arms, around her chest, and off her feet. Kenny Burton stood in front of her, facing away. He was looking directly into a huge mirror, speaking into it. "Enjoy the show," he heard him say.

Adrenaline shot through Rick. He turned his back against the wall and sank down into a crouch. *Oh, my God*, he silently prayed. *Please help me save her.*

Reaching to his collar, he clicked his radio. "I've got the subject in sight. He is in the back, right corner room of the burned-out Brecker place, ground level. He's holding Hope Spencer hostage. She's in imminent danger. Approach with caution as there may be an accomplice on foot outside. I can't wait. I'm going in."

Rick took a deep breath before hurrying around to the back of the house, pulling his weapon as he went. He raced to the back door and kicked it in.

Sixteen

"Why do I hate you?" Kenny replied as he considered the gleaming blade of his large hunting knife. He was still standing by the lantern he'd just lit near the kitchen sink. "You want to know why? That is an interesting question." Turning away from the sink, he faced her and brought the blade down, sliding the point carefully across Hope's upper lip. Without the voice in his head, though, he refused to make eye contact.

Hope jerked back and tensed, her eyes saucers of fright. Where was the thing in his head? He figured it would be soaking up her terror like gravy on a piece of biscuit. Instead, it had abandoned him once again, while it went off and did whatever it was it did when it was gone.

"The truth is, I don't hate you," Kenny said, "and I don't blame you, either. Not really."

"You don't blame me?" Hope blurted. "You killed my dog. You beat up my mom. You even tried to kill me. Maybe you still will. But, somehow, in this whole thing, you don't blame me? You don't blame me for what, exactly?"

"Your mother ruined my life. You're just an unintended consequence…sorta collateral damage, I guess."

"My mother loved you! She was devoted to you."

"No." He lowered his head and turned away. "She cheated on me. She had other men, other lovers."

"That's just stupid. She didn't have the time or the energy to cheat on you. She was either with me, cleaning the house, washing our clothes, or babysitting to earn extra money."

Deep inside his soul, the residual piece of conscience that hung on inside Kenny was desperate. That piece of himself was trying to claw his way back to the top, to make himself really think.

"No, no, no," Kenny countered. "I'm sure. She was cheating."

"How would you know? You were never around. You were either working or drinking. When you were around, you were drunk."

"I was told. I was told about her having other guys."

"Who told you? How would they know?"

Kenny couldn't answer that question. It had been that voice in his head. *It* didn't have a name. Instead, he changed course.

"She'd cheated when she had you. You aren't even my daughter. I thought you were, but now, I know you aren't. You're the result of someone else's seed."

***

Hope noticed he wouldn't look at her, not directly in the eyes. In fact, he looked anywhere *but* at her. She sensed he was feeling a touch of doubt, despite his words. Somehow, she had to get him to see her, to really see her. She had to convince him that he was working off a lie. "Daddy... Daddy, please look at me. Please, come over and look at me."

Slowly, Kenny raised his eyes. He hesitated as if he was afraid the view would burn his vision away. "I don't want to."

***

Inside, the remnant of conscience had fought against the alcoholic lube until it reached the pinnacle. It managed to grab Kenny's control wheel.

***

"Please, Daddy. Please look at me." As Kenny made eye contact, she added, "Do you remember that game we used to play when I'd sit on your lap? You'd pretend to steal my nose and I'd pretend to steal yours? Do you remember how people used to say that was silly because I already had your nose? Look at my eyes. Look at my hair. Look at my cheekbones. I'm a girl version of you. I'm even tall like you. If you'll just look, it's obvious."

Kenny did look, this time with unfiltered eyes. He saw her eyes. He saw her nose and her cheekbones. He saw it all, and he recognized himself in her face.

"I told mom just a little while ago that I still love you. I really did. And it's true, too. I do love you. Despite it all, I just can't help it. I love my daddy." Tears welled again in her eyes and slipped down across her cheeks.

All at once, Kenny's eyes opened wide. He knelt and sobbed against her knees. Using his knife, he sliced through the tape that bound Hope's feet. Then, he cut the bindings off her hands and her chest. "I'm so sorry," he said through spurts of emotion. "Oh, honey, I'm sorry." Tears welled and leaked from his eyes.

Her father was a broken man. She began pulling the tape off her wrists so she could wrap her arms around him.

***

"We've got to get you away from—"

Then his eyes changed.

Inside Kenny's head, his weak identity had briefly taken control. It had lasted only long enough for his mind to register the reality of the specter's lies and see his little girl for who she was— his daughter. Just as he had managed to free her, the evil force swept in and knocked his mind for a loop. That tiny, powerless voice was no more than a whispering breath beneath the booming, hyper-amplified sound of the specter.

His own mind shouted, "NO," over, and over again. His conscious and subconscious minds once again unified, Kenny felt like he was at the bottom of an oily steel cone. He tried to climb back to the top, but he couldn't get traction on the slippery slope of his own faculties. He had braced himself to keep from slipping out the bottom, but the alcohol prevented him from climbing back to the top.

"Little girl, you know what I'm going to do, right?" the thing inside Kenny said. *It* didn't wait for her to answer. "I'm going to get each of your friends, too. One by one. Then, I'm going to get your mother. I know what I'll do—" he emitted a high-pitched laugh. "I'll take them all back to that little shack by the quarry. I'll take them there and tie each of them to old chairs facing one another." He was enjoying the look on the little girl's face as he spoke. The fear was coming off her in waves. It was sweet like honey.

***

Hope didn't dare move, but whatever the thing inside her dad was, *it* didn't seem to notice that he had cut her bindings.

***

Slowly, the Kenny-puppet dragged the point of the knife around her face. Here and there, *it* jabbed a little as she tried to jerk away, just enough to puncture the skin. Little streaks of blood drizzled down around her chin like honey on a piece of toast.

"Then," he/*it* continued, "I'll make them watch each other as I slowly—"

The thing that was riding Kenny like a horse stopped in mid-sentence. *It* turned Kenny's head and looked at the mirror. *It*'d heard something. The specter was inhibited when *it* rode the human's form, but *it* could still see that the portal had been activated. Turning full around to face the glass, *it* could make out the shapes on the other side. Elves were watching. Terrified elves. *It* could taste their horror, like an appetizer. Delicious.

***

"Oh, we have an audience now," Kenny heard himself say. "I hope you enjoy the show."

***

The specter turned Kenny's body back to face the girl. *It* held the knife up in front of her face again. This time, though, the fear was gone from the girl's eyes. To *its* own horror, the fear had been replaced by something else. Determination.

It hated the taste of determination.

***

Hope watched as *it* manipulated her dad's body, playing with the large knife. She watched as *it* approached her and held the blade out to her face. Despite herself, she was terrified. The sparkle that she used to see in her dad's eyes had been replaced. The irises were pitch black now, but with just a hint of red in the middle.

Her mind was in full fight-or flight-mode, but it didn't lessen her fear. The determination to get away didn't lessen the pain each time he jabbed the point of the knife into her skin. The strategy she was developing didn't reduce the horror of watching the drool drip from her daddy's chin or the terror inside her as he described what he was going to do to her mother and her friends.

If he gave her an opening, she was going to take it. She might be able to escape if she could just get another chance. Maybe he would go on another errand and leave her alone one more time. *Maybe I can get away. Maybe I can still save myself. I only wish I could save my daddy, too.*

Like lightning flashes, her good times with her father shot through her mind. Riding on his shoulders, the times he tickled her until she couldn't breathe. Ice cream dripping down the cone and across her fingers while he laughed at her. Him pushing her on the swing or pulling her in her wagon. Giving her that bike with training wheels and holding her when she fell and skinned her knees. He'd kissed the tears away.

She loved her daddy despite all the pain. She loved him deeply. She loved him widely. She loved him completely. She loved him so much that it fed her determination like a spark to old newspaper. That determination flamed to life as that thing stopped in mid-sentence and turned her daddy's head as if *it* had heard something.

The dark being turned her daddy away from her. *It* was looking in the mirror, staring at *its* own reflection. *It* said something about an audience enjoying the show. Then, her daddy's rider turned him back to face her like a cowboy turns a stallion. *It* made a hideous grin. At that moment, Hope Spencer made a terrifying decision.

She would free her father—one way or another. To her new friends the elves, the mirror represented a doorway, but to her it was just a large pane of glass—fragile, sharp, and dangerous when broken.

"Get out of my daddy," Hope screamed as she drove herself headlong into her father's torso, catching him in the gut. She used all the strength in her athletic legs to drive herself forward. "You can't have him anymore," she bellowed.

Hope hit him hard. The knife flew from his right hand and stuck in the wall. The force of her impact knocked him back on his heels and he lost his balance. Her daddy's hands flailed in the air for something to grab. He fell back as if in slow motion.

As they fell, the kitchen door crashed open.

They hit the glass of the giant mirror as if diving into a still pond of water. Just as a pond swallows a tossed rock, the mirror swallowed Hope and Kenny. The reflections of the room even rippled as they disappeared into the solid surface of the glass. They were gone.

***

The back door broke from its latch and flew open. Rick with gun drawn, raced inside. He stood in an empty room. A chair with strips of duct tape attached was spinning on the floor. A knife was quivering in the wall above a kitchen table. Two lanterns illuminated the whole scene, giving it an eerie feel.

"Where'd they go?" he exclaimed.

He ran from the kitchen into the front room. There was no sign of them. Other vehicles were arriving, doors slammed, and footsteps approached.

Quickly, he returned to the kitchen. He considered the knife and the chair. He glanced at the footprints in the char and soot on the floor. Then, he studied the large, over-sized mirror, and in an instant, he knew where they went. He just didn't know if that was a good thing or a bad thing.

Rick also didn't know how he was going to explain it.

***

Josh's body was locked in a coma, but his soul continued to sit in the sand, surf washing over his feet. The superheroes were playing frisbee in the waves. Beside him, the Hulk had finished his hotdogs. A dribble of ketchup stained his huge green chin. The boy leaned back on his hands and gripped the sand with his fingers. The sun had angled into the western horizon.

"You know," said the Hulk, "you can stay here until the sun dips to the sea, but then you'll need to make a decision."

Josh frowned at the giant hero. "What kind of decision?"

"Which way to go," Bruce Banner's alter ego replied. Then he pointed one massive green finger up the beach before reversing and pointing it the other way. "You can go there…or you can go there."

When Josh looked up the beach, he saw a shimmering light. It was not unlike the shimmers he had seen when he was with his elfin friends in their world, but this one was more like a crack than a window. The light slipping through the crack was so brilliant it almost blinded him.

The view down the beach was different. The sand just went on and on and on. There was no apparent destination.

"What's the difference?" he asked the Hulk. "Is one better than the other?"

"The difference? Hmm." The Hulk contemplated that for a few moments. "Well, if you go up the beach and into that crack, then you will experience joy and peace and eternal rest. But, if you go down the beach, no one knows what's down there. You'll face only the uncertainty of life."

Rest and peace and joy sounded good to Josh.

MICHAEL DECAMP

Seventeen

As soon as they heard Sacqueal's bellow, Gavin, Gronek, and Smakal came running. They approached their mother's position in front of a large shimmer.

"Have you found them, Mother?" Smakal asked. He had barely spoken the words when a tangle of arms, legs, and torsos came plunging through the shiny portal, landing on the leaf-strewn grass at their feet.

"Keep back," Queen Hesed ordered. "No one touch them." She used both hands, her six fingers on each spread wide, motioning everyone to stand clear.

Sacqueal grunted, pawing the ground, growling at the fray.

Tomo leaned in, obviously struggling against a desire to act.

"Shouldn't we try to help her?" Gavin pleaded.

Hesed didn't immediately respond. Rather, she stood still, a look of amazement adorning her green-tinted face. "Remarkable," she finally said. "It appears that instinct has driven Nozomi to discern what I had not yet been able to explain."

"What do you mean, Mother?" Gronek asked, his body shaking as his eyes darted from his mother to the battle in front of him. "He is so much larger. We should help her."

"No," Hesed answered, sharply. "No, no, no. This is Nozomi's battle. If she is to truly win, she must win on her own. Watch and learn. See how the power of light and the power of dark struggle against one another."

Hope's father was twice the girl's size. In the normal human realm, he could have easily knocked her off himself with one massive blow to her head or a punch to the side of her gut, but, in the semi-spiritual realm of the trees and the elves, his arms and legs were flailing about, kicking and hitting against the earth and the air. It seemed that the specter was acting out of desperation, forgetting the physical advantage of Kenny's powerful body.

Hope, for her part, wrapped around her father like a button-down shirt put on backward. Her arms clinched around his neck, and her legs encircled his waist. She held him tight, her eyes squeezed shut and her teeth clenched with the effort to hold on.

"Get out of my daddy," she screamed. "Get out of him. You can't have him."

"He is mine," the specter bellowed. "I claimed him, and I will hold him."

"No, Get out of him now."

The dark entity was clearly visible in the Arboreal Realm as it billowed around Kenny Burton. Waves of darkness surged down Kenny's arms and legs, and a black fibrous sphere enveloped the man's face. Even as Kenny's human arms and legs beat against the ground and the air, the darkness extended from those extremities and slammed themselves against the aura of the girl.

For her part, Hope's aura had bloomed into such a bright glow that those watching could hardly maintain a view. The light only grew in intensity with each dark strike from the evil presence. Daggers of light shot from her eyes and blades of light extended from her arms and feet as the two struggled in the leaves.

"How is she doing that?" Tomo finally asked. "Where is that power coming from?"

Queen Hesed answered with only one word, "Love."

***

"They were here, but they're gone now," Anders told Deputy Jerry Steinkamp, outside the burned-out house's back door. Steinkamp had rushed to the scene based on Rick's earlier radio call. "Search the grounds. They couldn't have gotten far. His car is still here."

As crazy as it seemed, Rick was certain of where they had gone, but there was no way to explain it in a way that wouldn't make him look completely devoid of rational thought. No sane person would believe that they had somehow crossed over to another dimension through a portal that appeared in a mirror. *I'd be locked up in an institution.*

Other cruisers and official vehicles were arriving. Rick's deputy turned away and headed off to pass along the sheriff's instructions.

As he stood there, a small whirlwind seemed to come from nowhere and began to blow the downed leaves nearby. He couldn't feel the breeze, but he could see it. It picked up the fallen foliage and shifted it back and forth. Leaves skittered around as if they were in a mini maelstrom in the backyard.

How am I going to explain this to Maggie? Rick was a professional. He was fully trained and experienced. He had all the resources of the local, state, and federal law enforcement agencies to draw upon. Still, if they had really gone where he believed they had, there was nothing he could do. There was no way to investigate. He didn't even have a clue how the portals worked. *We may never see Hope again.*

"Where are they, Rick?"

Anders looked up to see Maggie approaching. She must have tagged along with Steinkamp. She looked haggard. Her eyes were swollen. One was badly bruised. Her lower lip was split and swollen. She wore sweatpants and a ragged flannel shirt. A pair of slip-on leather casual shoes covered her feet. Not a touch of makeup adorned her face. To Rick, she was a beautiful, yet fearful sight to behold. *I don't know how to do this. I don't know what to say.*

"Jerry told me to stay in the car, but I couldn't do it. Is she here?"

He was going to have to tell her. He was going to have to tell her now. He took her hands and gazed into her eyes.

"What is it?" she asked. "Where is she?"

"Come inside," he said. "I have something to show you."

***

Maggie's anxiety continued to rise as she followed Rick through the backdoor into the kitchen of the large, old house. Her hands were quivering. The acrid odor invaded her nose. Rick stepped through and leaned against the soiled counter on the far side of the room. He looked stricken. She read fear on his face.

"What's happened, Rick? Tell me."

He didn't reply at first but motioned for her to look around. "I saw them through that window," he eventually said as he pointed. "I saw her lunge at him, so I ran to the back door and kicked it in, but when I got in here...only seconds later...well...this is all I found."

She spotted the chair with pieces of duct tape stuck to the back and each of the legs. She saw the lanterns, one on the table and one on the counter that were still ablaze. A knife was sticking in the wall above the table. Finally, her eyes landed on the huge mirror. She walked over and placed her fingertips against the glass. She simply touched her own reflection. It was as solid as any mirror ever was.

"Do you think—" she stammered. "Have they both gone through?"

"I think so," Rick replied. "I can't see any other way. It was too quick. I was in here in seconds. I mean literally seconds."

Tears welled up in her already swollen eyes. She began to tremble. Her curly black hair hung limply around her face as she lowered her gaze to the floor.

Rick came to her, pulling her into his chest and wrapping his arms fully around her. The warmth of his body struggled to overcome the cold fear that had gripped her heart. Slowly, hesitantly, she returned his embrace.

"What do I do now, Rick? Is my Hope gone?" Tears brimmed in her stricken eyes. "Will she be back?"

They both turned together and stared at the mirror. The light of the lantern on the table flickered off the glass. The world, which had been rushing by at breakneck speed all day, suddenly slowed to a crawl. There was absolutely nothing they could do. Nothing.

"I used to pray," Rick broke the helpless silence. "When things seemed out of control, I'd pray. Do you pray, Maggie?"

***

When Hope took that dive into her father's torso, it was a last-ditch effort. The force driving her dad was that evil entity that had haunted Josh and influenced the Hicks. She didn't know what else to do, but she fully expected the glass of that massive mirror to shatter. Maybe, just maybe, one of those large shards of glass might injure him enough for her to escape. On top of that, if her father were significantly injured, maybe that thing would leave him, or maybe she could get him some real help. The last thing she expected was for the two of them to fall through and land with a thump on the ground outside—on the other side.

Once through, she could see darkness swirling around him. Her father's face was inside a black bubble. The ebony cloud extended down his flailing arms, and the red dots of the specter's eyes floated over her dad's face. He had no aura. She wrapped her arms around his neck and her legs around his waist. *It* was screaming at her, and she matched its screams right back.

"Get out of him," she shrieked. "You can't have him."

"He is mine," the spirit bellowed in return. "I will not let him go."

Hope sensed that others were nearby, but she dared not let up for even a second. Instincts told her to keep driving, keep pushing.

Her mind was flooded with negative thoughts. *You can't do this. You don't have the strength. You are weak. You will be swallowed up by the same darkness that has your father. It will take you, too. It is larger than you. It is stronger than you. It will kill you and eat your soul.* The thoughts were in her head, but they were not her own. She pushed back. *I am strong enough. I love my dad and you can't have him. I will not let go and I will not stop until you leave him. I love him.*

"You love him?" The dark power laughed. "Love is nothing but the candy of the weak," *it* lied. "Besides, he doesn't love you. Not anymore." The specter extended black clouds of hatred into the air and brought them down upon Hope's back in repeated blows.

"I love him despite it all," Hope answered. "I will always love him. I love him. I love him. I LOVE HIM!"

She felt the mental attack again. *He doesn't love you. He killed your dog. Remember? He tried to kill you. He beat your mother. HE HATES YOU!*

"It was you that killed my dog," Hope screamed, "and you're a liar." She redoubled her efforts, squeezing her father's neck with her arms, driving her cheek into the side of his face. She tightened her legs around his torso, driving her knees tightly into his side. "I love him, anyway. I LOVE HIM."

Hope suddenly realized she was holding her own. The specter was flailing at her, but her dad's arms and legs were just flopping around. The dark blows were not accompanied by any physical strikes. This battle was coming down to a struggle of wills—her will to love her father against the specter's power of hate. From somewhere, a voice said, "Love never fails."

"I will keep him," the darkness shouted. "I will hold him. I will use him. I will bend him to my will. He is mine."

Hope ignored the specter's words. She recognized them for what they were—empty lies. Instead, she continued to repeat one thought, over and over. "I. LOVE. HIM."

***

"Love?" the three brother elves replied to their mother in unison.

"Her power is from love?" Gronek asked.

The brothers were terrified for their friend. The specter itself could not hurt Hope, but if it broke down her defenses, the human man that it controlled could easily kill her.

"Is love really enough?" asked Gavin.

Queen Hesed herself was distressed, but she'd witnessed the power of pure love in the past, long ago. If the girl did not falter, the spirit would have no choice but to relent. If *it* could not break Nozomi's will, *it* would be forced away. "The darkness of hate cannot stand within the bright light of love," she said. "They cannot coexist. If Nozomi does not give in to the specter's attacks, she will prevail."

"What if she falters?" Tomo asked. "What then?"

Hesed did not reply. Instead, she turned her voice in support of the young, human girl. "Love him, Nozomi. Love him well. Love never fails!"

"I. LOVE. HIM," Hope enunciated each word.

The specter roared in response, and as he did, Kenny Burton's arms and legs found purchase on the ground and shoved his massive body upward. He spun over, reversed positions with Hope and pinned her beneath his huge frame. The dark form of the specter combined with the human body of Kenny Burton covered the girl, concealing her bright light of life. Only tiny shafts of light shot out from under the large man like flashlights from a cave.

Hesed fell to her knees. Sacqueal called out a mournful howl. Tomo pulled a knife from his belt. Gavin, Gronek, and Smakal held one another.

"Please, Nozomi, fight back. Do not give in to the hate. Love him!" Hesed cried. "Love him back to you."

"It is too much for her, my queen," Tomo exclaimed. "I will force the man off her." He raised his blade and surged forward.

***

Struggling with the dark entity, Hope felt her body suddenly rise into the air. Even as she felt her father lift her, she redoubled her grip on his neck and his waist, driving her face harder against his. Hope clung to him with every twist and turn, and then she plunged to the ground. He was on top of her now, the weight of his torso pressing against her own. She could barely breathe.

Thoughts of doubt and despair were again flooding her mind. *You have lost. You will suffocate. You have no chance. He will kill you. Can you feel your lungs beginning to burn?*

"I will not stop," she forced the words from taut lips. "I...love...him..."

Even as she said the words, the air leaked from her lungs. She couldn't inhale to replace it. Her lungs burned and her face began to tingle. She loosened her grip on his neck, pummeling Kenny's back. It was like punching a sandbag.

***

Deep down inside, what was left of the conscious Kenny Burton, combined with his residual conscience, watched the thing that sat up high and in control. From his hiding place in the corner, he could see what was going on. And he could hear all the terrible things the specter used his own lips to say. He could hear the responses from Hope. He saw her bright light fighting against the darkness that enveloped him. Through it all, his essence cowered in that corner at the base of the alcohol-slickened cone on which the dark spirit sat.

Kenny's remnant peered around. He studied the cone. Spots appeared where the alcohol had begun to evaporate. It had been a while since that last beer. The surface was not as slick as it had been. Still, he had tried to regain control before only to be knocked back into submission. There was no longer any reason to fight. To struggle against the darkness no longer served any purpose. *Maybe one day it will get tired of me and just leave.* All that was left of Kenny's essence, his conscience, hoped that was true. It would be his only chance, his only hope to live his own life again.

"I love him," he heard Hope shout. "Get out of him."

She still loves me? He could feel the truth of it. *Despite all I've done, she still loves me.*

That realization caused Kenny's essence to flare up yet one

more time. He watched the dark force above him. All its attention was focused on fighting the girl. The remnant piece of Kenny looked at the cone. The surface was nearly dry. *Do I dare?* Then he felt his body rise and twist.

"Ha," the specter shouted. "Now, I've got you. Give it up, girl. You cannot fight me. Your strength is gone. You will suffocate. Even now, your breath fades."

She still loves me, the residual Kenny thought again. *She loves me and he is going to kill her.*

It was then that Kenny felt something he had not felt in a long, long time—two things he'd forgotten about. The first was something that his grandmother called "righteous indignation." He'd been angry several times, but it had been a long time since he'd been angry because something wrong was being done to someone else. That white-hot anger was even more stoked because it was his own body doing the deed. The second thing he felt for the first time in a long time was love—love for someone else.

"I...love...him..." Hope choked out.

The residual essence of Kenny Burton charged the side of the cone and slammed into the back of the specter, knocking it off to one side. For a few seconds, Kenny took direct control of himself again. He used his physical arms to push up from the dirt, lifting the pressure off his daughter's chest. "I love her," he yelled at the dark thing. "And I won't let you do this."

The specter wailed at his loss of control. Immediately, it began to push against Kenny, shoving him, driving him back to his corner. Kenny was slipping, but he hung on this time. He fought back.

"I LOVE HER," Kenny screamed at it. "Get out now!"

***

Hope's mind was beginning to fade from lack of oxygen. Tingling took over her limbs and stars swirled in her eyes. She struggled to pull in air. Physically, her muscles weren't strong enough to overcome the weight of her father's body. Consciousness was slipping away, so she pushed one more time with her mind: *I love him. I will always love him. You can't keep him. Get. Out.*

All at once, the pressure on her chest released. She sucked in a huge gulp of air, and power resurged through her system. The tingles dissipated and the stars disappeared. "I. LOVE. HIM." She screamed one more time. "Get out."

***

Tomo was about to drive his knife into Kenny's back. He stepped forward and raised the blade high with both hands. Sacqueal was bellowing. All the elves, Hesed included, were crying out in fear. Just as the blade began its descent, something stopped him. He froze mid-strike.

Astonished, he watched Kenny Burton drive himself up with his arms and call out, "I love her! I won't let you do this."

Even as Kenny spoke, shafts of bright, white light replaced the darkness of his eyes. Similar shafts of light shot from the big man's ears, nostrils, and mouth.

"I love her! Get out of me now," the man shouted.

"I love him. Get out of him," Hope screamed simultaneously.

The group around the pair stood dumbfounded. As words of love echoed through the forest, a white-bright bloom of light emerged from beneath Kenny's body and surrounded the dark shape of the specter. It formed a bubble that encased the spirit. As it did, the shafts of light from Kenny's eyes sharpened into blades and began to cut at the dark bubble that was swirling around his face.

The specter wailed in its defeat.

Quickly, the bright bubble squeezed in on the darkness. Tighter, tighter, tighter. At the same time, the light from Kenny sliced at the compressing darkness.

"Ahh," *it* screamed, slowly releasing its grip on Kenny's mind and withdrawing its hold on his body.

"Look," Hesed exclaimed. "It has surrendered the man."

The brightness continued to condense the dark presence into a tiny orb not much larger than a green-hulled walnut. Kenny rose to his knees and looked at the small, black ball encircled in the bright, see-through cover. It looked like a transparent baseball. He grabbed it in his right hand and flung it with all his might into the trees. Propelled by Kenny's strong arm, it flew on a line toward the giant sycamore, a crack opened in the trunk to accept it. The specter was swallowed up. It was gone.

Kenny fell over on the ground beside his daughter. Their eyes locked, and they smiled at one another.

"I love you, Pumpkin Pie," Kenny said.

Hope smiled and rested her hand on his. "I love you, too, Dad."

The audience looked on, frozen in place.

Finally, Queen Hesed broke the silence. "There you have it. Love wins again—" She took a breath before finishing. "And, Nozomi has prevailed."

Eighteen

Josh continued to sit in the sand and watch the waves. One by one, the superheroes came over to say goodbye before going on their way. The last one to leave was Aquaman, who surged out of the water and gave a hearty wave before splashing back and zipping away. That only left Ironman sitting next to him. They both were letting the surf wash up over their feet.

"Are you gonna rust?" Josh asked. "If you do, you'll be just like the Tin Man."

"The suit is not actually iron—" the hero began to explain. "It's actually... Hey, there's a Tin Man? I don't know him. Sounds kinda weak."

Josh laughed. "Don't worry. That's a whole different kinda story."

They both leaned back on their elbows. The sun was hanging just above the horizon. *Funny that the tide hasn't changed. I guess not all the rules are the same here.*

"It's almost time for your decision," Tony Stark pointed out through his retracted mask. "The sun is almost down. What are you thinking?"

Josh didn't answer right away. He knew the implications of the decision. He knew that this beach and the heroes were all in his mind, figments of his imagination, but he also knew that the decision was real. He glanced to his left. The crack was still there. A bright light shone through and sparkled off the sand nearby. He looked to the right, but all he saw was endless beach. He didn't know where it went, and that was the point. Life is uncertain.

"Do you want to take a closer look?" the metallic hero asked. "You can get up now."

Josh wiggled his feet. His legs were free to move, so he stood.

The wet sand squeezed up between his toes. A light ocean breeze blew from his left, from the direction of the crack. Such a pleasant breeze. "Sure," he finally answered. "It doesn't hurt to look."

Ironman jumped to his feet. "I'll walk with you."

"Are you sure you won't rust?"

"I'm sure."

They ambled up the beach, wandering in and out of the surf until they stood right before the crack. It hung low in the air at eye level with no visible support, just like the shimmers in the dimension of the Elves. Josh leaned to his left to look behind it. Nothing there but more beach.

The crack itself was about as tall as Josh and wide enough for him to turn sideways and slip through to whatever was on the other side. He looked intently at the light but could see nothing but a few shadows moving around. Somehow, though, it felt warm and pleasant and safe. It was pulling at him, drawing him nearer.

"Can I look inside?" he asked his companion.

"No, Josh. I'm sorry. You can't. It's either all in or all out. You have to choose."

"Will I see people I know?"

"Probably."

"Will that thing leave me alone—that specter thing?"

"You will never have to worry about it again. Ever."

The boy turned around and looked the other way down the endless beach. The specter waited for him somewhere in that direction. He knew that for sure. He just didn't know where or when. As he stood there facing the uncertain course, the breeze shifted and began to blow into his face, as if a vacuum were sucking the air toward the crack behind him. He took a step back and felt the pull of the warmth and comfort drawing him inside.

"It's okay," Ironman said. "Either choice is allowed."

Josh closed his eyes, took a deep breath, and leaned back toward the bright light, enjoying the warmth on his shoulders.

***

Clem Downey was true to his word. He didn't wait long to fire a couple of tear gas cannisters into the mouth of the mine. He'd called out several times with no response. No more shots were fired at his position. The girl who was bound to the machine was drooping against her bindings. About twenty minutes after Rick left, Clem sent the noxious gas flying, but no one came out.

Two deputies wearing gas masks slipped in from the right side of the gaping hole. A couple of minutes later, they radioed that the mine was vacant. Mabel and her crew were nowhere to be found.

"Okay, boys," he said to Gator and Calvin, "Climb down there and pull that girl off that machine. Get her some help. Once that's done, join my guys inside. See if you can figure out where they went."

"Roger that," Gator replied.

"Yup," Calvin added.

Clem turned his back on the mine and faced the cages along the bluff. They hadn't yet located Mabel and her twisted family of miners, but it seemed the immediate danger had passed. He fingered his mic. "Deputy Blaine, you still at the motel?"

"Yessir, Sheriff."

"Are there any medics up there?"

"Yessir."

"Send 'em down that mine road. We've got some captives down here who're going to need some help."

He glanced back at the mine. Gator was using his knife to cut the bindings loose on the girl. She slumped against him, putting her arms around his neck. "People are nuts," he mumbled to himself, shaking his head. "Just freaking nuts."

The sun popped through the clouds and briefly brightened the day. Clem studied the clouds as they were moving briskly across the sky. One lone crow was soaring in circles high above. He removed his hat and rubbed the sweat off his brow before heading to the nearest cage to rescue the men behind the locked steel gates.

As Downey approached the first cage, he saw a man standing there with his fingers gripping the chain-link. The man looked healthy enough. He was dressed and standing strong with the breeze fluttering his thin hair. Clem could hear coughing coming from further along, but this guy looked like he was fresh meat.

"Clem," the man said. "Is that you?"

Downey took a closer look.

"Al? How'd you end up down here?"

The caged man rubbed his face. "I'm not sure. I went to bed last night in my room at the Notch Inn and I woke up here. I don't even know where *here* is."

"Well, I've gotta tell you," Sheriff Downey said, "the last thing I expected was to find one of my cousins locked up down here."

"Can you get me out of this cage? Please?"

"Sure, sure." Clem peered up the line. A medic was using a pair of bolt cutters at the first gate. "I'll be right back. I'm gonna go get those cutters and get you right outta there."

"Clem, where am I exactly?"

"The Robbins Stone mine site. Looks like you were about to become an unwilling part of their labor force." Clem hurried away to retrieve the bolt cutters.

A few minutes later, after helping the medic load Russell Bray on a gurney, he came back. He carefully placed the jaws of the tool on the loop of the gate's padlock. "Al, I haven't seen you in years. What are you up to these days?"

"I'm a drug rep," he replied. "I'm divorced, but I live over in the St. Louis area near my family. I don't get back here much." He bounced back and forth on the balls of his feet. "I was just here wrapping up some family business."

"Gotcha," Clem said. The jaws contracted and the loop snapped. The lock fell free of the gate, landing in the dirt near Clem's boots.

Moving quickly, Al Havener flipped the gate latch and swung it open. "It's good to see you, but I really need to get outta this cage. Which way do I go?"

"Just follow the trail and then walk up the road," the neighboring county's sheriff answered, pointing. "There'll be some folks up there who can give you a hand. One of my deputies will take your statement. We'll need a play-by-play of what happened to you. Good to see you, too, by the way. Don't be so scarce."

Al stopped and looked back at his cousin. "Oh, don't you worry," he replied. "I'll be around." He smiled, turned, and walked away.

***

Inside the mine, Calvin Churchill found a master switch that turned on all the lights. When he flipped it, the world of the underground mine lit up like a massively oversized basement. In one direction sat large flatbed trailers with slabs stacked on top. In another direction a strange machine sat next to a stone wall—some sort of stone slab cutter, he imagined. In a room adjacent, he found a collection of cars, vans, pickups, and SUVs lined up along a wall. But there was an open slot with tire tracks leading away.

He grabbed the attention of one of Clem's deputies, and together they followed the tire tracks in the dirt floor, taking them deeper into the mine, around a corner, and up a steep incline. There were no overhead lights along the way, so the men used their flashlights as they climbed the slope. After a couple more turns, daylight appeared way up the hill ahead of them. Eventually, the tracks led them through an open steel gate and onto a dirt road at the very top of the Cutters Notch bluff. They'd found the mine's back door.

Mabel, her son, and her crew were long gone.

***

Trick was watching all the activity in the parking lot through the large, plate-glass window in the motel lobby. His father sat wrapped in a blanket behind him on a sofa. His mother was doting on his dad, as a female deputy sat nearby, asking questions and taking notes. His father was constantly interrupting with violent coughing fits.

For his part, Trick was watching for them to bring his sister up from the mine. He'd been told that she was okay, that they had freed her, and that she'd be transported up the road soon. He paced in front of the window. Trick wanted more than anything for his family to be reunited. That night back in June was the last time they'd all been together.

The parking lot was active with ambulances and medics. Mixed in were the police vehicles—mostly county, but some state police, too. On the outer fringe, a line of yellow tape stretched out as a barrier. A lot of people stood gawking behind the tape. Most looked like regular people, but a few had notepads or cameras. Behind the trees a news crew was setting up along the highway.

Trick watched as one, lone, middle-aged, slightly balding man meandered up from the mine road and made his way calmly through the melee. He slipped around and between the cruisers, through the ambulances, and approached the yellow tape.

The man, about his parents' age, ducked under the yellow tape and passed through the crowd, unhindered. For some reason, the man's bald head caught Trick's eye. He followed the bobbing head's progress until it dipped out of sight behind a car.

***

Al Havener climbed into the driver's seat of the Chevy Impala that someone had left running along the road. He adjusted the seat and the mirrors, then picked up and flipped through the wallet he found in the console. Al put the car into drive and pulled away. In the rear-view mirror, he laughed at the man who darted into the street. Apparently, he saw his car drive off.

The man jumped up and down, but no one paid him any mind. With as many messes going on in Cutters Notch at the same time, one missing car was not high on the priority list. By the time someone finally listened to the man, Al Havener knew he would be in Illinois, headed west.

***

Rick Anders once again left Jerry Steinkamp in charge of a scene. This time Jerry was left to handle the search around the burned-out house while Rick drove Maggie home. He wasn't sure what to do after that. The Gillis and Flannery women were both at the hospital in Bloomington with their boys. *Maybe Maggie will let me call her folks.* One thing he did know for sure was that he simply couldn't leave her alone.

Maggie sat close to him, silent and shivering. Tears streaked her already swollen face. Her left hand clutched onto his right arm.

When they arrived at her house, she didn't immediately jump out, so Rick sat there with her, letting her talk first. He peered down at the hand holding his arm. Nails cherry red, recently manicured and beautifully shaped. Maggie leaned her head onto his shoulder.

"I feel so helpless," she choked out between sobs.

Rick shifted and put his arm around her, pulling her tight to his chest. "I understand," he whispered.

Maggie pulled back and looked at him. "There has to be something we can do." Her plaintive eyes begged him for some solution. "Do you really believe there's some other dimension and that's where they went? Really?"

Rick didn't know what to believe. He saw Hope launch herself into Kenny. And within seconds, they'd disappeared into thin air. It seemed crazy, but the only thing he could figure was that they crossed into the mirror. "Maggie," he replied, "I don't know what to believe. I saw one of those things hanging out of your living room mirror a couple of nights ago. And Hope and the boys claim to have been on the other side. They say they're friendly. Maybe we can send some sort of message to them."

"What? How?"

"I don't know, but the kids say they watch us through the mirrors. Maybe we can watch back. Maybe we can make it clear that we need to reach them." He shrugged. "Something." Rick paused. "Come on. Let's go inside. Let me make you some tea, or maybe some coffee?"

Maggie nodded and started to climb out. Then she stopped and touched Rick's arm. "Thank you." Her eyes welled up again. "You can't know what it means to have you with me right now."

Rick's own eyes began to tear. He leaned down and kissed her forehead. "I'll stay with you, Maggie. You can count on me." He slipped from her grasp and got out. Quickly, he circled the car and took Maggie's hand as she stepped onto the walk. Together, they went inside.

After leading her to the sofa, he went to the kitchen. It was a mess from the earlier fight, but after a little rummaging, Rick found the coffee and filters. Soon, he had the brew going. With that done, he sat down next to Maggie and stared at that mirror hanging on the wall. It was then that it occurred to him that the elves had sent him a written message on a tennis ball. *If they can write, then they can read.*

"Do you have a pen, notepad, and some adhesive tape?"

Once she retrieved the requested material, he started to scribble. Maggie was peeking over his shoulder and her breath tickled his neck. Rick liked it. He pushed that thought away.

"What are you going to do with that?" she asked.

"I'm going to tape it on the mirror." He showed it to her.

Elves, is Hope with you? Is she okay?
Please help us find her.

"Seriously?"

"Seriously." As he stood, something crashed in Hope's bedroom.

***

Once the specter was gone and Kenny and Hope had caught their breath, Hesed instructed that everyone return to the clearing near Hope's home. She was determined to hold an official council to deal with the matters at hand. It took them a few minutes to pass through the forest, but soon everyone was gathered around her. She sat in her chair with Gavin on her right. Gronek and Smakal stood to her left. Sacqueal towered behind her with his two swords. Tomo stood with the hairy guardian.

Kenny and Hope sat cross-legged at the queen's feet, and Hope had her arm hooked inside the crook of her father's elbow. Her head leaned against his shoulder. A smile rested on her face.

"Bring me the fallen ones," the queen demanded. "We will begin with them."

Immediately, Sacqueal departed. The group was silent as they awaited his return. Gavin, Gronek, and Smakal fidgeted but did not speak. Tomo kept eyeing the forest. The sasquatch was not gone long but came back with a fistful of elves in each of his hairy hands. He dropped them on the ground in front of the queen.

The two captive elves kneeled and fidgeted their hands, keeping their gaze toward the ground.

"Face me," Hesed demanded. "And stand up."

After a brief hesitation, they each stood and slowly raised their eyes to the queen. They visibly shook, their auras orange instead of the usual light green.

"The two of you have sold yourselves to a lie," she stated. "Bayal has no power and no strength. His only tool to convince his followers is a false tongue that promises what he cannot deliver."

The one on the right lowered his gaze.

"Look up at your queen," Hesed ordered. The elf sheepishly returned his eyes to hers.

"I could imprison you or I could banish you to the barren, frigid north. Yet, for some reason that I cannot fathom, my heart still holds hope for you. Return your allegiance to your people and to this realm, and I will release you to return to your homes."

The fallen elves chanced a glance at one another. "You would do this?" the one on the left asked. "You would release us?"

"Yes. All you need do is return your allegiance to its rightful place and promise to return home. Then, you may go. This is a day of celebration, and I do not wish to tarnish it with your punishment."

Again, it was the one on the left who replied. He crossed his arms across his chest and gave a respectful bow. "I belong to my people, to my queen, and to the path of right. I promise to return home."

"And you?" the queen eyed his companion. "Will you return your loyalty to its rightful place?"

"I will, your majesty." He then crossed his arms, gave a brief bow, and muttered the same words.

"You are free to go. Go straight home, and do not return to this place. I will not be so gracious if we meet again under similar circumstances."

The two bowed again before scampering away, disappearing into the forest.

"Now, for you two," the queen said to Kenny and Hope. She smiled so broadly that her lips split her face, ear to ear. "What joy you must be feeling."

***

Kenny did not immediately react. He was still mesmerized by the glittering forest, the furry Bigfoot, the Native American, and the green elves. It was a lot to take in, even for a guy who had just shrugged off the direct control of an evil specter.

Hope spoke first, "Dear Queen Hesed, I can't tell you how happy I am. I have missed him so much. My heart was broken, but now it's all put back together. I can see the love in his eyes again. I just want to hold him and have him hold me. I want to feel my daddy's arms hug me again and again and again."

"Kenny Burton," the queen said. "You have a remarkable daughter. Just look at the brightness of her aura. It was her love that made the difference in your battle."

Kenny stared at Hope. There were tears in his eyes. He brushed his awkward hand though her hair. His fingers disappeared into the light glowing from her scalp. For his part, his own arms were glowing a bright creamy white. He felt clean for the first time in years. Kenny addressed his words to his daughter, "You never gave up on me after all I did to you and to your mother. I'd given up on myself and I surrendered to that evil thing. Everyone else walked away from me, but not you. Why'd you hold on to me so hard?"

"I didn't know what was wrong with you," she replied, "but I knew something had changed you. You're my dad. I had to love you. I had to hope for the old daddy I knew to come back to me."

She reached up and kissed his cheek.

Kenny paused and gazed at Hope. Her bright aura illuminated everything around her. It was like she was oozing love for him. A tear trickled down his cheek.

"What's wrong?" Hope asked, using her hands to cup his whiskered chin.

He leaned his forehead against hers, his shoulders shook, and he sobbed. "My sweet girl, we can't be together when we go back. Maybe you can see me once in a while, but we'll be separated again."

A furrow wrinkled her forehead. "Why? Everything has changed now. We can do stuff together. I know I can convince Mom."

"Sweetie," he continued, "I will be arrested. I beat your mother...again. And I kidnapped you. I even punched my boss on my way out of Muncie this morning."

"But that wasn't you," Hope exclaimed. "It was that thing."

"Yes," he answered, "but that won't matter in our world. My parole will be revoked, and I'll be brought up on new charges. I'll be going back to prison for a long, long time...and I deserve it. I gave that thing access. I let it in, and I listened to its lies. And, early on, it wasn't controlling me. I chose to do some of those evil things—hurtful, mean, hateful things. Yes, it drove me in the end, but I chose to let it in."

Hesed gently broke into their conversation. "My dear Nozomi, your father is correct. He has guilt that must be atoned for. He is responsible for listening to the specter and giving it harbor in his heart."

"There is another option." Tomo interjected. "You could stay here and live with my people."

"Interesting idea." Hesed frowned and tapped a finger against her chin. "Interesting, indeed."

"Here?" Kenny asked. "How would that work?"

Tomo took a deep breath, then stepped forward, speaking up so that all could hear. "Kenny Burton, you would live as we live. You would assume chores as a member of our people. You would work very hard to earn your place in our society. Still, in this place, you would be near your daughter and free from the authorities in your realm. Hope could visit you through the shimmer from time to time."

Hope, slumped in her sadness, sat upright. "So, someone would come get me so I could see him?"

"That apparently will not be necessary," the queen said. "You seem to be able to pass through on your own."

"What do you mean?" Hope's eyes brightened.

"During your struggle with the specter, you drove your father through the shimmer on your own," Hesed explained. "It seems the Mighty One has granted you access to our realm. We will test to be sure, but you may be able to come and go as you wish."

While the queen was still speaking, a fairy fluttered into the group and landed lightly upon the queen's right forearm. Lifting it to her ear, she listened intently to the message. Concern appeared on her elfin face and her aura shifted from the greenish glow to a yellowish red tint. When the small creature had finished its message, it fluttered away.

"Nozomi," Hesed said, "when your friends were found and taken for medical care, I dispatched two fairies to watch over them. The one that just spoke to me has been watching over the smaller boy."

"Josh?" Smakal asked.

"Yes," she continued. "That is the one. Dear girl, you should go to him now. He is at a critical point and is considering moving on to the next life. His time of decision is very near."

Hope sprang to her feet. "What do you mean by 'next life'? Is he about to die?"

The queen rose and embraced the girl. The yellowish red concern of her aura disappeared into the brilliance of Hope's essence. "Yes, he is near death, but he is allowed the choice. He can go or he can come back. Perhaps, if you reach him in time, you can encourage him to come back to you, to his family."

Hope needed no further explanation. "I've gotta go," she exclaimed.

Without another word, she turned and leaped through the nearest shimmer, which happened to lead to her own bedroom. On the other side, she knocked her keepsake box and her collection of seashells off her dresser, which crashed to the floor alongside her.

With no hesitation, she stood and rushed into the hallway. Rick and her mother were standing there, staring at her with wide eyes.

She didn't wait for them to recover.

"We need to get to Josh. We have to go now!"

***

When Hope burst from her room, Rick and Maggie urged her to stop and give an explanation. They wanted to know where she'd gone, what had happened, and where Kenny was at that moment.

Maggie grabbed Hope to try to hold her in place, but Hope yanked herself free. "I'll tell you everything," she said, "—in the car…while we drive to see Josh. He's dying, Mom. We have to go now." Tears streamed down her face, and she choked back sobs. "Now."

Moments later, they were in Rick's county cruiser with the light bar flashing and the siren blaring as they passed through Cutters Notch on their way to Bloomington. They passed the General where a large black crow perched on top of one of the gas pumps. They passed the burned-out house where squad cars filled the lawn and drive.

"What's going on there?" Hope asked.

"Deputies are searching the surrounding woods for any sign of Kenny," Rick said.

"Well, they won't find him there," Hope muttered.

Finally, they passed the Notch Inn where TV news trucks were positioned with their broadcast antennae projecting into the sky. County and state police vehicles congregated in the parking lot, but the ambulances had already left.

What a weird and crazy day. Rick knew, as interim sheriff, that he should be at one of those sites, directing the investigations. Yet, he was going to have to invest some trust into his team because his personal responsibilities were trumping his professional. Whatever the consequences to his career, he was taking Hope to see Josh.

As they passed the town limits, Rick punched the accelerator. Glancing down, he saw the needle hit eighty miles an hour. He held it there. The roads were winding, so he couldn't go any faster until they hit the wider Highway 37.

"Where did you go, Hope?" Maggie asked from the front passenger seat, her black curls pulled back with a scrunchy. Even with no makeup, Rick was smitten with her beauty. "Where's Kenny? Did he hurt you?"

Rick glanced at Hope in the rear-view mirror. Hope was staring out the window, watching the ragged trees along the road as they whizzed by. Her lower lip was pulled in and she was biting down. She didn't answer right away.

"Hope," Maggie pleaded, "please answer me. Are you okay? Where's Kenny?"

Hope pulled her eyes from the window and focused on her mom. "I'm fine, Mom." A smile spread across her face. "Dad is finally free and safe, too."

"What do you mean?" Rick interjected.

"Do you remember me telling you about that specter thing that was so scary? You know, from when the Hicks grabbed me? The evil influence behind what they were doing?"

Maggie frowned, apparently not putting much stock in the concept. "Well, yeah. I remember."

"It was the specter that was making Dad do the things he was doing. *It* corrupted his mind and actually took control of his body, but he's free now."

Maggie's brow furrowed. "Honey, you can't know that. He's dangerous. He broke in, beat me up, and kidnapped you…just today."

"I can know. In the other dimension, you can see the specter…actually *see* it. I saw it with my own eyes. It's an ugly, whirling black thing. It was all around Dad, but it's gone now, and he's free of it."

Maggie looked over at Rick. Rick glanced back. "Where's your dad, now?" Rick prompted. "Did he stay on the other side?"

"Yeah. I had to leave him to go see Josh. Please, Rick, can we go any faster?"

"Sweetie," Maggie said in a softer tone, "how do you know Josh is dying?"

"I'm sure he's okay," Rick added. "He was stable when the helicopter carried him off this morning, and that Bloomington Trauma Center is top-notch."

"I just know," Hope said. "Please hurry." Then, she pulled her lower lip back between her teeth and returned her gaze to the passing scenery.

***

With the lights flashing and the siren blaring, the traffic moved out of the way, so they reached the Bloomington hospital in just under an hour. Hope leapt from the car and ran into the lobby ahead of Rick and Maggie. By the time the adults arrived, she had retrieved the location of Josh's room in the ICU.

On the ride up the elevator, Hope's hands were shaking as she nervously paced in front of the elevator doors. Each time the door opened on the wrong floor, she moaned. Maggie tried to pull her close, but she shrugged off the gesture. When they finally reached the floor, she burst out before the doors were all the way open.

Hope paused briefly at the doors to the ICU unit and read the sign about hours. It wasn't visiting hours. She rushed past the sign and slammed through the double doors anyway, with her mother and Rick on her heels.

The ICU was set up in a ring. A nurses' station was in the middle and the rooms were surrounding it. Each patient bed was behind a glass wall with curtains for privacy.

Hope quickly found the right room, but as she stepped inside, her heart sank. Roger Gillis was holding Cindy at the foot of Josh's bed. She was crying hysterically. Roger's face was stricken. Josh was lying still in the bed with bandages around his head. An oxygen tube that had been wrapped around his face to feed his nose was loose on his neck. His leg was wrapped and suspended slightly. His shirt was open with red marks on his chest. A doctor stood framed by a giant picture window on the far side of the bed, stethoscope draping her chest. She was replacing paddles into their fixture. Hope could see that the sky was growing dark and the horizon was a deep red from the setting sun. A nurse on the near side was busy clearing used materials. Most ominously, a monitor next to the bed contained zeroes and flat lines.

"Time of death—" the doctor began to say.

"No," Hope screamed as she rushed to his bedside. "Josh, don't go." She flung herself across his torso and put her face right up next to his. "Please don't go. Oh, please no!"

***

Josh leaned back against the crack and it supported him there. He would have to turn sideways to intentionally slip through. A comfortable warmth permeated his spine. It was pleasant—like standing on a heat register on a cold, cold morning.

As he enjoyed the sensation on his back, he looked down the beach toward the uncertainty that it held. Danny crossed his mind.

He would miss his best friend. *We had so much fun together.* He thought about his dad. *I wanted to be like him. He was an athlete and just the kind of guy I wanted to be, goofy or not.* His mother flashed into his thoughts. Her smile. Her quick temper. Her soft hugs. All those things pulled at him. They were waiting for him at the uncertain end of the long, empty beach.

Behind him, he thought he could hear his grandfather's voice. It was a little gruff, but in a playful way. He missed their fishing trips and piddling with him in his garage workshop. Together, they'd made fishing lures and little wooden trinkets. *I could see him again.* That idea seemed so appealing.

Without warning, the specter appeared in front of him, whirling and twirling, the black fog of its torso expanding and contracting. Its red eyes bore into Josh's own, as if they were drilling into his soul. It had haunted him every night since Hope's rescue, and it tormented him after his own failed escape from the silo. It was only the beach that had given him any respite. Now, here it was again. Josh pushed himself harder against the crack. He leaned his head back until his scalp slipped inside the warmth. It felt a little like a soft pillow.

"Do you see it?" he asked Ironman. "It's right there in front of me. I can feel the hatred. It wants to hurt me so much."

"I'm sorry," Ironman answered. "I can't see it. This is your vision and your decision."

"I can't take it anymore," Josh yelled. "Every time I close my eyes, I see its eyes. I hear its voice in my nightmares. It chases me and pulls at me and promises to get me—one way or another. It was that thing that put me in the silo. I have to get away from it. I have to!"

Ironman stepped in front of Josh, causing the specter to evaporate. "You can. You can leave it behind you. You can be safe again. All you have to do is turn a little to the side and let your body go. Just slip inside the warmth."

Josh turned to his left, facing the sunset. The sky was turning red on the horizon. His left arm slipped through the bright warm crevice. It felt so pleasant. *I'm gonna do it. I'm gonna go.* He felt a little sad for his parents, but he had to escape from that thing. He had to be safe…again.

He let his left hip slip inside and then his left shoulder. The soft warmth played against his cheek as it began to slip through. He lifted his left leg and stepped inside. *Oh, this feels so good.* It pulled him, tugged at him. Half of his face slid inside, and he could see images, clear and bright, no shadows. Birds soared above the ocean waves. Some of the images looked like people. A man was there. *Grandpa?* He thrust out his hand and Josh reached out to take it.

"Josh, no. Please don't go!"

He froze. *Hope?* For a moment, he was frozen in place—half in and half out. *Hope, is that you?*

"Oh, Josh, please come back to me."

Loud, bright, and clear, her voice called to him from down the beach. She seemed desperate. At the beckoning of her voice, his heart turned. He wanted to see her again. He needed to see her freckles and her blue eyes. He wanted to hold her hand and taste her lips again. He wanted to giggle and goof off with her.

His decision changed, but he was already halfway through. The warm, comfortable, safe place was still holding him, tugging at him like a giant vacuum cleaner. He tried to pull back out. To retreat. To return to the uncertainty of his life. Yet, his original choice was like a suction. It didn't want to let go. He dug into the sand with his right foot and his right arm flailed in the air.

"I've changed my mind," Josh screamed. "I don't want to go anymore."

"Oh, Josh," Hope's voice wailed. "Please come back to me." He could hear her sobs.

He pulled with all his might. He fought and pulled and yanked and jerked. Suddenly, something grabbed his arm. Ironman.

With a huge jerk, the superhero pulled him back out onto the sandy beach. Josh landed on his hands and knees.

"Thanks," Josh said, turning to look at the large man in the red armor. "That was close."

"No problem," Ironman replied.

Then, Josh jumped to his feet and ran down the beach. Sand flew up behind him. He ran toward uncertainty. He ran toward Hope. He ran until the beach faded and he opened his eyes. As his lids fluttered open, his gaze met the sparkling, wet gaze of Hope Spencer. Her eyes were warm and safe and comfortable. He smiled. This was where he really wanted to be.

NOZOMI'S BATTLE

Epilogue

Late that evening, after growing confident that Josh was back to stay, Maggie and Rick convinced Hope to go home and get some rest. But, rather than rest, she stood in front of the mirror in her bedroom. She was staring at her own reflection, at the smiling face looking back at her. Her hair was a mess, she was exhausted, but she was happy—happier than she'd been in close to three years.

Her mom was asleep in her own bedroom. Hope could hear her snoring. Rick had gone home. She was alone with her thoughts. Ignoring her reflection, she looked at the mirror itself and remembered the words of Queen Hesed. *I wonder if I can.*

Hope tentatively reached out her hand and focused her mind on that other realm. Slowly, she extended her fingers. When they met the glass surface, they passed through as if it were nothing more than water in a bowl. She jerked back. *I can.*

Smakal popped his head through. "Come on. What are you waiting for?"

Hope smiled, then climbed up on her dresser. Focusing her mind, she jumped through. It was like jumping through the blowing air of a fan. It tickled a little. Hope landed on the grass in her backyard, but in the other dimension, and her momentum drove her to her knees. Peering up, she saw a hand, her dad's hand, reaching down to help her up.

As she accepted his grasp and was pulled to her feet, she looked around. Surrounding them was an array of new friends. Gavin, Gronek, and Smakal were there. Queen Hesed stood behind her dad. Sacqueal and Tomo were in the rear. A fairy fluttered over and landed on Hesed's shoulder. Everyone wore broad smiles. Behind them, the forest glowed like a rainbow light collage.

"You made it in time," Kenny said as he gave her a big hug. "Your friend is okay. The fairy told us."

"Yes," Hope replied. "It was close, but he's okay. And, Dad, he's actually my boyfriend." Focusing on her father, she shifted the conversation. "Are you okay?"

"Boyfriend? I'm not sure how I feel about that," Kenny said. He pulled her into a bearhug. They turned together to face the queen. "I'm doing great. I haven't felt this good in a long, long time. Tomo took me to meet his people. They gave me a small place to stay and some incredible food to eat. Obviously, I'll need to get used to this place—" He waved his free arm at the glowing forest. "But I think I'm gonna like it here."

"Dear Nozomi," Queen Hesed interrupted, "you have had a remarkable day. You have saved both your father and your friend. Well done, indeed. The power of your pure love is evident in the brightness of your aura of life. I am well-blessed in knowing you."

"Thank you, my queen," she replied.

"You need not refer to my royalty. You are not from my realm. You may call me 'Agahpey' as you and I are now friends."

"Agahpey." Hope's smile broadened. "I like that. Thank you for taking my dad into your world. Thank you for accepting him."

"After what we witnessed," Agahpey answered, "we could do no less. Now, I must ask *you* a favor, young one."

"Anything," Hope promised.

"I must ask you to keep our world a secret. I know that you have spoken of it to your mother. That is to be expected. And, I know you have also spoken of it to the lawman—"

"Rick?" Hope said.

"Yes, Rick. However, please let our existence travel no further. This is both for your sake and for our own. We exist next to you in an overlapping universe, and we interact with your world from time to time. But, if we became widely known to your people, our civilization would be in grave danger."

"You have my promise," Hope confirmed. "I owe so much to you. I won't tell anyone else about you and I'll make sure everyone else keeps the secret too."

"Thank you, my friend. Now, we will leave you and your father. Why do you not take a walk together?"

"I'd like that," Kenny confirmed. He reached down and took

his little girl's hand.

"Me too," Hope responded with a warm smile. "I'd like that a whole lot."

"Oh, by the way," he added. "I don't think I'll be needing these anytime soon. Why don't you give them to your mom?" As he spoke, he fished his car keys from his pocket and dropped them in Hope's hand. "They go to a particular green and white Ford Gran Torino."

"Can I ride on your shoulders?"

Kenny laughed. "Are you tired already?"

Walking hand in hand, they passed through the group, skirted the forest edge, and turned into the trees along the double-rutted trail that in the human realm started behind the Hicks' privacy fence. In this realm, though, the trail was just a colorful, glowing, passageway to reunion.

***

The two miscreant elves that Queen Hesed had released to return to their homes made their way through the forest, traveling north along various streams and creek beds. Occasionally, they would follow the barren trails cut through the landscape by the roadways in the human realm, but mostly they kept to the trees. They didn't talk to one another much except to point out a potential food source or decide on a route change. One was eager to get home and start over, the other not so much. The aura of the eager elf had returned to a solid bright green. But the other elf's aura remained a pukey yellowish orange.

After a couple of days of journey, they ambled along the edge of a bluff above a large lake that wound through the hills. They had recently passed the barren lands that the humans called Bloomington. The colorful glow of the trees was beginning to illuminate the sky with the setting of the sun. The air was growing cold with a wind blowing in their face from the north. Suddenly, the eager elf shot his left hand out and stopped his companion.

"There are others ahead," he said. "They are coming our way. I see weapons."

"I see them," his fallen companion calmly replied. "From the color of their auras, they appear to be fallen, as well."

"Perhaps, we should hide ourselves," the no-longer-fallen elf suggested.

"Why should we do that?" the pukey elf gruffly replied. "We have nothing to fear from our own kind. And we should warn them of what they may encounter."

The question was settled, though, because the approaching group hailed them. "Ho there, brothers. Hold up and let us speak."

There were four of them, all with the same jaundiced aura as the grumpy elf of the pair. Each wore human clothing with not a leaf shirt in sight. Boots. Leather jackets. Camouflage ball caps. The elf in the front who had called out seemed to be the leader. A large knife poked out from a sheath strapped to his chest. Each of the other three sported a similar weapon.

The six elves gathered on a shelf outcropping high above the lake. Below, the water roiled in the wind, splashing against jagged rocks. The trees were mostly barren now, but the leaves that hung on were blowing strongly toward the south. The bluish aura of the trees swayed with the breeze.

The two travelers stood with their backs to the cliff. Both eyed their feet that were close to the edge. The new group of four circled around them.

"Where are you going and where have you been?" the leader asked. "At least one of you looks to be one of us. Were you traveling to the great rock to meet Bayal?"

"Yes, yes," the eager elf said. "We were, but we are returning to our homes now."

"But why?" the leader probed. "Bayal has not yet arrived, has he? We have not yet taken what we are due."

"The Queen was there with her sons and her guardian," The pukey elf explained. "They captured and threatened us until we promised to return to our homes."

"Oh, Hesed is there, is she?" the leader asked with an irreverent chuckle. "Well, that is good news, indeed. We will take care of her before Bayal even arrives, then we will be honored in his presence."

A look of disbelief claimed the eager elf's face as his mouth fell open. The pukey elf simply studied the new group of fallen elves, a slight smile creasing his sickly-colored cheeks.

"You would dare to attack the queen?" The eager elf asked. "Even with her sasquatch bodyguard? She also has humans around her. You would take that kind of risk? If you failed, you would be banished."

The pukey one was standing slightly behind the eager one. He turned his attention to the back of his traveling companion's head and frowned.

"Of course, we dare," the leader declared. "Bayal has called all of the fallen ones to band together. We shall throw off the tired theories of the royal domain and take what we want from the human realm. But, looking at you, you would not understand. You are not fallen. Look at your bright green aura. Why, you look almost like a newborn baby, you are glowing so green." His weaponized companions broke out in laughter.

Pulling the knife from his sheath, the leader stepped up close to the eager one. "Why are you here?" he demanded. "Are you some kind of spy? Are you working for that wretched she-elf?"

"No," he answered. "I am just a simple one. I was fallen, but I have renewed my loyalty and am returning home. I no longer want to stray. I want only to return to the peace of my home and my people, my family."

"So, you are no longer with us?" The leader pointed the tip of his knife under the eager elf's chin. "If you are not with us, then you are against us."

"But I am just going home. That is all. I am going to return to my family and renew my bonds. I have no desire to be more than—"

The eager one never finished his sentence. His pukey companion reached forward and grabbed the rear of his leafy shirt. Jerking him backward, he flung his eager fellow traveler over the edge of the precipice. As the eager elf fell, the five remaining fallen ones listened to his screams and stepped to the edge just in time to see him land hard on a jagged pile of rocks a hundred feet below. They watched as his green glowing blood splattered and flowed into the crevices of the various stones, eventually mixing with the surging water. The eager one's renewed aura began to fade and blink. Soon, the glow disappeared as his lifeforce was lost to eternity. It was the first elfin murder in over two thousand years.

"Well, look at you," the leader roared. "You have spunk. Friends, it appears that we have a new traveling companion."

The other fallen elves cheered, whooping and hollering and shaking their six-fingered fists in the air. "Well done. Well done, indeed."

The leader grabbed the murderous elf and pulled him in for a hug. "Welcome to our group, brother."

Turning away from the cliff, the group of five trudged on south toward Cutters Notch. Toward the great rock—the ancient Gate to Abandon. Toward their determined confrontation with the royal one, the great Queen Agahpey Hesed.

***

Above them, fluttering unseen in the treetops was a swirling darkness. It had slurped up the pain of the eager one's death like a delicious soup. Now, it decided to follow along and see what other meals this ridiculous little group of elves might be able to provide.

Michael DeCamp is the author of both fiction and non-fiction. A life-long resident of Indiana, he enjoys centering his stories around his home state. He began his work with short stores, a collection of which can be found in his work, *Cutters Notch Interludes*. Eventually, he moved on to write his first novel, *Abandon Hope*, which introduced the world to the strange, small town of Cutters Notch, Indiana. While in the middle of writing this sequel, *Nozomi's Battle*, he also published his first non-fiction work, *Loving Out Loud: Learning to Love in a Hate-Filled World*.

When not writing, he enjoys cycling, traveling, and podcasting. You can find his podcast (*Cutters Notch Podcast*) through any podcasting service platform.

Michael is married to his best friend, Nancy. They have two grown daughters and a ferocious miniature Australian shepherd, Leo. Michael and his family call Indianapolis home. Feel free to reach out to Michael through his website (www.authormichaeldecamp.com) or his email (michael@authormichaeldecamp.com).

I hope you didn't miss the first book, *Abandon Hope*.